I0652636

Praise for The Flame Imperishable

"McIntosh's comprehension of Tolkien's *Legendarium* is masterly; his appropriation of Aquinas is superb; his knowledge of the most important works in recent theology is staggering. A first-rate work of scholarship on a rarely explored aspect of Tolkien's work—the metaphysics of *Faërie*."
  —RALPH C. WOOD, author of *The Gospel According to Tolkien*

"*The Flame Imperishable* is a most valuable addition to Tolkien scholarship. Jonathan McIntosh explores Tolkien's implicit metaphysics of Middle-earth in the light of Thomism with skill and restraint, developing productive lines of argument. His focus on the creation story within the larger *Silmarillion,* combined with his attention to Tolkien's views on creation and sub-creation, allows him to develop a careful and insightful analysis that will greatly enrich our understanding of Tolkien's work."
  —HOLLY ORDWAY, author of *Tolkien's Modern Sources: Middle-earth Beyond the Middle Ages* (forthcoming from Kent State University Press)

"While many scholars have explored Tolkien's literary and philological influences, his philosophical and theological sources have attracted far less scrutiny—apart from general religious motives and themes. Jonathan S. McIntosh shines a brilliant light into this lacuna, revealing Tolkien's debts to St. Thomas Aquinas, and along the way situating Tolkien among the line of theological philosophers extending from antiquity, through the Middle Ages, and on into Tolkien's own day. *The Flame Imperishable* is surely the most thorough study to date of Tolkien's most cosmological works, and especially of his creation myth, the *Ainulindalë.* In a *tour de force* for religious and non-religious readers alike, McIntosh illuminates Tolkien's own metaphysical thought and how it pervades the entire fictive world of his legendarium."
  —JASON FISHER, editor of *Tolkien and the Study of His Sources: Critical Essays*

"Breathtakingly original, this book deserves to be a landmark. McIntosh makes a compelling case for the cosmological depth of Tolkien's world, arguing not only that it is a world founded on St. Thomas Aquinas, but that it is also a significant contribution to metaphysics in its own right. With a boldness supported closely by a wealth of reasoned argument, McIntosh highlights the singularity and magnitude of Tolkien's achievement both as an artist and as a speculative thinker."
  —MARK SEBANC, co-author of the *Legacy of the Stone Harp* series

"In this scholarly study of the philosophical basis of Tolkien's Middle-earth, Jonathan McIntosh demonstrates that metaphysics can be exciting. Far from detracting from the beauty and originality of Tolkien's writing, approaching it through the thought of Thomas Aquinas serves to all the more fully reveal its power over the reader. We know that, however deeply we engage with these stories, there is always more to discover. This is a trustworthy guide to the radiant sense of being in *The Lord of the Rings* and the *Silmarillion*, which truly illuminates the realism of Tolkien's project."

—ALISON MILBANK, author of *Chesterton and Tolkien as Theologians*

"In this exciting and lucidly written study, Jonathan McIntosh flings open a door that has remained all but sealed, bringing together the doctor of creation, Thomas Aquinas, with the artist of creation, J. R. R. Tolkien. In uncovering the influence of Aquinas on Tolkien's mythmaking, McIntosh lights up Tolkien's major themes — including the relationship between creation and sub-creation, the independence and 'otherness' of created reality, and the unity of world myth and fairy tale. Most importantly, he helps us recover the vision of a world made meaningful and whole by its Creator."

—CRAIG BERNTHAL, author of *Tolkien's Sacramental Vision: Discerning the Holy in Middle Earth*

"There have been many good books on Tolkien. There have even been several very good books on the philosophy of Tolkien. This book, however, is something else, something more, delving deeper. To borrow a phrase from C. S. Lewis, it goes further up and further in. Within these densely packed and brilliant pages, we journey to the core of Tolkien's Thomistic heart and mind. Reading this book engenders an unshakable conviction that one can no more separate Tolkien from Thomas than one can Dante from Thomas. Without Aquinas, there would have been no *Divine Comedy*. Without Aquinas, there would have been no Middle-earth. In short, and in sum, this book is absolutely essential reading to anyone who takes Tolkien seriously enough to want to understand him more deeply."

—JOSEPH PEARCE, author of *Tolkien: Man & Myth* and *Bilbo's Journey: Discovering the Hidden Meaning of The Hobbit*

"One does not merely dip into *The Flame Imperishable*. Rather, one immerses oneself in the very love McIntosh so vividly shares and radiates. Indeed, it is clear that the author holds a special place in his soul for Tolkien and Lewis as well as Sts. Augustine and Aquinas. Gloriously, McIntosh invites us to enter the art as well. *The Flame Imperishable* is not just another in a long line of books about J.R.R. Tolkien, but a truly seminal book that will be remembered as such long after the ephemera surrounding Peter Jackson's work has come and gone. It will be canon."

—BRADLEY J. BIRZER, author of *J.R.R. Tolkien's Sanctifying Myth*

THE FLAME IMPERISHABLE

THE *Flame* IMPERISHABLE

Tolkien, St. Thomas,
AND THE
Metaphysics of Faërie

JONATHAN S. MCINTOSH

ANGELICO PRESS

First published in the USA
by Angelico Press 2017
Copyright © Jonathan S. McIntosh 2017

All rights reserved:
No part of this book may be reproduced or transmitted,
in any form or by any means, without permission

For information, address:
Angelico Press, Ltd.
4709 Briar Knoll Dr.
Kettering, OH 45429
www.angelicopress.com

978-1-62138-315-4 pbk
978-1-62138-316-1 cloth
978-1-62138-317-8 ebook

Book and cover design
by Michael Schrauzer
Cover illustration based on "Drei Sonnen,"
Augsburger Wunderzeichenbuch — Folio 26, ca. 1552
Source: Wikimedia Commons

To Annie,
whose love is imperishable

Table of Contents

Acknowledgments

THIS BOOK BEGAN AS A RESEARCH DISSERTATION FOR THE PH.D. in philosophy completed at the University of Dallas, Texas in 2009. I would like to thank all the excellent faculty and staff in the U.D. Department of Philosophy, the Braniff Graduate School of Liberal Arts, the Institute of Philosophic Studies, and the Cowan-Blakley Memorial Library for their instruction, encouragement, and support during my studies and research there, and especially to my dissertation advisor, Professor Philipp Rosemann. I would also like to thank the Tolkien Estate and Christopher Tolkien in particular for their labor and scholarship in making available so great a volume of Tolkien's work, as well as for their assistance with some of the questions that came up in the course of my research.

Part of Chapter Three, *The Metaphysics of the Music and Vision*, was previously published in Heidi Steimel and Friedhelm Schneidewind, eds., *Music in Middle-earth* (Zollikofen, Switzerland: Walking Tree, 2010).

Abbreviations

BLT   *The Book of Lost Tales*, vol. 1

EBT   *Expositio super librum Boethii De Trinitate*

FOTR   *The Fellowship of the Ring*

L   *Letters of J.R.R. Tolkien*

LR   *The Lost Road*

MR   *Morgoth's Ring*

S   *The Silmarillion*

SD   *Sauron Defeated*

ROTK   *The Return of the King*

ST   *Summa Theologiae*

TL   *Tree and Leaf*

TR   *The Tolkien Reader* ("On Fairy-Stories")

TT   *The Two Towers*

Introduction

> He [St. Thomas] very specially possessed the philosophy
> that inspires poetry; as he did so largely inspire
> Dante's poetry. And poetry without philosophy has only
> inspiration, or, in vulgar language, only wind. He had,
> so to speak, the imagination without the imagery.
> G.K. Chesterton[1]

> I am sorry if this all seems dreary and "pompose." But so do all
> attempts to "explain" the images and events of a mythology.
> Naturally the stories come first. But it is, I suppose, some
> test of the consistency of a mythology as such, if it is capable
> of some sort of rational or rationalized explanation.
> J.R.R. Tolkien, letter to Major R. Bowen

> The tale is after all in the ultimate analysis a tale, a piece
> of literature.... Its economics, science, artefacts, religion,
> and philosophy are defective, or at least sketchy.
> J.R.R. Tolkien, letter to Peter Hastings

THE ARGUMENT OF THIS BOOK IS THAT J.R.R. TOLKIEN was a metaphysical thinker, that questions concerning the nature of both created and uncreated being significantly inspired and shaped his fiction, and that one of the foremost influences on Tolkien's metaphysical imagination was one of the greatest doctors of the Christian church, the thirteenth-century theologian St. Thomas Aquinas (1225–1274). Tolkien's philosophical and theological sources, like his literary ones, were many, and a good deal of attention has been given by Tolkien scholars to both the philosophical pedigree and significance of his writings. What there has not been to date, however, is a systematic approach to the metaphysical underpinnings of Tolkien's fiction generally, or any sustained investigation into the role Aquinas in particular may have had in shaping Tolkien's philosophical consciousness, and

---

1 Chesterton, *St. Thomas Aquinas: "The Dumb Ox,"* 152–53.

this despite a general acknowledgement that the Catholic Doctor represented an important and formative influence on the Catholic don. The aim of this book, accordingly, is to begin to fill in these lacunae by initiating a conversation of sorts between Tolkien and Thomas in the form of a philosophical commentary on Tolkien's most metaphysical work, the *Ainulindalë* or "Music of the Ainur," his creation-myth from the posthumously published *Silmarillion*. By bringing to bear on Tolkien's fiction many of the central metaphysical questions posed by St. Thomas, I hope to shed some light on the profound metaphysical subtlety of the latter and, in the process, give us a better sense of the scope and nature of Thomas's influence on Tolkien.

J.R.R. Tolkien, Metaphysician

WHAT IS *METAPHYSICS*? TO GET AN AT LEAST PRELIMINARY sense of what this word would have conveyed for Tolkien, and hence how it is being used in this study, we could do no better than to begin, in good Tolkienian fashion, with its etymology. The origins of this exotic-sounding word are actually quite prosaic, coined as it was in antiquity by librarians as a means for cataloguing Aristotle's book on first philosophy. The practice was to place Aristotle's text *after*—"*meta*" in Greek—Aristotle's book on *Physics*, hence the name *Meta-physics*. Eventually this designation came to be associated with the subject matter of Aristotle's book itself, which he defines in one place as the study of "being *as* being." Aristotle's view was that all science or knowledge is concerned with some aspect or part of being or existence. Zoology, for example, studies *animal* being; biology is more comprehensive in its study of all *living* being; physics is broader still in its investigation of all *physical* or material being, and so forth. In this scheme metaphysics finally enters as the most comprehensive and penetrating — and hence most divine — science of all, for it undertakes to study not this or that kind of being, but the universal principles of all being simply insofar as it has or is being. It was in these terms, moreover, that the discipline of metaphysics would be primarily understood throughout much of the subsequent philosophical tradition, especially during that industrious and momentous convergence of Aristotelian and Catholic thought known as medieval scholasticism, a convergence in which St. Thomas Aquinas would play no insignificant role.

As for Tolkien's own use and sense of metaphysics, although he explicitly denies in one letter that he is a metaphysician himself, in the same passage he also explicitly recognizes that his stories about Middle-earth contain a "metaphysic"

(L 188), and the text that will be providing the framework for our present study, his creation myth *Ainulindalë,* reveals an author quite conscious of the concept of *being* and deliberate in his use of it. Yet one might reasonably wonder why Tolkien, a philologist and professor of Old English and writer of fantasy literature and fairy stories, would have been concerned at all with being and metaphysics. And even if his mythology should "contain" a metaphysics, of what importance might this fact be for a proper understanding of his mythology? To properly answer this question, however, it may prove worthwhile to introduce or review some of the better known or familiar motives that animated Tolkien in the crafting of his Middle-earth mythology, or "*legendarium,*" as he referred to it.[2] To begin, it should be noted that Tolkien's stated aims for writing his stories are as diverse as the stories themselves, varying widely depending on the occasion or the audience whom he is addressing at the moment. In one famous (and infamously long) letter written to Milton Waldman, a potential publisher for *The Lord of the Rings,* Tolkien declares his aim to have been that of providing a mythology for his mother England.

> Do not laugh! But once upon a time (my crest has long since fallen) I had a mind to make a body of more or less connected legend, ranging from the large and cosmogonic, to the level of romantic fairy-story — the larger founded on the lesser in contact with the earth, the lesser drawing splendour from the vast backcloths — which I could dedicate simply to: to England; to my country. (L 144)

Some five years later, Tolkien wrote of his aspirations in a similar vein: "Having set myself a task, the arrogance of which I fully recognized and trembled at: being precisely to restore to the English an epic tradition and present them with a mythology of their own" (L 230-1).

In another context, Tolkien identifies his motive for creating Middle-earth as essentially linguistic: he realized that he needed a home-world in which his invented languages (a hobby he began as an adolescent) might be spoken, along with a history in which those languages could change and develop: "It was just as the 1914 War burst on me that I made the discovery that 'legends' depend on the language to which they belong; but a living language depends equally on the 'legends' which it conveys by tradition" (L 230). In another place, by comparison,

---

2 *Legendarium* was a medieval term used for a volume of collected lessons or legends. Leclercq, *The Love of Learning and the Desire for God,* 162.

Tolkien speaks of his objective as moral as well as metaphysical: "I would claim, if I did not think it presumptuous in one so ill-instructed, to have as one object the elucidation of truth, and the encouragement of good morals in this real world, by the ancient device of exemplifying them in unfamiliar embodiments, that may tend to 'bring them home'" (L 194). Some indication of what "good morals" constituted for Tolkien may be seen in yet another statement of his literary goals, in which he gives an overtly theological meaning to his mythology: "In *The Lord of the Rings* the conflict is not basically about 'freedom,' though that is naturally involved. It is about God, and His sole right to divine honour" (L 243). This claim in particular has puzzled some readers, inasmuch as *The Lord of the Rings* famously contains no overt or at least readily recognizable reference to a divine being. As I hope to show in this study, however, an understanding of the underlying metaphysics — inherited from St. Thomas — of Tolkien's mythical world promises to go a long way in explaining the fundamental coherence of this and many other paradoxes surrounding Tolkien's work.

A further significant factor in the shaping of his Middle-earth *legendarium*, and one that begins to address more fully the role of metaphysics in his fiction, was Tolkien's desire to do what he believed all fairy stories must do, namely fashion a coherent "secondary world" into which the reader may imaginatively enter and even "escape." As Tolkien argues in his programmatic essay "On Fairy-Stories," one of the fundamental criteria of any sub-created, secondary world is that it must possess what he calls the "inner consistency of reality." Fantasy on Tolkien's analysis involves the "making or glimpsing of Other-worlds" which, like our own world, must have a logic or order of their own, so that

> a successful "sub-creator"…makes a Secondary World which your mind can enter. Inside it, what he relates is "true": it accords with the laws of that world. You therefore believe it, while you are, as it were, inside. The moment disbelief arises, the spell is broken; the magic, or rather art, has failed. You are then out in the Primary World again, looking at the little abortive Secondary World from outside. (TR 60)

This particular feature of fairy story was so important to Tolkien that, in first developing and then afterward explaining and revising his own lengthy fairy-story about Middle-earth, he was often preoccupied — one might dare say obsessed — with ensuring and defending the rational coherence of his mythical world. Aware of his own compulsive tendencies in this regard, and after having momentarily indulged them while writing to one correspondent, Tolkien concluded his letter with the apology quoted in the epigraph at the beginning of this Introduction: "I am sorry if this all seems dreary and 'pompose.' But so do all attempts to 'explain' the images and events of a mythology. Naturally the stories come first. But it is, I suppose, some test of the consistency of a mythology as such, if it is capable of some sort of rational or rationalized explanation" (L 260).[3] In Tolkien's mind, the artistic success of his fiction hinged in part on his ability to demonstrate the rational coherence of his mythology. It was thus an authentic unity of artistic and mythic imagination (*mythos*) on the one hand and philosophical rationality (*logos*) on the other that Tolkien sought to achieve in his own mythology. Tolkien even went so far as to give symbolic representation to this synthesis of imagination and reason in one of the central images of his *legendarium*, the Light of the Two Trees of Valinor, from which the primary sources of light in Tolkien's fictional world — the sun, moon, stars, Silmaril jewels, and even the phial of Galadriel which Frodo takes with him into Mordor — would eventually take their origin. As Tolkien writes, "The Light of Valinor (derived from light before any fall) is the light of art undivorced from reason, that sees things both scientifically (or philosophically) and imaginatively (or subcreatively) and 'says that they are good' — as beautiful" (L 148n). For Tolkien, good fairy-stories may be as much a matter of reason as they are of the imagination, so that good fantasy necessitates good philosophy, and good mythology requires a good metaphysics.

Because of the expansive scope of Tolkien's mythology, however, the demand of rational consistency presented a significant practical problem, compelling him at times to go to extreme lengths to reconcile real or apparent tensions in his work. This exercise particularly involved him in a careful consideration of the metaphysical intricacies and implications of his imaginary world. Accounting for the long delay, for example, of *The Silmarillion*'s publication after the remarkable success of *The Lord of the Rings*, Tolkien's son and literary executor Christopher wrote of his father:

> Meditating long on the world that he had brought into being and was now in part unveiled, he had become absorbed in analytic speculation concerning its underlying postulates. Before he could prepare a new and

---

3 After waxing metaphysical in another letter, Tolkien similarly confessed to his correspondent: "Now (you will reasonably say) I am taking myself even more seriously than you did, and making a great song and oration about a good tale, which admittedly owes its similitude to mere craft. It is so. But the things I have scribbled about, arise in some form or another from all writing (or art) that is not careful to dwell within the walls of 'observed fact'" (L 196). Even Tolkien had second thoughts about his own metaphysical digressions, as the letter ultimately went unfinished and unsent. He wrote in explanation at the top of the draft, "It seemed to be taking myself too importantly" (L 196).

final *Silmarillion* he must satisfy the requirements of a coherent theological
and metaphysical system, rendered now more complex in its presentation
by the supposition of obscure and conflicting elements in its roots and its
tradition. (MR viii)[4]

We will see what some of these "conflicting elements" in Tolkien's mythology
were in the chapters to follow. The point to be made here is that the attention
Tolkien gave to the metaphysical details of his mythology was by no means a
consideration irrelevant to the meaning or value he placed on his own work, for he
saw the latter's coherence on these matters as an indication of its validity as a true
work of art. The ideal role of such myths or fairy-stories was to present a secondary
world with the inner consistency of reality, a consistency that Tolkien hoped to
reflect even at the very deepest metaphysical level of his own sub-created reality.

If the aim of creating a secondary world is to imitate something of the *consistency* of the primary world's own reality, for Tolkien this is because it also has the
higher aim of reflecting or revealing something of the *truth* of that reality. An
alternative, secondary reality, after all, is still part of our own world and as such
has the duty of "recovering" the truth of that reality, something Tolkien also
argues in his essay: "Creative fantasy is founded upon the hard recognition that
things are so in the world as it appears under the sun; on a recognition of fact,
but not a slavery to it" (TR 74-5). Thus, beyond the above-mentioned regional,
linguistic, moral, narrowly theological, and aesthetic or artistic objectives of
his writing, a further motive behind Tolkien's fiction involves his purpose to
explore the real-world relationship between the divine "art" of creation on the
one hand and, subordinate to it, the human art of "sub-creation" on the other.
Tolkien's interest in this relationship was something he particularly shared with
Thomist scholar and philosopher Jacques Maritain and a coterie of other early
to mid-twentieth century Catholic lay artists who were influenced by him, as
I discuss further below. In the same letter to Waldman cited above, Tolkien
writes of his *legendarium*: "It is, I suppose, fundamentally concerned with the
problem of the relation of Art (and Sub-creation) and Primary Reality" (L 145n).
As Tolkien admits here, at the heart of his mythology lies a concern with the
being of "Primary Reality" and the basis this reality provides for the secondary
worlds or realities of human imagining. In another letter written to a Catholic
acquaintance, Peter Hastings, Tolkien reiterates this point when he says that "the
whole matter" of his mythology "from beginning to end is mainly concerned with

4 See also MR 271.

the relation of Creation to making and sub-creation," and therefore "references to these things are not casual, but fundamental" (L 188). For Tolkien, not only was it the case that all human sub-creation must presuppose and is made possible and meaningful by a prior, divine act of creation, but, as we shall see, it was his express purpose to foreground this relationship within his own mythology by making it one of the central themes of his fiction.

Another place where Tolkien makes explicit the metaphysical foundation of myth and fairy-story is his unfinished and not well-known time-travel fantasy, *The Notion Club Papers*, in which an allusion is made to the same Aristotelian and hierarchical understanding of being mentioned earlier. When one character asks what is the source or soil of "ancient accounts, legends, myths, about the far Past, about the origins of kings, laws, and the fundamental crafts," if these accounts are to be something more than "wholly inventions" or "mere fiction," another character gives the following, rather philosophical reply: "In Being, I think I should say…and in human Being; and coming down the scale, in the springs of History and in the designs of Geography — I mean, well, in the pattern of our world as it uniquely is, and of the events in it as seen from a distance" (SD 227).[5] Again, for Tolkien mythology has its roots in the fertile soil of metaphysics, in a certain insight into and feeling for the being of things, and this certainly holds true of Tolkien's own mythology. As Tolkien scholar Verlyn Flieger has gone so far as to suggest, the whole of Tolkien's *Silmarillion* represents an "exploration of the implications and ramifications of the one word *Eä*,"[6] the Elvish word the Creator Ilúvatar speaks when he brings into being the physical world, and which has the meaning either of the indicative "It is" or the imperative "Let it be" (or both simultaneously). The reason metaphysics is relevant to Tolkien's *legendarium* is that metaphysics is the science of being, and for Tolkien, myths, legends, and fairy-tales are concerned ultimately with the reality or being of things.

In overview, then, there are at least four distinguishable levels at which Tolkien's Middle-earth tales are inextricably bound up with metaphysics, four distinct levels, moreover, that we will be touching on in various ways in the pages

---

5 Tolkien alludes to this same hierarchy or "scale" of being and its "patterns" of being in a letter to Camilla Unwin, the daughter of his publisher Rayner (discussed in chapter two), answering Camilla's question as to the purpose of life: "As for 'other things' their value resides in themselves: they ARE, they would exist even if we did not…. If we go up the scale of being to 'other living things,' such as, say, some small plant, it presents shape and organization: a 'pattern' recognizable (with variation) in its kin and offspring…. And since recognizable 'pattern' suggests design, [human curiosity] may proceed to WHY? But WHY in this sense, implying reasons and motives, can only refer to a MIND" (L 399).

6 Flieger, *Splintered Light: Language and Logos in Tolkien's World*, 59.

to follow. First, as a writer Tolkien was particularly self-conscious of the kind of real-world, creation metaphysics or philosophy of being he believed he and his art were ultimately a part of, and hence whose truth he saw as necessary if sub-creation as a human endeavor was to be a possible and meaningful activity in the first place. Second, in his own writing and revising Tolkien endeavored to construct a secondary world that would reflect the kind of internal consistency he believed to constitute the world around us. Third, insofar as his fictional world was intended to picture not so much an alternative reality as an alternative *history* of our world in its mythical, primeval past, the reality Tolkien sought to illustrate was not a *different* world but the *same* one as ours. Fourth and finally, as Tolkien mentions in his letters to Waldman and Hastings above, this relationship between the primary world and the secondary worlds of our sub-creating is itself one of the central themes of Tolkien's particular work. Tolkien's Middle-earth *legendarium*, in sum, not only presupposes, contains, and presents a metaphysics, as all art, on Tolkien's view, must, but, on his own reckoning, it is also funda-mentally and paradoxically *about* that very metaphysics.

Approaches to Tolkien
CHRISTIAN, CATHOLIC, MEDIEVAL, PHILOSOPHICAL, AND THOMISTIC

IN LIGHT OF THIS IMPORTANT ROLE I HAVE SUGGESTED metaphysics plays in Tolkien's literary project, we might at this point survey what attention this aspect of his writings has received to date. One of the earliest recognitions of Tolkien's sophisticated metaphysical sensibility also contains, significantly enough, one of the first references to Tolkien's alleged Thomism. In 1972, the year before Tolkien's death, professor and literary critic Paul H. Kocher raised the question as to "how far Tolkien wishes his treatment of evil to be considered not only moral but metaphysical."[7]

> Without using blatantly theological terms his ideas are often clearly theo-logical nonetheless, and are best understood when viewed in the context of the natural theology of Thomas Aquinas, whom it is reasonable to suppose that Tolkien, as a medievalist and a Catholic, knows well. The same is true in the area of metaphysics. Some of Thomas's less specifically Christian

---

7 Kocher, *Master of Middle-earth: The Fiction of J.R.R. Tolkien*, 76.

> propositions about the nature of evil seem highly congruent with those which
> Tolkien expresses or implies in laymen's terms in *The Lord of the Rings*.[8]

In his commentary on Tolkien's creation-myth in particular, the *Ainulindalë*, Kocher describes the angelic Ainur's longing for the world to be created as a wish that it should be given "full metaphysical Being (in the Thomistic sense)."[9] His perceptive point that Tolkien's philosophy may be "best understood" in light of the thought of St. Thomas notwithstanding, Kocher goes on to say very little himself in regards to the role of Thomas's ideas in Tolkien's thought. Over forty years later, the question of Tolkien's Thomism is in much the same state in which Kocher left it.

What has generated a good deal of attention (and even some debate) is the question of the extent and nature of the Christianity and Catholicity of Tolkien's work.[10] Of late there has also been a surge of interest in Tolkien's medievalism on the one hand and in the general philosophical import of and sources behind his work on the other. A few recent books addressing Tolkien's medieval antecedents are *Tolkien the Medievalist* and *Tolkien's Modern Middle Ages*, both edited by Jane Chance, and *The Keys of Middle-earth: Discovering Medieval Literature through the Fiction of J.R.R. Tolkien* by Stuart Lee and Elizabeth Solopova. Focused as these works primarily are on the literary influences on Tolkien, the thirteenth-century intellectual giant, Aquinas, receives nary a mention, nor is Tolkien's philosophy or theology (with a couple of exceptions discussed below) given much serious attention. In the recent *J.R.R. Tolkien Encyclopedia*, edited by Michael Drout, Thomas fares slightly better, receiving his own article by Brad Birzer, who rightly observes that it is an "implicit rather than explicit Thomism"

---

8 Ibid., 77.

9 Kocher, *A Reader's Guide to The Silmarillion*, 18.

10 For an introduction to the issues and a survey of some of the more important literature, see the following (often overlapping) articles and their associated bibliographies in Drout, ed., *J.R.R.T. Encyclopedia*: "Bible," "Catholicism, Roman," "Christ," "Christian Readings of Tolkien," "Christianity," "Theological and Moral Approaches in Tolkien's Works," and "Theology in *The Lord of the Rings*." (For a discussion of other important trends in the past fifty years of Tolkien scholarship in the *J.R.R.T. Encyclopedia*, see the three articles by Brian Rosebury, Richard C. West, and Hilary Wynn respectively, listed under "Tolkien Scholarship.") Some of the more notable studies on the religious impulse behind Tolkien's writings include Pearce, *Tolkien: Man and Myth*; Birzer, *Tolkien's Sanctifying Myth: Understanding Middle-earth*; Wood, *The Gospel According to Tolkien: Visions of the Kingdom in Middle-earth*; and Caldecott, *The Power of the Ring: The Spiritual Vision Behind "The Lord of the Rings."* For a critique of such religious appreciations of Tolkien's work, however, see, for example, Catherine Madsen's (incoherent, in my view) "'Light From an Invisible Lamp': Natural Religion in *The Lord of the Rings*." On the question of the Catholic nature of Tolkien's creation-myth, the *Ainulindalë*, which this book will be focusing on, see Purtill, "Tolkien's Creation Myth" and Devaux, "The Origins of the *Ainulindalë*: The Present State of Research."

one finds in Tolkien's work.[11] Birzer makes the further point as to how it would have been impossible for a traditionalist and pious Roman Catholic of Tolkien's generation to have escaped the influence of Thomism, not to mention one who received his education during the decades immediately following the first Vatican Council's revitalization of the study of St. Thomas in Catholic schools around the world. Oddly, however, Birzer locates "the first and most significant Thomistic element" of Tolkien's *oeuvre* in Aragorn's Christ-like kingship, and the convergence between Thomas and Tolkien in matters of philosophical theology, that area where Thomas's own legacy has arguably been the most lasting and influential, is left unconsidered. Nearer to the mark in this regard is a second brief mention St. Thomas receives in the *Encyclopedia* in Matthew Dickerson's article, "Theological and Moral Approaches in Tolkien's Works," which makes the claim that "Tolkien's Aristotelian and Thomist outlook can be seen in his emphasis on the orderliness of creation and the view of all creation having its source and purpose in the mind of God; the Ainur were the offspring of Ilúvatar's thought, and Eä, the creation, arose from the music or Theme of Ilúvatar."[12]

There have been a couple of essays, however, that have ventured a bit further into the relation between Thomas and Tolkien. Andrew Nimmo's article, "Tolkien and Thomism: Middle-earth and the States of Nature," takes up the five states of nature distinguished by Aquinas, namely the "hypothetical" states of (1) pure nature and (2) integral nature, and the "historical" states of (3) innocence or original justice, (4) fallen nature, and (5) restored or repaired nature, and correlates these (albeit in a rather underdeveloped fashion) with the different species of rational beings and their respective states found in Tolkien's mythology.[13] Perhaps the most extensive treatment of Tolkien in conjunction with Thomas to appear to date is a study by Peter Candler, which suggestively situates Tolkien at the "intersection" of Aquinas and Nietzsche.[14] Candler's argument concerning the theoretical or conceptual relationship between the philosophies of Thomas and Tolkien revolves chiefly around Tolkien's premise that the activity of human sub-creation is grounded in the divine activity of creation proper. He writes:

> Whatever the case, Tolkien, while not straightforwardly "Thomist," is quite clearly, like Flannery O'Connor, at least "a Thomist thrice-removed." This is evident in the way in which the human activity of poiesis is explicitly

---

11 Birzer, "Aquinas, Thomas," in Drout, ed., *J.R.R.T. Encyclopedia,* 22.

12 Ibid., 644.

13 Nimmo, "Tolkien and Thomism: Middle-earth and the States of Nature."

14 Candler, "Tolkien or Nietzsche, Philology and Nihilism."

bound up with creation, particularly in the sense that all human making
reflects the gratuity of the creation itself, and forms not a discrete set of
activities of an agency of purely human propriety, but rather participates
in the divine creation itself.[15]

These are points to which we will have occasion to return in the chapters that
follow.

While there have been a couple of other noted Thomists who have been published on Tolkien — Thomas Hibbs in his article on "Providence and the Dramatic
Unity of *The Lord of the Rings*" in *"The Lord of the Rings" and Philosophy*, and
Peter Kreeft in *The Philosophy of Tolkien* — neither mentions anything about
the possibility of Tolkien's Thomism (Plato and C.S. Lewis are Kreeft's philosophical interlocutors of choice). John Milbank, founder of the contemporary
intellectual movement known as "Radical Orthodoxy" and coauthor of *Truth
in Aquinas,* in an essay-review of Rowan Williams's book on Thomist Jacques
Maritain's aesthetics, *Grace and Necessity: Reflections on Art and Love*, briefly
credits Tolkien and G.K. Chesterton with having developed "a Catholic and
even a Thomistic aesthetic."[16] These comments anticipated his wife Alison Milbank's book, *Chesterton and Tolkien as Theologians: The Fantasy of the Real*,
which draws attention to the metaphysical realism and the consequent belief in
the freedom or independence of the created order that Chesterton and Tolkien
both inherited from St. Thomas.[17] A more incidental parallel between Aquinas
and Tolkien pointed out by Milbank is the one she makes between, on the one
hand, Chesterton and Hilaire Belloc's social theory of "distributism," which had
its origins in Thomas's teaching on social issues such as property-ownership, and
on the other hand the kind of communitarianism idealized by Tolkien in his
depiction of the Shire.[18] Finally, theologian and literary critic Ralph Wood has
noted a certain affinity between Tolkien and St. Thomas in their understanding
of divine providence, concurrence, and miracles.[19]

15 Ibid., 8.
16 Milbank, "Scholasticism, Modernism, and Modernity," 663.
17 A condensed version of Alison Milbank's discussion may also be found in her article "Tolkien,
Chesterton, and Thomism."
18 Milbank, *Chesterton and Tolkien as Theologians*, 13. For more on Tolkien's social philosophy,
see Caldecott, *The Ring of Power,* 119–21, and Richards and Witt, *The Hobbit Party*. For a brief
discussion of St. Thomas's own ruralist and hobbitic ambivalence towards the emergent urbanism
and commercialism of the thirteenth century, see Courtenay, "The King and the Leaden Coin: The
Economic Background of 'Sine Qua Non' Causality," 206.
19 "There is, in fact, an implicit Thomism at work in Tolkien's understanding of miracles. As
Brian Davies observes, Aquinas '*thinks that miracles come about by virtue of the creative activity of*

As to more general studies that have been made on the philosophy of Tolkien, a relatively early instance is Howard Davis's "The Ainulindalë: Music of Creation." Although Davis notes that Tolkien's *Ainulindalë* has both "biblical origins and Eddic roots,"[20] much of Davis's article is oddly preoccupied with comparing Tolkien's cosmogonic myth with the Eastern thought of the Indian yogi Paramahansa Yogananda (Davis was writing in the early 1980s, if that is any explanation). The parallels noted by Davis are actually not far-fetched, if only because none of them seems especially unique to or characteristic of Eastern thought.[21] Later in his essay, Davis finds a more plausible antecedent for Tolkien's creation-music in the ancient Greek philosopher and mathematician Pythagoras and rightly observes that "there is an actual metaphysical principle behind [Tolkien's] literary depiction of the creation of Middle-earth."[22] In agreement with this statement is the title of Robert Collins's similarly eclectic, yet more occidentally-oriented, survey of Tolkien's possible philosophical influences, "Ainulindalë: Tolkien's Commitment to an Aesthetic Ontology," in which the names of Pythagoras, Pseudo-Dionysius, Prudentius, Edmund Spenser, John Milton, Sir Philip Sydney, composer Igor Stravinsky, G.W.F. Hegel, and Friedrich Nietzsche all receive mention.

The couple of references made to Nietzsche thus far bring to mind a number of considerations of Tolkien's philosophy that have been informed by a more postmodern focus. On the side of philosophy of language, we might include here

God and nothing else. The whole point about them is that nothing subject to God's providence, i.e. no cause other than God (no secondary cause), is at work in their occurrence.' This is not to say that God does violence to the created order, or that he 'intervenes' to disrupt its natural processes. On the contrary, St. Thomas insists that God is totally present to every existing thing, so that all events are always the effect of God's will. Yet miracles are not worked through secondary causes, not even through their divine compression, as Lewis argues: they are brought about by God alone…Aquinas described miracles, therefore, as those events which, because their divine source is hidden from us, excite admiration — the wonder which existentially and etymologically lies at the root of the word miracle." Wood, "Conflict and Convergence on Fundamental Matters in C.S. Lewis and J.R.R. Tolkien," 325 (emphasis original).

20 Davis, "The Ainulindalë: Music of Creation," 6.

21 For example, after noting Tolkien's identification of the *Ainulindalë*'s Secret Fire with the Holy Spirit, Davis uses Yogananda to explain Tolkien's understanding of the relationship between the Trinity and the created universe (ibid., 8), when a more recognizably Western theologian such as Augustine or Aquinas would seem to be the more logical choice. Another questionable attempt at comparing Tolkien with Eastern thought is Jennifer L. McMahon and B. Steve Csaki's "Talking Trees and Walking Mountains: Buddhist and Taoist Themes in *The Lord of the Rings*." As the authors themselves conclude their study, "as we hope to have shown, while aspects of *The Lord of the Rings* call to mind ideas and themes evident in the Buddho-Taoist tradition, close examination reveals that many of these similarities are merely apparent. In fact, many of the similarities that exist between Tolkien and Taoism are, while quite striking, somewhat superficial" (ibid., 191). Indeed.

22 Davis, "The Ainulindalë: Music of Creation," 8.

Verlyn Flieger's *Splintered Light: Logos and Language in Tolkien's World,* which uses the linguistic theory of marginal Inkling member Owen Barfield to elucidate Tolkien's views on the integral and co-constitutional relationship between words and reality. Flieger, however, betrays a certain hesitance in suggesting that the beauty of Tolkien's created universe necessarily tells us anything ultimately true about the beauty of the real universe ("Whether there really is such a universe is less important than the undeniable truth that we need one badly"[23]). On this issue, Peter Candler — in his aforementioned study juxtaposing Tolkien's Frodo Baggins and Nietzsche's Zarathustra in their competition for the title of the ideal human form — comes closer to capturing Tolkien's confidence in the real-world, metaphysical implications of his aesthetics. According to Candler, there is indeed an "inescapably linguistic character of all revelation and truth," and yet Tolkien's own contribution to the postmodern "linguistic turn" is best understood against the backdrop of the medieval belief in the absolute convertibility of the transcendental properties of truth and beauty: "The Christian appeal is, with a certain element of charm (if not 'glamour'), to a story that is in some way more attractive because more beautiful, and beautiful because *true.*"[24] The contrast between Tolkien's humble hobbits and Nietzsche's Zarathustrian philosophy of the will to power is also the subject of Douglas Blount's essay, "*Über*hobbits: Tolkien, Nietzsche, and the Will to Power." Tolkien's hostility towards modernity in general and its manifestation in the technological mastery of nature in particular has invited comparison with another eminent German philosopher of the last century, Martin Heidegger.[25] Also addressing the theme of power in Tolkien's writings is Jane Chance's *"The Lord of the Rings": The Mythology of Power,* which examines Tolkien's *magnum opus* in light of Michel Foucault's important work on the nature of power structures and relationships. In an essay by Robert Eaglestone, Emanuel Levinas is the post-modern French philosopher of choice, as Eaglestone analyzes the invisibility-inducing effects of Sauron's Ring in light of Levinas's logic of the "other."[26] Finally, Hayden Head has found in Tolkien's fiction a worthwhile application of the theory of imitative desire propounded by the contemporary French philosopher René Girard.[27]

Of those studies specifically addressing the philosophical antecedents of Tolkien's work, however, interest has naturally tended to gravitate towards the

23 Flieger, *Splintered Light*, xii.
24 Candler, "Tolkien or Nietzsche," 6 (emphasis added).
25 Malpas, "Home."
26 Eaglestone, "Invisibility."
27 Head, "Imitative Desire in Tolkien's Mythology: A Girardian Perspective."

foundational philosophies of Platonism and Neoplatonism. There have been, as one might expect, the obligatory comparisons of Tolkien's invisibility-inducing ring with the famous Ring of Gyges from Plato's *Republic*,[28] and Gergely Nagy and Frank Weinreich have each looked at the similar roles that myth serves in the thought of Tolkien and Plato.[29] I have already alluded to the prominent role Plato serves in Kreeft's *The Philosophy of Tolkien,* and Mary E. Zimmer has argued that behind Tolkien's depiction of magic in his stories is what twentieth-century German philosopher Ernst Cassirer describes as "the assumption that the world of things and the world of names form a single undifferentiated chain of causality and hence a single reality," an assumption that Zimmer correlates with what she describes as the "Christian-Neoplatonic belief that language first created that reality."[30] Of particular note in connection with Tolkien's alleged Platonism are a couple of essays written thirty years ago by Mary Carman Rose and Verlyn Flieger.[31] Rose's article identifies Tolkien as a Christian Platonist in general and his *Ainulindalë* in particular as a "Christian Platonist account of creation."[32] The three specific Platonic elements she finds common to Lewis, Williams, and Tolkien are "the reality and availability of suprasensory aspects of creation; the modes of our coming to know these aspects of creation; and the ideal copresence of truth, beauty, and goodness in all aspects of creation."[33] Although Rose recognizes that, as Christians, the Platonism of these three thinkers does differ in some notable ways from all forms of non-Christian Platonism, she nevertheless implies that the "psychophysical dualism" and "other-worldliness" she finds explicit in Lewis and Williams are also dimly present in Tolkien. Ralph Wood, on the other hand, has more recently made the point that, in comparison with his friend Lewis, Tolkien was in fact "no sort of Platonist at all. He espoused what might be roughly called an Aristotelian metaphysics. For him, transcendent reality is to be found in the depths of this world rather than in some putative existence beyond it."[34] While Wood's emphatic denial of any

---

28 See Katz, "The Rings of Tolkien and Plato: Lessons in Power, Choice, and Morality"; De Armas, "Gyges' Ring: Invisibility in Plato, Tolkien, and Lope de Vega"; Eaglestone, "Invisibility"; and Herbert, "Tolkien's Tom Bombadil and the Platonic Ring of Gyges."

29 Nagy, "Saving the Myths: the Re-creation of Mythology in Plato and Tolkien" and Weinreich, "Metaphysics of Myth: The Platonic Ontology of 'Mythopoeia.'"

30 Zimmer, "Creating and Re-creating Worlds with Words: The Religion and Magic of Language in *The Lord of the Rings,*" 50, 52.

31 Rose, "The Christian Platonism of C.S. Lewis, J.R.R. Tolkien, and Charles Williams," and Flieger, "Naming the Unnameable: The Neoplatonic 'One' in Tolkien's *Silmarillion.*"

32 Rose, "Christian Platonism," 205.

33 Ibid., 206. Unfortunately Rose doesn't apply any of these elements to Tolkien in much detail.

34 Wood, "Conflict and Convergence," 325.

Platonism in Tolkien is perhaps slightly overstated, he is certainly right that the latter's metaphysical sympathies run in a decidedly more Aristotelian than directly Platonic direction.[35]

As for Flieger's article on Tolkien's Neoplatonic influence, she focuses on Tolkien's identification of God, or "Eru," as "the One" (*Eru* being the Elvish word for "the One"), pointing out that a "central idea, indeed a major element, in Neoplatonic thought is the concept of God as the One, the Monad beyond human knowing or naming."[36] Of prime interest to Flieger, accordingly, is the "unsolvable problem" she finds common to Tolkien, Plotinus, and the Christian Neoplatonist Pseudo-Dionysius: "They are confined to the separable and limited vocabulary of human language to talk about inseparable, unlimited being. They must express the inexpressible."[37] Approaching Tolkien in light of the Plotinian and Dionysian tradition of Neoplatonism, Flieger both here and in her *Splintered Light* stresses the apophatic or negative dimension of Tolkien's fictional theology at the expense of its more cataphatic or positive aspects, going so far as to represent Tolkien's Eru as an almost deistic entity who has abdicated the real work of creation to the intermediate agency of the angelic Ainur.[38] Following in Flieger's footsteps, while offering an even deeper analysis of the overlap between the themes of Tolkien and those of Platonic and Neoplatonic philosophy, is John Cox's insightful but similarly flawed "Tolkien's Platonic Fantasy."[39] As I will argue, in contrast to both of these studies, Tolkien is in fact far more balanced, biblical, and Thomistic in his philosophies of God and creation than a one-sidedly Platonic and Neoplatonic interpretation of Tolkien would seem to allow.

In the handful of studies that have approached Tolkien first and foremost as a *Christian* Neoplatonist, St. Augustine and Boethius have naturally had feature-roles. John Houghton has drawn out a number of illuminating parallels between Tolkien's creation-myth and Augustine's literal commentary on the

---

35 As we will see in chapter four, for example, contrary to Rose's claim, Tolkien explicitly rejects the psychophysical dualism of Plato in favor of the hylomorphic understanding of the soul's relationship to the body advanced by Aristotle and St. Thomas.

36 Flieger, "Naming the Unnameable," 127.

37 Ibid., 128–29.

38 "It is the Ainur, not Eru, who actually create Tolkien's world. They sing its plan in the Great Music which they make from the themes Eru propounds to them, and from that plan fabricate the material world. The rest of Tolkien's vast mythology is enacted without Eru, involving chiefly the Ainur and the Children of Ilúvatar. Father of All he may be, but he has no further role in the action.... He remains throughout the Unknown God, unknowable and unreachable in his oneness, perceivable and approachable only to the extent by which the part can represent the whole." Ibid., 132.

39 Cox, "Tolkien's Platonic Fantasy."

Book of Genesis.[40] Matthew Fisher has written an article placing Tolkien at the "crossroads" of Augustinian theology and anthropology on the one hand and, on the other, the Northern, Beowulfian theme of courage in the face of impossible opposition,[41] while Kathleen Dubs has traced the important themes of providence, fate, and chance in *The Lord of the Rings* to Boethius's *Consolation of Philosophy*.[42]

Augustine and Boethius have also made prominent appearances in a debate that has been waged over Tolkien's philosophy of evil. While readers have long recognized a certain Neoplatonism in Tolkien's representation of evil as a corruption or privation of the otherwise inherent goodness of being, Tolkien expert Tom Shippey has argued that Tolkien's fiction in fact embodies a syncretistic, even contradictory, union of the historically opposed views of Neoplatonic monism on the one hand and, on the other, a Manichean dualism according to which evil is a subsistent reality in its own right, coequal and equipotent with the good.[43] While Shippey's argument has gained a significant following, Scott Davison and the late British theologian Colin Gunton have each written pieces attempting to defend the consistent Augustinianism of Tolkien's theology of evil, and John Houghton and Neal Keesee have together argued that the tensions in Tolkien's presentation of evil noted by Shippey are in fact tensions already present in Boethius's treatment of evil.[44] We will take up the question of evil in the concluding chapter of this book in an effort to see how understanding Tolkien's philosophy of evil in light of his Thomistic metaphysics of creation promises to resolve the issue.

Tolkien's Thomism

AS FOR ST. THOMAS AQUINAS'S PARTICULAR INFLUENCE ON Tolkien's metaphysics, the case for this may be broadly divided into two parts, the first (addressed below) having to do with the real-life, religious, theological, historical, and cultural connection that may be inferred to have existed between these two individuals. The second motive for inquiring into St. Thomas's possible

---

40 Houghton, "Augustine in the Cottage of Lost Play: The *Ainulindalë* as Asterisk Cosmology."
41 Fisher, "Working at the Crossroads: Tolkien, St. Augustine, and the *Beowulf*-poet."
42 Dubs, "Providence, Fate, and Chance: Boethian Philosophy in *The Lord of the Rings*."
43 Shippey, *J.R.R. Tolkien: Author of the Century*, 112–60.
44 Gunton, "A Far-Off Gleam of the Gospel: Salvation in Tolkien's *The Lord of the Rings*"; Davison, "Tolkien and the Nature of Evil"; and Houghton and Keesee, "Tolkien, King Alfred, and Boethius: Platonist Views of Evil in *The Lord of the Rings*."

role in shaping Tolkien's philosophical thought has to do, of course, with their discernible theological and philosophical affinities, which will be the primary focus of the present study, and the main outlines of which I would like to rehearse briefly here. The first point that might be made in this regard is the fact that both men begin their metaphysical thinking in the same place, which is to say, in the beginning, when God began everything. St. Thomas, for example, has been widely celebrated as *the* theologian of the doctrine of creation.[45] As G.K. Chesterton once quipped, a fitting Carmelite epithet for Thomas, similar to John "of the Cross" or Thérèse "of the Child Jesus," would be *Thomas a Creatore,* "Thomas of the Creator." Commenting on Chesterton's remarks, Aquinas scholar Rudi te Velde has noted that "it is, indeed, true that the theme of creation is basic to Thomas's thought," as it "provides the general metaphysical framework of most of his theological, anthropological, and ethical inquiries. The whole of what exists, in all its multiplicity and diversity, is regarded as a good creation of God."[46] In this evaluation, Velde reiterates the judgment rendered by the twentieth-century German Thomist, Josef Pieper, concerning the central place the doctrine of creation enjoyed in St. Thomas's thought:

> In the philosophy of St. Thomas Aquinas, there is a fundamental idea by which almost all the basic concepts of his vision of the world are determined: the idea of creation, or more precisely, the notion that nothing exists which is not *creatura*, except the Creator Himself; and in addition, that this createdness determines entirely and all-pervasively the inner structure of the creature.[47]

As Pieper continues, much as the concept of createdness for St. Thomas characterizes the "inner structure" of every existing thing, so also "the notion of creation determines and characterizes the interior structure of *nearly all* the basic concepts in St. Thomas's philosophy of Being."[48] Even when the doctrine of creation is not

---

45 Kerr, *After Aquinas: Versions of Thomism,* 39.

46 Velde, *Aquinas on God: the 'Divine Science' of the "Summa Theologiae,"* 123. On the importance and unique role of the doctrine of creation in Thomas's thought (including another enthusiastic appraisal of Chesterton's above comment), see also Torrell, *Saint Thomas Aquinas, Volume 1: The Person and His Work,* 161–62.

47 Pieper, *The Silence of St. Thomas,* 47.

48 Ibid., 48. In a related fashion, Jean-Pierre Torrell explains in his biography of St. Thomas: "He is certainly not the only Christian thinker to have developed a creationist view of the universe following the book of Genesis, but he has probably done it with the greatest rigor, not only in dealing with questions relative to the beginning of the world or to its eternity, but even more perhaps in unfolding all the implications that stem from the biblical teaching. To say that the world is created

explicitly mentioned or even alluded to by Aquinas, it is almost always present, silently guiding him into many of his profoundest insights.

As for Tolkien, not only does he begin his *legendarium*, in evident imitation of the Bible, with his own genesis narrative, the *Ainulindalë*, but, as we have seen, the interplay of the themes of creation and sub-creation raised there were held by Tolkien to be integral to the meaning of his entire Middle-earth corpus. The programmatic statement from his letter to Peter Hastings cited earlier bears repeating: "since the whole matter from beginning to end is mainly concerned with the relation of Creation to making and sub-creation…, it must be clear that references to these things are not casual, but fundamental" (L 188). If Thomas has sometimes been referred to as the "theologian of creation," Tolkien might with equal justification be described as the "mythologist of creation."

This leads us to a second, related point upon which the metaphysics of Thomas and Tolkien call for comparison, which is that, contrary to much modern, including theistic philosophy, the metaphysical thought of Tolkien, like Thomas's, is deeply and ineluctably *theological*, attempting to see all of reality as implicating the infinite, reality-enriching plenitude of the divine being. As I hope to show, for example, it is the same kind of profound theological intuition of all created being discussed by Pieper above that will allow Tolkien to say that *The Lord of the Rings* is fundamentally about God without God ever being mentioned in it. Much as the centrality of the doctrine of creation made possible those places in his thought and writing where St. Thomas is otherwise "silent" on the matter, I want to suggest that it is similarly the centrality of God in Tolkien's metaphysical thought that, within his fiction, allows for what we might here refer to as the theological "silence of J.R.R. Tolkien."

Related to this, a third principle common to Thomas and Tolkien is what we will find to be their shared metaphysical realism. Contrary to the idealism and phenomenalism of much modern philosophy, seeking to reduce things (or at least what is held to be most important about them) to their mere representational or phenomenal appearances, for Tolkien and Thomas, things, being created by a God who is himself Being, are inescapably real. Things are *there*, they exist, they have their own mind-independent reality, yet a reality which, because dependent upon the divine mind by virtue of their createdness, at the same time has a constitutional affinity with those human minds (created in God's

---

signifies that it is entirely, in each and every element, in a relationship of total dependence on God: everything that is, is from God, God giving to each existing thing not only being, but being what it is, and the power of acting according to the nature he has given it." Torrell, *Saint Thomas Aquinas, Volume 1: The Person and His Work*, 163.

image) that know and experience them. Through his Elves in particular, as we shall see, Tolkien lays great stress on the goodness and consequent desirableness of the "otherness" of things. It is this awareness of the simultaneous kinship and otherness of things, their at-once familiarity yet strangeness, their sameness and difference, that Tolkien argues is one of the chief tasks for all fairy-stories to cultivate and maintain (TR 77).

On a less doctrinal note, a further justification for bringing Thomas and Tolkien into dialogue with each other has to do with the common catholicity or universality with which they labored in their respective areas of study and writing. Thomas and Tolkien were both men of tremendous powers of synthesis, for their shared religious convictions led them to believe that, because truth is truth and God is the Creator of all, the best that pagan learning and experience had to offer — whether it be the sublime principles of Greek philosophy or the sublime beauties of heathen myth and fairy-tale — was not to be neglected, but appropriated and sanctified for Christian (and in the case of Tolkien's audience, even non-Christian) edification. Thomas writes in his commentary on the *Metaphysics* of Aristotle, the philosopher whose thought he especially helped harmonize with Christian revelation, that "we should love both: those whose opinion we follow, and those whose opinion we reject. For both have applied themselves to the quest for the truth, and both have helped us in it."[49] As for those distinctly philosophical conclusions that Thomas was able to demonstrate by reason alone, as Étienne Gilson argued in the last century, it was Thomas's faith in divine revelation, providing him, as it were, with an "inside track," that first prompted and thus made possible many of these insights.[50]

In a similar spirit, yet working in the reverse direction to what Philipp Rosemann has described as the medieval scholastic project of re-inscribing Greek *logos* within the Christian *mythos*,[51] Tolkien's work draws upon not only the inherited mythology of the Western world, but also its philosophical and theological resources

---

49 Aquinas, *Commentary on Aristotle's Metaphysics* 12.9, trans. Rowan.

50 In his 1931 Gifford Lecture, Gilson defended the existence of an authentic and intelligible "Christian philosophy" in the Middle Ages, a philosophy that operated on its own terms but which took for its inspiration and guiding light the truths of revelation, a philosophy, furthermore, that Gilson believed above all manifested in the thought of St. Thomas: "the Bible is full of ideas about God and His divine government which, although not properly philosophical in character, only needed to fall into the right soil to become fruitful of philosophic consequences. The fact that there is no philosophy in Scripture does not warrant the conclusion that Scripture could have exerted no influence on the evolution of philosophy.... Why should we refuse to admit *a priori* that Christianity might have been able to change the course of the history of philosophy by opening up to human reason, by the mediation of faith, perspectives as yet undreamt of?" Gilson, *The Spirit of Medieval Philosophy*, 11–12.

51 Rosemann, *Understanding Scholastic Thought with Foucault*, 50–54.

as well. Tolkien's purpose in doing so, moreover, was to construct an entirely new mythology that would at the same time resonate powerfully with Christian revelation, yet without (at least formally or explicitly) presupposing it. One place where this may be seen is found in Tolkien's description of the Valar, his fictional angels who shape and govern the world of Middle-earth, as entities that were "meant to provide beings of the same order of beauty, power, and majesty as the 'gods' of higher mythology, which can yet be accepted — well, shall we say baldly, by a mind that believes in the Blessed Trinity" (L 146). In his attempted synthesis of the truth of Christian angelology and the "beauty, power, and majesty" of pagan polytheism, we have just one example of Tolkien's mission to assimilate the good of pagan myth within an otherwise Christian narrative. Much as the biblical creation "myth" provided Thomas and medieval scholasticism more generally with a crucial datum in developing a unique and powerful metaphysical system, so also did the *philosophia perennis* represented by Thomas provide Tolkien with a tacit guide in the development of a rational Christian mythology.

Tolkien's Thomistic Sources

THE ABOVE POINTS—THEIR CREATIONISM, THEIR REALISM, AND their scholastic synthesis of pagan and Christian learning — provide only the barest sketch of the kinds of parallels between Thomas and Tolkien's thought we will be examining in greater detail in the chapters to follow. At this point we turn to the question of what may have been some of the concrete means by which Thomas's ideas would have been communicated to Tolkien. To begin, it has to be said that there is admittedly very little direct or obvious evidence linking these two thinkers. Tolkien, for example, never so much as alludes to St. Thomas in any of his writings, yet this by itself is hardly conclusive, for neither does he ever mention Augustine, Boethius, Plato, Nietzsche or any other major thinker whose works Tolkien was certainly aware of, and in the light of whose thought his stories have been insightfully examined by others.

What we do know is that Tolkien was in possession of, and at some point in his life spent some time consulting, his personal copy of a four-volume 1787 Latin edition of Thomas's *magnum opus*, the *Summa Theologiae*.[52] Beyond this point of

---

52 According to Alison Milbank, Tolkien's copy of the *Summa* includes marginal notes which she believes to be those of Tolkien's godfather, Fr. Francis Morgan, from whom Tolkien apparently inherited the set. She says that it also has "marks on sections that might easily be by Tolkien — book marks are made of Anglo-Saxon booklists! They also mark sections on marriage and obedience, which

contact, we are more or less left to informed conjecture as to the avenues by which Thomas's influence might have been mediated to Tolkien. Peter Candler, in his essay on Tolkien and Nietzsche, notes the profound influence that Pope Leo XIII's 1879 encyclical *Aeterni Patris*, with its call for Catholic intellectuals to return to the thought of St. Thomas, had on the education and consciousness of Catholics of Tolkien's generation.[53] In particular, Candler conjectures that the Birmingham Oratory, where Tolkien went to school as a boy — established by Cardinal John Henry Newman in 1849 and the place where Tolkien's guardian and godfather, Fr. Francis Morgan, ministered — was the sort of place where the ripples of this burgeoning interest in Thomas would have been felt.[54] Alison Milbank has made the further point, no less worth repeating for its obviousness, that Tolkien sat through sermons every week by those trained in the thought of St. Thomas.[55]

Additional evidence of an even more indirect source of Thomas's possible influence on Tolkien lies in the parallels existing between Tolkien's whole approach to art or sub-creation and that found in other lay Thomists during the early and mid-twentieth century. Here Jacques Maritain's *Art and Scholasticism* may be of some significance. A treatise attempting to develop a Thomistic theory of art based in turn on Thomas's theory of being, it had a particularly galvanizing effect on many Catholic artists and writers during this period. Maritain's little text was adopted, for example, as a sort of manifesto by the Catholic art guild at Ditchling in East Sussex in the 1920s, an affiliation that included artist Eric Gill, poet David Jones, and Fr. John O'Connor, the co-translator of the first English edition (1923)

---

fit with Tolkien's early marriage against Fr. Morgan's advice." Tolkien Library, "Interview with Dr. Alison Milbank author of *Chesterton and Tolkien as Theologians*." According to my colleague Ben Merkle, who has also examined Tolkien's *Summa*, the volumes are mostly unmarked except for a few spots in the more ethical matters of the *secunda pars*, where there has been some underlining and an occasional scribbled word.

53 Candler, "Tolkien or Nietzsche," 8.

54 Paul E. Sigmund similarly concurs that it was through institutions such as the Birmingham Oratory that the social and political teaching of the First Vatican Council was widely promulgated: "In the nineteenth century the Catholic church drew on Aquinas' political thought to respond to the challenges of industrialism, liberalism, and socialism.... The Catholic political parties and trade unions that had emerged in many European countries used the encyclicals and Thomist categories of thought to develop a 'communitarian' or 'personalist' alternative both to socialism and to free-enterprise capitalism that claimed to provide for both the individual and social aspects of private property. In these organizations, as well as in seminaries, universities, and secondary schools run by the church, Thomism provided the structure through which political and ethical questions were articulated and analyzed." *St. Thomas Aquinas on Politics and Ethics*, ed. Sigmund, xxiv. On the other hand, while the influence of the Birmingham Oratory on the formation of the young Tolkien's mind was certainly not limited to the time of Tolkien's formal education there, his own studies at the Oratory lasted only a few months before he resumed his education at King Edward's Academy. Carpenter, *Tolkien: A Biography*, 26–27.

55 Milbank, *Chesterton and Tolkien as Theologians*, 15.

of Maritain's text, as well as the purported inspiration behind Chesterton's famous clerical sleuth, Fr. Brown.[56] Chesterton probably had the Ditchling group in mind when, in his biography of St. Thomas, he alluded to the existence of a contemporary Thomistic renaissance: "In this not very hopeful modern moment, there are no men so hopeful as those who are today looking to St. Thomas as a leader in a hundred crying questions of craftsmanship and ownership and economic ethics. There is undoubtedly a hopeful and creative Thomism in our time."[57]

   Although we can only speculate as to the possibility and extent of Tolkien's own familiarity with Maritain's work, Alison Milbank in her *Chesterton and Tolkien as Theologians* has pointed to a number of broad but legitimate parallels between Tolkien's and Maritain's views on art. Some of the similarities I have observed in my own reading of Maritain and Tolkien include their agreement on the simultaneous practicality yet integrity and dignity of the work of art;[58] art's freedom from and yet imitation of nature;[59] the responsibility of art both

---

56 MacCarthy, *Eric Gill: A Lover's Quest for Art and God*, 161. See also Candler, "Tolkien or Nietzsche," 9–14.

57 Chesterton, *St. Thomas Aquinas*, 189. Chesterton also bears witness in his biography to a more general resurgence of interest in and work being done on Thomas at the time of his writing (1933). As Chesterton self-effacingly writes, "this book, I hope (and I am happy to say I believe) will probably be lost and forgotten in the flood of better books about St. Thomas Aquinas, which are at this moment pouring from every printing-press in Europe, and even in England and America." Ibid, 197.

58 According to Maritain, "Art belongs to the practical order. It is turned towards action, not towards the pure interiority of knowledge." Maritain, *Art and Scholasticism*, 6. Tolkien, as we have seen, similarly identifies a very practical or moral aim to his fiction: "I would claim, if I did not think it presumptuous in one so ill-instructed, to have as one object the elucidation of truth, and the encouragement of good morals in this real world…" (L 194). At the same time, however, Maritain argues that, as a *productive* action, "Making" was contrasted by the medieval schoolmen with mere "Doing," for whereas in mere Doing the action or result of the action is a means used for some further end, in Making the art product is an end in itself. Maritain, *Art and Scholasticism*, 8. Tolkien also allows for the distinction between Doing and Making when he describes the attitude of Elvish art toward the natural world: "they have a devoted love of the physical world, and a desire to observe and understand it for its own sake and as 'other' — sc. as a reality derived from God in the same degree as themselves — not as a material for use or as a power-platform" (L 236). The Elvish love of the world "for its own sake and as 'other'" which lies at the heart of their art is also shared by Tom Bombadil, whom Tolkien describes as desiring "knowledge of other things, their history and nature, *because they are 'other'* and wholly independent of the enquiring mind, a spirit coeval with the rational mind, and entirely unconcerned with 'doing' anything with the knowledge" (L 192, emphasis original). Alison Milbank has further suggested that the two races of Elves and Men basically correspond to Aristotle's distinction between *poesis* and *praxis* respectively. Milbank, *Chesterton and Tolkien as Theologians,* 20.

59 On the freedom of art, Maritain writes: "Doing, in the restricted sense in which the Schoolmen understood this word, consist in *the free use, precisely as free,* of our faculties, or in the exercise of our free will, considered not with regard to the things themselves or to the works which we produce, but merely with regard to the use which we make of our freedom." Maritain, *Art and Scholasticism*, 7. And because the artist must be free, "servile imitation is absolutely foreign to art" (56). The purpose behind art's freedom from nature, however, is not so that it might despise nature, but rather so

to communicate truth to the intellect and simply to delight the will;[60] the consequent rationality or intelligibility of art; its likeness and submission to the Creator's act of creation on the one hand and the antithesis between it and the technological tendency towards the domination of one's artistic "medium" on the other; and, more concretely, even the role of art in acting as a "prism" through which the light of divine beauty may be further refracted. Beyond these and other similarities, it is also noteworthy how the Ditchling community influenced by Maritain also shared with Tolkien an idealization of rural, agrarian living, a wariness toward modern technology, and what Elizabeth Ward in her biography of David Jones identifies as a "passion for the home-made or authentically crafted artefact," idiosyncrasies all of which the members of the Ditchling guild in one way or another saw as being rationally defensible in terms of, and even mandated by, the common-sense sacramental realism of St. Thomas Aquinas.[61]

Another means by which Thomas's influence may have impressed itself on Tolkien was by those same allusive avenues through which so many of Tolkien's other influences were mediated to him. To quote Candler again:

> One can only, again, speculate on the influence of a figure like Aquinas on someone like Tolkien, but in any case there is no doubt that some kind of mediated Thomism was certainly in the air Tolkien breathed — delivered, perhaps, through the pipe-bowl. Perhaps the metaphor is apt — Tolkien's extra-philological influences seem to have been, so to speak, tobacco- or ale-mediated through the conversations in pubs, drawing-rooms, college quarters (not to mention letters) which were so formative on his imagination.[62]

---

that it might be an agent in its beautification. For Tolkien, the importance of free will in art or "sub-creation" is so great that the two terms are used interchangeably by him, as may be seen in his letter to Peter Hastings: "having mentioned Free Will, I might say that in my myth I have used 'subcreation' in a special way.... Free Will is derivative.... So in this myth, it is 'feigned'...that He gave special 'sub-creative' powers to certain of His highest created beings..." (L 195). And like Maritain, Tolkien also believes that art, especially as represented in Fantasy literature, is "founded upon the hard recognition that things are so in the world as it appears under the sun; on a recognition of fact, but not a slavery to it" (TR 75).

60 According to Maritain, following Aquinas, "the beautiful is what gives delight — not just any delight, but delight in knowing; not the delight peculiar to the act of knowing, but a delight which superabounds and overflows from this act because of the object known. If a thing exalts and delights the soul by the very fact that it is given to the soul's intuition, it is good to apprehend, it is beautiful." Maritain, *Art and Scholasticism*, 23. Compare this with the following statement by Tolkien describing a good fairy-story: "But first of all it must succeed just as a tale, excite, please, and even on occasion move, and within its own imagined world be accorded (literary) belief. To succeed in that was my primary object" (L 233).

61 Ward, *David Jones: Mythmaker*, 32.

62 Candler, "Tolkien or Nietzsche," 8.

The most famous of these intellectual gatherings of Tolkien's was, of course, the Inklings, the informal literary and philosophical group revolving around Tolkien, C.S. Lewis, and Charles Williams. It was in this venue that Tolkien, over the years, had the opportunity to read significant portions of his Middle-earth corpus, and whose membership at times included the likes of Gervase Matthews, a Catholic priest from Blackfriars, the Oxford house of the Dominicans (St. Thomas's order).[63] The Thomist who probably exerted the greatest influence on the Inklings, however, was Chesterton, to whom the thought and imagination of both Tolkien and Lewis were much indebted. Tolkien's essay "On Fairy-Stories," in which he sets forth many of the literary principles behind his own fiction, owes much in particular to the philosophical outlook articulated by Chesterton in "The Ethics of Elfland," the third chapter of *Orthodoxy*.[64] Whether Tolkien was familiar with Chesterton's actual biography of Thomas is not known for sure, yet the common metaphysical emphases between the two men are certainly suggestive. Raymond Dennehy, for example, identifies three main metaphysical emphases in Chesterton's study of St. Thomas — the goodness of creation contra the doctrine of the Manichees, his philosophical realism, and the primacy of the doctrine of being[65] — all three of which, as we shall see, enjoy a central importance in the literature of Tolkien.

Even if Tolkien never did read Chesterton's work on Thomas directly, the nature of, first, Chesterton's influence on Tolkien's imagination, and second, Chesterton's own somewhat curious relationship to St. Thomas, together may provide an instructive analogy for how Tolkien's own Thomism is best to be understood. One of the surprising aspects of Chesterton's little book on Thomas is that, although it has been lauded by such eminent twentieth-century Thomists as Maritain, Gilson, Anton Pegis, James Weisheipl, and even the Master-General of the Dominican Order at the time, Père Gillet,[66] Chesterton's profound insight into the thought of St. Thomas does not seem to have been the product of his own careful research.[67] In his biography of

63 Carpenter, *Inklings*, 186. Matthews even seems to make an appearance in Tolkien's time-travel story and "apocryphal imitation of the *Inklings' Saga Book*," "The Notion Club Papers," in the character of Dom Jonathan Markison, whose "polymathy" is described as extending "to some very recondite knowledge of Germanic origins" (SD 149, 151). (Matthews, by comparison, was an expert on Byzantine history.)

64 For Alison Milbank's discussion of the influence of Chesterton's *Orthodoxy* on Tolkien, see Milbank, *Chesterton and Tolkien as Theologians*, x.

65 Dennehy, "Introduction" to Chesterton, *St. Thomas Aquinas*, in *G.K. Chesterton: Collected Works*, vol. 2, 414–17.

66 Pearce, *Wisdom and Innocence: A Life of G.K. Chesterton*, 431–34.

67 Dennehy, "Introduction" to Chesterton, *St. Thomas Aquinas*, in *G.K. Chesterton: Collected*

Chesterton, Joseph Pearce comments on the "carefree approach to the writing of the book," and how Chesterton had "dictated half the biography without consulting any books whatsoever," and that, even when he did finally acquire a list of classic and more recent studies on St. Thomas, according to his secretary Dorothy Collins, Chesterton "'flipped them rapidly through' and then proceeded to dictate to her the rest of his own book without consulting any of them again."[68] Instead, R.V. Young is probably correct when he characterizes Chesterton's text on Thomas as "the result not of diligent scholarly labor, but of intuition and intellectual sympathy.... In other words, the brilliance of Chesterton's study of the Common Doctor of the Church comes from a flash of insight ignited by an innate philosophical affinity."[69] Or in Pearce's own words, Chesterton "*loved* St. Thomas with both his heart and mind, and he *understood* St. Thomas's teaching with both his heart and mind. This, he hoped, would be sufficient."[70] It is in similar terms, finally, that I suggest that Tolkien's own Thomism might be appreciated, for regardless of what might be conjectured about Tolkien's direct or indirect exposure to the writings of Thomas or other Thomists, in the end the thing calling for analysis and comment is the undeniable fact of just such an "innate philosophical affinity" and "intellectual sympathy" between Tolkien and St. Thomas, whatever the historical causes might have been in producing it.

Method and Outline

THIS BRINGS US AT LAST TO THE METHOD AND OUTLINE I WILL be pursuing in the argument to follow. Although my analysis will cover much of the fictional history recorded in Tolkien's *legendarium* and a number of Tolkien's texts and various commentaries, the argument will focus on and will be largely organized around the structure of Tolkien's creation-myth, the *Ainulindalë*. An extraordinarily dense and subtle text in terms of both its literary and its metaphysical content, the *Ainulindalë* touches directly or indirectly on virtually all of the themes I wish to discuss here. Chapter one, accordingly, focuses on the nature of Tolkien's God, Eru, the creative source of all being who is introduced by Tolkien in the very opening line of *The Silmarillion*. The chapter

---

Works, vol. 2, 414–17.
68 Ibid., 423–24.
69 Young, "Chesterton's Paradoxes and Thomist Ontology," 67.
70 Ibid., 424.

also inquires into the general character of theistic belief and the question of faith and reason in Middle-earth, questions in which St. Thomas was also deeply interested. The second chapter extends the theological analysis of the first, taking as its starting point the very first act of creation, in which the angelic Ainur are brought into being and are subsequently taught the original musical theme by Ilúvatar the Creator. Here the question of creative and sub-creative possibility is discussed against the backdrop of the medieval debate over divine omnipotence and the Augustinian doctrine of the divine ideas. Chapter three moves on to a consideration of the metaphysical significance of the two central events in Tolkien's "cosmogonical drama" (as he termed it), namely the Music of the Ainur, a subject that has received a good deal of attention from commentators, and the Vision of the Ainur, whose importance for understanding Tolkien's metaphysics has gone largely unnoticed. Chapter four picks up with the next stage of Tolkien's creation-drama, when the Creator speaks the word that at last brings the physical world into being and he commissions those Ainur who are willing, the "Valar," to enter into the world and fashion it according to the Music and Vision. This chapter will thus round out chapter two's discussion of the question of sub-creative *possibility* with its study of Tolkien's and Thomas's theological and metaphysical conditions of sub-creative *actuality*. Chapter five, as I have mentioned, will involve us in an analysis of Tolkien's metaphysics of evil, a central theme both in the *Ainulindalë* and throughout Tolkien's Middle-earth corpus. By approaching Tolkien's view of evil in terms of his underlying Thomistic understanding of creation, I attempt to navigate a debate that has arisen over Tolkien's Augustinianism on the one hand and his alleged Manichaeism on the other, and I argue that Tolkien suggests a much more radical synthesis of these traditions than has hitherto been appreciated. In the conclusion, finally, I proffer some closing remarks about the significance of Tolkien's Thomism, not only for understanding Tolkien but possibly also for facilitating a contemporary retrieval of St. Thomas, and how, if there is a sense in which mythology has its roots in metaphysics, as Tolkien so clearly says that it does, there may nevertheless be an equally important sense in which sound metaphysical reasoning also has its roots in myth and the imagination.

While the argument of this book, as I have said, will focus on the *Ainulindalë,* I also draw freely from Tolkien's essay "On Fairy-Stories" and especially his published letters, two sources of invaluable authorial commentary on the meaning and intention of his work. In keeping with a dominant trend in current literary criticism, some Tolkien scholars have questioned the validity of using authorial intent as a definitive or even reliable measure of authorial achievement, a debate into which it is not my purpose to enter here.[71] Suffice it to say that the primary object of this study is Tolkien's own understanding of the metaphysics of his fiction, though throughout the reader is of course left with the responsibility of determining for himself the level to which Tolkien may have actually succeeded in achieving the rationally and metaphysically coherent and cogent mythological system he was at times aiming for. I will also from time to time be referring to select passages from Tolkien's *History of Middle-earth*, edited by his son Christopher, and in particular volume ten of that series, *Morgoth's Ring*, which contains some of Tolkien's most developed and sophisticated musings on the metaphysics of his *legendarium*.

It is also to be recognized at the outset that, although this study of Tolkien is a metaphysical inquiry, Tolkien's work is, of course, first and foremost a work of literature, and of fantasy literature at that, and obviously *not* a philosophical treatise, and thus the ultimate significance of this study for understanding the man and his writings as a whole will obviously have its limitations. It thus goes without saying that nothing said here or in the analysis to follow is by any means intended to imply that the metaphysics of Middle-earth is the most important (much less the *only*) dimension to Tolkien's mythology. Here, rather, I would simply echo a parallel point made by Christian Moevs in his study of *The Metaphysics of Dante's Comedy*, which is that, in focusing on the metaphysics of Tolkien, the aim is "to address a neglected sphere of inquiry in order to balance, complement, and enrich, not set aside, what has been amply treated" in other readings of Tolkien.[72] However, it is also to be recognized that, as we have already begun to see, the difference between telling a story and doing good philosophy was a distinction that Tolkien himself was not terribly concerned with making. Taking Tolkien's own commentaries on his work as our guide, therefore, our goal, for good or for ill, will be to take his stories with the same kind of metaphysical seriousness as Tolkien himself did, which, as we shall see, is saying quite a lot. We scarcely need worry about out-doing Tolkien in this regard. As for St. Thomas, I have chosen to rely primarily on his *Summa Theologiae* (with references made to other works as the occasion merits), as it represents his most accessible and influential work, and is the one work of St. Thomas's we know Tolkien owned and had ready access to.

A brief word, finally, might also be said on the varying nature of the comparisons I will be making in the course of this study. Because my overall objective is

71 See, for example, Drout, "Towards a Better Tolkien Criticism," 15–29. For a brief critique of Drout, however, see Bratman, "The Year's Work in Tolkien Studies 2005," 278.

72 Moevs, *The Metaphysics of Dante's Comedy*, 12.

in fact twofold — first, to take Tolkien seriously as a metaphysician, or at least to take seriously the metaphysics of his mythology, and second, to show the affinity between Tolkien's metaphysics and that of St. Thomas's — sometimes the comparisons I will be making between the two will be less to suggest an important parallel between the two than simply to use Thomas's thought as a helpful foil for illustrating some point of interest in Tolkien's work. Thus, even when Tolkien's stories involve him in metaphysical suppositions that St. Thomas would never have entertained, even here Thomas, whose powers of intellectual taxonomy and metaphysical penetration are rightly legendary, will often prove to be a useful dialogue partner in raising the kinds of questions that might be instructively posed to Tolkien's work and in that way lead us to a new appreciation of the depth and breadth of Tolkien's own metaphysical sophistication. In some cases, Thomas's usefulness in helping elucidate precisely Tolkien's originality may even point to a more profound kind of agreement.

The Metaphysics
of Eru

There was Eru, the One,
who in Arda is called Ilúvatar....

IKE THE INAUGURAL VERSE OF THE BIBLE, "IN THE beginning *God*," so the opening line of Tolkien's mythology intro-duces us to what is arguably its most important character: "There was Eru, the One, who in Arda is called Ilúvatar" (S 15). I say "arguably," for it is not immediately obvious that the Creator is a significant character at all in Tolkien's mythical history, much less the most important one. After creating the angelic Ainur, to whom much of the work of fashioning and then governing the physical world is delegated, Eru seems to play very little role in Tolkien's tale, so that, after the first few chapters of *The Silmarillion*, references to him are few and far between, and, in *The Lord of the Rings*, they are virtually non-existent. Yet, as was noted in the Introduction, Tolkien characterized *The Lord of the Rings* as a story basically "about God, and His sole right to divine honour" (L 243). Part of the purpose of this chapter, accordingly, is to show how a metaphysical approach to the theology of Tolkien's fiction can help explain how God can (as Tolkien put it) be simultaneously "never absent and never named" (L 253). My claim is that what undergirds Tolkien's view of the "common being" (*ens commune*) of things, giving them their uncommon depth and reality, is a broadly Thomistic appreciation of the infinite profundity of the One who is self-subsisting being itself (*ipsum esse per se subsistens*). As I hope to show, it is a radically theological reckoning of being which he shares with St. Thomas that allows Tolkien in his fiction to be paradoxically everywhere and nowhere silent about God.

To this end, the order I propose to follow in the present chapter is to analyze the theology of Tolkien's *legendarium* in light of some of the central questions raised by St. Thomas in the *Summa Theologiae*'s famous and influential opening treatise on God. The first question we will consider, accordingly, concerns the

respective roles that faith and reason play in the theology of St. Thomas, comparing
this with the function that faith and reason — or their near equivalents — serve
within both Tolkien's fiction and his literary theory more generally. Following
this, our first test case of St. Thomas's and Tolkien's views on faith and reason
will be an examination of how each in his own way approaches the central issue
in the philosophy of religion, namely God's existence. Here we will look at the
Summa's fifth proof for God's existence in particular, his so-called "teleological
argument," and compare it with the way Tolkien in a couple of notable places
deals with much the same issue. After this, and again tracing the progression
of St. Thomas's argument in the *Summa,* we will follow our consideration of
the question of *whether* God exists with the question of *what* this God is. It is
this deliberation on the nature of the divine being that will in turn lead to our
reflection on the respective views of Tolkien and Thomas on the question alluded
to above, namely the paradox of how a transcendent Creator can nevertheless
be intensely present or immanent within his creation. Finally, we will conclude
the chapter with a second test case of their views on faith and reason through a
comparison of how each of these orthodox theologians handles one of the great
mysteries of the Christian religion in their respective writings, the doctrine of
the Holy Trinity.

Faith and Reason in St. Thomas

ALTHOUGH THE SUBJECT WITH WHICH WE ARE CONCERNED IN
this study is the metaphysical thought of Tolkien and St. Thomas — that is, with
their philosophical or *rational* perspectives and reflections on the nature and
structure of being, of what exists — as we shall shortly see, for neither of these
individuals can the question of reality be separated from a consideration of those
peculiar and proper modes by which we as specifically human inquirers have
been made to perceive and apprehend that reality. So it is that our investigation
into the metaphysics of St. Thomas and Tolkien must sooner or later — in this
case, sooner — lead us to a consideration of those means of faith and reason by
which, they both believed, we are able to respond to and apprehend the nature
of ultimate being.

As with the ambiguity surrounding God's presence within Tolkien's fiction,
the relevance of the relationship between faith and reason in Tolkien's *legendarium* is similarly complex and far from straightforward. Tolkien conceived of
his mythical history, after all, as belonging to a "pre-Christian" era, so that in

his stories, as he writes in one letter, "there are no churches, temples, or religious rites and ceremonies" (L 220). In another letter, he says of the Hobbits in particular that he did not think they "practiced any form of worship or prayer (unless through exceptional contact with Elves)" and of the Númenórean race of Men he says that, after their fall, "religion as divine worship" played only a "small part," as when in *The Two Towers* "a glimpse of it is caught in Faramir's remark on 'grace at meat'" (L 193-94 n). As in the case of Ilúvatar's (seemingly) diminishing presence after the first few chapters of *The Silmarillion*, Tolkien's intent seems to have been to make religious belief as invisible or unobtrusive as possible. While readers may be accustomed to seeing profound acts of hope on display in Middle-earth, this does not seem to be the case with her sister theological virtue of faith.

That having been said, one of the objectives Tolkien set for himself in setting his tale in a mythical, pre-Christian past, as I shall discuss more fully below, is the freedom it afforded both him and his readers to revisit imaginatively, and hence with renewed vision, certain aspects of the inhabited world that have in modern times grown so familiar as to become "trite." It was for this reason, for example, that Tolkien found the Arthurian cycle inadequate as a proper myth, as it was "involved in, and explicitly contains the Christian religion," something he considered "fatal" to the true purpose of myth and fairy-story, which he says in this context is to "reflect and contain in solution elements of moral and religious truth (or error), but not explicit, not in the known form of the primary 'real' world" (L 144). The problem with an overtly Christian mythology, in other words, is not its containing "moral and religious truth," but that by presenting such truth in the recognizably Christian categories already familiar and well-worn to us in "our present situation," the original, transformative force and mystery of such truth is deprived of its full force. In this sense, for Tolkien the studied *non*-religious character of his mythology has in fact a deeply religious and strategically apologetic motive: by approaching certain moral and religious themes in a mythical and unfamiliar setting, his hope was in part to recover something of their ancient clarity and potency. Included in these "elements of moral and religious truth" that Tolkien aspired to provide "in solution," as we shall see, is the age-old question of the relationship of faith and reason. Tolkien's challenge, in short, was to address the question while at the same time making the question invisible; of making it a "non-question," in other words, by placing it at a mythical point in history that long antedated our own times, in which we allowed it first to become a "question," and then a neglected or misunderstood question at that.

As to Tolkien's personal views on the relationship between faith and reason, one position he doubtlessly would have been aware of and which certainly would have held some authority for him was the famous synthesis promulgated by St. Thomas Aquinas and which Pope Leo XIII had made virtually the official position of the Roman Catholic Church in his 1879 encyclical *Aeterni Patris*. One of the things Pope Leo particularly commended in St. Thomas was his "clearly distinguishing, as is fitting, reason from faith, while happily associating the one with the other," and thus "both preserved the rights and had regard for the dignity of each."[1] Some of Thomas's more well-known statements along these lines appear in the opening articles of the *Summa,* in which he emphasizes the distinct spheres in which faith and reason have their proper operation. In the very first article of the *Summa* ("Whether, besides philosophy, any further doctrine is required"), Thomas explains how Scripture, which is to be received by faith and which provides the first principles or axioms of the otherwise demonstrative science of sacred doctrine or theology, "is no part of the philosophical sciences, which have been built up by human reason" (ST 1.1.1 *sed contra*). The necessity of sacred doctrine, moreover, lies in man's double spiritual need: the created fact, on the one hand, that man is by nature directed towards God as to an end that surpasses the grasp of his reason, and the historical fact, on the other, that man has fallen from his supernatural estate and so is in need of salvation. In the second article of the second question ("Whether it can be demonstrated that God exists"), Thomas further writes: "the existence of God and other like truths about God, which can be known by natural reason, are not articles of faith, but are preambles to the articles. For faith presupposes natural knowledge, even as grace presupposes nature" (ST 1.2.2 *ad* 1). Not only are faith and reason distinct modes of knowing, and therefore theology and philosophy distinct sciences or bodies of knowledge, there is a sense in which reason and philosophy even exercise a certain epistemic priority or at least immediacy over faith and theology, insofar as the latter "presuppose," build upon, and to that extent may be said to depend upon the former. For Pope Leo and the tradition of Leonine Thomism stemming from him, accordingly, much of the virtue of St. Thomas's position lay in his giving both faith and reason their due and his acute sense for distinguishing and not confusing the distinct domains or spheres in which these two have their proper operation.

As straightforward as these statements may seem, however, Thomas's distinction between faith and reason has nonetheless been subject to a wide array of incompatible interpretations, prompting Aquinas scholar Rudi te Velde to

---

1 Leo XIII, *Aeterni Patris*.

go so far as to state that "the subtle balance and interplay between reason and faith, philosophy and theology in the *Summa* undoubtedly constitutes one of the main challenges for any serious interpretation of Aquinas's thought."[2] Rejecting both modern and postmodern interpretations that have tended to read Aquinas by turns as a rational foundationalist on the one hand and a fideistic anti-foundationalist on the other, Velde represents a recent trend in Aquinas scholarship seeking to soften and nuance such stark dualisms as grace-vs.-nature and faith-vs.-reason. As Velde reads him, the divine revelation of faith for Aquinas consists in something far more than a mere positivist, factual claim that "escapes any verification by reason," but constitutes instead an entire body of truth invested with its own intrinsic, intelligible meaning,[3] a point that might be illustrated by Thomas's insistence that, while sacred doctrine does not depend upon the philosophical sciences to *prove* any of its principles, it can and does "take from the philosophical sciences…in order to make its teaching clearer" (ST 1.1.5 *ad* 2). Theology and faith are thus capable of and receive a "*manifestatio* through philosophy," that is to say, "a rational clarification of a truth of revelation by means of philosophical arguments."[4] Velde summarizes Thomas's purpose in the opening passages of the *Summa* in these words:

> The truth of Christian doctrine is not simply taken for granted, but neither does he attempt to prove its divine origin and, consequently, its truth from the external standpoint of reason…. For Aquinas, there is no such external standpoint from which the way reality is pictured in the Christian tradition might be compared to reality itself. Aquinas places himself within the particular tradition of Christian faith, not simply by identifying himself with the particularity of its "truth," but by arguing for the intelligibility of the Christian self-understanding. In this way he opens a universal perspective of truth, from within the particular tradition of Christianity, in so far as he aims to show that the notion of revelation has an intelligible sense.[5]

On this interpretation, accordingly, we do wrong to think of Thomas as assuming an autonomous, neutral rationality from which a "pure" natural theology might be constructed, even if it should leave room for, and even need completing by, a later revealed theology supernaturally added by grace. Rather, for Thomas,

2 Velde, "Understanding the *Scientia* of Faith," 53.
3 Ibid., 59.
4 Ibid., 71.
5 Ibid., 60.

Christian truth represents a comprehensive, coherent, and integrated worldview comprised of both a natural *and* a revealed theology, of both a way of faith *and* a (perfected) way of reason, which are and must be taken together and whose coherence or intelligibility must be appreciated not from some supposed outside, "objective" perspective, but "from the inside," as it were. In this way, as we shall see more fully later, the natural theology of Thomas's *Summa*, while not written specifically for the unbeliever, nevertheless has an important and inescapable application to him. It makes a rational claim upon the non-believer, in other words, without on that account making a concession to the pretended autonomy of his rationality. As we will see, in this arrangement we have an instructive parallel for understanding the apologetic dimension to Tolkien's own work.

To illustrate further this reading of Aquinas on the relationship between faith and reason, and to anticipate some of the related subtleties we shall find in Tolkien's writings, we may consider in further detail one of Thomas's earlier discussions of faith and reason found in his commentary on the sixth-century Boethius's *On the Trinity*. In this work, Thomas accords a more prominent place to St. Augustine's famous theory of "divine illumination" in the act of knowing than he typically does in later works such as the *Summa*.[6] According to St. Augustine, all human knowledge, including that of sense-particulars, is made possible by the mind's being directly and supernaturally illumined from above by God.[7] In his commentary on Boethius's *On the Trinity,* Thomas gives a broad endorsement of this view, though he naturalizes Augustine's notion of divine illumination by attributing its activity to, or at least mediating it through, the rational soul's own immanent power of (what Aristotle referred to as) the "agent intellect." Thus, in his argument defending the integrity of the natural powers of human reason to know truth, Thomas states that "the human mind is *divinely* illumined by a *natural* light" (EBT 1.1).[8] Thomas further emphasizes that the divine gift of the

---

6   In the *Summa*, Aquinas associates Augustine's doctrine with its Platonic antecedent, contrasting, on the one hand, Augustine's and Plato's position that "intellectual knowledge is not brought about by sensible things affecting the intellect, but by separate intelligible forms being participated by the intellect," with Aristotle's theory of abstraction (favored by Thomas), on the other hand, according to which it is the agent intellect, immanent within and natural to the individual perceiver, that sheds the intelligible light by which sensible things are known (ST 1.84.6). As Gareth B. Matthews observes, "the chief ancient rival to the doctrine of illumination is the Aristotelian idea of abstraction." Matthews, "Knowledge and Illumination," 181.

7   As Augustine writes in his *Literal Meaning of Genesis*, just as "air has not been given its own luminosity, but it becomes luminous" through the action of light, "in a similar way, man is illuminated when God is present to him, but when God is absent, darkness is immediately upon him." Augustine, *The Literal Meaning of Genesis* 8.12.26.

8   As John Milbank has aptly described the process, the "Augustinian and Neoplatonic construal of truth as inner *illuminatio*" hasn't been so much replaced by Aquinas as rerouted through

natural light of the intellect is not a one-time, once-for-all divine donation, as though after positing the intellect in its existence God then leaves it to itself. Instead, as Thomas comments on Augustine's teaching on divine illumination,

> just as air is illuminated by the presence of light, which in its absence leaves air in continual darkness, so also the mind is illuminated by God. God is always the cause of the soul's natural light — not different lights but one and the same. He is the cause not only of its coming into existence but of its existence itself. In this way, therefore, God is constantly at work in the mind, endowing it with its natural light and giving it direction. So the mind, as it goes about its work, does not lack the activity of the first cause. (EBT 1.1 ad 6)

Here we have the epistemological application of Thomas's more general meta-physical doctrine of divine concurrence (discussed below): the natural powers of the human mind are not set over against or separated from God's own power and operation, but are rather viewed as a particular, regular, integral, dependable, and natural form of that power and operation. Natural knowledge, in short, is already in a sense "supernatural," thus guaranteeing its mutual compatibility and support with the divine light of faith.

More than their mere compatibility, however, and notwithstanding the *Summa*'s later claim that "faith presupposes natural knowledge," Thomas further suggests in his commentary on Boethius that there is a deeper sense in which reason also presupposes faith. Having shown that a "new," supernatural illumi-nation is not necessary for the human mind to know truth by its own power, Thomas returns in a later passage to ask in what sense faith nevertheless might be "necessary for the human race" (EBT 3.1). One of his arguments here points to a profound irony and tension in the order of human knowledge: although we only come to know what is most knowable in itself, namely the uncreated "divine and necessary realities," through a consideration of what is known "first for us," i.e., those created, sensible objects of nature, it is only in their relationship to what is known "last" (God) that those creatures known "first" receive their ultimate ground of intelligibility or truth. Thus, unless *some* knowledge of these divine and necessary realities is given and apprehended from the outset, no such intellectual ascent could ever properly get underway. Thomas states the problem, and its solution, in these words:

---

an "Aristotelian detour through the truth embodied in finite creatures and conveyed to us only via the senses." Milbank, "Truth and Vision," 23.

> But what we first know is known on the strength of what we eventually
> come to know; so from the very beginning we must have some knowledge
> of those things which are more knowable in themselves, *and this is possible
> only by faith*. The sequence of the sciences makes this clear, for the science
> that concerns the highest causes, namely metaphysics, comes last in human
> knowledge, and yet the sciences that precede it must presuppose certain
> truths that are more fully elucidated in that science. As a result, every
> science has presuppositions which the learner must believe. Consequently,
> since the goal of human life is perfect happiness, which consists in the full
> knowledge of divine realities, the direction of human life from the very
> beginning requires faith in the divine, the complete knowledge of which we
> look forward to in our final state of perfection. (EBT 3.1, emphasis added)

If faith presupposes reason in the opening of the *Summa*, there is another sense,
at least for the Thomas of the commentary on Boethius, in which reason at the
same time and even more deeply presupposes faith. Although the theme is much
more characteristic of earlier medieval thinkers such as St. Anselm,[9] there is a
sense in which, for Aquinas, too, it is faith that leads us to greater understanding
(*fides quaerens intellectum*).

In summary, then, the picture of the relationship between faith and reason that
emerges is not that of two isolatable, compartmentalized, or mutually-exclusive
modes of knowing, but that of two coordinate rays of "light" simultaneously
radiating from a shared, divine source, each of which serves in its own way to illuminate the human intellect, and, in doing so, serves to illuminate and support the
other. Faith thus not only completes reason by offering the promise and guarantee
of that which reason desires but cannot on its own attain, namely the vision of
God in his essence, but is also what sets reason on the right path in the first place
by providing it with its initial, orienting trajectory towards the divine.[10] At the
same time, it is this faith-informed and infused reason that first enlightens man
as to his *natural* limits and consequent need for something beyond reason, and
afterward helps explicate the inner intelligibility of faith once faith has arrived.
Faith and reason thus continually key-off of and give traction to each other, as

---

9 Anselm, *Proslogion*, prologue.

10 As Velde writes, "without a sort of revelation by which the ultimate goal of human life
is disclosed in the manner of a promise, thus as beyond what is humanly attainable, the infinite
aspiration, which underlies the process of humanization, would always be frustrated. Revelation is
necessary in so far as it offers human life in this world a concrete orientation to the transcendent
horizon of the good and the true." Velde, "Understanding the *Scientia* of Faith," 62.

the intellect makes its incremental ascent along the path towards its final end of the beatific vision of God, when both faith and reason are at last superseded by the unmediated, intuitive experience of God in his essence.

Faith and Reason in Middle-earth

THIS UNDERSTANDING OF THOMAS'S APPROACH TO THE ISSUE of faith and reason, as I hope to show, gives us an ideal framework for appreciating how Tolkien deals with these and related issues in his own thought and writing. The theme of faith and reason makes perhaps its most express appearance in his work in the *Athrabeth Finrod ah Andreth* ("The Debate of Finrod and Andreth"), a little-known dialogue Tolkien wrote after the publication of *The Lord of the Rings* and in which he addresses many of the philosophical and theological principles underlying his *legendarium*.[11] According to his son Christopher, the dialogue held some "authority" for his father as to how his mythical history as a whole was to be interpreted, and thus his intention was that it should be included as an appendix in the published *Silmarillion* (MR 303 and 328–29). A record of an exchange between the Elf-lord Finrod and a mortal woman named Andreth, the *Athrabeth* represents one of the earliest conversations in the history of Middle-earth between two representatives of these respective races, in which the two participants attempt "to fathom the relations of Elves and Men, and the part they were designed to play in...the *Oinekarmë Eruo* (The One's perpetual production), which might be rendered by 'God's management of the Drama'" (329). In a commentary he wrote on the dialogue, Tolkien spells out at even greater length many of the Elvish "basic beliefs" presupposed by Finrod in the course of his conversation with Andreth, beliefs which the Elves had acquired from their "created nature; angelic instruction; thought; and experience" (330). Of some relevance to our present discussion is the reference to "angelic instruction," as it suggests that part of the foundation of Elvish knowledge consisted in truths known neither intuitively, discursively, nor experientially, but simply on authority, in particular, the authority of a higher, spiritual being. Thus, despite the absence of any formal or official divine revelation in Tolkien's mythical history, the Elves' relationship of trusting subordination to the angelic Valar would seem to contain something of the New Testament's characterization of the Old Testament as a time when God's people were under the tutelage of angelic

---

11 Christopher Tolkien places the *Athrabeth*'s composition sometime in 1959 (MR 304).

administration and revelation, a dispensation that was afterward surpassed by
God's direct revelation through his Son (Acts 7:53, Gal. 3:19, Heb. 2:2–3). As
we shall see in the conclusion of this chapter, it is a similar biblical logic and
progression of history that the *Athrabeth* anticipates as well.

Of the aforementioned sources of Elvish basic beliefs, however, possibly of
even greater import is Tolkien's reference to the Elvish "created nature," which
he implicitly distinguishes from both Elvish "thought" and "experience." What
exactly he means by "created nature" is not made clear in his commentary, but in
the *Athrabeth* itself Finrod credits the Elvish nature as the source of their faith
or *estel,* which he defines as "trust," a condition that is "not defeated by the ways
of the world, for it does not come from experience, *but from our nature and
first being*" (320, emphasis added). This is interesting, as it implies that, for the
Elves at least, the exercise of faith or trust is not something "supernatural" in the
sense of it being adventitious or superfluous to the Elvish nature, but instead as
emerging from, rooted in, and thus necessary for the completion or perfection
of the Elvish "nature and first being." And while Tolkien here emphasizes the
naturalness of faith as far as its origins in the individual are concerned, the
orientation of this faith has an unmistakably supernatural dimension. When
Andreth, for example, despairingly speculates that the Creator has abandoned
Men because of their rebellion, Finrod identifies as the "last foundation" of his
own faith in the goodness and providential care of Ilúvatar the fact that Elves
and Men are indeed the "Children of the One" and that the fatherly Eru will
therefore "not suffer Himself to be deprived of His own, not by any Enemy, not
even by ourselves" (320). In this way, like Thomas, Tolkien implicitly challenges
an overly facile and modern division between the natural and the supernatural,
inasmuch as hope and trust in God and his ability to intervene supernaturally in
human (or Elvish) history is something eminently natural and necessary to us as
"children" of God. In a word, our nature was *made* to have faith.

This natural necessity for faith, however, is not something limited to the
Elves, for, in *The Silmarillion* proper, the question of trust both in "angelic
instruction" and in the Creator's good intentions is brought to bear directly
on human history in Tolkien's retelling of the Atlantis myth, the *Akallabêth.*
In this story, the men of Númenor, fearing death and coveting the immortality
of the Elves, bitterly complain that "of us is required a blind trust, and a hope
without assurance, knowing not what lies before us in a little while" (S 265).
The theological context behind the complaint (as the *Athrabeth* also helps to
make clear) is the fact that the difference between human mortality and Elvish
immortality is the result of a free decision or creative choice on the part of

Ilúvatar the Creator. Because the origin of this difference between Men and Elves lies ultimately in the inscrutable freedom of the divine will, this means there is no discernable *rational* necessity behind what turns out to be the contingent fact of human mortality. Indeed, from the perspective of the Elves, whose own nature is such that they must continue to endure forever in a world they love but cannot prevent from changing, human mortality — for men a tragedy — is in their view nothing less than a "gift" that the Creator has granted to Men alone. For the Men themselves, however — who know their own mortality by direct experience but are left in ignorance as to their fate beyond death — to accept their mortal nature as a gift requires an exercise of faith or trust in the good purposes of the Creator, an acknowledgement that they have not in fact been cheated of the unending life given to the Elves as their created, natural right. Refusing to rest in such "hope without assurance," and seduced into rebellion by Sauron, the Númenóreans at last break the ban laid upon them by the Valar and foolishly sail to Valinor in order to win by force the immortality that only Ilúvatar can bestow. As a consequence of their rebellion, Númenor is destroyed in an act of direct divine judgment.[12] In Tolkien's re-writing of the legend, accordingly, it was, after a fashion, a fundamental failure of both faith and reason that brought about the downfall of the ancient kingdom of Atlantis: of reason, because the Númenóreans neglected to discern rightly their own proper nature; of faith, because they failed to receive this God-given nature as a gift whose goodness and wisdom, even if not perfectly evident at the present, might nevertheless be made plain to them in the future.[13]

---

12 Tolkien distinguishes several stages leading up to the Númenóreans' eventual breaking of the ban: "They must not set foot on 'immortal' lands, and so become enamoured of an immortality (within the world), which was against their law, the special doom or gift of Ilúvatar (God), and which their nature could not in fact endure. There are three phases in their fall from grace. First acquiescence, obedience that is free and willing, though without complete understanding. Then for long they obey unwillingly, murmuring more and more openly. Finally they rebel — and a rift appears between the King's men and rebels, and the small minority of persecuted Faithful" (L 154–55).

13 For a further comparison and contrast between Tolkien's *legendarium* and Plato's *Timaeus,* including the latter's myth of ancient Atlantis, see chapter four. As Verlyn Flieger summarizes the theme of mortality in its relationship to the question of faith in this episode, "release from bondage to the circles of the world comes not with immortality but with death, the Gift of Ilúvatar to Men. But it is release with no promise. Tolkien's text gives no guarantees; what's to come is still unsure. Indeed, Tolkien explicitly stated that he was concerned with death as belonging to the nature of humanity, and wanted to illustrate the necessity of accepting 'hope without guarantees.' There is in his story no assurance of any future beyond death. The unknown must be accepted in faith. This is exactly the point. The ability to let go, to trust, is the ability to rely on faith. To cling to the known, the tangible — even if it is a Silmaril — is to be bound." Flieger, *Splintered Light*, 144. Flieger also sees the question of faith implicit in the Elves' differing responses to the summons, issued by the Valar, that they should leave their home in Middle-earth and come to Valinor, where they would be

So much for the play of faith and reason *within* Tolkien's *legendarium*; there is another, very different level, however, at which Tolkien's literary project also touches on this subject, and that is the role he assigns to belief and reason in the very acts of sub-creating, receiving, and appreciating the successful fairy-story. In his essay "On Fairy-Stories," Tolkien introduces the idea of "literary belief," the act whereby the reader enters imaginatively and sympathetically into an author's world and accepts it on its own terms. As Tolkien makes clear, this is not a subjective attitude that the reader brings to the story, but is rather an objective dimension of the "story-maker's art [that] is good enough to produce it" (TR 60). He goes on to criticize (though not by name) Samuel Taylor Coleridge's characterization of this state of mind in terms of a "willing suspension of disbelief." As Tolkien comments:

> But this does not seem to me a good description of what happens. What really happens is that the story-maker proves a successful "sub-creator." He makes a Secondary World which your mind can enter. Inside it, what he relates is "true": it accords with the laws of that world. You therefore believe it, while you are, as it were, inside. The moment disbelief arises, the spell is broken; the magic, or rather art, has failed. You are then out in the Primary World again, looking at the little abortive Secondary World from outside.... But this suspension of disbelief is a substitute for the genuine thing.... A real enthusiast...is in the enchanted state: Secondary Belief... [and] if they really liked it, for itself, they would not have to suspend disbelief: they would believe—in this sense. (60–61)

For Tolkien, then, secondary or literary belief in the sub-creator's tale is no fideistic, irrational leap, a romantic state the reader artificially conjures up to overcome his default state of natural skepticism towards such stories. Rather, the natural, or at least healthy, disposition towards such tales is one of desire and even willing credulity—a desire to be "enchanted." The sub-creative story-teller, however, far from presuming upon or taking for granted such secondary belief in his reader, actually has the sober and difficult task of first eliciting and then sustaining the reader's literary "faith" within the fictional world he has fashioned.

---

free from the threat of Melkor: "The Avari are those Elves who reject the light and choose to remain in Middle-earth, 'preferring the starlight...to the rumour of the Trees' (S 52). The word 'rumour' is important. The Avari are unwilling to predicate action on the basis of a rumour, of something they have not themselves experienced.... The three Elven kindreds who go to Valinor...represent the spectrum of human spirituality and response to the light." Ibid., 78, 98.

He does this, moreover, by fashioning a "secondary world" whose elements of fantasy and unreality are achieved not in the face or at the expense of human reason or other principles of credibility, but through a careful observation of them. Tolkien defines "Art" in this context as "a special skill, a kind of elvish craft" whereby the sub-creator imbues his fictional world with "the inner consistency of reality," that is to say, with its own internal integrity and immanent truth (68). The conviction is that just as the primary world is characterized by a rational, intelligible order, being the product of an intelligent, purposeful Creator, so our finite, sub-created realities must similarly reflect an analogous internal harmony and rationality. Tolkien explains:

> Fantasy is a natural human activity. It certainly does not destroy or even insult Reason; and it does not either blunt the appetite for, nor obscure the perception of, scientific verity. On the contrary. The keener and the clearer is the reason, the better fantasy will it make. If men were ever in a state in which they did not want to know or could not perceive truth (facts or evidence), then Fantasy would languish until they were cured. If they ever get into that state (it would not seem at all impossible), Fantasy will perish, and become Morbid Delusion. (TR 74–75)

While a kind of "faith," then, is required of the reader or audience to enter imaginatively into the world of a story and to accept it on its own terms, "reason" is not on this account suspended or ignored. It has an integral role to play, first on the part of the author in elucidating, and on the part of the reader in afterward comprehending, the "inner consistency," credibility, and rationality of that world. Reason, in other words, would seem to play a role in fairy-stories analogous to the function of *manifestatio* that St. Thomas assigns to it in sacred doctrine.[14] As we found Tolkien relating these matters in the Introduction, while it is true that the "stories come first," it is "some test of the consistency of a mythology as such, if it is capable of some sort of rational or rationalized explanation" (L 260).

Thus far we have seen some of the ways in which both Tolkien's fiction and his literary theory presuppose and display a quasi-scholastic distinction and harmonization of faith and reason in their proper roles. And yet, at an even

---

14 Or as Peter Candler has put it, "there is an implicit Thomism to Tolkien's understanding of philology as it seeks not to recover a lost antiquity, but to create an imaginary world in which the aspirations of this world may be glimpsed with greater luminosity." Candler, "Tolkien or Nietzsche, Philology and Nihilism," 22.

deeper level still, one of the purposes behind Tolkien's mythical pre-history
of the world was to reach back imaginatively and reconstruct a time prior to
such later distinctions or dualisms. As I noted in the Introduction, Tolkien's
mythology is quite literally a *mytho-logy*, a unity, that is, of the sub-creative and
mythic imagination (*mythos*) on the one hand and of philosophical rationality
and rigor (*logos*) on the other. This unity Tolkien went so far as to symbolize in
one of *The Silmarillion*'s central images: "The Light of Valinor (derived from
light before any fall) is the light of art undivorced from reason, that sees things
both scientifically (or philosophically) and imaginatively (or subcreatively) and
'says that they are good' — as beautiful" (L 148n). Here Tolkien seems to have in
mind the epistemological equivalent to the "ancient semantic unity" that English
philologist, mythologist, philosopher, and sometime Inkling Owen Barfield
argues to have once existed within human language and perception. Verlyn Flieger
summarizes Barfield's position in her study of the latter's influence on Tolkien:

> Language in its beginnings made no distinction between the literal and the
> metaphoric meaning of a word, as it does today. Indeed, the very concept of
> metaphor, or one thing described in the terms of another, was nonexistent.
> All diction was literal, giving direct voice to the perception of phenomena
> and humanity's intuitive mythic participation in them.... Humankind in
> its beginnings had a sense of the cosmos as a whole and of itself as a part
> of that whole, a sense that has long since been left behind. We now per-
> ceive the cosmos as particularized, fragmented, and entirely separate from
> ourselves. Our consciousness and the language with which we express that
> consciousness have changed and splintered. In that earlier, primal worldview
> every word would have had its own unity of meaning embodying what we
> now can understand only as a multiplicity of separate concepts, concepts
> for which we (no longer able to participate in the original worldview) must
> use many different words.[15]

Put differently, and as Tolkien explains in his essay "On Fairy-Stories," one of the
functions of fairy-stories is that of "Recovery," or the regaining of a clear view
of reality in all of its original wonder and strangeness, and part of this retrieval,
in the case of myth in particular, is the reinvestment of language with a sense

---

15 Flieger, *Splintered Light*, 38. Similar views to Barfield's on the interrelationship between myth,
language, and reality were developed about the same time in the 1920s in Germany by Ernst Cassirer
and later in France by Vernant. For a discussion of Tolkien and Cassirer on the relationship between
language and magic, see Zimmer, "Creation and Re-creating Worlds with Words."

of its ancient immediacy and primitive literality. In this way myth helps heal the partially artificial breach between philosophic and mythic perception, by tracing these two now-splintered lights back to an imaginatively reconstructed moment of primordial confluence.

For Tolkien, however, this retrieval of a unified vision of reality went beyond a merely nostalgic and romantic literary reconstruction of a tragically lost, mythical past; for, as a Christian, it also involved for him a forward-looking hope of an as-yet future fulfillment. This is glimpsed, for example, in a letter he wrote to his son Christopher describing his own almost mystical experience of direct, intellectual illumination when he first came to realize that "Man the story-teller would have to be redeemed in a manner consonant with his nature: by a moving story," namely, the Christian Gospel. Tolkien writes:

> I was riding along on a bicycle one day, not so long ago, past the Radcliffe Infirmary, when I had one of those sudden clarities which sometimes come in dreams (even anaesthetic-produced ones). I remember saying aloud with absolute conviction: "But of course! Of course that's how things really do work." But I could not reproduce any argument that had led to this, though the sensation was the same as having been convinced by reason (if without reasoning). And I have since thought that one of the reasons why one can't recapture the wonderful argument or secret when one wakes up is simply because there was not one: but there was (often maybe) a direct appreciation by the mind (sc. reason) but without the chain of argument we know in our time-serial life. (L 101)

Tolkien took it as some indication of his success, accordingly, when, toward the end of his life one reader, a self-described "unbeliever, or at best a man of belatedly and dimly dawning religious feeling," wrote telling him how Tolkien had "create[d] a world in which some sort of faith seems to be everywhere without a visible source, like light from an invisible lamp" (L 413). Tolkien reported these words to another correspondent who had made a similar observation, and to whom Tolkien replied, "of his own sanity no man can securely judge. If sanctity inhabits his work or as a pervading light illumines it then it does not come from him but through him. And neither of you would perceive it in these terms unless it was with you also" (413). Not unlike St. Thomas, then — for whom, as we have seen, there is a sort of planned obsolescence or provisionality to the distinction between faith and reason, one that is to diminish asymptotically until the day it dissolves altogether in the completely unified and unifying vision of God (and vision of all things else) in his essence — Tolkien looks both backward *and* forward to what is for him a simultaneously ancient and eschatological vision of things in their created glory.

The Existence of God
IN ST. THOMAS AND TOLKIEN

HIS DESIRE TO RECONSTRUCT A PRE-SCIENTIFIC AND PRE-philosophical vision of reality notwithstanding, the fact remains that, as has been noted, Tolkien's mythical world is, ironically, almost entirely devoid, not only of recognizably Christian, but of *any* explicit religious or cultic expression or sentiment whatsoever. Instead, Tolkien describes the world of *The Lord of the Rings* in one place as a "monotheistic world of 'natural theology'" (L 220), implying the presence of a certain scholastic, rational theology without, curiously enough, any overt and animating religious faith behind it. And typically the very first question in any philosophical or natural theology, of course, is the question of God's existence, of whether it can be known, and if so, how. In keeping with this, in his commentary on the *Athrabeth,* the first of the aforementioned "basic beliefs" of the Elves listed by Tolkien is their conviction that "there exists Eru (The One); that is, One God Creator, who made (or more strictly designed) the World, but is not Himself the World" (MR 330).

More than this, as we shall see, the *manner* in which the Elves know God to exist bears a certain likeness to the kind of rational, natural theology developed by St. Thomas in the opening pages of the *Summa*. Although Thomas gives five distinct arguments for God's existence in the *Summa,* it is his celebrated Fifth Way, the so-called "teleological argument" or argument from design, that has the greatest bearing on our present interest in Tolkien and which I will accordingly focus on here. According to Thomas,

> We see that things which lack knowledge, such as natural bodies, act for an end, and this is evident from their acting always, or nearly always, in the same way, so as to obtain the best result. Hence it is plain that they achieve their end not by chance, but by design. Now whatever lacks knowledge cannot move towards an end, unless it be directed by some being endowed with knowledge and intelligence, as the arrow is directed by the archer. Therefore some intelligent being exists by whom all natural things are ordered to their end; and this being we call God. (ST 1.2.3)

In short, we experience in nature non-intelligent things acting purposefully, for an end, and if there is a purpose, there must be, if you will, a "purposer."

As for the natural theology of Tolkien's fiction, we have already noted that, although inhabited, shaped, and governed by powerful beings whom he refers to as "gods," his fictional cosmos is nevertheless a strictly monotheistic world. More than a monotheistic world in principle, he further indicates that it was also known and experienced to be a monotheistic world by its principal inhabitants. Of the ancient Númenórean race of men, for example, from whose lineage Aragorn and his fellow Dúnedain of *The Lord of the Rings* are descended, Tolkien writes: "They thus escaped from 'religion' in a pagan sense, into a pure monotheist world, in which all things and beings and powers that might seem worshipful were not to be worshipped, not even the gods (the Valar), being only creatures of the One" (L 204). Of the Elves Tolkien similarly writes in his commentary on the *Athrabeth* that, even amongst the most rebellious of their race, "not one had ever entered the service or allegiance of Melkor himself, nor ever denied the existence and absolute supremacy of Eru" (MR 334). As noted above, that God existed and that he was the supreme authority over all things, in short, was a foundational tenet of the Elvish worldview.

Nor was this belief in God's existence a mere fideistic affair, but, as Tolkien's reference to the presence of a "natural theology" within his fictional world suggests, there seems to have been a rationally reflective or philosophical character to it. Of the faithful men who escaped the destruction of Númenor, Tolkien does indicate in one place that their belief in God had more to do with "religion as divine worship" than it did with "philosophy and metaphysics" (L 194n). The theism of the Elves, by comparison, seems to have been of a more speculative or rational nature, as we see in the case of Finrod in the *Athrabeth* dialogue. Here we may recall Tolkien's summary of the latter as an exchange between two "enquiring minds" attempting to understand — through a critical reflection upon evidence ranging from oral legends to the most fundamental structures of reality — something of the Creator's perplexing purpose in creating two distinct yet closely related races of rationally incarnate beings. One of the persistent assumptions throughout Finrod's remarks in particular is a kind of Thomistic confidence that, first, if Eru has done something (in this case, create the closely similar yet significantly differing species of Elves and Men), it was done for a *purpose* — otherwise Men "would have been simply Elves, and their separate introduction later into the Drama by Eru would have no function" (MR 333); and second, the purpose of God in question is one that a finite, created mind can, in principle, discover and comprehend. Again, as Tolkien summarizes the dialogue, it is an attempt to "*to fathom* the relations of Elves and Men, and the part they were *designed to play*" in the divine "Drama" of creation (329, emphasis added). For Finrod, the created cosmos is one in which means and causes have been divinely ordered towards their ends and effects "so as to obtain," as Thomas puts it in his fifth way, "the best result."

Although God's existence is presupposed rather than proved in the *Athrabeth,* we see something of this same Elvish teleological reasoning in an argument Tolkien himself provided for the existence of a divine being. In a letter responding to his publisher Rayner Unwin's daughter, Camilla, who had written to him as part of a school assignment asking his "opinion" on the "purpose of life," Tolkien offered the following broadly Thomistic reply:

> I do not think "opinions," no matter whose, are of much use without some explanation of how they are arrived at.... I think that questions about "purpose" are only really useful when they refer to the conscious purposes or objects of human beings, or to the uses of things they design and make.... If we go up the scale of being to "other living things," such as, say, some small plant, it presents shape and organization: a "pattern" recognizable (with variation) in its kin and offspring; and that is deeply interesting, because these things are "other" and we did not make them, and they seem to proceed from a fountain of invention incalculably richer than our own.
>
> Human curiosity soon asks the question HOW: in what way did this come to be? And since recognizable "pattern" suggests design, may proceed to WHY? But WHY in this sense, implying reasons and motives, can only refer to a MIND. Only a Mind can have purposes in any way or degree akin to human purposes. So at once any question: "Why did life, the community of living things, appear in the physical Universe?" introduces the Question: Is there a God, a Creator-Designer, a Mind to which our minds are akin (being derived from it) so that It is intelligible to us in part. (L 399, emphasis original)

What we see in this letter is the question of the purpose of life naturally leading for Tolkien into the question of God's existence. He also takes for granted that we experience things in terms of "recognizable patterns" and that therefore these exist in the world independent of ourselves, patterns that imply "design," design that implies "reasons and motives." These motives, however, in their turn imply a "MIND," or what St. Thomas describes in his fifth way as "some being endowed with knowledge and intelligence." Or as Chesterton imaginatively reformulated the same argument in his discussion of the whole philosophical purpose of fairy-stories — a discussion that had some influence on Tolkien[16] — "this world... is magic,...magic must have a meaning, and meaning must have some one to mean it."[17] Like Thomas in his five ways, then, we find Tolkien moving confidently from the sensible experience of nature to the character of the first cause that must exist if such experience is to be both possible and meaningful. The world is magic, so there must be a divine magician. As Tolkien goes on to explain toward the end of his letter to Camilla, expressing in his own way the Thomistic principle that "from the effect we proceed to the knowledge of the cause," as well as alluding to the principle that there are some things about God known only by revelation:

> Our ideas of God and ways of expressing them will be largely derived from contemplating the world about us. (Though there is also revelation both addressed to all men and to particular persons.)
>
> So it may be said that the chief purpose of life, for any one of us, is to increase according to our capacity our knowledge of God by all the means we have, and to be moved by it to praise and thanks. (400)

One of things that is interesting about this exchange is that Tolkien evidently assumed this kind of reasoning to be intelligible and appreciable even to a child, for, like the fairy-stories whose relegation to the children's nursery he laments in his essay (TR 57–58), Tolkien was also well-aware that such arguments for God's existence and significance were something that many of his modern readers no longer found persuasive.[18] Thus, at the beginning of his commentary

16 On Chesterton's influence on Tolkien, see Alison Milbank, *Chesterton and Tolkien as Theologians.*

17 Chesterton, *Orthodoxy*, 70. On Chesterton's natural theology or "religion" of fairyland, see Milbank, *Chesterton and Tolkien as Theologians,* 9–11.

18 Chesterton noted a related irony between what a child was able to recognize in his innocent wisdom and what the enlightened, "adult," modern mind could not: "When a child looks out of the nursery window and sees anything, say the green lawn of the garden, what does he actually know; or does he know anything? There are all sorts of nursery games of negative philosophy played round this question. A brilliant Victorian scientist delighted in declaring that the child does not see any grass at all; but only a sort of green mist reflected in a tiny mirror of the human eye.... Men of another school answer that grass is a mere green impression on the mind; and that he can be sure of nothing except the mind. They declare that he can only be conscious of his own consciousness; which happens to be the one thing that we know the child is not conscious of at all.... St. Thomas Aquinas, suddenly intervening in this nursery quarrel, says emphatically that the child is aware of *Ens.* Long before he knows that grass is grass, or self is self, he knows that something is something. Perhaps it would be best to say very emphatically (with a blow on the table), 'There *is* an Is.' That is as much monkish credulity as St. Thomas asks of us at the start. Very few unbelievers start by asking us to believe so little. And yet upon this sharp pin-point of reality, he rears by long logical processes that have never really been successfully overthrown, the whole cosmic system of Christendom."

on the *Athrabeth*, for example, Tolkien admits that the central "argument" of the dialogue — an argument, as we have seen, based on God's existence and his purposeful governance of the world — would likely not have "any cogency for Men in their present situation (or the one in which they believe themselves to be)" (MR 329). Tolkien recognizes himself, in other words, to be writing for an audience that has by and large lost not only its faith in God, but also its confidence in reason's ability even to discern God's presence and purposes in the world. In his discussion of the "recovery" role of fairy-stories in his essay, Tolkien evinces a similar taciturnity: "I do not say 'seeing things as they are' and involve myself with the philosophers, though I might venture to say 'seeing things as we are (or were) meant to see them' — as things apart from ourselves" (TR 77). As Paul Kocher has commented on this passage, in stating that fairy-stories help us to see things merely as we were "meant" to see them, Tolkien is not avoiding entanglements with the philosophers so much as he is exchanging a frontal attack for a more subversive and indirect approach:

> Yet of course Tolkien cannot escape metaphysics. By introducing the word *meant* he implies intention, and only a person of some kind can have an intent for mankind. He is merely turning an epistemological problem into a theological one. Without using blatantly theological terms his ideas are often clearly theological nonetheless, and are best understood when viewed in the context of the natural theology of Thomas Aquinas.[19]

Instead, therefore, of pitting the natural theology of St. Thomas against the skeptical idealism and phenomenalism of modern philosophy directly, Tolkien's "'response' to modernity," as Peter Candler has aptly observed,

> is to re-enshrine narrative, particularly the "fairy tale," as the medium of Christian persuasion to beauty. That is, it is not apodictically that Tolkien seeks [to] make a case for Christianity; rather he "argues" for Christianity by making an appeal to the beautiful in the form of the story.... After modernity (or at least, within its death-throes) the Christian appeal is, with a certain element of charm (if not "glamour"), to a story that is in some way more attractive because more beautiful, and beautiful because true.[20]

Chesterton, *St. Thomas Aquinas: "The Dumb Ox,"* 165–66.

19 Kocher, *Master of Middle-earth*, 77.

20 Candler, "Tolkien or Nietzsche, Philology and Nihilism," 6. As Tolkien himself states, following St. Thomas, on the ultimate convertibility of truth and beauty or of intelligibility and

This basic apologetic method Tolkien would also have been familiar with from his reading in *Orthodoxy*, in which Chesterton makes the point that, although the modern unbeliever, whom Chesterton represents under the image of the "madman," might indeed be "vanquished in mere reason, and the case against him put logically," his curse is not that he has lost his reason but that he has in fact lost everything but his reason. Thus, the case against him might "be put much more precisely in more general and even aesthetic terms."[21] As we saw earlier being said of St. Thomas, there is no neutral, autonomous, secular reason upon which the question of God's existence might be adjudicated without bias, for to suppose such an account of reason is already to enthrone reason as God, a peculiar form of "mental evil" which, as Chesterton observes, one cannot simply "think himself out of…for it is actually the organ of thought that has become diseased, ungovernable, and, as it were, independent. He can only be saved by will or faith."[22] Here it is possible to see Chesterton as echoing St. Thomas's statement, reviewed earlier, that "what we first know is known on the strength of what we eventually come to know; so from the very beginning we must have some knowledge of those things which are more knowable in themselves, *and this is possible only by faith*" (EBT 3.1, emphasis added).[23]

To return to Tolkien, the suggestion here is that one of his self-appointed (though implicit) tasks in his fiction is to help re-awaken a sense of religious faith in his modern audience by first kindling in them the analogous and perhaps even preparatory posture of "literary" or "secondary" belief. Through his own powerful combination of faith, imagination, and reason, in other words, Tolkien seeks to re-enchant the world in such a way that, when taken on the world's own internally consistent terms, the kind of metaphysical and theological vision outlined by such Christian thinkers as St. Thomas might once again be glimpsed not only as plausible or intelligible, but as even beautiful and highly desirable, a vision in which the Christian synthesis of faith and reason might not be merely theorized about, but delightfully and enticingly imagined and experienced.

---

aesthetic desirability, in a letter discussing his admiration for the Eden story in Genesis, "the beauty of the story while not necessarily a guarantee of its truth is a concomitant of it, and a *fidelis* is meant to draw nourishment from the beauty as well as the truth" (L 109).

21 Chesterton, *Orthodoxy*, 27. As Chesterton puts it, in a passage the echoes of which we might faintly discern in Tolkien's declining to involve himself with the philosophers, "curing a madman is not arguing with a philosopher; it is casting out a devil." Ibid., 26.

22 Ibid., 26.

23 As Chesterton similarly puts it, "it is idle to talk always of the alternative of reason and faith. Reason is itself a matter of faith. It is an act of faith to assert that our thoughts have any relation to reality at all." Ibid., 38.

Eru
PLOTINIAN ONE OR THOMISTIC *ESSE*?

"WHEN THE EXISTENCE OF A THING HAS BEEN ASCERTAINED," Aquinas writes in his *Summa* following his arguments for God's existence, "there remains the further question of the manner of its existence, in order that we may know its essence" (ST 1.3, prologue). So we are led to ask who or what is this God the belief in whom Tolkien's pre-Christian, pagan mythology would restore us to? The name *Eru*, as the opening line of *The Silmarillion* informs us, simply means "the One," and the index to the book gives the additional sense of "He that is alone" (S 329).[24] This emphasis on the utter unity and solitariness of the Creator has understandably led some readers to interpret the theology of Tolkien's *legendarium* in terms of the One (*to hen* in Greek) of classic Neoplatonism.[25] As I hope to show, however, the picture Tolkien presents of the divine nature owes much more to the biblically informed Christian Neoplatonism of such influential theologians as Augustine and Aquinas—with their comparative balance of positive and negative theology—than it does to the pre-Christian, pagan, and predominantly negative theology of classic Neoplatonism. In contrast to the third-century AD Neoplatonist philosopher Plotinus, for whom the One is "beyond being" and thus beyond all human knowing and naming, in the thought of Augustine and Aquinas, by comparison, God is conceived not so much as "beyond being" as he is identified as pure, essential being itself (*ipsum esse*). By identifying God as being, these theologians were still concerned to preserve God's supreme transcendence and consequent mystery while at the same time taking seriously the Bible's disclosure of a self-revealing, personal, present, knowable, nameable, and, indeed, now incarnate God. According to the influential interpretation of twentieth-century Thomist Étienne Gilson, Christian theologians such as Augustine and Aquinas were led to break with the apophatic "beyond being" tradition of Plato and Plotinus partly on the authority of such scriptural passages as Exodus 3:14, in which the Lord God reveals himself to Moses as "I am who I am." In Gilson's apt summary of this tradition of the "metaphysics of Exodus," "no Christian needs to draw from this statement

---

24 Michaël Devaux observes that, absent in earlier editions of the *Ainulindalë*, "the inclusion of the name Eru is a unique feature of the 1977 *Silmarillion*." Devaux, "The Origins of the *Ainulindalë*: The Present State of Research," 91.

25 See, for example, Flieger, "Naming the Unnameable," and *Splintered Light*, 53–55, and Cox, "Tolkien's Platonic Fantasy."

['I am who I am'] any metaphysical conclusions, but if he does, he can draw only one, namely, that God is the supreme principle and cause of the universe. If the Christian God is first, and if He is Being, then Being is first, and no Christian philosophy can posit anything above Being."[26]

Thomas himself addresses God's identity as self-subsisting being in his discussion of divine simplicity in the third question of the *Summa*. In the fourth article on "whether essence and being are the same in God," he gives three arguments in the affirmative, the first of which makes the case that God's essence must be identical with his existence, since, if it were not, God's existence would have to be either caused by his essence (thus making God self-caused, which Thomas holds to be impossible), or else caused by something other than God himself (a fact contradicted by God's status as the first cause). Therefore God's essence must be the same as his existence. Second, Thomas argues that, because the existence or being of a thing is "the actuality of every form or nature" and therefore "being must be compared to essence, if the latter is distinct from the former, as act to potency," God's essence cannot be distinct from his existence since it is impossible (as the first of Thomas's five ways had shown) that there should be any unrealized potency in God. Again, God's essence *is* his existence. Finally, Thomas argues that a thing has its existence either *essentially*, i.e., through itself, or it has its existence only by *participation* in another, just as that which "has fire but is not itself fire is on fire by participation." As the first cause, God cannot participate in anything else for his being, and so God must exist essentially: his essence *is* his existence, which is to say, God is being itself. It is this understanding of God as pure being or actuality, finally, that leads Thomas on the one hand to deny that we can know God's essence in this life, while on the other hand to affirm that, first, God is nevertheless "in Himself supremely knowable," since "everything is knowable according as it is in act" (ST 1.12.1); second, that we can name God, since "we can give a name to anything in as far as it can be known by our intellect" (ST 1.13.1); and third, that the "He Who Is" of Exodus 3:14 is "the most proper name of God," since "the being of God is His essence itself, which can be said of no other" (ST 1.13.11).

As to the nature of the supreme deity in Tolkien's *legendarium*, as we have already seen, unlike the Neoplatonic One, Eru is no mere, emanative source of all existence, but, more like Aquinas's First Being, is a personal agent who has self-consciously designed and created the world in such a way as to enable his creatures to learn something of his own mind through the study of his effects.

---

26 Gilson, *Being and Some Philosophers*, 30.

Yet perhaps the most striking and specifically Thomistic image provided of the divine nature in the *Ainulindalë* is Tolkien's characterization of it in terms of the "Flame Imperishable" and, its alternate appellation, "the Secret Fire." After creating the angelic Ainur and teaching them a new, "mighty theme," Ilúvatar informs them that, "since I have kindled you with the Flame Imperishable, ye shall show forth your powers in adorning this theme, each with his own thoughts and devices, if he will" (S 15). Based on this passage, some readers have interpreted the Flame Imperishable as specifically Ilúvatar's creation of individual free will and creativity, and in some cases have identified it with the created gift of free will and sub-creation itself. Yet, while these certainly are some of the crowning *effects* of the Flame Imperishable, the latter nevertheless has an even wider metaphysical significance in the *Ainulindalë*. A little after the above scene, for example, it is told how Melkor, the mightiest of the Ainur, began to "interweave matters of his own imagining that were not in accord with the theme of Ilúvatar, for he sought therein to increase the power and glory of the part assigned to himself," and so he began to go "often alone into the void places seeking the Imperishable Flame; for desire grew hot within him to bring into Being things of his own.... Yet he found not the Fire, for it is with Ilúvatar" (S 16). Two things may be noted about the Flame Imperishable here: first, it is, at least as viewed by Melkor, the only means by which one's own thoughts might be "brought into Being," suggesting that it is a kind of power to create *ex nihilo*, to bestow, that is, existence as such. Second, it is said that Melkor does not find the Flame Imperishable, "for it is with Ilúvatar," indicating that this power to create *ex nihilo* is something exclusive to the Creator himself.

This understanding of the Flame Imperishable is confirmed later in the *Ainulindalë*, when, after the Vision of the world has been taken away, but before the world has actually been brought into being, Ilúvatar tells the Ainur:

> "And I will send forth into the Void the Flame Imperishable, and it shall be at the heart of the World, and the World shall Be; and those of you that will may go down into it." And suddenly the Ainur saw afar off a light, as it were a cloud with a living heart of flame; and they knew that this was no vision only, but that Ilúvatar had made a new thing: Eä, the World that Is. (S 20)

In this passage, the fire being kindled by the Imperishable Flame, more than the mere donation of life and sub-creative freedom, involves the very gift of being or existence itself, in this case the existence of the physical world. The Imperishable Flame, in sum, is nothing less than the creative force or power of the Creator whereby he gives the gift of being — whether it be the gift of material existence, in the case of the physical world, or the gift of free, spiritual, sub-creative existence bestowed on rational yet finite beings. The Imperishable Flame, in short, is the power whereby Ilúvatar brings things "into Being."

Finally, we have Tolkien's own interpretation in his commentary on the *Athrabeth* when he writes that the Flame Imperishable

> appears to mean the Creative activity of Eru (in some sense distinct from or within Him), by which things could be given a "real" and independent (though derivative and created) existence. The Flame Imperishable is sent out from Eru, to dwell in the heart of the world, and the world then Is, on the same plane as the Ainur, and they can enter into it. (MR 345)

Above we saw that Melkor, when he went into the void seeking the Flame Imperishable, could not find it because it was "with Ilúvatar." Here Tolkien, by expressly identifying it as the "Creative activity of Eru" that is "in some sense distinct from" him, almost seems to imply another sense in which the Flame Imperishable is *not* distinct from but is in fact identical with Ilúvatar, a point we will return to at the end of the chapter. The Flame Imperishable is not only "with" Ilúvatar, but as Tolkien puts it here, it is also "within Him."

Thus, while Eru is initially introduced to us in the *Ainulindalë* simply as "the One," he is afterward revealed in his creative capacity and activity as the sovereign wielder of the Flame Imperishable, by which he "kindles" or bestows the being of his creatures, a characterization of the divine being that would seem to suggest a much stronger influence of the Bible and the Christian intellectual tradition on Tolkien's theological imagination than some of his commentators have recognized. Fire is an image frequently associated in Scripture with the divine presence, especially in the theophanic appearances in which God reveals himself to his people as their covenant Lord. The very first appearance of the word *fire* in the Old Testament, incidentally, occurs when the Lord covenants himself with Abraham (much as Ilúvatar does with the Ainur) in a vision in which he manifests himself as a "burning lamp and a torch of fire" (Gen. 15:17).[27] During the Israelites' wandering in the wilderness after their exodus from Egypt, the Lord again appears as a "cloud of smoke" by day and a "pillar of fire" by night (Exod. 3:21). In the New Testament, the Holy Spirit descends upon the heads of

---

27 Vine, *Vine's Complete Expository Dictionary of Old and New Testament Words*, 82. On the "dialectic of fire" in the Old Testament, see Balthasar, *The Glory of the Lord,* vol. 6, *Theology: The Old Covenant,* 47–50.

the disciples in the upper room at Pentecost as "tongues of fire" (Acts 2:3), God
is described as a "consuming fire" (Heb. 12:29; see also 10:27), and the eyes of
the Son of God in the Book of Revelation are "as a flame of fire" (Rev. 1:14, 2:18,
19:12).[28] Perhaps the most suggestive passage in connection with Tolkien's image
of the Imperishable Flame, however, especially given the Exodus imagery pervasive
throughout *The Silmarillion* (it may be worth noting here that Tolkien taught
the *Old English Exodus* throughout the 1930s and 40s[29]), is the prophet Moses's
famous encounter on the slopes of Mt. Horeb/Sinai, where the Lord appeared to
him as a "flame of fire out of the midst of a bush" that "burned with fire" and
yet "was not consumed" (Exod. 3:2).[30] It is hard to imagine that this scene, in
which the Lord declared himself to Moses as "I am that am," had no influence
on Tolkien's depiction of Ilúvatar under the guise of the Flame Imperishable,
burning "at the heart of the World," not consuming it, but kindling it to "Be."[31]
If so, Tolkien's image of the Flame Imperishable might be taken to reflect something of his own inheritance in the Augustinian and Thomistic "Metaphysics of
Exodus," as well as providing a powerful image of Thomas's understanding of God
as that dynamic, fully actualized conflagration of existence — what Chesterton

28   There is an allusion to the Book of Acts when "tongues of fire" appear on the heads of the
disciples at Pentecost in Tolkien's poem "Mythopoeia," when he describes the saints in their future
state of glory as "poets" who will "have flames upon their head."

29   L.J. Swain, "*Exodus*, Edition of," in Drout, ed., *J.R.R.T. Encyclopedia*, 180-1.

30   In many ways *The Silmarillion* is a retelling of the Old Testament narrative in general and
of the Exodus story in particular. Beginning, like the Bible, with the creation of the world, *The
Silmarillion* moves on to tell the story of the Elves' migration out of Middle-earth where they were
under constant threat of becoming enslaved to the tyrannical Pharaoh-figure of Melkor, and their
journey to the idyllic Valinor, a veritable "promised land" of milk and honey. The Elves entry into
Valinor, moreover, is preceded by representatives from each of the heads of the different Elvish
lines, an echo of the twelve spies from each of the twelve tribes of Israel who enter the land of
Canaan in advance of the rest of the Israelite host. Leading the Elves in their journey, moreover, is
the Moses-figure Oromë, messenger of the Valar. Once in Valinor, the Elves rebel, being persuaded
that the hardships endured in Middle-earth were preferable to their current fortunes, much as the
Israelites complain that the freedom they enjoy in the wilderness is incomparable to the luxuries
and securities they enjoyed back in Egypt. The Elves' return to Middle-earth, accordingly, also
becomes their "exile," from which many of them do not return to Valinor except through violent
death, comparable to the curse laid on the first generation of Israelites coming out of Egypt that
they would all die before seeing the land of Canaan.

31   As Stratford Caldecott comments on the "Secret Fire" of Iluvatar, "The fire that is of God
burns without consuming. Lesser fires may give light, and they may be used to give life and form
to other creatures, but at the same time they consume the fuel on which they depend. Thus all
lesser fires depend on God's gift of being, of fuel, of substance, continually renewed." Caldecott,
The Power of the Ring, 104. In this we have a specifically theological example of the more general
pattern identified by one scholar of how "Tolkien makes biblical metaphors literal and recombines
biblical elements to be particular to Middle-earth." Christian Ganong Walton, "Bible," in Drout,
ed., *JR.R.T. Encyclopedia*, 63.

described as "the great Dominican's exultation in the blaze of Being"[32] — in
which all creatures participate for their own being.

Divine Presence
IN ST. THOMAS AND TOLKIEN

IN ADDITION TO THE KNOWABILITY AND NAMEABILITY OF GOD,
a further divine attribute involved in the question of God's identity with his own
act of existence concerns the issue of his divine presence within those things for
which he is creatively responsible. For St. Thomas, one important and almost
immediate application of God's existence as pure, self-subsisting being is the
fact of his unmediated involvement within and presence to the created order.
Thus, in his argument for the being of God in things, Thomas hearkens back
to his earlier argument concerning the identity of essence and existence in God:

> Now since God is being itself by his own essence, created being must be his
> proper effect; just as to ignite is the proper effect of fire. Now God causes
> this effect in things not only when they first begin to be, but as long as
> they are preserved in being; as for instance light is caused in the air by the
> sun as long as the air remains illuminated. Therefore as long as a thing
> has being, God must be present to it, according to its mode of being. But
> being is innermost in each thing and most deeply inherent in all things....
> Hence it must be that God is in all things, and most intimately. (ST 1.8.1)

Again, Thomas's fire-imagery is highly suggestive. As St. Thomas writes in the
above passage, just as the proper effect of fire is to ignite fire in other things, so the
"proper effect" of God as "being itself by his own essence" is his communicating
to or igniting other things with something of his own nature, namely with their
own act of being or existence. It is precisely this principle, I submit, that Tolkien
quite effectively dramatizes in the *Ainulindalë*, when the Ainur first glimpse the
newly created world immediately following Eru's sending forth of the Flame
Imperishable to burn "at the heart of the World," causing it to be: "And suddenly
the Ainur saw afar off a light, as it were a cloud with a living heart of flame; and
they knew that this was no vision only, but that Ilúvatar had made a new thing:
Eä, the World that Is" (S 20). For Thomas, "every agent produces an effect like

---

32 Chesterton, *St. Thomas Aquinas*, 190.

itself" (*omne agens agit sibi simile*), so that, like the Flame Imperishable, which *is* the act of and power to confer existence itself, God's "proper effect" is to set aflame his creatures with the blaze of being that is his own existence.

As Thomas further explains in his article on God's presence in things, the embers of existence are not something that, once ignited, God then withdraws from in deistic, watchmaker-like fashion, but are a flame that the Creator is continually "stoking" into being, as it were: "Now God causes this effect in things not only when they first begin to be, but as long as they are preserved in being; as for instance light is caused in the air by the sun as long as the air remains illuminated." As we shall examine further in chapter four, for both Thomas and Tolkien, because created being is literally "from nothing" (*ex nihilo*), it has no other fuel for the flames of its existence than the constant, sustaining power of the Creator. What this implies for God's presence, Thomas continues, is that "as long as a thing has being, God must be present to it, according to its mode of being." In his earlier argument for the identity of essence and existence in God, Thomas made the point that the existence of every being for which its essence is distinct from its existence is caused by "some exterior agent" (*aliquo exteriori*), namely God, who is the first cause of all being. The further point Thomas makes here is that, because the very being or act of existence of a thing (which it is God's proper effect to produce in creatures) is also that which is most *internal* and proper to the things he creates, it follows that God, as the immediate cause of this effect, must also be "inside" things in a most profound way: "But being is innermost in each thing and most deeply inherent in all things…. Hence it must be that God is in all things, and most intimately." As pure being itself, God is simultaneously most unlike, other than, outside of (*aliquo exteriori*), and thus transcendent to his creatures, yet it is precisely this divine otherness that at the same time paradoxically enables God to be most like, present to, and immanent within his creatures.[33]

It is a similar dialectical balance of the simultaneity of divine transcendence and immanence that pervades Tolkien's depiction of the Creator as the Flame

---

33 As Robert Wood comments on the dialectical interplay of divine immanence and transcendence, "God as both the top of the hierarchy and its ground is Wholly Other, being infinitely infinite. But precisely that Otherness is linked to His absolute Presence to all things." Wood, *A Path into Metaphysics*, 198. In a similar vein, John Milbank explains Thomas's understanding of divine omnipresence in terms of a divine act of "self-exteriorization": "God's omnipresence simply is God himself…. Such omnipresence is seen as the direct effect of divine goodness, and elsewhere [ST 1.20.2 ad 1] Thomas cites Dionysius's 'daring to say' that God on account of his goodness exists 'as it were outside of himself'. For only this impossible self-exteriorization will explain how there can be something other to God participating in God, when God is in himself the repletion of being." Milbank, "Truth and Vision," 37.

Imperishable, which, as we have seen, is both "with Ilúvatar" (and so undiscoverable by Melkor) as well as "sent forth" into the Void to burn "at the heart of the World." As Tolkien writes in his commentary on the *Athrabeth*, the Flame Imperishable "refers rather to the mystery of 'authorship,' by which the author, while remaining 'outside' and independent of his work, also 'indwells' in it, on its derivative plane, below that of his own being, as the source and guarantee of its being" (MR 345). Tolkien even coined an Elvish expression capturing the above Thomistic principle that God causes being in things "not only when they first begin to be, but as long as they are preserved in being," calling it the *"Oienkarmë Eruo,"* "The One's perpetual production" and "management of the Drama" (MR 329).[34]

If God is in all things, this is of course because all things are rather *in* God, a point that, as we saw in the third of Thomas's above three arguments for the identity of essence and existence in God, Thomas expresses in terms of the Platonic concept of "participation," an idea for which Tolkien too seems to have had some affinity.[35] For Thomas, as we saw, God is essential being, whereas everything else has merely "participated being," a distinction that is further related to Thomas's famous doctrine of analogy: because God and creatures exist in these fundamentally divergent manners, we can only ever predicate being of God and creatures in an analogous fashion (ST 1.13.5). It is the same idea of creatures participating in the Creator, not only for their form, but for their existence itself, that Tolkien represents in his creation-myth. In the earliest *Book of Lost Tales* version of the *Ainulindalë,* Eru informs the Ainur that, in creating the world first sung by the Ainur in their Music and then beheld by them in the Vision, he has in fact "caused [the world] to be — not in the musics that ye make in the heavenly regions, as a joy to me and a play unto yourselves, alone, but rather to have shape and reality even as have ye Ainur, *whom I have made to share in the reality of Ilúvatar myself"* (BLT 54-5, emphasis added). In creating things, Ilúvatar causes them to have a "share" or participation in his own reality, yet this does not mean that creation has the same, univocal *kind* of reality as Ilúvatar. It does mean, however, that its reality, by virtue of its participation in Ilúvatar, is analogous to his, being related to it as effect to cause. As Tolkien differentiates

---

34 As the twentieth-century Thomist Herbert McCabe explains this point in imagery notably similar to the *Ainulindalë's*: "This God cannot be a Top Person summoned to fill the gaps in the natural order; this God must be at the heart of every being, acting in every action (whether determined or free), continually sustaining her creation over against nothing as a singer sustains her song over against silence — and that too is only a feeble metaphor, for even silence presupposes being." McCabe, *God Matters*, 59–60.

35 On the notion of participation in St. Thomas's thought, see Velde, *Participation and Substantiality in Thomas Aquinas.*

these matters in one letter, the reality enjoyed by creation is a "secondary reality, subordinate to his [God's] own, which we call primary reality" (L 259).

For both Thomas and Tolkien, then, God is most immanent to his creatures, even closer, as St. Augustine once put it, to creatures than they are to themselves. Not surprisingly, given this common emphasis, Tolkien also shares with Thomas something of his concern to distinguish at the same time the divine intimacy with creation from any form of pantheistic heterodoxy. Thomas, for example, opens his discussion of the being of God in things in the *Summa* with the clarification that "God is in all things; not, indeed, as part of their essence, nor as an accident, but as an agent is present to that upon which it works. For an agent must be joined to that wherein it acts immediately, and touch it by its power; hence it is proved in the *Physics* that the thing moved and the mover must be together" (ST 1.8.1). Although things participate in God for their being, creatures are not on that account "made out of" or composed of God's own substance. God is in things, instead, not as the material but as the *efficient* cause of their being (ST 1.4 4.1-2). Wherever things exist, God is there, perpetually "on site," not as the raw resource of their being, but as the agent or effecting cause of their being.

Taking for granted the same Platonic logic of participation as St. Thomas, Tolkien, too, exhibits a similar concern to differentiate unambiguously the Platonic participation of things in God for their reality from the pantheistic identification of things with God's own reality. In his commentary on the *Athrabeth,* Tolkien describes the Elvish "basic belief" in Eru in these words: he is the "One God Creator, who made (or more strictly designed) the World, but is not Himself the World" (MR 330). Within the text of the *Athrabeth* itself, moreover, Andreth acknowledges, despite her doubts, that Eru is the "One, alone without peer," who "made Eä, and is beyond it," yet is nevertheless "already in it, as well as outside," a statement Finrod further clarifies by adding, in good, scholastic fashion, that "indeed the 'in-dwelling' and the 'out-living' are not in the same mode" (321-22). Andreth, apparently comprehending Finrod's meaning, responds by saying: "Truly... So may Eru in that mode be present in Eä that proceeded from Him." Tolkien offers his fullest explanation of the subject, however, when in his commentary on the *Athrabeth* he introduces his above metaphor of divine authorship: Eru "must as Author always remain 'outside' the Drama, even though that Drama depends on His design and His will for its beginning and continuance, in every detail and moment" (335). Finally, in the passage from the commentary cited earlier, we found Tolkien to explain once more: "It [the Flame Imperishable] refers rather to the mystery of 'authorship,' by which the author, while remaining 'outside' and independent of his work, also 'indwells' in it, on its derivate plane, below that of his own being, as the source and guarantee of its being" (345). For Tolkien, in summary, Eru is indeed "inside" creation, not in the sense that creation is made out of God, which, contrary to Tolkien's express claim, would effectively raise it to the same "plane" of being as himself, but in the sense that an author is "inside" his story. As author, he is immediately present to and causative of the being of every creature, while his own being is identifiable with the being of none of them.

The Metaphysics of Eucatastrophe

IF TOLKIEN'S REPRESENTATION OF THE DIVINE IMMANENCE OR presence should turn out to be rather orthodox and traditional so far as its metaphysics is concerned, this is not to say that the way in which he employs the doctrine of divine immanence in his fiction is at all unoriginal. On the contrary, it is precisely his radical conception of divine presence that, I want to suggest, enables Tolkien paradoxically—and for his own literary and theological purposes, which we will turn to shortly—to suppress references to Eru's presence throughout much of the narrative. As Tolkien expressly acknowledges in one letter, the Creator in his mythology is "immensely remote" (L 204), and in another letter he stresses that Eru is "outside the World, and only directly accessible to the Valar or Rulers" (235), meaning that, as he puts it in yet another letter, it is instead the Valar and not Ilúvatar who are the "immediate 'authorities'" of the world (193). Yet an important distinction needs to be made (and which not all of Tolkien's readers have succeeded in making) between Eru's unquestionable, palpable presence in Tolkien's fictional world at the *metaphysical* level, that is to say, at the level of the world's being or existence, and Eru's comparative absence at the *narrative* or *historical* level. Tolkien himself implies such a distinction when he explains in another letter still that, in his mythology, "We are in a time when the One God, Eru, is known to exist by the wise, but is not approachable save by or through the Valar, though He is still remembered in (unspoken) prayer by those of Númenórean descent" (387). In other words, while creation's dependence upon the immediate, creative presence of Eru is a matter of constant, metaphysical necessity, Tolkien's *legendarium* is nevertheless dealing with a particular historical epoch or dispensation — "we are in a *time*," as he puts it — in which Eru, for his and for the author's good purposes, has deigned not to reveal or relate himself to his creatures in a direct or personal way.

Tolkien's reasons for portraying the divine being in this way may be approached from a number of different directions. One point to be made is that, contrary, for example, to the suggestion made by Flieger that Eru's remoteness necessarily sets him apart from the biblical God,[36] in one sense it actually makes them quite similar, inasmuch as the Bible itself represents the vast majority of human beings (the "Gentiles") as having been without any direct knowledge of or access to God until the Christian era, when the "good news" of the gospel, "hidden from ages and generations" (Col. 1:26), was at last to be preached to all peoples and nations without distinction. Inasmuch as Tolkien conceived of his mythical history as taking place *before* the sacred history recorded in Scripture, the relative silence of his mythology concerning the Creator is, after a fashion, actually quite consistent with the historical record found in Sacred Scripture.

Even so, on the narrative and historical level of Tolkien's mythology, Eru is not nearly as aloof as some readers have assumed. In the *Ainulindalë,* for example, after promulgating the first theme of the Music to the Ainur and inviting them to develop it as they see fit, Ilúvatar continues to contribute a great deal to the Music, especially in redirecting it in response to the corruptions of Melkor, contributions which, we are led to understand, anticipate and correspond to Ilúvatar's later and similarly direct involvement in human history. Tolkien explains in one place the significance of Ilúvatar's involvement in the Music of the Ainur:

> The Creator did not hold himself aloof. He introduced new themes into the original design, which might therefore be unforeseen by many of the spirits in realization; there were also unforeseeable events (that is happenings which not even a complete knowledge of the past could predict).
>
> Of the first kind and the chief was the theme of the incarnate intelligences, Elves and Men...[b]eing other than the Spirits, of less "stature," and yet of the same order. (L 260)

Corresponding to the "second theme" introduced by Ilúvatar in the Music is the part of world-history containing the creation and consequent free choices of the "incarnate intelligences" of Elves and Men, beings in whose making it is instead the Valar who would have no direct role to play. In addition to this, however, Tolkien alludes in his letter above to other "unforeseeable events (that is happenings which not even a complete knowledge of the past could predict),"

36 Flieger, *Splintered Light,* 53–55.

an apparent reference to those miraculous events in Middle-earth's history that transcend the natural order, events that Tolkien says elsewhere not even the Valar, for all their immense power, are able to perform.[37] As Tolkien clarifies in another place, although the Valar may be the "immediate authorities" in the world,

> the One retains all ultimate authority, and (or so it seems as viewed in serial time) reserves the right to intrude the finger of God into the story: that is to produce realities which could not be deduced even from a complete knowledge of the previous past, but which being real become part of the effective past for all subsequent time (a possible definition of a "miracle"). According to the fable Elves and Men were the first of these intrusions, made indeed while the "story" was still only a story and not "realized"; they were not therefore in any sense conceived or made by the gods, the Valar, and were called the Eruhíni or "Children of God," and were for the Valar an incalculable element: that is they were rational creatures of free will in regard to God, of the same historical rank as the Valar, though of far smaller spiritual and intellectual power and status. (L 235–36)

The image of Eru "intrud[ing] the finger of God into the story" is alluded to in *The Silmarillion* itself when it says how the Valar Manwë in a vision "saw that all was upheld by the hand of Ilúvatar; and the hand entered in, and from it came forth many wonders that had until then been hidden from him in the hearts of the Ainur" (S 46). The "hand" of Eru, in other words, is always immanently present (at the "metaphysical level," as I have termed it), "upholding" the world in its very being and in every particular, while the "finger" of Ilúvatar, we might say, signifies those moments (at the "historical" or "narrative level") when Eru further deigns to make his unfailing presence manifest in an unmistakable way, by specially "intruding" into the story and interrupting or redirecting the natural course of events.[38] What Tolkien refers to as Eru's "absence," therefore, is in fact a form of feigned absence whereby he (and Tolkien as author) create the historical and literary conditions for an even more radical display of his immanent presence. Providing as he does this vision of Manwë's toward the beginning of his *legendarium,* I submit that part of what Tolkien is doing here

---

37 For a discussion of Valaric power, see chapter four's comparison of Tolkien's and Thomas's respective angelologies.

38 As Thomas Fornet-Ponse describes this passage, it is an expression of "Eru's sovereignty and his *creatio continua*..." Fornet-Ponse, "Freedom and Providence as Anti-Modern Elements," 181.

is providing his reader with the necessary metaphysical framework and herme-
neutic for rightly interpreting the subsequent, less theologically explicit, yet still
theologically significant, portions of his mythology.

Another point to be made in this regard is that for Tolkien, as for Aquinas, the
delegated, secondary, or intermediate agency of angels and Valar is not something
that *displaces* the Creator's immediate causality, as though creaturely secondary
causality was something that "intervened" between him and his effects in such
a way as to place his agency at a further level of remove. As we have already seen
in his Thomistic view of the "being of God in things," for Tolkien, following
St. Thomas, the interaction of divine and creaturely causality is not a zero-sum
game, as though God's line of action operated on the same plane and therefore in
competition with his creatures, even if his causal power should always infinitely
transcend theirs. As St. Thomas explains in his commentary on *The Book of
Causes (Liber de Causis)*, a Proclean, Neoplatonic text of anonymous authorship,
in a hierarchy of causes, every higher cause is *more* rather than less the cause of
a given effect than any intermediate secondary cause, inasmuch as the higher
primary cause is the cause of both the effect *and* the secondary cause together.[39]
The higher cause, in other words, does not cause the intermediate secondary
cause in isolation from the latter's effects, but causes the secondary causes *along
with* its effects: in causing the secondary cause, in other words, it also causes the
entire causal order, or the very *causality*, of the secondary cause. God is the first
cause, meaning he is the very cause of other causes *in* their causing.

Similarly, for Tolkien, the highly mediated character of his fictional universe is, properly understood, evidence not of a divine indifference towards and
absence from the world, but is rather precisely the particular form in which the
divine presence and personalism manifests itself.[40] Of special significance here is
Tolkien's habit in his letters of referring to the Valar and their vassals, the Maiar,
as "angels" or "angelic beings," as well as his reference to the Istari or "wizards"
(e.g., Gandalf and Saruman) as "guardian angels" (L 159n). In a letter written to
his son Christopher — as notable for its sentiments of fatherly concern as for its
creative theological speculation — Tolkien articulates his personal philosophy
of angelic mediation in which he gives us a clue to how the angelic mediation
within his fiction is best to be interpreted:

---

39 Aquinas, *Commentary on the Book of Causes,* trans. Guagliardo, et al., prop. 1.

40 Similar to Flieger, Madsen also incorrectly sees creaturely agency as displacing divine agency:
"without the possibility of direct supernatural intervention it is the natural beings, incapable of being
entirely good, who must bring everything about. Therefore all triumphs are mixed; every victory
over evil is also a depletion of the good." Madsen, "Light from an Invisible Lamp," 41.

Your reference to the care of your guardian angel...reminded me of a sudden vision (or perhaps apperception which at once turned itself into pictorial form in my mind) I had not long ago when spending half an hour in St Gregory's before the Blessed Sacrament when the Quarant' Ore was being held there. I perceived or thought of the Light of God and in it suspended one small mote (or millions of motes to only one of which was my small mind directed), glittering white because of the individual ray from the Light which both held and lit it. (Not that there were individual rays issuing from the Light, but the mere existence of the mote and its position in relation to the Light was in itself a line, and the line was Light). *And the ray was the Guardian Angel of the mote: not a thing interposed between God and the creature, but God's very attention itself, personalized.* And I do not mean "personified," by a mere figure of speech according to the tendencies of human language, but a real (finite) person. Thinking of it since — for the whole thing was very immediate, and not recapturable in clumsy language, certainly not the great sense of joy that accompanied it and the realization that the shining poised mote was myself (or any other human person that I might think of with love) — it has occurred to me that (I speak diffidently and have no idea whether such a notion is legitimate: it is at any rate quite separate from the vision of the Light and the poised mote) this is a finite parallel to the Infinite. As the love of the Father and Son (who are infinite and equal) is a Person, so the love and attention of the Light to the Mote is a person (that is both with us and in Heaven): finite but divine: i.e. angelic. Anyway, dearest, I received comfort, part of which took this curious form, which I have (I fear) failed to convey: except that I have with me now a definite awareness of you poised and shining in the Light — though your face (as all our faces) is turned from it. But we might see the glimmer in the faces (and persons as apprehended in love) of others. (L 99, emphasis added)

To Tolkien's Proclean and Thomistic way of thinking, the highly mediated character of his fictional cosmology does not displace the divine presence from the world, but rather is again a particular form and evidence of that presence. The mediating role of the Ainur, the Valar, the Maiar, and the Istari in the world of Middle-earth are not, therefore, in competition with or a threat to the Creator's involvement, but are a guarantee and sign of that involvement. As Tolkien puts it, they are "God's very attention itself, personalized."

Tolkien further mentions that that the realization of this profound truth concerning angelic causality produced in him a "great sense of joy," a comment

that helps link his metaphysics of mediated divine presence to another central
theme in his writing. Earlier it was noted how Eru's temporary absence from the
narrative of *The Silmarillion* is what makes possible an even more "disruptive"
manifestation of his ever-abiding presence. This divine intrusion into the story,
undertaken for a specifically salvific purpose, is of course the metaphysical and
theological framework behind Tolkien's well-known concept of *eucatastrophe*
(literally "good catastrophe"), a neologism Tolkien coined in his essay "On
Fairy-Stories" to describe the literary device of the "happy ending," that is to
say, the "sudden joyous 'turn'" that is the "mark of a good fairy-story" (TR
86–87). Tolkien describes the existential experience of eucatastrophe this way:
"however wild its events, however fantastic or terrible the adventures…when the
'turn' comes, [there is] a catch of the breath, a beat and lifting of the heart" (TR
86). More than a mere literary device, Tolkien believes that the effect that the
eucatastrophes in our tales have upon us points to a profound metaphysical truth,
namely the prospect that there might really occur a "sudden miraculous grace:
never to be counted on to recur." As Tolkien described the same phenomenon
in the above letter to his son Christopher, eucatastrophe is "that sudden glimpse
of the truth behind the apparent Anankê [Greek for *necessity, constraint*, or
what Tolkien refers to immediately beforehand as 'nature chained in material
cause and effect, the chain of death'] of our world, but a glimpse that is actually
a ray of light through the very chinks of the universe about us" (L 100–1). The
identity of this "ray of light" shining "through the very chinks of the universe"
Tolkien clearly reveals in another letter defining the role of divine presence and
providence in *The Lord of the Rings* in particular:

> I have purposely kept all allusions to the highest matters down to mere hints,
> perceptible only by the most attentive, or kept them under unexplained
> symbolic forms. So God and the "angelic" gods, the Lords or Powers of
> the West, only peep through in such places as Gandalf's conversation with
> Frodo: "behind that there was something else at work, beyond any design
> of the Ring-maker's" or in Faramir's Númenórean grace at dinner. (L 201)

Tolkien expresses the same principle, finally, in his account of the eucatastrophe
that occurs at the end of *The Lord of the Rings* when Frodo fails to destroy the
Ring of his own free will. Of the Creator's personal involvement at that moment
Tolkien writes: "Few others, possibly no others of his time, would have got so
far [as Frodo did]. The Other Power then took over: the Writer of the Story (by
which I do not mean myself), '*that one ever-present Person who is never absent*

and never named' (as one critic has said)" (L 253, emphasis added).[41] For Tolkien, in summary, fairy-stories represent one of the highest of human art forms; one of the essential devices of "a good fairy-story" is the eucatastrophe; and at the heart of Tolkien's understanding of the eucatastrophic turn is his Thomistic recognition of an eminently personal, involved God, who nonetheless deliberately hides himself under the veil of natural, secondary, and even angelic causality, so that he might then tear aside the veil of his own devising — like a child in a cosmic game of peek-a-boo — and show himself present, strong, and faithful to those who know and serve him.

St. Thomas on the Trinity

THE LAST TOPIC I WISH TO TOUCH ON THIS CHAPTER, THE Christian doctrine of the Trinity, represents yet another notable dimension both to St. Thomas's and Tolkien's philosophical theologies and to their wider philosophies of being as a whole. The doctrine of the Trinity holds an important place in St. Thomas's understanding of both God and creation, and, as we shall see, this article of the faith has an important application to issues of central concern to Tolkien as well. We may begin by noting that, in contrast to God's existence, which we saw for Thomas is knowable by natural reason and constitutes a preamble to the articles of faith, Thomas holds that it is "impossible to attain to the knowledge of the Trinity of divine Persons by natural reason" (ST 1.32.1). The basis for this judgment, Thomas explains, is that we gain our knowledge of God by means of his creatures, and so we can only know as much about God as is manifested in his creatures. Because the creative power of God is not unique to any of the individual persons of the Trinity, but is common to

---

41 Here we might contrast Tolkien's own self-understanding with Madsen's deistic, secularized reading of the eucatastrophes of Tolkien's fiction: "Tolkien never forces cosmology into these moments of attention.... For that moment, the unexpected presence of beauty in the midst of desolation is enough to assure that beauty will endure forever — because of the otherness of the other, because of its very distance, perhaps (could one see it as beauty) because of the very distance of God." Ibid., 44. Christopher Garbowski, however, I think gives a more accurate account of the ultimately divine pattern behind Tolkien's concept of eucatastrophe: "the concept becomes closely associated with his concept of 'sub-creation,' which is introduced in the same essay ["On Fairy-Stories"]. In subcreation, by telling stories or inventing worlds the artist effectively imitates the 'Primary Creator.'...Consequently, since the Primary Creator ultimately intends humans to be happy, the artist that evokes eucatastrophe is creating in consonance with God. Moreover, if the deepest sense of story is consonant with revelation, the concept approaches natural theology with a Christian humanist perspective." Christopher Garbowski, "Eucatastrophe," in Drout, ed., *J.R.R.T. Encyclopedia*, 176.

all three, we can only learn of God from his creatures what is common to the entire godhead. Furthermore, the very attempt to prove the Trinity rationally, Thomas thinks, only detracts from its mystery as a truth transcending the power and reach of human reason.

At the same time, and in response to the Trinitarian proofs of Richard of St. Victor and St. Anselm, St. Thomas does admit that, even if reason is not able to "furnish a sufficient proof of some principle," it can nevertheless "confirm an already established principle, by showing the congruity of its results" (ST 1.32.1 ad 2). It is in this second way that reason can "avail to prove the Trinity; because, that is, when assumed to be true, such reasons confirm it." Here we have the classic example of the *manifestatio* role of reason within sacred doctrine mentioned at the beginning of the chapter, according to which reason helps clarify or rationally articulate the inner intelligibility of the truth of revelation, and which I suggested is paralleled in Tolkien's view of reason's role in story-making, where it helps construct fictional secondary worlds that enjoy the "inner consistency of reality." For Thomas, the most significant "confirmation" of the Trinity is the psychological analogy developed by St. Augustine. As Thomas presents the argument, if there is indeed a procession of persons within the godhead as Sacred Scripture teaches, the closest creaturely approximation or analogy to such a procession would not and could not be the "outward procession" involved in God's creation of lower, bodily creatures, in which there is a "tending to external matter," but the comparatively more perfect, "inward procession corresponding to the act remaining within the agent" (ST 1.27.1). This "appears most conspicuously" (*maxime patet*), in Thomas's view, in the case of a concept or mental word whereby an intellect understands a thing and that proceeds from the intellect, all the while remaining entirely within it. In an analogous way, Thomas wagers, the divine "Word" must proceed from the divine "intellect," all the while remaining, in its perfection, within and identical with it. This Word, of course, is the divine Son, the second person of the triune godhead. A second case of "inner procession" is the way in which love for an object similarly proceeds from the will of an agent while also remaining within the agent (ST 1.27.4). In God, the divine Love both proceeds from God while at the same residing within and in a relationship of identity with him, so that, as we found even Tolkien recognizing, "the love of the Father and Son (who are infinite and equal) is a Person."[42]

---

42 On Aquinas's interpretation and use of the psychological analogy, see Matthew Levering, "Scripture and the Psychological Analogy for the Trinity."

It is this understanding of God as triune, moreover, that Thomas presupposes and imports into the *Summa*'s later consideration of creation. In his response to the question as to "whether to create is proper to any of the persons" (ST 1.45.6), after a brief, initial paragraph rehearsing his argument that creation belongs to the being and essence of God that the three persons are in common, Thomas goes on to devote the lengthier portion of the corpus of the article to arguing that "the divine persons, according to their procession, nevertheless have a *causality* respecting the creation of things." In an analogy which we will return to in the next chapter's consideration of Tolkien's metaphysics of sub-creative possibility, Thomas argues that, just as "the craftsman works through the word conceived in his intellect, and through the love of his will regarding some object," so also "God the Father made the creature through his Word, which is his Son, and through his Love, which is the Holy Ghost. And so the processions of the Persons are the types of the productions of creatures in so far as they include the essential attributes, which are knowledge and will." The "emanation" *from* God that is creation, in short, is made possible by, and is imitative of, the "procession" *within* God that constitutes the triune godhead. While not "proper" to any one member of the godhead, creation is nonetheless very much a Trinitarian affair, the consequence of which is that, as Thomas argues in the following article, "traces" (*vestigii*) of the Trinity are necessarily to be found in creatures (ST 1.45.7).[43] Even the ancient philosophers who lacked revelation and faith, according to Aquinas, were nonetheless able to catch some small glimpse of the doctrine (ST 1.32.1 ad 1).

Trinity in Middle-earth

AS FOR TOLKIEN, AS WE HAVE SEEN, THE THEOLOGY OF HIS mythical world is a decidedly "pre-Christian" and "natural theology," and thus a world in which the explicitly Christian and divinely revealed idea of God as a unity of three equal, co-eternal, and "consubstantial" persons might seem to have little place or relevance. As Tolkien wrote of his mythical Valar, however,

43 The examples of these vestiges of the Trinity given by Thomas are, first, the aforementioned powers of intellect and will among rational creatures, in which "there is found the representation of the Trinity by way of image, since there is found in them the word conceived, and the love proceeding." Second, Thomas finds a "trace" of the Trinity in irrational beings as well, inasmuch as they exist as substances (showing the Father), have form and belong to species (showing the Son), and have a certain order (showing the Spirit).

they were "meant to provide beings of the same order of beauty, power, and majesty as the 'gods' of higher mythology, which can yet be accepted—well, shall we say baldly, by a mind that believes in the Blessed Trinity" (L 146). The point to be made here is that, if Tolkien saw it as important that his fictional gods be consistent with the Christian doctrine of the Trinity, we may assume that he understood his fictional representation of the Creator at the very least to have met the same criterion.[44] What significance, if any, we might ask, could this theological fact possibly hold for our understanding of Tolkien's broader theory of being?

It was noted above how for St. Thomas, although the doctrine of the Trinity was not liable to philosophical demonstration, with the knowledge of the Trinity in hand by means of special revelation, "traces" of its effects were nonetheless to be clearly discerned not only in creation, but within the Old Testament itself. As Fergus Kerr, for example, points out, for Thomas, "given the historical dispensation of the New Covenant and thus the revelation of God as Trinity…[w]e can discover prefigurings in the Old Testament and elsewhere."[45] It is something like a "trace" of the Trinity that I want to suggest Tolkien likewise gives us in his *legendarium*. Like the Old Testament, as Ralph Wood has observed,

> Tolkien's pre-Christian world does not know God as Trinity, but rather as the One. Just as the Old Testament is monotheistic, so is there but one God of Middle-earth. Yet in Genesis we hear God somewhat strangely declaring, "Let *us* make man in our image" (1:26). The pronoun may point to the heavenly court, as if God employed intermediate beings to assist him in his action. Christians have rightly seen this plural reference as a foreshadowing of the Trinity, as a sign that God is never alone but that he always exists in triune community.[46]

However, while Wood recognizes that "Tolkien has a similar conception of God as acting communally," he seems to downplay a Trinitarian interpretation of the *Ainulindalë* when he writes that, "unlike the Son and Holy Spirit, who are co-creators with the Father, Ilúvatar employs his Valar as ancillaries in the

---

44 As Michaël Devaux has suggested, "Tolkien speaks of the Ainur as gods that can be accepted 'by a mind that believes in the Blessed Trinity.' This notion of acceptability can no doubt be extended to the *Ainulindalë*." Devaux, "The Origins of the *Ainulindalë*: The Present State of Research," 98.

45 Kerr, *After Aquinas*, 194.

46 Wood, *The Gospel According to Tolkien*, 12.

act of creation."[47] On the contrary, I submit that Tolkien deliberately imbues his portrayal of the divine being in the *Ainulindalë* and elsewhere with just the kind of Old Testament ambiguity that would allow for — if not in fact positively require — a later Trinitarian interpretation.

The primary example of this intentional, mythical ambiguity appears in the *Ainulindalë*'s image of the Flame Imperishable discussed earlier. As the "Creative activity" or power of Ilúvatar that is simultaneously "with" and "within" him and yet "sent forth" from him, the Flame Imperishable is, as Tolkien writes in his commentary on the *Athrabeth*, "in some sense distinct from" Ilúvatar (MR 335, 345). Tolkien here implies the presence of "distinction" or difference within the Creator, while at the same time implying another "sense" in which the Flame Imperishable is in fact *not* distinct from but is the same as or identical with Ilúvatar. This reading is dimly indicated in the *Athrabeth* itself, when at one point in their conversation Andreth tells Finrod about a "rumour" reported amongst those Men of the "Old Hope" that one day "the One will himself enter into Arda, and heal Men and all the Marring [of the world] from the beginning to the end" (321). Andreth, who for her part does not believe the rumor of the Men of the Old Hope, since "all wisdom is against them," raises the following, reasonable objection: "Eru is One, alone without peer, and He made Eä, and is beyond it; and the Valar are greater than we, but yet no nearer to His majesty…. How could Eru enter into the thing that He has made, and than which He is beyond measure greater? Can the singer enter into his tale or the designer into his picture?" (321–22). Finrod replies by reminding Andreth of the simultaneity of Eru's immanence and transcendence, stating how Eru is in fact "already in it, as well as outside," to which Andreth agrees but replies that the legend speaks rather of Eru "*entering into Arda,* and that is a thing wholly different." When Andreth asks how this could be possible without the Earth — indeed, without created reality itself — being "shattered," Finrod pleads ignorance, though he does not doubt that, should Eru purpose to accomplish it, "he would find a way," but that, if "he were to enter in, He must still remain also as He is: the Author without." In his commentary on this exchange, Tolkien says that, in recognizing the possibility of Eru being both "'outside' and inside," Finrod further "glimpses the possibility of complexity or of distinctions in the nature of Eru, which nonetheless leaves Him 'The One'" (335), something Tolkien further

---

47 Ibid. As Wood himself goes on to admit, the Flame Imperishable by which Ilúvatar creates the world is none other than "his own Spirit" with which he has "imbued the entire cosmos." Ibid., 12–13. For my critique of the common interpretation of the Valar as creative agents in the proper sense of the term, see chapter four.

claims to be "actually already glimpsed in the *Ainulindalë*, in which reference is made to the 'Flame Imperishable'" (345). True to St. Thomas's discovery (following St. Augustine) of evidence of the Trinity in the opening words of Genesis, so Tolkien finds evidence of Trinitarian-like structures within Eru in his own retelling of Genesis.[48] For Tolkien, Eru's ability to be simultaneously immanent within while transcendent to his creation, as his metaphysics of eucatastrophe requires, is directly connected with a kind of Trinitarian complexity or distinction within Eru's own being.

Corroborating Tolkien's claim that the distinction within Eru is already to be discerned in the *Ainulindalë* is the interpretation Paul Kocher gave in 1985, eight years before the publication of the *Athrabeth* and its commentary in *Morgoth's Ring*. As Kocher argued then, in calling the One "Ilúvatar,"

> Tolkien is suggesting that Ilúvatar, as Father, is merely the most active
> member of a more complex deity known as Eru, who is the only Lord of
> all.... [T]he description of the Flame as "Imperishable" gives it divinity
> in its own right. Only God is eternal and cannot die. The Flame is not
> a possession of Ilúvatar but is co-equal with him in the Being of Eru the
> One.... God the Father is the maker of the universe, but the Flame Imper-
> ishable, his coadjutor, infused it with life. Surely the "Secret Fire" or "Flame
> Imperishable" which "giveth Life and Reality" is very much like the Holy
> Spirit which works in the New Testament miracles underlying the whole
> Christian faith?[49]

As it turns out, Tolkien himself answered Kocher's very question in an interview he gave with Clyde Kilby, in which he divulged that the Secret Fire was none other than the Holy Spirit.[50] Thus, as is consistent with St. Thomas, while there is certainly no explicit awareness of, much less rational inference to, the triunity of God in Tolkien's fiction, again, what we do see, especially in the case of Finrod, is an instance of philosophical reasoning — ever so dimly illumined

---

48 According to Thomas, following Augustine, the statement "In the beginning God created heaven and earth" is to be expounded to mean that God created heaven and earth "in the Son. For as the efficient principle is appropriated to the Father by reason of power, so the exemplary principle is appropriated to the Son by reason of wisdom, in order that, as it is said (Ps. 103:24), *Thou hast made all things in wisdom*, it may be understood that God made all things in the beginning — that is, in the Son; according to the word of the Apostle (Col. 1:16), *In him* — namely, the Son — *were created all things*" (ST 1.46.3).

49 Kocher, "Ilúvatar and the Secret Fire," 36–37.

50 Kilby, *Tolkien and The Silmarillion*, 59.

by the conceptual possibilities opened up by the "revelation" or rather "rumour" of those of the "Old Hope" — arriving at some "trace" of this divine mystery.[51] To adapt and apply a statement made by Tolkien in a very different context, "I have thought it best in this Tale to leave the question a 'mystery,' not without pointers to the solution" (L 190).

While Tolkien deliberately mutes — much as he does the fact of God's presence — the Trinitarian character of the Creator in his mythology, we have also seen that, again, similar to the point concerning the divine presence, far from this representing a departure from the Christian and biblical traditions, Tolkien has both profound Scriptural and theological reasons for doing so. Tolkien's relative silence on the question of this "possibility of complexity or of distinctions in the nature of Eru," therefore, is no reason for thinking it unimportant for a right understanding of the theology and metaphysics of his fiction. While such complexity or distinction may not be properly knowable by unaided, natural reason, Tolkien, like St. Thomas, clearly ties God's status as Creator with his identity as divine difference. Eru creates, in short, by sending to burn at the heart of the world the Flame Imperishable that both is and is not himself.[52] Eru thus may be the "One alone," but he is not *alone* in his aloneness, and as the case of Melkor in his self-imposed isolation indicates, complete solitude is as much a metaphysical vice as it is an ethical one (a point we shall return to in the concluding chapter on evil).[53] For Tolkien, following Aquinas, God creates a world other than himself because he is the God who is other than himself, meaning that the difference or "otherness" that constitutes creation in its very being receives its own significance and ground in the deepest possible source, the God who is being.[54]

---

51 While I have focused on the image of the Flame Imperishable, Zimmer has seen a possible allusion to the Word of God, the second person of the Trinity, in Eru's speaking the word *Eä!*, which brings the world into being: "While in non-Christian-Neoplatonic thought the eternal act that constitutes the divine mind is termed the 'nous,' in the Christian tradition the *nous* is reformulated as the Word. Like the *nous*, the Word contains within itself all of creation as it exists eternally in the form of archetypal ideas.... This double quality of the Word as both the intelligible structure and the willed act of creation is expressed in *The Silmarillion* by the single word 'Eä,' which means both 'It is' and 'Let it be'...." Zimmer, "Creation and Re-creating Worlds with Words," 53.

52 As Devaux puts it, in the *Ainulindalë* the Holy Spirit is "distinct from God but also in Him." Devaux, "The Origins of the *Ainulindalë*," 106.

53 Peter Candler writes: "It is not enough simply to say that the world is created *ex nihilo* by an eternal 'simplicity,' but by a Holy Trinity who in its primordial fecundity is not threatened by any kind of 'original' violence, strife, or chaos. For this reason Tolkien's 'creation myth' in *The Silmarillion* depicts a prior, though learned, harmony among the Ainur." Candler, "Tolkien or Nietzsche, Philology and Nihilism," 23.

54 Again, as Candler observes, for Tolkien the "appearances" and "surfaces" of created beings "can therefore be like one another but truly different from one another because they are created by the One God, who in His eternal tri-unity, creates the world from nothing." Ibid., 37.

Conclusion

IN ADDITION TO THIS DIVINE, TRINITARIAN-LIKE DIFFERENCE being a condition for the possibility of *creation* in Tolkien's world, it also turns out to be a condition for the possibility of the world's future *re-creation*. For, as Finrod also confesses in the *Athrabeth*, unless Eru should indeed specially "enter in" and take upon himself the hurts of the world wrought by Melkor, all the while remaining "the Author without"—the simultaneity of which, as we have seen, is made possible by this difference within the divine being—Finrod says he cannot at all "conceive how else this healing could be achieved" (MR 322). Equally inconceivable to the faith or "*estel*" of Finrod, however, is the thought that Eru should leave the world he loves forever unredeemed. As Tolkien thus concludes the matter in his commentary, "since Finrod had already guessed that the redemptive function was originally specially assigned to Men, he probably proceeded to the expectation that 'the coming of Eru,' if it took place, would be specially and primarily concerned with Men: that is to an imaginative guess or vision that Eru would come incarnated in human form" (335). In Tolkien's mythology, then, it is the Creator's own difference, whereby he is "other" even to himself, that leads him first to produce the "other" that is the created order and, consequent to that created order's fall and corruption, to restore it eventually to an even greater state of perfection. Beneath the creaturely otherness that, as we shall see repeatedly in the chapters to follow, so transfixed Tolkien's attention, lie the infinite depths of the divine "otherness" in which all things participate for their being, and therefore from whom they must one day receive it back again.

TWO

The Metaphysics
of the Ainur

*And [Eru] spoke to [the Ainur], propounding to them themes
of music; and they sang before him, and he was glad.*

HE LAST CHAPTER EXAMINED THE CREATOR OF TOLKIEN'S
fiction, Eru, in light of the opening questions of St. Thomas Aquinas's *Summa Theologiae*, in which the angelic doctor investigates,
first, the question whether God exists, and second, the manner of his existence.
There I argued that St. Thomas's programmatic discussions of such topics as
the relationship between faith and reason, God's existence, his identity as
pure, self-subsisting being, his presence in all things, and lastly, his identity as
a Trinity are all vital issues touched on in some way or another by Tolkien in
his fiction: the relation between literary belief and rational story-telling, the
nature of theistic belief in Middle-earth, the discernibility of Ilúvatar's purposes in the world, his identity as the "Prime Being" upon whom all creation
depends, the dialectic of divine presence and absence at the heart of Tolkien's
concept of "eucatastrophe," and finally the ultimately divine ground or origin
of creaturely otherness or difference.

The purpose of this second chapter is to extend and deepen the theological
analysis of the first with a consideration of St. Thomas and Tolkien's understanding
of God as he relates to a further issue of central importance to Tolkien, namely the
relation between the divine act of creation and the human act of sub-creation. Our
present argument, accordingly, takes as its point of departure the *Ainulindalë*'s
account of Eru's creation of the Ainur and his tasking them to improvise the
original theme of the Music according to their desire and ability. This episode I
propose to analyze in light of the third and final part of the *Summa's* discussion
of the divine essence, namely God's "operations" of knowledge, will, and power.
One of Tolkien's primary objectives with his fictional Ainur, of course, is to explore
imaginatively — on the heightened plane of myth and on a cosmic, metaphysical

scale — the vast scope or latitude of creaturely, sub-creative possibility and free-dom. As I will argue, while Tolkien's central preoccupation in his writings is with the integrity, freedom, and (in a properly qualified sense) "independence" of the creaturely act of sub-creation, sub-creative possibility and freedom for Tolkien ultimately has its ground in a broadly Thomistic understanding of God's own creative possibility and freedom. Thus, the hope is that, through a consideration of Thomas's teaching on divine knowledge, will, and power, we may come to a better understanding of both Tolkien's theory of sub-creation and his mythical dramatization of that theory within the pages of the *Ainulindalë*. More than merely using Thomas to elucidate certain aspects of Tolkien's thought and writing, however, in the second half of the chapter, dealing with the operation of divine power in particular, I will attempt to show that it is actually *Tolkien*, especially with his criteria for the sub-creative imagination, who may have something import-ant to teach us about the role of the theological imagination at the heart of the medieval debate Aquinas was engaged in over the divine ideas and omnipotence.

St. Thomas on the Divine Ideas

AFTER INTRODUCING THE READER TO "ERU, THE ONE, WHO IN Arda is called Ilúvatar," the *Ainulindalë* reports how "he made first the Ainur, the Holy Ones, that were the offspring of his thought" (S 15). In his representation of Eru as creating the angelic Ainur according to a pattern in the divine mind or "thought," Tolkien would seem to allude to the classical and Christian-Platonic doctrine of the divine mind and ideas.[1] In his own creation-myth, the *Timae-us* — a work that, as I will show in chapter four, Tolkien parallels in a number of places and ways in the *Ainulindalë* — Plato represents the benevolent but not omnipotent creator-god, the world-craftsman or "demiurge," as fashioning the existing universe by first looking outside of himself to the "eternal model" of the forms, and then imposing that form, beauty, and order onto an other-wise chaotic array of unformed, pre-existing matter.[2] Taking for granted that the demiurge must have had a model in mind when he fashioned the world, Timaeus, the eponymous spokesman of the dialogue, asks whether the model the demiurge looked to was "the one that does not change and stays the same," i.e., the eternal, unchanging model of the forms, "or the one that has come to

---

1 For a good history of the doctrine of divine ideas from Plato to St. Thomas, see Boland, *Ideas in God According to Saint Thomas Aquinas*.

2 On the divine ideas in the *Timaeus*, see ibid., 17–22.

be," i.e., the changing realm of becoming grasped not by a "reasoned account" but by mere "opinion" and "unreasoning sense perception."[3] Because the physical cosmos "is the most beautiful, and of causes the craftsman is the most excellent," Timaeus concludes that it must have been the eternal model that the demiurge looked to in crafting the world.

Although St. Augustine, following in the train of the middle and later Neo-platonist schools, internalized the divine ideas within the mind of God himself, like Plato he emphasized their role in accounting for the intelligibility, beauty, and general order of the created universe.[4] As Augustine inquires in one place,

> Who would dare to say that God has created all things without a rational plan? But if one cannot rightly say or believe this, it remains that all things are created on a rational plan, and man not by the same rational plan as a horse, for it is absurd to think this. Therefore individual things are created in accord with reasons unique to them. As for these reasons, they must be thought to exist nowhere but in the very mind of the Creator.[5]

It is in reference to the Augustinian-Platonic theme of the fundamental intelligibility of creation, finally, that St. Thomas Aquinas first introduces his discussion of the divine ideas in the *Summa Theologiae*.[6] Thomas's opening article on the subject asks if there are in fact any ideas in God, to which he replies that, "as then the world was not made by chance, but by God acting by his intellect…, there must exist in the divine mind a form to the likeness of which the world was made. And in this the notion of an idea consists" (ST 1.15.1).

One of the issues Augustine did not directly address, but which became a point of contention in later scholastic discussions of the subject (as well as more recent debates over how St. Thomas is best to be interpreted on the matter), involves the problem of reconciling the multiplicity of divine ideas within the divine intellect with the simplicity of the divine essence.[7] We will have occasion to

3 Plato, *Timaeus* 28a–29a, trans. Zeyl.

4 On the doctrine of divine ideas in Augustine, see Boland, *Ideas in God,* 36–48.

5 Augustine, *Eighty-three Different Questions,* q. 46, trans. Mosher.

6 For an extensive treatment of the doctrine of divine ideas in St. Thomas, in addition to Boland, see Doolan, *Aquinas on the Divine Ideas as Exemplar Causes.* For an analysis of Thomas's discussion of divine ideas in ST 1.15 in particular, see Boland, *Ideas in God,* 210–14.

7 On the debate over whether or not St. Thomas in fact believed in a multiplicity of divine ideas, see Ross, "Aquinas's Exemplarism; Aquinas's Voluntarism"; Maurer, "James Ross on the Divine Ideas: A Reply"; Dewan, "St. Thomas, James Ross, and Exemplarism: A Reply"; Ross, "Response to Maurer and Dewan"; Martin, "Reckoning with Ross: Possibles, Divine Ideas, and Virtual Practical Knowledge"; and Doolan, "Is Thomas's Doctrine of Divine Ideas Thomistic?"

consider in particular William of Ockham's (1288–c.1347) drastic reformulation of the traditional doctrine of divine ideas for the sake of the divine simplicity in our later discussion of divine omnipotence. For the present we observe that, like Augustine, Aquinas also affirmed a multiplicity of ideas in the mind of God, though he clarifies that what gives the ideas their multiplicity is the role they play in God's own self-knowledge. As Thomas explains:

> Since God knows his own essence perfectly, he knows it according to every mode in which it can be known. Now it can be known not only as it is in itself, but as it can be participated in by creatures according to some degree of likeness. But every creature has its own proper species, according to which it participates in some degree in likeness to the divine essence. So far, therefore, as God knows his essence as capable of such imitation by any creature, he knows it as the particular type and idea of that creature; and in like manner as regards other creatures. So it is clear that God understands many particular types of many things, and these are many ideas. (ST 1.15.2)

The divine ideas after which God patterns his creatures are the result of God's knowledge of himself in his own essence. In knowing himself, God invariably knows the infinite number of ways in which his essence might be "imitated" by or participated in by his creatures, and it is this knowledge that comprises the divine ideas. It is precisely because God is supremely one, without limit, and hence infinite and capable of infinite imitation on the part of his finite creatures, that God must have an infinite number of ideas by which he grasps his own essence as infinitely imitable by his possible creatures.

For Aquinas, then, following Augustine and Plato, the doctrine of divine ideas is important for understanding the nature of divine artistry or craftsman-ship: when God creates the world, he does so not arbitrarily or irrationally, but beautifully and in orderly fashion through the intelligible exemplars that he intellectually conceives beforehand, indeed, from all eternity. As I argued in the last chapter, moreover, it is this fundamental vision of God and reality into which Tolkien sought in part to induct his modern readers through his mythology. Before turning, however, to our consideration of how Tolkien represents this divine exemplarism in his own writings, I want to examine some competing claims as to what the legacy of the traditional, Augustinian-Thomistic understanding of God's own making has had, or at least is *able* to have, for our understanding of our own acts of making or sub-creating. After all, according to Martin Heidegger's influential critique of the last century, such traditional, exemplarist theories of God and reality, far from circumventing the kind of technological approach to nature that Tolkien so lamented and from which he sought to provide escape in his fiction, instead unwittingly enfranchised the technological outlook at the deepest metaphysical and theological level. In his influential essay, "The Question Concerning Technology," Heidegger makes the case that the commonplace definition of technology in terms of an instrumental alignment of causes and effects or means and ends — as Tolkien, for example, arguably does when he defines the modern "Machine" as an instrument designed for "making the will more quickly effective" (L 145) — actually fails to get at the essence of technology, inasmuch as the definition itself presupposes the very causal and instrumental paradigm that lies at the heart of technology. The very *definition* of technology, in other words, is itself infected with the technological. And yet it is in terms of just this technological, causal framework that theology has traditionally articulated God's relation to creation, according to Heidegger, with the result that theology and the doctrine of creation, far from offering a true alternative to the technological form of making, is instead a form of it. As a consequence, as Heidegger put it, "even God can, for representational thinking, lose all that is exalted and holy, the mysteriousness of his distance. In the light of causality, God can sink to the level of a cause, of *causa efficiens*. He then becomes, even in theology, the god of the philosophers, namely, of those who define the unconcealed and the concealed in terms of the causality of making, without ever considering the essential origin of this causality."[8] While Heidegger in his essay is resigned to the inevitability of technological thinking, he hopes modern man might nonetheless find his "saving power" by "confronting" and "questioning" the technological paradigm through the cultivation of an alternative mode of thinking and "revealing," namely that of *poiesis* or art.[9]

Others, however, have argued that, properly understood, the traditional Christian doctrine of creation, especially as defended by St. Thomas, and in particular, the role the divine ideas play within that doctrine, far from exemplifying the kind of technical thinking and making criticized by Heidegger, in fact does provide us with the only true alternative to them. As Robert Miner has stated the problem in his study of creative knowledge in later medieval and early modern philosophy and theology, what is basically at issue here is the "relation between knowing and making."[10] Following the analysis of R.G. Collingwood, Miner distinguishes on the one hand the "paradigm of craft" or "technical making,"

---

8 Heidegger, *The Question Concerning Technology and Other Essays*, trans. Lovitt, 26.
9 Ibid., 34–35.
10 Miner, *Truth in the Making*, 2.

which "involves a distinction between planning and execution, where 'planning' means precise foreknowledge of what is to be made, before the making is executed."[11] In craft or technical making, in other words, the relation between knowing and making "is one of dependence: making (understood as the execution of the means through the transformation of matter) depends upon an antecedent knowledge of the form. *The activity of making does not provide knowledge* of the formal cause of the artifact, but presupposes this knowledge."[12] On the craft model, consequently, instead of the produced artifact providing a new or authentic avenue for being to reveal itself (the task Heidegger had assigned to true *poiesis*), the produced artifact represents merely a "mimetic" and hence superfluous or redundant overflow from a prior act of knowing or speculative vision. An alternative form of making to the craft model, accordingly, would be one in which "the activity of making does not merely devise means for the sake of giving material embodiment to what is already known, but actually contributes to our knowledge."[13] Contrary to the suggestion, finally, that the exemplarism of Thomas's doctrine of divine ideas makes God into a kind of demiurgic "super-technician," Miner argues that it in fact gives us a true basis for thinking alternatively about human making.

To be sure, as Miner points out, God's knowledge of the divine ideas for Thomas "in the first instance, is a speculative knowledge," that is to say, a knowledge of God's essence in itself and without reference to his doing anything with that knowledge. Yet this knowledge is not a "sterile" knowledge, as it immediately gives rise to, and is implicative of, the divine practical knowledge, or God's knowledge as directed to operation, in this case, the operation of creation. As we noted earlier, in knowing his own essence, God at the same time knows his essence as imitable by his creatures, so that, while God's practical knowledge of the divine ideas is conceptually distinct from his speculative knowledge of his essence, the two are nevertheless inseparable from each other. As Miner explains:

> Thus God's knowledge of ideas may be either entirely speculative, or both
> speculative and practical. When they are known speculatively, as principles
> of knowledge, they are "types" (*rationes*). When they are not only known
> speculatively, but also directed to the making of something, they attain
> the status of an *exemplar*, that is, the "principle of the making of things"
> (*principium factionis rerum*). A distinction between speculative and practical

11 Ibid., 1.
12 Ibid., 2 (emphasis added).
13 Ibid.

knowledge of ideas is necessary, because Aquinas allows that God knows some types of created things but chooses not to actualize them. But he does not sever practical knowledge of exemplars from speculative self-knowledge. "In speculative knowledge of himself, he possesses both speculative and practical knowledge of all other things," Aquinas concludes the final article of Question 14. Thus God's knowledge of exemplars is essentially different from the craftsman's knowledge of forms, because the former is a function of perfect self-knowledge, and the latter is not.[14]

For Aquinas, then, while God's speculative knowledge may precede and so be distinguishable from God's practical knowledge in a logical sense, his speculative knowledge nevertheless always involves his practical knowledge. There is no craft-like process or series of stages, therefore, which God goes through in which he is first a seer or knower and only afterward a doer or maker, for in the very act of knowing himself, God knows himself *as* maker, or at least as a potential or possible maker, which is another way of saying that only in knowing himself as a (possible) maker does God know himself as God.

Corroborating this account is the almost creativity or artistry which Aquinas, at least in one place, attributes to the otherwise speculative act whereby God knows the divine ideas in the first place. In his argument for a plurality of divine ideas in his *Disputed Questions on Truth,* Thomas writes: "The one first form to which all things are reduced is the divine essence, considered in itself. Reflecting upon this essence, *the divine intellect devises* — if I may use such an expression — different ways in which it can be imitated. The plurality of ideas comes from these different ways."[15] According to Aquinas's divine "psychology," God's ideas are the result of his first understanding his own essence, and consequent (logically) to that, understanding all the ways in which his essence may be imitated by created being. The act by which God knows the divine ideas, however, Thomas again depicts not merely in terms of a passive, speculative, and hence "technological" gaze at his own essence in order to understand the possible ways of it being imitated, but more than that, in terms of an active process of "devising" those ways in which his essence might be imitable. The word Thomas uses here is *adinvenit,* which W. Norris Clarke interprets as an act of divine "invention." On Clarke's reading, the divine ideas are the result of God's "infinitely fecund, artistically inventive activity, which does not find them somehow ready-made in

14 Ibid., 5.
15 Aquinas, *Truth* 3.2 ad 6, trans. Mulligan.

His essence (what could that possibly mean ontologically?) but literally 'invents,' 'excogitates' them, using the infinitely simple plenitude of *Esse* that is His essence as supreme *analogical* model or norm."[16] In a similar vein, John F. Wippel writes how, for Aquinas, "in knowing his own essence, [God] also knows (or 'discovers') the many ways in which it is imitable and, therefore, the divine ideas and the possibles."[17] On this understanding, the divine ideas emerge as a form of divine self-interpretation: they are not merely God's *knowledge,* but his *interpretation* of himself as imitable by his creatures. What all of this suggests is that God is not merely an artist in his *ad extra* act of creation, but, more radically, for St. Thomas God is a kind of artist as he knows and therefore relates to his own self. God is an artist *essentially.*

In developing just how Thomas's divine-exemplarist conception of creation makes possible an alternative way of thinking about human making, Miner turns to the thought of Jacques Maritain, whose Thomistic theory of art, as was pointed out in the Introduction, influenced many lay Catholic artists and writers in the early to mid-twentieth century, including possibly Tolkien. As Miner notes, while God's knowledge of his creative exemplars through an act of perfect self-knowledge must remain essentially different from a human maker's knowledge of the forms he makes, according to Maritain, the "creative intuition" of the poet, like God's knowledge of the exemplars, but unlike the form apprehended by the mere craftsman, does involve a kind of "obscure grasping of his own Self and of things in a knowledge through union or through connaturality which is born in the spiritual conscious, and which fructifies only in the work."[18] Thus, there is a kind of "free creativity of the spirit" on the part of the poet that makes him like a god, albeit a "'poor god' because he does not know himself," and, of course, because his creative insight "depends on the external world," whereas "God's creative Idea, from the very fact that it is creative, does not receive anything from things."[19] As to how the poet first comes by this knowledge of the artistic form, for the medieval Schoolmen, at least, it could not have been by mere abstraction, since, in Maritain's words, the form in question is "in no way a *concept*, for it is neither cognitive nor representative."[20] Instead, the "creative idea is an intellectual form, or a spiritual matrix, containing implicitly, in its

16 Clarke, "What is Really Real?," 85n45.
17 Wippel, "Thomas Aquinas, Henry of Ghent, and Godfrey of Fontaines on the Reality of Non-existing Possibles," 172n19.
18 Maritain, *Creative Intuition in Art and Poetry*, 115.
19 Ibid., 112–13.
20 Ibid., 135–36.

complex unity, the thing which, perhaps for the first time, will be brought into actual existence."[21] The result is that for neither God nor man is the Thomist exemplar a mere "ideal model sitting for the artist in his own brain, the work supposedly being a *copy* or portrait of it. This would make of art a cemetery of imitations." Rather, "the work is an original, not a copy."[22] Miner finds particular support for this reading of Thomas in *Prima Pars*, question 44, article 3 of the *Summa*, in which the angelic doctor illustrates his point concerning God's exemplar causality of all things with the example of the human craftsman who "produces a determinate form in matter by reason of the exemplar before him, whether it is the exemplar beheld externally, or the exemplar interiorly conceived in the mind." In Thomas's notion of a human artificer producing form in matter through an "exemplar interiorly conceived in the mind," Miner sees the suggestion of an analogy between a particular kind of human making on the one hand and the act of generation within the divine mind on the other:

> The conception of an exemplar in the mind is like the utterance of an inner word, a *verbum* which proceeds from the mind, but is not distinct from the mind. Maritain notes the importance of the *verbum mentis* doctrine for Aquinas's account of making: "before the work of art passes from art into the matter, by a transitive action, the very conception of the art has had to emerge from within the soul, by an immanent and vital action, like the emergence of the mental word." He quotes a pertinent text from Aquinas's commentary on the *Sentences*: "the procession of art is twofold, that is, from the soul of the artificer to his art, and from his art to his artifacts."[23]

In summary, then, in Thomas's divine "psychology," including his doctrine of divine ideas and his theory of creation as determined by that doctrine, Thomas makes possible an alternative way of thinking about human making that rescues it from the banal nihilism towards which the technological model has been alleged to lead by dignifying it with real metaphysical significance in its participation in and mirroring of the profundity of God's own Triune life.

---

21 Ibid., 136.

22 Ibid. (emphasis original). For a related discussion as it applies to Tolkien directly, see also Candler, "Tolkien or Nietzsche, Philology and Nihilism," 16.

23 Miner, *Truth in the Making*, 8–9. As Maritain himself summarizes the resulting analogy between human and divine making in Thomas's account, "in a way similar to that in which divine creation presupposes the knowledge God has of His own essence, poetic creation presupposes, as a primary requirement, a grasping, by the poet, of his own subjectivity, in order to create." Maritain, *Creative Intuition,* 113.

One final corollary to St. Thomas's doctrine of divine ideas that we will want to consider, on account of the important appearance it makes in Tolkien's own thought, involves Thomas's notion of "theological truth" or the "truth of things."[24] In the *Summa,* after his discussion of the divine ideas, the very next question entertained by St. Thomas concerns the subject of truth, with the very first article asking "whether truth is only in the intellect?" (ST 1.16.1). Thomas's reply is that, although truth is principally in, being first and foremost a property of, the intellect, because truth establishes a relation between the intellect and the thing known — "the true [existing] in the intellect in so far as it is conformed to the thing understood" — there is an important sense in which "the aspect of the true must pass from the intellect to the thing understood, so that also the thing understood is said to be true in so far as it has some relation to the intellect." In other words, when an intellect becomes truthfully related to a thing, the thing itself is not left unaffected, but reciprocates by likewise entering into a truthful relationship with the knowing intellect.[25] And even when a thing is not actively being known by any intellect, it still exists in a state of potentiality for being known, a potentiality that is no mere accidental feature of, but is constitutive of, the thing in its very being. As Josef Pieper has aptly described Thomas's teaching concerning truth's status as a "transcendental" property of all being,

> every being, as being, stands in relation to a knowing mind. This relational orientation toward a knowing mind represents the same ontological reality as the very being of a thing.... With all "being" thus related to a knowing mind, we further state that this relationship is actualized in the process of mental perception or intellection. "The mind's act of intellection itself constitutes and completes that relation of 'conformity' which is the nature of truth."[26]

24 For a history of the doctrine of the "truth of things," see Pieper, *The Truth of All Things.* Pieper traces the doctrine as far back as the pre-Socratic philosopher Pythagoras, through Aquinas, and forward to its dissolution in modernity. On Thomas's doctrine of the truth of things in particular, see also Phelan, "*Verum Sequitur Esse Rerum*" and Pickstock, "Truth and Correspondence."

25 As Catherine Pickstock explains the dynamic reciprocity involved in Thomas's theory of truth, the intellectual apprehension of truth "is not an indifferent speculation; it is rather a beautiful ratio which is instantiated between things and the mind which leaves neither things nor mind unchanged.... If, for example, one were to know a willow tree overhanging the Cherwell, our knowing of it would be just as much an event in the life of the form 'tree' as the tree in its willowness and in its growing." Pickstock, "Truth and Correspondence," 9.

26 Pieper, *The Truth of All Things,* 35, citing St. Thomas's *Commentary on the Book of Sentences* 1.19.5.1.

Although a thing always exists in this state of "relational orientation toward a knowing mind," or rather precisely on account of it, there is a very real sense in which it is only by being known that a thing is finally allowed to reach its completion or perfection. By knowing things and thus realizing their potential for being known, the human intellect gives things the opportunity to be what they truly are, providing them, so to speak, with the stage upon which they might enact their foreordained part. As Catherine Pickstock has observed, there is thus an almost redemptive dimension to the intellect's role in actualizing the truth potential of things, their innate capacity, that is, for being known:

> one must think of knowing-a-thing as an act of generosity, or salvific compensation for the exclusivity and discreteness of things.... It is a *corrective* or *remedy*, according to Aquinas in *De Veritate*, for the isolation of substantive beings.... [T]he very notion of a "thing itself" is radically otherwise, for it is only "itself" in its being conformed to the intellect of the knower.... The thing-itself is only itself by being assimilated to the knower, and by its form entering into the mind of the knower.[27]

Here Maritain is also worth mentioning again, as he connects, in a way that we will find echoed in Tolkien, this Thomistic sense of the radical co-belongingness of the human mind and things with the reason why human beings can have an aesthetic experience of the natural world: "Take the objects of aesthetic delight which are the most completely remote from any impact of humanity.... Everywhere in reality, man is there, under cover. Man's measure is present, though hidden All these nonhuman things return to man a quality of the human mind which is concealed in them."[28]

Yet the primary basis for Thomas for both the knowing intellect's truthful orientation towards things and the truthful orientation of things towards the knowing intellect is that each is ultimately oriented towards the divine intellect in which both intellect and things have their origin. Because all things owe their existence to the divine intellect, making them "essentially" related to it, Thomas concludes that "in the same way natural things are said to be true in so far as they express the likeness of the species that are in the divine mind. For a stone is called true, because it expresses the nature proper to a stone, according to the

27 Pickstock, "Truth and Correspondence," 9 (emphasis original). As Maritain has similarly written, "object and objectivity are the very life and salvation of the intellect." Maritain, *Existence and the Existent*, 23.

28 Maritain, *Creative Intuition*, 6.

preconception in the divine intellect" (ST 1.16.1). In short, because things have
been created and patterned after their corresponding idea or exemplar in the
divine mind, things exist in this state of continuous conformity to that mind,
the consequence of which is that things are by nature not alien or indifferent
to, but fundamentally akin and so intelligible to the knowing mind. As Pieper
again elaborates on this relationship, "things can be known by us because God
has creatively thought them; *as* creatively thought by God, things have not only
their *own* nature ('for themselves alone'); but *as* creatively thought by God,
things have also a reality 'for us.'"[29]

Tolkien and the Divine Ideas

WITH THE ABOVE ACCOUNT OF THOMAS'S DOCTRINE OF DIVINE
ideas in view, and its implications for a theory of human making, we turn to the
Ainulindalë in an effort to make a more thorough survey of the possible influence
of the divine ideas tradition of St. Thomas on Tolkien's creation-myth. We began
the chapter with the *Ainulindalë*'s statement that Ilúvatar "made first the Ainur,
the Holy Ones, that were the offspring of his thought." The narrative goes further
to describe how the Ainur at first "sang only each alone, or but few together,
while the rest hearkened; for each comprehended only that part of the mind of
Ilúvatar from which he came, and in the understanding of their brethren they
grew but slowly. Yet ever as they listened they came to deeper understanding, and
increased in unison and harmony" (S 15). As intellective beings having their origin
in the divine "thought" of Ilúvatar, each of the Ainur in his beginning knows
only "that part of the mind of Ilúvatar from which he came." As St. Thomas
explains, the divine thought or ideas after which all things are patterned are simply
God's knowledge of himself insofar as he is imitable by his creatures, meaning
that creatures themselves are nothing other than so many finite imitations of
the divine essence and being. Consequently, in knowing themselves, the Ainur
are able to know, to the extent that their own natures allow, something of the
mind of Ilúvatar after which they have been made.

Yet, through their music-making, the Ainur come into increasing contact
and communion with each other — creatures like and yet different from each
other, who have also been modeled after the Creator — and so come into an
increasing knowledge of the mind of Ilúvatar, in which each of them originally

---

29 Pieper, *The Silence of St. Thomas*, 55.

had a unique share. In the Ainur's Music, accordingly, we are treated to an excellent example of the kind of knowing-through-making discussed by Miner, an authentic form of making that is not threatened but preserved by the divine exemplarism in which both the Ainur and their Music have their provenance. Having their origin in the mind of Ilúvatar, what the Ainur represent, not only in their own being and essence, but also in the music they perform, are so many dim, finite, yet authentic reflections of the otherwise infinite brightness of the Creator's own thought and being. Verlyn Flieger captures this understanding of the *Ainulindalë* well (her own Neoplatonic and apophatic reading of Tolkien's theology notwithstanding) when she writes: "As 'offspring' of Eru's thought, the Ainur are aspects of whole mind, differentiations of Eru's undifferentiated nature. They are divided parts of that which is undivided, thoughts springing outward from the mind, assuming life of their own. As parts, they express, but cannot encompass, the whole."[30] Robert Collins likewise points out how, as the "offspring" of Ilúvatar's thought, the Ainur also represent so many "interpretations of the mind of the One," something Collins connects further with the apparent etymological inspiration behind the name of *Ilúvatar* itself:

> Indeed, the Creator's name among the denizens of Middle Earth — Ilúvatar — obviously incorporates not only the Indo-European "father" (Sindarin *atar*/Sanskrit *pitar*) but also the Latin "vates" — poet/seer — emphasizing the character of the Creator as artist, and that of his creation as art object, the substantive image in time and space of the artist's thought. His symphonists, the Ainur, are clearly individual avatars of the various aspects of his own aesthetic fecundity.[31]

As Maritain similarly observes, "the Latin *vates* was both a poet and a diviner," a point he relates back to his Thomistic claim that human art, like divine art, involves a kind of self-knowledge, and hence represents a "kind of divination."[32]

It is not only in and through each other, however, that the Ainur are able to "divinize" or reveal the creative purposes or possibilities of the Creator. When the Ainur receive in the Vision their first glimpse of the coming of the "Children of Ilúvatar," the race of Elves and Men, the astonishment of the Ainur is captured in these words: "Therefore when [the Ainur] beheld them, the more did

---

30 Flieger, "Naming the Unnameable," 131.

31 Collins, "'Ainulindalë': Tolkien's Commitment to an Aesthetic Ontology," 257. On the etymology of *Ilúvatar,* see also Flieger, *Splintered Light,* 50.

32 Maritain, *Creative Intuition,* 3.

they love them, being things other than themselves, strange and free, wherein they saw the mind of Ilúvatar reflected anew, and learned yet a little more of his wisdom, which otherwise had been hidden even from the Ainur" (S 18). As further "reflections" of Ilúvatar's mind, yet different from the Ainur, the Children of Ilúvatar in their very being and essence embody a new perspective or insight into the divine nature and "wisdom" after which both the Ainur and the Children of Ilúvatar have been patterned. It is also worth noting here that this identity-in-difference — a property I suggested at the end of the last chapter as having its ultimately theological ground for Tolkien, similar to St. Thomas, in his Trinitarian conception of the divine being — is also the basis for the Ainur's affection or "love" for the Children of Ilúvatar. It is for love of the Creator that the Ainur love their fellow creatures.

In Tolkien's fictional world, then, both angelic and incarnate rational beings are created after a pattern in the Creator's own mind, with the result that they both are able to reveal, in their very being, something of that mind. As for the rest of creation, the *Ainulindalë* of course departs significantly from the exemplarism of both the classical Platonic and Christian traditions in its depiction of the rest of the created order as having been fashioned by the Ainur — not after some unchanging archetype in the divine mind or in the "eternal model," but after the sub-created pattern of the Ainur's own Music. Yet even here, as we will see later, Tolkien's narrative never ceases to take for granted the fact that the sub-creative possibilities or potentialities discovered by the Ainur are not independent of, but find their ultimate meaning in, Eru's own creative possibility.

And while a more complete treatment of the matter will have to wait until our discussion of Tolkien's account of sub-creative possibility at the conclusion of this chapter, a word might be said here by way of relating Tolkien to Miner's Maritainian interpretation and application of Thomas to the whole problem of human making. Although Tolkien does not expressly develop the kind of distinction drawn, for example, by Maritain between the "poet" and the "craftsman," he does articulate the sort of concern raised by Heidegger in regard to technological or representational thinking as it contrasts with that of true, authentic art. In his essay "On Fairy-Stories," for example, Tolkien argues that one of the purposes of such fantasy is the "recovery" of the strangeness or mystery of things from the "dreary" or "trite" "familiarity" into which they fall through our "appropriation" of them. By "appropriation," Tolkien does not necessarily limit himself to the kind of practical or technological mastery or domination of things that he criticizes elsewhere, though it would certainly include that. Rather, "appropriation" would apply to that even more subtle, intellectual, and even aesthetic and artistic form of possessiveness, the kind of thing, for example, Tolkien thematizes in his *legendarium*, most notably in the character of the Elves. On the one hand, while the Elves symbolize "a devoted love of the physical world, and a desire to observe and understand it for its own sake and as 'other,'" as well as embody a "'subcreational' or artistic faculty of great excellence," on the other hand Tolkien sees them as for that reason being peculiarly susceptible to what he refers to as the "will to preservation," i.e., the desire "to arrest change, and keep things always fresh and fair" (L 236).[33] Thus, Tolkien too recognizes the ease and sometimes imperceptibility with which the true, selfless artistic impulse — which ideally seeks only communion with and knowledge of things through a sub-creative process that simultaneously brings things to their own completion or fulfillment — can slide into the self-interested imposition of one's own purposes or plans; the ease, that is, one might say, with which "art" or "poetry" can devolve into mere "craft" or "technological making," and hence the necessity for the one to be distinguished from the other. Here I submit we also gain a further perspective into Tolkien's well-known preference of myth or fairy-story over allegory. In allegory's "purposed domination of the author," as Tolkien puts it in the foreword to the second edition of *The Lord of the Rings*, we seem to have exactly the kind of "bad exemplarism" associated with the craft-model of making, in which the act of making is preceded and almost wholly predetermined by a prior act of knowing. In contrast to the "domination" of allegory, Tolkien juxtaposes the "discovery" and "applicability" of fairy-story and myth, a form of knowing, in other words, that takes place only in and through the act of making. As we shall see later, however, unlike Heidegger, or even William of Ockham, for that matter, this good kind of knowing-through-making for Tolkien is to be secured not through a *rejection* of the Augustinian tradition of divine exemplarism, but through a recognizably Thomistic embracing of it.[34]

At this point we might further connect, so far as may be possible, Tolkien's remarks on the nature of sub-creative "discovery" with what was said earlier about the psychology of creative-concept formation. As was observed above, according

33 We will return to this theme at greater length in chapter five's study of Tolkien's metaphysics of evil.

34 If Michael Allen Gillespie is correct, Heidegger's and, as we shall see later, Ockham's common rejection of the exemplarism of Aquinas may be more than mere coincidence, insofar as Heidegger's own notion of being arguably has its historical roots in the "dark god" of Ockham's nominalism. Gillespie, "Temporality and History in the Thought of Martin Heidegger." For Gillespie's more in-depth account of the tradition of nihilism running from Ockham to Heidegger's predecessor, Nietzsche, see his *Nihilism Before Nietzsche*.

to Maritain, taking his cue from St. Thomas, the "creative intuition" of the poet is the result of a kind of god-like "free creativity" on the part of the poet (made in the image of God) as he draws from the "spiritual matrix" produced by his knowing at once "his own Self and of things in a knowledge through union or connaturality," and so, as Miner put it, the "conception of the art…emerge[s] from within the soul, by an immanent and vital action, like the emergence of the mental word." Here one may also be reminded of the words Ilúvatar first speaks to the Ainur when he enjoins them to develop the musical themes he originally taught to them: "And since I have kindled you with the Flame Imperishable, ye shall show forth your powers in adorning this theme, each with his own thoughts and devices, if he will. But I will sit and hearken, and be glad that through you great beauty has been wakened into song" (S 15). As we saw in the last chapter, the Flame Imperishable is Ilúvatar's own creative power whereby he "kindles" his creatures with their very act of being or existence, and this fire of existence includes the gift of sub-creative freedom that Ilúvatar has granted to his rational creatures. What this means is that creatures, in sum, are able to sub-create because they have been kindled with and by the Creator's own creativity.

A more obvious application of Maritain's notion of creative intuition, however, is perhaps to be found in Tolkien's account of the sub-creative imagination in his essay "On Fairy-Stories." As Tolkien writes there:

> The incarnate mind, the tongue, and the tale are in our world coeval. The human mind, endowed with the powers of generalization and abstraction, sees not only *green-grass*, discriminating it from other things (and finding it fair to look upon), but sees that it is *green* as well as being *grass*. But how powerful, how stimulating to the very faculty that produced it, was the invention of the adjective: no spell or incantation in Faërie is more potent. And that is not surprising: such incantations might indeed be said to be only another view of adjectives, a part of speech in a mythical grammar. The mind that thought of *light, heavy, grey, yellow, still, swift*, also conceived of magic that would make heavy things light and able to fly, turn grey lead into yellow gold, and the still rock into swift water. If it could do the one, it could do the other; it inevitably did both. When we can take green from grass, blue from heaven, and red from blood, we have already an enchanter's power — upon one plane; and the desire to wield that power in the world external to our minds awakes. It does not follow that we shall use that power well upon any plane. We may put a deadly green upon a man's face and produce a horror; we may make the rare and terrible blue moon

to shine; or we may cause woods to spring with silver leaves and rams to wear fleeces of gold, and put hot fire into the belly of the cold worm. But in such "fantasy," as it is called, new form is made; Faërie begins; Man becomes a sub-creator. (TR 48–49)[35]

As Tolkien observes, by "the power of generalization and abstraction" the mind is able to see not only *green grass*, but *green* as distinct from *grass*. Abstraction, however, is not invention, or as Tolkien implies, it is not "incantation."[36] Creative intuition is no mere passive, speculative beholding of form, but is a kind of "magic," an "enchanter's power" similar to God's that can — if not literally (and thus unlike God's power), then at least imaginatively — "make heavy things light and able to fly, turn grey lead into yellow gold, and the still rock into swift water." As Tolkien further observes, the fact that we have this power does not mean that "we shall use that power well"; as Maritain has it, we can be very "poor gods." What accounts for the difference is the use one makes of the faculty of Imagination, or what Tolkien defines as "the power of giving to ideal creations the inner consistency of reality." It is something like this capacity to grasp the manifold "implications" of a given image that Maritain seems to have at least partially in view in his account of the kind of occult sympathy or intuition of things that the artist must have in the development of the creative form or concept.

As for Thomas's afore-discussed doctrine of the "truth of things," while we will consider in a moment the role of this idea within the pages of the *Ainulindalë*, its most prominent appearance in Tolkien's writings actually occurs in the same letter to young Camilla, the daughter of Tolkien's publisher Rayner Unwin, that we considered in the last chapter. Camilla had written Tolkien, it may be recalled, asking his opinion concerning the "purpose of life," and in his initial, clarifying remarks Tolkien had made the point that "questions about 'purpose' are only really useful when they refer to the conscious purposes or objects of human beings, or to the uses of things they design and make" (L 399). At first,

---

35　On this passage, see also Candler, "Tolkien or Nietzsche, Philology and Nihilism," 14–16.

36　As Maritain puts it, "in the spiritual unconscious the life of the intellect is not entirely engrossed by the preparation and engendering of its instruments of rational knowledge and by the process of production of concepts and ideas...which winds up at the level of the conceptualized externals of reason. There is still for the intellect another kind of life, which makes use of other resources and another reserve of vitality, and which is free, I mean free from the engendering of abstract concepts and ideas, free from the workings of rational knowledge and the disciplines of logical thought, free from the human actions to regulate and the human life to guide, and free from the laws of objective reality as to be known and acknowledged by science and discursive reason." Maritain, *Creative Intuition,* 110.

this statement might appear to have a somewhat modern and even evolutionary ring to it, restricting as it seems the sphere in which questions of purpose may be legitimately raised to the subjective realm of human consciousness: purposes apply to human matters, implying — or so one might infer — that they do *not* properly apply elsewhere. Tolkien's intended meaning, however, turns out to be quite different: "As for 'other things,'" he continues, "their value resides in themselves: they ARE, they would exist even if we did not. But since we do exist one of their functions is to be contemplated by us." In chapter three we will consider more fully the question of Tolkien's metaphysical realism, his conviction that there is a world of things that exist in their own ontological right, independent of the human beings who perceive and experience them. Here I merely want to point out how, contrary to modern realism, which presupposes an alienating dualism between the subjectivity of human consciousness on the one hand and an isolated, objective world of non-mental things on the other, Tolkien's realism is thoroughly anti- and pre-modern, even Thomistic. As he tells Camilla, although things are such that they "would exist even if we did not," he goes further to conclude from this that therefore their "*value* resides in themselves," independent of human beings as well. Thus, while "purposes" may be a mind-dependent or relative phenomena for Tolkien, "values" apparently are not. What precisely Tolkien means by "value" is not immediately evident ("moral value"? "truth value"? "aesthetic value"?), though we may perhaps recall here the passage from the *Ainulindalë* cited above as to how the Ainur loved the Children of Ilúvatar simply for being "other" than themselves. As Tolkien writes in another letter, moreover, "all things and deeds have a value in themselves, apart from their 'causes' and 'effects'" (L 76), a statement perhaps intended to express Tolkien's Aristotelian conviction, shared by St. Thomas, that creatures, having received their being as a gift from the Creator himself, are no mere Platonic shadow-realities, but have real ontological consequence, dignity, and weight. Things exist, and thus are to be intellectually reckoned with. Yet, as Tolkien goes on to point out in his letter to Camilla, human beings also exist, a fact that things themselves must reckon with in their own turn, so that, "since we do exist one of their [i.e., non-human things'] functions is to be contemplated by us." This contemplatable "function" of things, I submit, is none other than Thomas's notion of the "truth of things," or what Pieper referred to as their "relational orientation towards a knowing mind." Tolkien thus may be seen to reiterate the very sentiment he may have read in G.K. Chesterton's biography of St. Thomas, where Chesterton explains how for Thomas, in the act of knowing, the object becomes a part of the mind; nay, according to Aquinas, the mind actually becomes the object. But, as one commentator acutely puts it, it only becomes the object and does not create the object. In other words, the object *is* an object; it can and does exist outside the mind, or in the absence of the mind. And *therefore* it enlarges the mind of which it becomes a part. The mind conquers a new province like an emperor; but only because the mind has answered the bell like a servant. The mind has opened the doors and windows, because it is the natural activity of what is inside the house to find out what is outside the house. If the mind is sufficient to itself, it is insufficient for itself. For this feeding upon fact *is* itself; as an organ it has an object which is objective; this eating of the strange strong meat of reality.[37]

As Tolkien himself explains later in his letter to Camilla, "we are individuals (as in some degree are all living things) but do not, cannot live in isolation, and have a bond with all other things, ever closer up to the absolute bond with our own human kind." For Tolkien, there exists a special "bond" between human minds and other things, a claim we may relate back to his earlier statement in the same letter that the Creator of all things is "a Mind to which our minds are akin." For Tolkien, as for Thomas, things are intelligible to or truthful for the human intellect because they exist in a truthful relationship and hence kinship to the divine mind from which all things originate. Again, as Tolkien writes, things exist so as to be "contemplated by us," yielding the same "for us" character with which Pieper characterizes Thomas's doctrine of truth. Finally, for both Thomas and Tolkien, the potentiality things have for being known means that human beings have a real, ontologically redemptive role to play in bringing things to their full realization in their act of being known, for as Tolkien concludes in his letter to Camilla Unwin: "So it may be said that the chief purpose of life, for any one of us, is to increase according to our capacity our knowledge of God by all the means we have, and to be moved by it to praise and thanks.... And in moments of exaltation we may call on all created things to join in our chorus, speaking on their behalf" (L 400). As Augustine himself remarks in his *Confessions*, "animals and physical matter find a voice through those who contemplate them."[38] In knowing, praising, and thanking God, we not only fulfill our own being, but as kings and priests — as Aragorns and Gandalfs — of this world, we also help fulfill the being of the created things around us.

37 Chesterton, *Saint Thomas Aquinas*, 183–84.
38 Augustine, *Confessions* 5.1.1, trans. Chadwick.

As for the *Ainulindalë*, while Tolkien's Thomistic doctrine of the truth of things does not receive so express a statement as it does in his letter to Camilla, vestiges of the idea may be discerned there as well. As we saw in the last chapter, the created world has its existence through the Creator giving being or reality to the Music and Vision of the Ainur, meaning that the physical world has its existence in a state of harmony and conformity with the Music and Vision from which it receives its meaning and intelligibility. Yet there is an important escha-tological and theological component to this conformity, for, as Tolkien's tale indicates, not even the Ainur fully understand their own Music, much less the world patterned after it, so that there is prophesied a time when a greater Music still

> shall be made before Ilúvatar by the choirs of the Ainur and the Children of Ilúvatar after the end of days. Then the themes of Ilúvatar shall be played aright, and take Being in the moment of their utterance, for all shall then understand fully his intent in their part, and each shall know the compre-hension of each, and Ilúvatar shall give to their thoughts the secret fire, being well pleased. (S 16)

Owing first to their finitude and secondly to the corrupting influence of Melkor, the correspondence or "adequation" between the Ainur's Music, itself patterned after the original divine themes or ideas in the mind of Eru, and the world in its actual existence is an imperfect correspondence, or at least initially an imperfectly *conceived* correspondence. It is anticipated in the *Ainulindalë*, however, that this imperfection is one that will at last be rectified "at the end of days" in the fulfillment of the sub-creative equivalent to man's desire for the beatific vision (the paradoxical, natural desire for the supernatural vision of God in his essence), when the artistic purposes of the sub-creator are given the supernatural gift of being by the Creator himself.

In creating the physical world, moreover, Eru does not simply impose the beautiful and intelligible form of the Music and Vision onto an otherwise unin-telligible and recalcitrant array of matter, much as Plato's demiurge does in the *Timaeus*. Instead, and as we saw in the last chapter, Eru is rather depicted as sending his own self, under the guise of the Flame Imperishable, to kindle the world, including its matter, in its very being. The result of this is that, when the physical world is first brought into existence, and even before it has been given any of its defining form by the Ainur, it is told how "suddenly the Ainur saw afar off a light, as it were a cloud with a living heart of flame; and they knew that this was no vision only, but that Ilúvatar had made a new thing: Eä, the World that Is" (S 20). For Tolkien following Aquinas, all created existence, including the as-yet unformed material existence of the physical world, has its being by participating in the uncreated being of the Creator. Tolkien fittingly conceives the clarity and radiance of the One as penetrating into and thus shining from within the being of created reality, which has its being by participating in the One who is the Flame Imperishable, so that the physical world first presents itself to the Ainur as "a cloud with a living heart of flame." Thus, in Pieper's following characterization of Thomas's doctrine of the truth of things, we also find an apt commentary on Eru's creation of Eä, "the World that Is":

> Things have their intelligibility, their inner clarity and lucidity, and the power to reveal themselves, because God has creatively thought them. This is why they are essentially intelligible. Their brightness and radiance is infused into things from the creative mind of God, together with their essential being (or rather, as the very essence of that being!). It is this radiance, and this alone, that makes existing things perceptible to human knowledge.[39]

Divine Freedom
IN ST. THOMAS AND TOLKIEN

AFTER THE DIVINE KNOWLEDGE, THE NEXT OPERATION OF GOD discussed by St. Thomas in the *Summa,* and the one actually to receive the greater emphasis in the pages of the *Ainulindalë,* is that of the divine will. In contrast with a tendency in Plato and later Platonists to view the physical cosmos as an inexorable process or emanation prompted by the divine being's own internal necessity, the orthodox Christian confession has been to affirm the complete freedom and consequent gratuity of the creative act. For this reason, in his discussion of the divine will in the *Summa*, in response to the claim that, because God's will is identical with his essence and therefore whatever he wills he must will essentially, Thomas carefully distinguishes between two kinds of necessity in

---

39 Pieper, *The Silence of St. Thomas*, 55–56. At the same time, Pieper cautions, the very luminescence of created being is also what ensures that it can never be completely grasped or comprehended by the finite, human mind: "Accordingly, for St. Thomas, the unknowable can never denote something in itself dark and impenetrable, but only something that has so much light that a particular finite faculty of knowledge cannot absorb it all. It is too rich to be assimilated completely; it eludes the effort to comprehend it." Ibid., 60. Having this dual origin in God on the one hand and sheer nothingness on the other, both of which are unfathomable, there is a sense in which creatures are themselves unfathomable.

God's willing (ST 1.19.3). His willing of his own existence and goodness is indeed absolutely necessary, whereas his willing of creaturely existence and goodness is necessary only "by supposition." In other words, it is not necessary that God should will anything besides himself, but, if he should in fact freely will something besides himself, then and only then is it in fact necessary that he should will it, and what is more, that he should will that it be "ordered to his own goodness as [its] end." And in response to the objection that God, as the first cause of all things, must always act according to his nature and essence and therefore never cause things by his will, here Thomas counters by arguing that the same infinite yet simple perfection that he had earlier argued to necessitate a plurality of ideas in God also necessitates that the creation act be entirely voluntary. Being perfect and undetermined within himself, God cannot have any need to produce something outside of himself, and so God's "determined effects" of creation must "proceed from his own infinite perfection according to the determination of his will *and* intellect" (ST 1.19.4).[40]

While it is the freedom not of Ilúvatar but of his finite, rational beings that is of primary interest in Tolkien's writings, the latter nevertheless recognized that the question of creaturely freedom was inseparable from the Creator in whose image finite sub-creators have been made. In his letter to Peter Hastings, for example, Tolkien writes that in order for "Free Will" to exist, "it is necessary that the Author [i.e., God] should guarantee it" (L 195), and in another letter Tolkien goes so far as to identify God alone, in the absolute sense, as "the one wholly free Will and Agent" (L 204), themes that we will develop at greater length in chapter four. And one of the places, not surprisingly, where the theme of divine freedom appears in Tolkien's *legendarium* is in the context of the act of creation itself. As Tolkien defines it in his letter to Hastings, creation in Middle-earth is primarily conceived in terms of an "act of *Will* of Eru the One that gives Reality to *conceptions*" (L 190n, emphasis added), a definition echoing St. Thomas's aforementioned argument from the *Summa* that creation proceeds from God "according to the determination of his will and intellect."

In addition to Eru's freedom in bringing the physical world into being, there is also the unrivaled freedom Eru exercises during the course of the Ainur's

---

40 Later in the *Summa*'s discussion of creation proper, we get what is perhaps the most famous application of Thomas's own theological voluntarism, where, in the first two articles of question 46, Thomas refers to the divine will some fifteen times in arguing his dual thesis that, because creation is an act of divine will, neither the eternality nor the temporal beginning of the world can be philosophically demonstrated. Since creation is free, God could have created the world either way, and so the truth of the matter is something that can only be known by divine revelation.

Music. After communicating to the Ainur the original themes of the Music, Eru at first is content to "sit and hearken" to their Music, and it is only when Melkor introduces his musical disruptions that Eru makes his entrance again into the Music with a new theme, "like and yet unlike to the former theme, and it gathered power and had new beauty" (S 16). When Melkor persists in his rebellion, however, Eru responds with a "third theme," which is "unlike the others. For it seemed at first soft and sweet, a mere rippling of gentle sounds in delicate melodies; but it could not be quenched, and it took to itself power and profundity." We learn later in the narrative, during the Ainur's Vision, that these second and third themes introduced specially by Eru correspond to the future advent of the Elves and Men. One of the practical consequences of this direct involvement on Eru's part in the Music is that the Ainur, for all their wisdom and the foresight provided by their Music and the Vision, are never able fully to anticipate Eru's providential plan:

> Yet some things there are that they cannot see, neither alone nor taking counsel together; for to none but himself has Ilúvatar revealed all that he has in store, and in every age there come forth things that are new and have no foretelling, for they do not proceed from the past. And so it was that as this vision of the World was played before them, the Ainur saw that it contained things which they had not thought. And they saw with amazement the coming of the Children of Ilúvatar.... For the Children of Ilúvatar were conceived by him alone; and they came with the third theme, and were not in the theme which Ilúvatar propounded at the beginning, and none of the Ainur had part in their making. Therefore when they beheld them, the more did they love them, being things other than themselves, strange and free. (S 18)

Thus, in contradiction to the deistic interpretation that some readers have given to Ilúvatar's involvement in the created world, Ilúvatar reserves for himself the greatest part in the Music and in doing so guarantees his continued involvement throughout the subsequent course of the world's history. As Tolkien himself writes in one commentary:

> The [Elves] held that Eru was and is free at all stages. This freedom was shown in the Music by His introduction, after the arising of the discords of Melkor, of the two new themes, representing the coming of Elves and Men, which were not in His first communication. He may therefore in

stage 5 [of the creation process, "the Achievement, which is still going
on"] introduce things directly, which were not in the Music and so are
not achieved through the Valar. It remains, nonetheless, true in general to
regard Eä as achieved through their mediation. (MR 336)

As Tolkien was keen to stress, Eru remains "free at all stages" of the creation
process, a freedom that is first exhibited in his involvement in the Music and
later executed in his privilege, after the world has been created, to "introduce
things directly" without the "mediation" of the Ainur, even though that is his
normal or usual way of operating.[41]

St. Thomas on Divine Possibility

THIS BRINGS US AT LAST TO THE THIRD OF THE THREE DIVINE
operations distinguished by St. Thomas in his treatment of God in the *Summa*,
namely that of divine power or omnipotence, an important topic in the history
of philosophical theology, to which I hope to show that Tolkien, while not
dealing with it much directly, nevertheless has a significant contribution to
make. To begin, for Tolkien as much as for Thomas, as we have seen, God's
act of creation is entirely free, being an act of divine *will*. In the later medieval
era, however, the debate among schoolmen such as St. Thomas and William of
Ockham raged not over *whether* God had the freedom and power to create or
not to create, but over the *extent* of God's freedom and power to create things
or worlds other than what he has created, a debate, moreover, that would have
enormous repercussions for the future development of theology and, indeed, for
the advent of the modern era itself.[42] It has only been in the last half-century or
so, however, that historians have begun to realize the important role that the

---

41 As Tolkien further comments on Eru's freedom in a passage reviewed in the previous chapter:
"But the One retains all ultimate authority, and (or so it seems as viewed in serial time) reserves the
right to intrude the finger of God into the story: that is to produce realities which could not be
deduced even from a complete knowledge of the previous past, but which being real become part of
the effective past for all subsequent time (a possible definition of a 'miracle'). According to the fable
Elves and Men were the first of these intrusions, made indeed while the 'story' was still only a story
and not 'realized'; they were not therefore in any sense conceived or made by the gods, the Valar,
and were called the Eruhíni or 'Children of God,' and were for the Valar an incalculable element:
that is they were rational creatures of free will in regard to God, of the same historical rank as the
Valar" (L 235–36).
42 For a recent study on the theological origins of modernity in changing views on divine
freedom and power in the late medieval period, see Gillespie, *The Theological Origins of Modernity*.

question of divine omnipotence and, in particular, the scholastic distinction between God's "absolute power" (*potentia absoluta*) and his power as it is actually manifested in the created order (*potentia ordinata*) played in the development of late medieval thought. Although Augustine, as early as the fifth century, introduced the conceptual distinction between divine capacity and volition, or between what God wills to do and what he can do (*potuit, sed noluit*), according to William Courtenay, it was not until around the year 1245 that the distinction between God's absolute and ordained powers received the standard formulation that would be adopted by thinkers as otherwise diverse as Aquinas and Ockham.[43] And although the distinction was certainly emphasized more in the thought of Ockham and later nominalists, Thomas's own interest in the subject of divine power is indicated in the fact that he convened an entire *disputatio* on the topic, the proceedings of which were published in his *Disputed Questions on Power*. As for the distinction of powers itself, Courtenay observes that Thomas used "far more than has been realized, both the actual language of *potentia absoluta/ ordinata* and more frequently the concept that lies behind it."[44]

As has been further observed by historian Heiko Oberman, the distinction of powers originally functioned as a dialectical apparatus allowing theologians to consider simultaneously the divine omnipotence that infinitely transcends the created order and God's commitment and loyalty to that order.[45] The distinction, in other words, was a conceptual device designed for balancing a consideration of the radical contingency of creation with a recognition of its stability and dependability. Because of the dialectical character of the distinction of powers, it has been pointed out, neither the "ordained" nor the "absolute" pole of the distinction was ever intended to be taken and applied in isolation from its dialectical counterpart.[46]

Thomas's own statement of the distinction of powers in the *Summa* appears in his response to the question of article five, question 25, as to "whether God can do what he does not." In his reply to the first objection, Aquinas reasons that,

> because power is considered as executing, the will as commanding, and the intellect and wisdom as directing, what is attributed to his power considered in itself, God is said to be able to do in accordance with his absolute

43 Courtenay, *Capacity and Volition,* 74.

44 Ibid., 88.

45 Oberman, *The Harvest of Medieval Theology: Gabriel Biel and Late Medieval Nominalism,* 30–56.

46 Oakley, *Omnipotence and Promise,* 13.

power. Of such a kind is everything which has the nature of being, as was said above. What is, however, attributed to the divine power according as it carries into execution the command of a just will, God is said to be able to do by his power as ordained. In this manner, we must say that God can do other things by his absolute power than those he has foreknown and preordained himself to do. (ST 1.25.5 ad 1)

By God's "absolute power," Aquinas means "his power considered in itself," or his power in abstraction from or without consideration of how God actually does exercise his power in the created order. On this traditional understanding of *potentia absoluta*, the latter represents an admittedly human way of regarding or thinking about God's power, and is not to be understood as a particular kind or avenue or exercise of divine power. Rather, *potentia absoluta* refers only to those hypothetical and therefore non-actualized possibilities that theoretically lie open to God, but that he nevertheless does not choose to implement. In fact, it might be less misleading to describe divine *potentia absoluta* as a kind of divine *in*activity, a way in which God can but does *not* act, and what is more, *will* not act. God's *potentia ordinata*, by contrast, Aquinas identifies as that power of God as it actually finds itself exercised by the divine will in the world. *Potentia absoluta,* in short, refers to what God can do but does not and will not do; *potentia ordinata* refers to what God wills to do and in fact does do.

Given that for Thomas God's ordained power does not exhaust his absolute power, the question arises as to what kinds of things, beyond those which he has in fact already created, God's power actually does or might extend to. What, in short, are the parameters of divine possibility? For starters, for the entire tradition that took up the question of divine omnipotence, one of the fundamental "limits" on God's absolute power is the law of non-contradiction. Thomas writes:

> Now nothing is opposed to the notion of being except non-being. Therefore that which implies being and non-being at the same time is incompatible with the notion of an absolutely possible thing, within the scope of the divine omnipotence. For such cannot come under the divine omnipotence, not because of any defect in the power of God, but because it has not the nature of a feasible or possible thing. Therefore, everything that does not imply a contradiction is numbered amongst those possible things, in respect of which God is called omnipotent; but whatever implies contradiction does not come within the scope of divine omnipotence, because it cannot have the aspect of possibility. (ST 1.25.3)

God cannot create or do anything that would involve a logical contradiction. Yet the thing to note here is how St. Thomas defines logical contradiction in terms of an *ontological* contradiction, that is to say, in terms of "that which implies being and non-being at the same time," thereby rendering it "incompatible with the notion of an absolutely possible thing." What is possible, therefore, is "everything which has the nature of being," meaning that possibility in its first instance is more than a mere modality of thought or conceptual consistency: it is a modality of *being*, a point Thomas makes in a statement immediately preceding the above passage, in which he says that "whatever can have the nature of being is numbered among the absolutely possible things in respect of which God is called omnipotent." But, as Aquinas explains even earlier in the same article, what has "the nature of being" is determined by the divine being itself, which "is infinite, and is not limited to any genus of being but possesses beforehand within itself the perfection of all being." Thus, just as the logically possible is reducible to the ontologically possible, so the ontologically possible turns out to reduce to the theologically possible, meaning that the answer to the question of what God can *do* is a function of what God *is*.[47]

Filling out Thomas's account of divine possibility even further is his point that, because God is not only being itself but also goodness and wisdom itself, "God can do nothing that is not in accord with his wisdom and goodness," and therefore "whatever is done by him in created things, is done according to a fitting order and proportion, in which consists the notion of justice. Thus justice must exist in all God's works" (ST 1.21.4). Because what is possible for God to do or create is reducible to that which is capable of imitating his own being, and because God's being simply *is* his wisdom and justice, it follows that what is possible for God to do or create must likewise be characterized by the "fitting order and proportion" that is his wisdom and justice.[48] This condition of a "fitting order and proportion"

47 Or as Wippel has put it, "the possibility in question is not merely linguistic, nor merely logical, but ontological. Like the principle of noncontradiction itself, for Thomas possibility in its most fundamental sense is grounded in being, in this case in the divine being." Wippel, "The Reality of Non-existing Possibles," 168.

48 Far from such absolute conditions imposing an undue constraint upon divine power, for Thomas the situation is quite the reverse, as when he argues *from* the premise of divine wisdom *to* the conclusion of divine omnipotence. Thomas thus concludes his fifth article on divine power, "Whether God can do what he does not?," with the following telling inference: "And so the divine wisdom is not so restricted to any particular order that no other course of events could happen. Therefore we must simply say that God can do other things than those he has done" (ST 1.25.5). Not only does wisdom mark all of God's actual deeds, but because what God actually does do cannot possibly exhaust his wisdom, this infinite surplus of wisdom guarantees that God can always do more, infinitely more, than what he does do. For Thomas, the divine wisdom, characterized in terms of divine action that is always "according to a fitting order and proportion," not only does not infringe

required by justice is significant, as it implies an important aesthetic dimension to Aquinas's whole approach to the question of divine omnipotence not always recognized in discussions of the subject, and which will provide the basis for our introduction of Tolkien into this issue later. As Aquinas argues earlier on in the *Summa,* the notion of proportionality is an essential aspect of beauty:

> Beauty and good in a subject are the same, for they are based upon the same thing, namely, the form; and consequently good is praised as beauty. But they differ logically, for good properly relates to the appetite (good being what all things desire), and therefore it has the aspect of an end (for the appetite is a kind of movement towards a thing). On the other hand, beauty relates to the knowing power, for beautiful things are those which please when seen. Hence beauty consists in due proportion, for the senses delight in things duly proportioned, as in what is after their own kind. (ST 1.5.4 ad 1)

Although Thomas never expressly identifies beauty as one of the transcendental attributes of being, its intrinsic relationship to the good (which is a transcendental property of being) means that, where there is being, there must also be a corresponding level of beauty.[49] This suggests in turn that what is possible for divine omnipotence to do or make is that which has the nature of the beautiful. God can do what is beautiful, and only what is beautiful, because only the beautiful has the nature of being, and hence of possibility.

The aesthetic dimension to Thomas's requirement that divine omnipotence be conformed to the "fitting order and proportion" of divine justice is further indicated in that this is also one of the choice places where Thomas likens God to an artist. In response to the question, "Whether the justice of God is truth?," Thomas writes:

> But when the intellect is the rule or measure of things, truth consists in the squaring of the thing to the intellect; just as an artist is said to make a true work when it is in accordance with his art.
>
> Now as artificial things are related to the art, so are works of justice related to the law with which they accord. Therefore God's justice, which establishes things in the order conformable to the rule of his wisdom, which

---

upon divine power, but is in fact what positively guarantees that power.

49   On Thomas's doctrine of the transcendentals, including an argument for the non-transcendental status of beauty, see Aertsen, *Medieval Philosophy and the Transcendentals: The Case of Thomas Aquinas.*

is his law, is suitably called truth. Thus we also in human affairs speak of the truth of justice. (ST 1.21.2)

Divine justice means that God always does what he does in conformity to a rule or law, even if that rule or law is ultimately derived from the perfection of his own being. And although the exact order and law we find in *this* world would not necessarily apply in any alternative possible world that God might have created, it is nevertheless the case that *some* order and law, one presumably analogous to our own, would have to apply there. To put this in terms of the distinction of powers, what God is capable of doing by his *potentia absoluta*, and therefore capable of doing outside of the *potentia ordinata* of this world, would nevertheless still have to be consistent with the ordained power established or determined for the alternative possible world under conjecture. To put it differently still, what it means to say that God could do or create x according to his absolute power is simply to say that there is *some* possible order such that it would fall within the ordained power of that order for God to do x. Or in Boyd Talor Coolman's apt statement, "Power is not first and foremost a *potentia absoluta*, unconstrained by anything other than itself; rather, it is the ability to communicate goodness fully without diminishment."[50]

What this means is that any hypothesis as to what God is capable of doing or creating according to his absolute power must presuppose an order in which the actualization of that hypothesis would be rendered something just and wise for God to do; that is to say, it must presuppose a rule or law to which the actualization of that hypothesis on the part of God may be seen to conform. As one can see, for Aquinas God's ordained power, which is his power as it is actually exercised in this world, while clearly not exhaustive of God's absolute or unactualized power, is nevertheless an important indication of its nature. And this means that, for Aquinas, actuality or actual existence is our concrete measure of possibility or possible existence.[51] As for this order according to which the divine wisdom does all things, as Alice Ramos has helpfully pointed out, it is not merely "the static order of coordination, that is, the right arrangement of parts making a systematic whole or a universe, but also as a dynamic order of subordination whereby there is a right arrangement of means to the end. Order in the dynamic sense refers to the return of all things to their initial principle, that is, to the unity from

50 Coolman, "General Introduction," in Coolman and Coulter, eds., *Trinity and Creation*, 36.
51 John Milbank, for example, writes: "For Aquinas logical possibility is only a faint version of real substantive actuality. It is designed to 'intend' this actuality, and guaranteed only by this actuality." Milbank, "Truth and Vision," 45.

whence the multiplicity or diversity of beings proceeded."[52] This is another way of saying that what is possible and therefore creatable by God is anything that has God as its final end, goal, or fulfillment. As we found Thomas putting it in his discussion of the divine will, it is *necessary* that what God wills (and hence what is possible) should be "ordered to his own goodness as [its] end."

Ockham on Divine Possibility

FOR AQUINAS, THEN, THERE IS A CLEAR CORRESPONDENCE between God's own being and his knowledge of his own being on the one hand and what God is able to do or make on the other. In the generation of thinkers immediately following Aquinas, however, discussions of the possibles and God's ideas grew increasingly more subtle and complex, as theologians labored in particular to reconcile conceptually the multiplicity of divine ideas required by creation with the fact of divine simplicity.[53] The debate finally reached a point of crisis in the mid-fourteenth century in the thought of William of Ockham, whose radically revised account of the divine ideas and divine possibility, regarded by a number of intellectual historians as a critical development in the advent of modern thought, provides a useful foil for our understanding of what is at stake theologically and metaphysically, first, in St. Thomas's own understanding of these matters, and second, in Tolkien's approach to the question of sub-creative possibility.[54]

Ockham's most important consideration of the question of divine ideas appears in his commentary on Peter Lombard's *Sentences,* part 1, d. 35, q. 5.[55] Ockham begins his discussion with Henry of Ghent's statement of the traditional views that "the divine essence itself is the ground and exemplary form of creatures,"

---

52 Ramos, "Ockham and Aquinas on Exemplary Causality," 208.

53 On the development of the doctrine of divine ideas and possibility between Aquinas and Ockham, see Wippel, "The Reality of Non-existing Possibles"; Adams, *William Ockham,* vol. 2, 1037–43, 1068–76; and Cunningham, *Genealogy of Nihilism: Philosophies of Nothing and the Difference of Theology,* 13–17.

54 On Ockham's doctrine of divine ideas and omnipotence, see Pegis, "Concerning William of Ockham"; Wolter, "Ockham and the Textbooks: On the Origin of Possibility"; Adams, *William Ockham,* vol. 2, 1033-83; Klocker, *William of Ockham and the Divine Freedom,* 77–89; Ramos, "Ockham and Aquinas on Exemplary Causality"; Maurer, *The Philosophy of William of Ockham in the Light of its First Principles,* 205–65, 295–337; and Cunningham, *Genealogy of Nihilism,* 17–26.

55 Ramos, "Ockham and Aquinas on Exemplary Causality," 200. The following quotations from Ockham's *Commentary on the Sentences* 1.35.5 are taken from Stephen Chak Tornay's translation of the passage in Tornay, *Ockham: Studies and Selections,* 137–64.

and that a divine idea, "formally considered, is nothing else than an aspect of imitability in the divine essence itself, in so far as it is considered by the intellect." Against this traditional position, Ockham argues that, given the utter simplicity of the divine essence on the one hand and the admitted multiplicity of the divine ideas on the other, the divine ideas cannot in fact be identical with the divine essence as had been traditionally held to be the case. Thus, while Ockham grants with Augustine that God must create according to some intelligible exemplar if the act of creation is to avoid being "irrational," he breaks both with Augustine (though without drawing attention to the fact) and the entire tradition based on him when he says that the exemplary role provided by the divine ideas "is not applicable to the divine essence itself, nor to any aspect of reason, *but to the created thing itself.*" In other words, the divine ideas to which God looks in the act of creation and after which creation is patterned are in fact not truly divine at all, but are rather themselves created entities. Or rather, the ideas to which God looks in producing creatures are nothing other than the creatures themselves as known or foreknown by God in their producible aspect: as Ockham himself puts it, "the created thing itself is the idea…. Therefore, [God] really looks to the creature and by looking to it he can produce." However, because the number of things that God can produce are infinite and known by him from all eternity, it follows for Ockham that God's otherwise created ideas are themselves infinite in number and eternal in duration.[56] Not only are God's ideas not identical with his essence, neither do his ideas even have any kind of imitative *ground* in his essence, as when Ockham approvingly cites the view "according to some" that "the created things existed from eternity in the potentiality of God but not in his nature, so that in their view the created things existed and did not exist."

For Ockham, then, God's ideas of what he can create are to be understood in reference not to the divine nature, but to the divine power, not to divine *essence,* but to divine *omnipotence,* a fact that has far-reaching implications for the kind of thing Ockham allows to be possible for God to do or to make, as we shall see. As was the case for Aquinas, for Ockham the "divine" ideas are an exhaustive register or index of divine possibility: in a word, the ideas are the possibles. This means, however, that in exporting the ideas outside the mind of God by identifying them with his creatures, either potential or actual, Ockham also effectively locates the ground of divine possibility in a source external to God as well. Like

---

56 On the infinitude of God's ideas Ockham writes, "it follows that God has an infinite number of ideas, as there are infinitely many things which can be produced by him," and on the eternality of the ideas he says that "the ideas are eternal in the divine mind; that is, they are eternally and unchangeably understood by [God]."

Aquinas, Ockham affirms the law of non-contradiction as a negative limit on divine power. Yet, whereas Aquinas, as we saw, articulates logical possibility in terms of its determining ground within an ontological and ultimately theological possibility, Ockham by contrast roots possibility not in terms of the divine but in terms of the creature's own being.[57] Thus, according to Allan Wolter, what is logically possible for God to do or to make in Ockham's view is "not something that a creature has by reason of some relation to an active potency in God. It is something which the creature has of itself."[58] In other words, the logical possibility of a creature is not something determined by its relationship to God's own power, much less to God's own being, but is rather a property or principle intrinsic to the creature and therefore apart from any reference to God. In short, it is only by first being immanently and logically possible on its own terms that a possible being is afterwards to be related to God, yet not necessarily in terms of his own essence or nature, as we have seen, but rather simply in terms of his power to bring that possibility into being. This is not to say, however, that the possibles themselves have some kind of being or existence independent of God, for while the *possibility* of the possibles is determined independently of God, Ockham says that the possibles are, by themselves, literally a "nothing" (*nihil*), inasmuch as they have their being only as objects thought by God. Were God to "cease" thinking them, they would not exist at all.[59] Thus, possibility belongs to things themselves, which in themselves are nothing. To summarize, then, instead of God's power and (what for Aquinas was identical with it) God's essence being the determining ground of the possible, for Ockham God's power is measurable by an extrinsically determined logical possibility. In contrast with Aquinas, according to whom the goodness, wisdom, justice, and beauty of God's ordained power as manifest in actual existence provide the rule or "law" for the endless possibilities of God's absolute power, Ockham endorses an abstract logical

---

57 On the law of non-contradiction as a limit on divine power, Ockham writes that, in contrast to his ordained power, God's absolute power "is taken as 'power to do anything such that its being done does not involve a contradiction,' regardless of whether or not God has ordained that he will do it." Ockham, *Quodlibetal Questions* 6.1, trans. Freddoso.

58 Wolter, "Ockham and the Textbooks," 262. Armand Maurer makes this same point when he writes that, on Ockham's view, "we should not say that possible being *belongs* to a creature, but that the creature *is possible,* not because of anything pertaining to it, but because it can exist in the real world…'to be possible' does not belong to a creature from God, but from itself." Maurer, *The Philosophy of Ockham in Light of its Principles,* 254.

59 "Hence, from eternity God saw all the things that were able to be created, and yet at that time they were nothing." Ockham, *Quodlibetal Questions* 6.6, trans. Freddoso. On Ockham's curious doctrine that the possibles are, in themselves, nothing, see Adams, *William Ockham,* 1059–61; Maurer, *The Philosophy of William of Ockham,* 219–28; Ramos, "Ockham and Aquinas on Exemplary Causality," 203; and Cunningham, *Genealogy of Nihilism,* 19–20.

possibility that is the measure of God's absolute power, and which in its turn is the measure of the actuality of God's ordained power.[60]

The practical import of Ockham's having thus denuded logical possibility of what had been for Aquinas its ontological and theological content is that it allowed him far more latitude in indulging in the kind of outrageous counter-factual speculation with which late medieval thought has come to be associated, as when he suggests that God, for example, could have saved the human race through an ass, or have caused the moral law to require rather than forbid murder, or have eternally accepted an individual who was entirely lacking in the habit of grace, or even have made it meritorious for an individual to hate God, and so on. Behind each of these hypotheses, moreover, and intimately related to his rejection of divine exemplar causality, is Ockham's further denial, again, contrary to Aquinas, of any necessary final causality within the created order: not having its originating, exemplary cause in the divine being or essence, it follows for Ockham that neither does creation necessarily have its destinating, final cause in the divine being or essence either.[61]

Tolkien on Sub-Creative Possibility

WHAT, FINALLY, WE MAY ASK, DOES THIS MEDIEVAL DEBATE over divine power and possibility have to do with Tolkien's fiction and theory of sub-creation? As has been said, Tolkien did not really concern himself with the medieval problem of divine possibility as such; yet the basic issues involved were surely ones he was familiar with. The thesis, for example, that not even God can produce a logical contradiction would have been a topic raised and possibly even discussed amongst the Inklings when C.S. Lewis, for example, read through his book, *The Problem of Pain*.[62] In his chapter on divine omnipotence, Lewis writes:

---

60 As Cunningham writes, for Ockham "the possible is no longer defined by the actual, but is now more defined than the actual. This is the ascendancy of the law of non-contradiction." Cunningham, *Genealogy of Nihilism*, 24.

61 As Ramos points out, because for Ockham "it cannot be proved that God knows all effects and their operations, and that he has in his wisdom ordered them to an end,...[i]n the non-rational universe Ockham explains order simply by referring to the intrinsic determinism of nature, which does not point to anything outside of itself.... We have then in Ockham the disappearance of the idea of natural inclination, of the Aristotelian doctrine which is taken by St. Thomas of the tendency of nature toward the good; this tendency is for Ockham a faith proposition." Ramos, "Ockham and Aquinas on Exemplary Causality," 209.

62 Purtill, "Tolkien's Creation Myth," 95. See also Whittingham, "The Mythology of the '*Ainulindalë*': Tolkien's Creation of Hope," 218.

> His Omnipotence means power to do all that is intrinsically possible, not
> to do the intrinsically impossible. You may attribute miracles to Him,
> but not nonsense. This is no limit to His power. If you choose to say "God
> can give a creature free will and at the same time withhold free will from
> it," you have not succeeded in saying *anything* about God: meaningless
> combinations of words do not suddenly acquire meaning simply because
> we prefix to them the two other words "God can."[63]

And in one passage commenting on Eru's freedom to intrude "new themes" into
the Ainur's Music and, after the creation of the world, to introduce new "things"
and new, "eucatastrophic" turns of events, Tolkien gives as precise a statement of
the whole scholastic concept of God's ordained power as one could ask for: "The
additions of Eru, however, will not be 'alien'; they will be accommodated to the
nature and character of Eä and of those that dwell in it; they may enhance the past
and enrich its purpose and significance, but they will contain it and not destroy
it" (MR 336). For Tolkien, following the traditional scholastic formulation of the
distinction of powers, even God's acts of supernatural power, as in the case of miracles, are not counter-instances to the universal order by which God has elected to
govern his creation, but are themselves a further, even deeper manifestation of it.

The primary relevance of the medieval discussion of divine power to the thought
and work of Tolkien, however, concerns less his explicit views on creative than
it does his views on *sub*-creative possibility; yet the point I wish to make here is
that these two issues for Tolkien are closely connected. The prevailing paradigm
or metaphor in Tolkien's thinking about God's relation to his creation, after all,
is that of an "author" or "writer" (see, for example, L 195, 252, 253, 215), with
Tolkien in one instance referring to God as "the supreme Artist and Author of
Reality" (L 101). In the epilogue to his essay "On Fairy-Stories," moreover, he
characterizes "History and the primary world," especially after the Incarnation
and Resurrection of Christ, as nothing less than a great fairy-story in which
the Creator has seen fit to fulfill the aspiration of all human fairy-stories. All
of this is to suggest that, for Tolkien, the same considerations that are to guide
our understanding of the sub-creator's power and freedom have an inevitable
analogue and application in how one is to understand the Creator's own power
and freedom, and vice-versa. As Tolkien is fond of saying, "we make still by the
law in which we're made."[64]

---

63 Lewis, *The Problem of Pain,* 25.
64 The line is from Tolkien's poem "Mythopoeia," which he also quotes in his essay (TR 74).

Not surprisingly, then, given his views on the interrelationship between creation and sub-creation, when the question of the limits of legitimate, sub-creative possibility was posed by Hastings in his letter mentioned earlier, Tolkien had the same medieval criterion of logical non-contradiction to offer: "Are there any 'bounds to a writer's job' except those imposed by his own finiteness? No bounds, but the laws of contradiction, I should think. But, of course, humility and an awareness of peril is required" (L 194). As Tolkien observes at the very end of his reply to Hastings, the sub-creator is indeed free to take his art beyond the "walls of 'observed fact,'" but this of course does not mean that he is permitted to make mere gibberish, for there are criteria to which the sub-creator, for all his freedom, must submit. One criterion that Tolkien hints at here and to which we will return later is a moral one: "humility and an awareness of peril is required." Another limitation noted, similar to what we saw earlier in Maritain, is that the sub-creator's freedom of necessity will be conditioned by his "finiteness." Yet, what Tolkien is primarily asking in this instance is whether there are any limits "*except*" those natural to creaturely finitude, any limits, in other words, common to both the finite sub-creator and the infinite Creator. The answer Tolkien gives, echoing Aquinas, Ockham, and his friend C.S. Lewis, is that neither God in his creating nor man in his sub-creating may produce a logical contradiction.

A further, at least apparent, similarity between Tolkien and Ockham on this point is the seeming permissiveness of the limit of mere logical possibility in allowing for all manner of outrageous speculations as to how God might have made or done things otherwise. In Tolkien's account of sub-creative fantasy, for example — one similar to that given by his mentor in the ways of fairy land, Chesterton — the theme of creaturely contingency is so accentuated that one might almost be led to wonder if it isn't Ockham rather than Aquinas who is the more significant philosophical influence. In his chapter from *Orthodoxy* on "The Ethics of Elfland," a passage that made a deep impression on Tolkien's essay "On Fairy-Stories," Chesterton gives us the following account of the philosophical import of fairy-stories, which might sound more like a page lifted from Ockham's Enlightenment counterpart, the nominalist David Hume, than it does from a man who would later write the world's most famous biography of St. Thomas:

> We have always in our fairy tales kept this sharp distinction between the science of mental relations, in which there really are laws, and the science of physical facts, in which there are no laws, but only weird repetitions...

> All the terms used in the science books, "law," "necessity," "order," "tendency," and so on, are really unintellectual, because they assume an inner synthesis, which we do not possess. The only words that ever satisfied me as describing Nature are the terms used in the fairy books, "charm," "spell," "enchantment." They express the arbitrariness of the fact and its mystery. A tree grows fruit because it is a magic tree. Water runs downhill because it is bewitched. The sun shines because it is bewitched.[65]

Later on in the same chapter, Chesterton spells out explicitly the theology implicit in this philosophy of fairyland, a philosophy that, again, would seem to channel more the spirit of the "unconquerable doctor" (*doctor invincibilis*) than that of the angelic doctor:

> the fairy-tale philosopher is glad that the leaf is green precisely because it might have been scarlet. He feels as if it had turned green an instant before he looked at it. He is pleased that snow is white on the strictly reasonable ground that it might have been black. Every color has in it a bold quality as of choice; the red of garden roses is not only decisive but also dramatic, like suddenly spilt blood. He feels that something has been *done*.... So one elephant having a trunk was odd; but all elephants having trunks looked like a plot.... But the repetition in Nature seemed sometimes to be an excited repetition, like that of an angry schoolmaster saying the same thing over and over again.... But perhaps God is strong enough to exult in monotony. It is possible that God says every morning, "Do it again" to the sun; and every evening, "Do it again" to the moon. It may not be automatic necessity that makes all daisies alike; it may be that God makes every daisy separately, but has never got tired of making them.... I had always vaguely felt facts to be miracles in the sense that they are wonderful: now I began

65 Chesterton, *Orthodoxy*, 56, 58. Chesterton's distinction between the "science of mental relations" and the "science of physical facts" derives from Hume's well-known distinction between "relations of ideas" and "matters of fact" as the two fundamental classes of human knowledge. Hume, *An Enquiry Concerning Human Understanding*, 15. (Alison Milbank draws a similar comparison between Chesterton and Hume in *Chesterton and Tolkien as Theologians*, 9.) In Chesterton's claim, moreover, that in nature we do not find "laws" but "only weird repetitions," we also see something of Hume's occasionalist theory of causality, also anticipated by Ockham, according to which our experience of causality is never that of "necessary connection" but merely of "constant conjunction." As Chesterton himself writes a couple of pages later, "a forlorn lover might be unable to dissociate the moon from lost love; so the materialist is unable to dissociate the moon from the tide. In both cases there is no connection, except that one has seen them together." Chesterton, *Orthodoxy*, 58.

to think them miracles in the stricter sense that they were *willful*. I mean that they were, or might be, repeated exercises of some will. In short, I had always believed that the world involved magic: now I thought that perhaps it involved a magician.... There was something personal in the world, as in a work of art; whatever it meant it meant violently.[66]

While Tolkien's particular approach to fairy-land is perhaps less exaggerated than Chesterton's, his own fairy-tale speculations about the kind of metaphysical "magic" able to "make heavy things light and able to fly, turn grey led into yellow gold, and the still rock into swift water," are similarly evocative of the brand of outlandish, counter-factual hypotheses about divine absolute power associated with Ockham. In the comparatively more sober, tidy, predictable, and reserved Aristotelian outlook of Aquinas, after all, where knowledge is primarily a matter of intellectually apprehending the immutable essences of things as they actually exist, one is much more disposed (as Aquinas is) to dwell on the naturalness, the fittingness, and in some sense even the *necessity* of created structures. In the fairyland of Tolkien, by contrast, a very different spirit dwells, one in which knowledge of a thing is almost a knowledge of its contingency, of its *lack* of necessity. Finally, in his ability to produce "new form" by the mere command of his "will," as he puts it in his essay, the Tolkienian sub-creator might seem to resemble in small-scale the voluntarist God of Ockham, that supremely free and powerful deity, whose sovereign and unfettered will not only freely posits the created world itself, but also the very forms or divine ideas according to which the world is created. In a world so conceived, the forms or universals by which the human mind gains knowledge are in fact nothing *real* independent of the mind that conceives or "names" them, but are rather mere "fictions" of the mind, *fictional* in the etymological sense of things having been "made."

Yet, as we saw earlier, for Tolkien, the fact that the human imagination has this "enchanter's power" to imagine possibilities other than those realized in the present world is no guarantee that we shall "use that power well," and therefore, as Tolkien puts it in his letter to Hastings, a sense of "humility and an awareness of peril is required." The need for this humility is made clearer earlier on in his reply to Hasting's objection to Tolkien's conceit of Elvish reincarnation. As Hastings had cautioned,

66 Ibid., 64–70.

God has not used that device in any of the creations of which we have
knowledge, and it seems to me to be stepping beyond the position of a
sub-creator to produce it as an actual working thing, because a sub-creator,
when dealing with the relations between Creator and created, should use
those channels he knows the Creator to have used already.... "The Ring"
is so good that it is a pity to deprive it of its reality by over-stepping the
bounds of a writer's job. (L 187–88)

Where Hastings saw Tolkien's idea of reincarnate Elves as transgressing the limits
of legitimate sub-creation imposed by the Creator, Tolkien replied that such
a conceit was in fact a deliberate and self-conscious exercise of precisely those
sub-creative prerogatives *granted* by the Creator. In his response Tolkien writes:

I have, of course, already considered all the points that you raise. But to
present my reflexions to you (in other form) would take a book.... We
differ entirely about the nature of the relation of sub-creation to Creation. I should have said that liberation "from the channels the Creator is
known to have used already" is the fundamental function of 'sub-creation,'
a tribute to the infinity of His potential variety, one of the ways in which
indeed it is exhibited, as indeed I said in the Essay. I am not a metaphysician; but I should have thought it a curious metaphysic — there is not
one but many, indeed potentially innumerable ones — that declared the
channels known (in such a finite corner as we have any inkling of) to have
been used, are the only possible ones, or efficacious, or possibly acceptable
to and by Him! (L 188–89)

According to Tolkien, the essence of sub-creation lies in the "liberation" the
sub-creator enjoys in imagining (and further, exploring the implications of)
possibilities that go beyond the actual "channels the Creator is known to have
used already"; as Tolkien puts it in his essay, at the very "heart of the desire" of
Fantasy or fairy-stories lies "the making or glimpsing of Other-worlds" (TR
64). These "channels" that the Creator has *not* in fact used, however, along
with the individual yet potentially innumerable "metaphysics" to which these
hypothetical channels belong, do not occur in a shallow, theologically independent and de-ontologized infinite logical space, as in the case of Ockham, but
instead seem to find their home in the kind of ontological depths that Aquinas
attempts to plumb in his consideration of divine omnipotence. The "channels"
of possibility, in short, are a function of, and indeed, when explored by the

sub-creator, become a *"tribute to* the infinity of [God's] potential variety." In this way, according to Tolkien, sub-creation in fact becomes "one of the ways in which indeed it [i.e., God's infinite variety] is exhibited," a point he further claims to have made in his essay. Tolkien would thus appear to approximate St. Thomas's definition of possibility as that which is capable of divine imitation or participation, only now applied to the realm of human making: what constitutes a legitimate sub-creation is that which is capable of "imitating" (Thomas) or "exhibiting" (Tolkien) some aspect of God's infinite "perfection" (Thomas) or internal "variety" (Tolkien). To put it differently still, like the primary, divine act of creation upon which it is based, sub-creation is a peculiar form or exten-sion of natural revelation.[67] It is for this reason, finally, as Tolkien puts it in his essay (the same passage, presumably, referred to in his letter to Hastings), that the Christian sub-creator "may now perceive that all his bents and faculties have a purpose, which can be redeemed. So great is the bounty with which he has been treated that he may now, perhaps, fairly dare to guess that in Fantasy he may actually assist in the effoliation and multiple enrichment of creation" (TR 89). In this way Tolkien arrives at the very conclusion that Miner claims St. Thomas's philosophical theology makes possible, namely the "elevation" and dignifying of human making by granting it a true participation in, and even an agency for the fulfillment of, God's own act of creation.[68]

It is this same understanding of sub-creative possibility as rooted in God's own act of creation, moreover, which is in its turn rooted in God's own essence or internal "variety," that Tolkien brings to bear on and gives poetic expression to in his literary writings. In his poem "Mythopoeia," for example, Tolkien characterizes the work of sub-creation in terms of a lens through which the "white light" of God's creation becomes "splintered" into "many hues, and endlessly combined / in living shapes that move from mind to mind" (TL 101). The image of the sub-creator as God's agent for refracting God's own light of creation parallels Maritain's account in *Art and Scholasticism* of how the artist's concepts find in God "their sovereign analogue" and how therefore they represent a "dispersed and prismatized reflection of the countenance of God."[69] Consistent with this sentiment, in the conclusion of his poem where he describes man's future state

67 Here we have the specifically theological dimension to the point Alison Milbank makes about relationality in general: "enchantment is a mode of relationality as well: neither Tolkien nor Chesterton has the nominalist individualism that would see each thing as totally separately named from every other." *Chesterton and Tolkien as Theologians*, 12.

68 We will be returning to this point in chapter four's consideration of St. Thomas's and Tolk-ien's metaphysics, not of sub-creative possibility, but of actuality.

69 Maritain, *Art and Scholasticism*, 30.

of glory, Tolkien indicates that the light of creation from which the sub-creator takes his inspiration is itself only one ray within the infinite, uncreated light that is God's own being:

> In Paradise they look no more awry;
> and though they make anew, they make no lie.
> Be sure they still will make, not being dead,
> and poets shall have flames upon their head,
> and harps whereon their faultless fingers fall:
> there each shall choose for ever from the All. (TL 101)

Sub-creative freedom involves, both now and forever, a choosing from the divine "All," in whom all possibility is contained.

And it is this same theology of sub-creation, finally, that Tolkien presupposes and in part dramatizes in his *Ainulindalë* through the Ainur's sub-creation of their Music. On the one hand, while the Ainur are able and invited to sub-create beyond the original theme taught them by Ilúvatar, the sub-creative possibilities that they discover through their Music are in no way independent of Ilúvatar. Rather, as Tolkien describes the Ainur's sub-created themes in one letter, they represent so many "interpretations of the mind of the One" (L 284). In their act of sub-creation, accordingly, the Ainur are best seen as imitating something of God's own act, as Thomas puts it, of "inventing" or "devising" the divine ideas through the self-knowledge or interpretation that constitutes the divine Word and "art of God." David Bentley Hart indirectly illustrates well the affinity here between Tolkien and St. Thomas in his account of the traditional view of divine possibility held by Thomas, yet using the same musical imagery employed by Tolkien:

> The "theme" of creation is the gift of the whole, committed to limitless possibilities, open to immeasurable ranges of divergence and convergence, consonance and dissonance (which always allows for the possibility of discord), and unpredictable modulations that at once restore and restate that theme. The theme is present in all its modifications, for once it is given it is recuperated throughout, not as a return of the Same but as gratitude, as a new giving of the gift, as what is remembered and as what, consequently, is invented. The truth of the theme is found in its unfolding, forever. God's glory is an infinite "thematism" whose beauty and variety can never be exhausted, and as the richness of creation traverses the distance of God's

infinite music, the theme is always being given back. Because God imparts the theme, it is not simply unitary and epic but obeys a Trinitarian logic: it yields to a contrapuntal multiplicity allowing for the unfolding of endlessly many differing phrases, new accords, "explicating" the "complication" of divine music.[70]

Ilúvatar himself hints at this respect in which the Ainur's sub-creative discoveries, for all their freedom and lack of coercion, are nevertheless already anticipated within and pre-contained by the divine mind, when he tells them how, in the Vision of the history of the world corresponding to the Ainur's Music, each of them will behold "all those things *which it may seem* that he himself devised or added" (S 17, emphasis added). In the earlier version of the *Ainulindalë* from *The Book of Lost Tales*, Ilúvatar is slightly less subtle about the source of the Ainur's sub-creative possibility when he gives them the command to develop the original theme he has taught them: "I have not filled all the empty spaces, neither have I recounted to you all the adornments and things of loveliness and delicacy *whereof my mind is full*. It is my desire now that ye make a great and glorious music and a singing of this theme" (BLT 53, emphasis added). As Michaël Devaux has observed — and quoting from Aquinas's discussion of Augustine's notion of angelic "morning knowledge," or their "knowledge of the primordial being of things…according as things are in the Word" (ST 1.58.6) — "to perceive the Word, before the creation, is precisely the situation which the Music has made possible for the Ainur."[71]

Yet, in *The Silmarillion* edition, Ilúvatar makes matters plain enough when he explains to Melkor how, despite the latter's efforts to achieve true novelty through his musical innovations, or rather deviations, in the Vision he will come to learn that all sub-creative possibility finds its home in the Creator himself: "And thou, Melkor, shalt see that no theme may be played that hath not its uttermost source in me, nor can any alter the music in my despite. For he that attempteth this shall prove but mine instrument in the devising of things more wonderful, which he himself hath not imagined" (S 17). In his effort to go beyond the boundaries established by the beautiful rhythms of Ilúvatar's original theme, Melkor succeeds not, as is his intent, in discovering or creating hitherto unfathomed musical possibilities, so much as he does in nihilistically negating or distorting those possibilities provided for by the infinite perfection of Ilúvatar's own being. What Melkor produces, in other words, is not music but *anti*-music, not an "interpretation" of Ilúvatar's original theme, but an "alteration" of it (L 284). Yet even here, because his musical distortions are parasitic upon those rhythms and melodies that derive their possibility from the divine "mind" or "variety" of Ilúvatar, it follows that the ultimate meaning even of Melkor's distortions are likewise beyond his control, but fall under the sovereignty of Ilúvatar. To the extent, in other words, in which evil is "real" and therefore possible, its own significance is determined by the one who is the God of the possible.[72]

In the *Ainulindalë,* then, the sub-creative activity of the Ainur presupposes a recognizably Thomistic understanding of sub-creative possibility in terms of imitability of the divine mind or essence, yet the question remains as to how this theoretical outlook might practically inform the sub-creative act. One application, as we have seen, is that "humility and an awareness of peril is required": the function of sub-creation is to explore imaginatively the possible, which is to say, that which is *creatable* by and therefore imitable of God. As Tolkien implies in his letter to Hastings, a "possible" or "efficacious" world is one that is "possibly acceptable to and by Him!" This means that the act of sub-creation is never a merely theoretical enterprise, a theologically neutral or indifferent speculation into the artistically or aesthetically possible. Rather, every sub-created reality is an implicit statement about who the Creator is and what he is like — a "perilous" venture indeed. In his essay "On Fairy-Stories," Tolkien develops his criteria for distinguishing good from bad sub-creativity in the realm of Fantasy in more immediately aesthetic or artistic terms, yet the above account enables us to appreciate the theological subtext behind his remarks. As we saw in the last chapter's discussion of the role of faith and reason in Tolkien's fiction, while the reader of a fairy-story must exercise the literary virtue of "secondary belief" when he voluntarily submits himself to the world of the author's imagining, taking it on its own terms, the author at the same time has the responsibility of imbuing his sub-created, secondary worlds with the kind of "inner consistency of reality" that we find in our own world. The example Tolkien gives is that of a "green sun," which is relatively easy to imagine but

---

72 As David Harvey observes, "the [Ainur] are always second to Ilúvatar. The foundation of all that they do is within His design. Any incursion by Evil powers, any attempts to change the theme or the design, are taken and skillfully worked into the Theme so that the conclusion is exactly as it was intended." Harvey, *The Song of Middle-earth: JR.R. Tolkien's Themes, Symbols and Myths,* 32. We will be returning to this theme in chapter five's discussion of Tolkien's metaphysics of evil.

exceedingly difficult to render "credible." In using the consistency of *this* world as a measure of any possible sub-created world, Tolkien reflects something of his own Thomistic "actualism," his conviction, that is, that the world in its actuality is the standard for determining what is possible, and not vice-versa.[73] On the other hand, Tolkien's requirement that a sub-created world invite and sustain secondary belief by exhibiting the inner consistency of reality may be further appreciated as a literary application of Aquinas's three conditions of beauty of integrity, harmony, and splendor, mentioned earlier, a fact brought out rather precisely in Rowan Williams's summary of these three principles: "integrity, the inner 'logic' of a product; then 'proportion' or consonance, its harmony and adaptation to the observer's receptive mind; then *splendor* or *claritas,* the active drawing-in of the observing mind."[74] It was argued above how, for Aquinas, any hypothesis that God can do something other than what he in fact does do must of necessity presuppose a context, an alternative, ordained, created order, in terms of which the actualization of that hypothesis might be rendered just or wise. In like manner, we find Tolkien here demanding that the fantastical inventions of a sub-creator be situated within a secondary world in which those inventions might be rendered proportionate. As with God's own creativity, so with the finite maker's sub-creativity: the possible is one with the beautiful. Similar to Aquinas, then, who essentially maintains that what God can do or make is the beautiful because only the beautiful has the nature of being and hence of possibility, Tolkien maintains that only an internally consistent and hence beautiful world is to be sub-created because only such a world is creatable by and imitative of the Creator himself. For both Thomas and Tolkien, in sum- mary, every possible world is an ordered world, a world arranged and governed according to a rule or law, and so a world reflecting the justice, wisdom, and goodness of its actual or would-be Maker.[75]

73 As Tolkien puts it in his essay, "creative fantasy is founded upon the hard recognition that things are so in the world as it appears under the sun; on a recognition of fact, but not a slavery to it" (TR 74–75).

74 Williams, *Grace and Necessity*, 12.

75 Randel Helms represents this fact well in a relatively early study of Tolkien: "My point is that fantasy literature is based on an aesthetic as demanding and uncompromising as any realism. The realistic writer must, to maintain his credibility, make clear (however implicitly) how his events *could* have happened, for realism stands upon an ontology that grants reality only on a basis of cause-and-effect sequences. Fantasy stands upon a different theory of reality, but one demanding with equal rigor that the fantasist keep always in mind his aesthetic principles: that what happens in his world accord not with his daydreams nor with our own world's laws of common sense, but with the peculiar laws of the sub-created cosmos." Helms, *Tolkien's World*, 77.

Conclusion

THIS BRINGS US AT LAST TO WHAT I THINK WOULD BE TOLKIEN'S
Thomistic critique of Ockham and the late medieval, voluntarist position on
divine power. I have suggested that, as Tolkien would see it, the theological
speculation of the late medieval period over what God can do or make is fundamentally a question of the sub-creative imagination. As a number of intellectual
historians have suggested, moreover, it was precisely this new kind of theological
imagination practiced by voluntarists such as Ockham—with their emphasis
on the utter contingency of the world—that helped prepare the way for the
scientific revolution in the modern era.[76] As has also been noted, however, even
comparatively conservative theologians like Aquinas entertained such possibilities as the Father or the Spirit having become incarnate instead of the Son, that
God could have become incarnate in any creature he wished to, including an
angel or a woman, and that the head of a man could have been made lower on
his body and his feet higher, though, as Lawrence Moonan points out, Aquinas
was in general not one to "encourage unsatisfiable expectations."[77] Similarly, for
Tolkien, while God is truly all-powerful, and the world correspondingly radically contingent, and while speculation about how the world might have been
differently constituted is not only a legitimate, but, at some level, an essential
human activity—indeed, one that has been divinely sanctioned as a means for
bringing to completion *this* world—not every imaginable creature or world
is equally valid. Successful sub-creation, as Tolkien puts it in his essay, requires
"labour and thought, and will certainly demand special skill, a kind of elvish
craft" (TR 70). When achieved, however, the result (as Maritain acknowledged)
is something almost godlike: "narrative art, story-making in its primary and
most potent mode." Tolkien goes on to caution that such Fantasy "is a thing
best left to words, to true literature," rather than to other art forms such as
painting, where "the visible presentation of the fantastic image is technically
too easy; the hand tends to outrun the mind, even to overthrow it. Silliness or
morbidity are frequent results."

Yet the problem with much late medieval counterfactual speculation, from a
Tolkienian perspective, involves more than an arguably "silly" or "morbid" failure
of the sub-creative imagination, a failure, that is, to contextualize sufficiently

---

76 See, for example, Funkenstein, *Theology and the Scientific Imagination from the Middle
Ages to the Seventeenth Century*, 117–201.

77 Lawrence Moonan, *Divine Power*, 292–93.

speculations about what God could do or make according to his absolute power within a theological "secondary world" capable of exhibiting that action as something good, wise, or just for God to perform. For, as we have seen, what is ultimately at issue here is the whole question of the theology of possibility, of whether the perfections and possibilities contained within the divine essence, in other words, are in fact exhaustive of the possible, or if divine power and possibility extend beyond even these. For Ockham, the possible is the logically possible, a determination vacuous and permissive enough in itself to suggest to Ockham the possibility, as was noted, that God could, according to his absolute power, just as easily reverse the moral order by endorsing instead of prohibiting blasphemy, murder, theft, and adultery.[78] If Aragorn's well-known statement to Éomer might be applied here, however, Ockham's hypothesis is one that Tolkien would be unwilling to countenance in any possible world: "Good and ill have not changed since yesteryear; nor are they one thing among Elves and Dwarves and another among Men. It is a man's part to discern them, as much in the Golden Wood as in his own house" (TT 41).[79] Thus, for Tolkien every sub-created world should doubtless have the same goal he set for himself in constructing his mythology, namely "the elucidation of truth, and the encouragement of good morals in this real world, by the ancient device of exemplifying them in unfamiliar embodiments, that may tend to 'bring them home'" (L 194). Ockham and the theological and philosophical tradition stemming from him, by contrast, in divorcing the question of a thing's intrinsic, logical possibility from a consideration of its possibility with reference to other created entities, to the created order as a whole, and above all, to the nature of the Creator himself, effectively places both human art and science — by placing the domain of sub-creative possibility upon which these human enterprises depend — in an amoral and ultimately atheological sphere.

For Tolkien, following Aquinas, as should by now be clear, no such sphere does nor can exist. There are only two options, then: either one will take inspiration for one's sub-creative imaginations from the Flame Imperishable, by which the existence of all creation has been kindled (as the faithful Ainur do), or one will attempt (after the fashion of Melkor) to seek out one's own personal "secret fire" in the Void. The two possible sources for the possible, in short, are the God who is being or the non-being that is nothing. As we have seen, it is a dilemma already somewhat anticipated by Ockham, and one that Umberto Eco

---

78 Ockham, *Commentary on the Sentences* 2.19, in Tourney, *Ockham: Studies and Selections,* 180–81.

79 Similarly, Tolkien writes elsewhere: "Evil is not one thing among Elves and another among Men" (MR 224).

captures well in his novel *The Name of the Rose*, when the Ockhamist William
of Baskerville is asked by his novice, Adso of Melk, whether affirming God's
absolute omnipotence and freedom, even with respect to his own essence, isn't
"tantamount to demonstrating that God does not exist?"[80] The lesson of the
Ainulindalë, however, is that sub-creative possibility is not even to be discovered
in the Void and that the only alternative to the humble, sub-creative "interpretation" of the "mind of the One" and the themes of his creation is the violent
"alteration" and distinctly *un*imaginative negation of those themes, yielding
a kind of "possibility on the cheap." For Tolkien, in conclusion, our human
making either will involve an enabling and ennobling "Enchantment" of creation through its imitation of the Creator, an account of human making that,
as we have seen, St. Thomas provides for, or will involve rather the tyranny of
"Magic" that "is not an art but a technique" and whose "desire is *power* in this
world, domination of things and wills" (TR 73).

---

80   Eco, *The Name of the Rose*, 493. William's reply, I think, is intended to be unsatisfying: "How
could a learned man go on communicating his learning if he answered yes to your question?" On
the alleged, Thomistic philosophical sub-text behind Eco's novel, see Sweeney, "*Stat rosa pristine
margine*: Umberto Eco on the Role of the Margin in Medieval Hermeneutics and Thomas Aquinas
as a Comic Philosopher," 255–69.

THREE

The Metaphysics of the Music and Vision

Then Ilúvatar said to them: 'Of the theme that
I have declared to you, I will now that ye make
in harmony together a Great Music....'

'Behold your Music!' And he showed to them a vision,
giving to them sight where before was only hearing....

AT THE CENTER OF J.R.R. TOLKIEN'S *AINULINDALË* IS
the eponymous "Music of the Ainur," the beautiful, cosmic composition sung by the angelic host together with the Creator before the
creation of the world and the pattern according to which the history of the world
later unfolds. We have already seen, in the previous chapter, the respect in which
the Ainur's Music serves to dramatize in part Tolkien's Thomistic theology of
sub-creative possibility, according to which the human art of sub-creation, no less
than the divine art of creation, has as its dignified task the "interpretation" and
"imitation" of the divine mind and essence. In this chapter, by comparison, we are
interested in the Music of the Ainur in its own right and for the significance this
particular image may hold for Tolkien's general Thomistic philosophy of being.
Before we consider some of its more Thomistic dimensions, however, it is worth
briefly surveying another important and oft-cited source of Tolkien's Music of the
Ainur, namely, the *musica universalis* tradition of such eminent earlier thinkers
of the philosophical tradition as Pythagoras, Plato, Augustine, and Boethius.

Ainulindalë *and* *the* Musica Universalis

ALTHOUGH THE IDEA OF THERE BEING A KIND OF CELESTIAL
music before or behind the cosmos is perhaps more often associated with ancient

classical rather than specifically scriptural sources, Tolkien's conceit of angelic beings helping to fashion the world through music—an idea admittedly absent from the book of Genesis—is not entirely without biblical precedent. In the book of Job, for example, the heavenly host are described as having accompanied the creation of the world with their singing: "Whereupon are the foundations thereof fastened? Or who laid the corner stone thereof; When the morning stars sang together, and all the sons of God shouted for joy?" (Job 38:6–7).[1] In the Book of Chronicles, moreover, King David enjoins the entirety of creation to lift up its praises to God: "Sing unto the Lord, all the earth; shew forth from day to day his salvation...Let the heavens be glad, and let the earth rejoice... Let the sea roar, and the fullness thereof: let the fields rejoice, and all that is therein. Then shall the trees of the wood sing out at the presence of the Lord..." (1 Chron. 17:23, 31–33; see also Ps. 96:11–12 and 98:4–8). The Book of Revelation, finally, depicts in similar fashion the angels singing and praising God in the company of his martyred saints (Rev. 5:8–12). As David Bentley Hart summarizes the scriptural data on the subject, "there are abundant biblical reasons, quite apart from the influence of pagan philosophy, for Christians to speak of the *harmonia mundi*: in Scripture creation rejoices in God, proclaims his glory, sings before him; the pleasing conceits of pagan cosmology aside, theology has all the warrant it needs for speaking of creation as a divine composition, a magnificent music, whose measures and refrains rise up to the pleasure and the glory of God."[2]

It was presumably in reference to such passages as the above, combined with his reading of Pseudo-Dionysius's treatise on *The Celestial Hierarchy*, that Pope Gregory the Great in the sixth century propounded the influential medieval idea that the redeemed human race, in the final consummation of all things, would constitute with the angels a tenth choir and so make up for the loss suffered from the rebellion of Satan and his company.[3] Tolkien himself would seem to echo such an idea in the opening page of the *Ainulindalë*, where it is already anticipated that "a greater [music] still shall be made before Ilúvatar by the choirs of the Ainur and the Children of Ilúvatar after the end of days" (S 15). And while we're on the topic of the Bible, more than one reader has suggested a resonance between the Music at the inception of Tolkien's mythology and the *Logos* that is "in the beginning" of the Apostle John's Gospel. Verlyn

---

1 All passages from the Bible are taken from the King James Version.

2 Hart, *The Beauty of the Infinite*, 275.

3 Gregory the Great, *Forty Homilies on the Gospels*, Homily 34. Thanks to Stephen Maddux for drawing my attention to this point.

Flieger, for example, in her commentary on the *Ainulindalë*, observes how the word *logos*, carrying with it a sense of *order, principle of organization,* and *harmony,* thus originally

> meant something very close to music in the Pythagorean sense. In Tolkien's fictive world, the creative principles of Genesis and John are combined. Light and music are conjoined elements made manifest in the visible world sung as the Music of the Ainur. The Word *Eä*, which in Elvish means, "It is," or "Let it Be," is listed in the Index to *The Silmarillion* as "the word of Ilúvatar when the World began its existence." It thus becomes the imperative form of the Great Music, the vision as both light and *logos*.[4]

To turn, finally, to the classical philosophical tradition, as the above quotation from Flieger illustrates, a number of readers have noted the possible significance of the fifth-century mathematician and philosopher Pythagoras for Tolkien's idea of the Ainur's cosmic music, as it is to the latter's school that the popular idea of the "music of the spheres" has been traditionally ascribed.[5] Aristotle, for example, writes of the Pythagoreans that "they took the elements of numbers to be the elements of all things, and the whole heaven to be harmony and number,"[6] and that according to them "the movement of the stars produces a harmony, i.e., that the sounds they make are concordant."[7] Leo Spitzer has gone so far as to suggest that the Pythagorean concept of world or cosmic "harmony" was more than a mere metaphor derived from human vocal or instrumental harmonies, but was in fact conceived as the reality from which human music was ultimately derived. The Pythagoreans thus

> inverted the order by admitting that the human lute (as imagined in the hands of the god Apollo) was an imitation of the music of the stars; human activities had to be patterned on godly activities, i.e., on the processes in nature: human art, especially, had to be an imitation of the gods, i.e., of reasonable nature. Thus we...witness [in Pythagoreanism] a continuous flow of metaphors from the human (and divine) sphere to nature and back

---

4 Flieger, *Splintered Light*, 59.
5 For other references to Pythagoras in the Tolkien literature, see also Grubbs, "The Maker's Image: Tolkien, Fantasy & Magic"; Davis, "'Ainulindalë': The Music of Creation"; and Collins, "'Ainulindalë': Tolkien's Commitment to an Aesthetic Ontology."
6 Aristotle, *Metaphysics*, 1.5.986a., trans. Hope.
7 Aristotle, *On the Heavens*, 2.9.290b12, trans. Stocks.

again to human activities, which are considered as imitating the artistic orderliness and harmony of nature.[8]

It is a similar kind of Pythagorean "inversion," in any event, that Tolkien performs in the *Ainulindalë*, as when he writes, for example, how "the voices of the Ainur, like unto harps and lutes, and pipes and trumpets, and viols and organs, and like unto countless choirs singing with words, began to fashion the theme of Ilúvatar to a great music; and a sound arose of endless interchanging melodies woven in harmony that passed beyond hearing into the depths and into the heights" (S 15). As we saw in chapter one's discussion of Tolkien's image of the Flame Imperishable, the literary genre of myth or fairy-story allows for a reinvesting of metaphors and images such as fire and music with a degree of ancient, pre-Enlightenment literality, so that the Creator's power of creation is not "like" fire, but simply *is* the Fire from which all fires originate. In like manner, neither is the Ainur's and Ilúvatar's Music "like" the music we human beings play and experience, but, in Pythagorean fashion, simply *is* the Music to which all our music is a remote hearkening and response.

As for those philosophers coming after Pythagoras, although Aristotle himself was somewhat dismissive of the idea of the music of the spheres, his teacher Plato's attraction to the notion is made evident in his *Timaeus*, a work that, as we shall see more fully in the next chapter, Tolkien had at least partially in mind in the development of his creation-myth. In one of the more challenging passages of the dialogue, the character Timaeus, himself a Pythagorean mathematician and philosopher, alludes to the notion of the music of the spheres when he suggests that an analogous structure was placed by the demiurge in the World Soul: "Now while the body of the heavens had come to be as a visible thing, the soul was invisible. But even so, because it shares in reason and harmony, the soul came to be as the most excellent of all the things begotten by him who is himself most excellent of all that is intelligible and eternal."[9] In addition, the way in which the Ainur's Music antedates and pre-contains the entire history of the world resembles, as noted in the last chapter, Plato's famous realm of the forms, in which the physical world of sensible things participates, or, as the *Timaeus* has it, the eternal model according to which the demiurge-creator has fashioned the material world. As Plato's later disciple Plotinus applied the master's theory to music some six-hundred years later,

8 Spitzer, *Classical and Christian Ideas of World Harmony*, 8–9.
9 Plato, *Timaeus* 36e–37a, trans. Zeyl.

"certainly all music, since the ideas which it has are concerned with rhythm and melody, would be of the same kind, just like the art which is concerned with intelligible number," and thus like the other arts would have "its principles from the intelligible world."[10]

Plotinus is particularly worth mentioning here as it was principally through his works that the thought of Plato was mediated to St. Augustine, whose treatise *De musica* was the first Christian work to shape significantly the way music was studied in the Latin West. Although the bulk of Augustine's *De musica* is devoted to matters of musical theory, the sixth and final book of his treatise addresses some of the more psychic and cosmic implications of music. As the title of book six has it, Augustine discusses the Neoplatonic "ascent from rhythm in sense to the immortal rhythm which is in truth."[11] In the course of his discussion, Augustine enumerates five different kinds of rhythm, the highest and most "immortal" of which he calls "Judicial Rhythm" (*iudiciales numeri*), a form of rhythm that, "if not entirely without limitation by durations of time," is nevertheless in some sense "eternal," and resides "in the soul," enabling it "to judge what is presented, approving the rhythmic and condemning the irregular."[12] The Judicial Rhythm within the soul enabling it to judge the presence or absence of rhythm outside of the soul, however, is also a property of the cosmos as a whole:

> Every living thing in its own kind, and in its due relation to the whole (*proportione uniuersitatis*), has been endowed with a sense of magnitude in space and time, so that as its body is in a certain proportion to the universal body of which it is a part, so its permitted life-time (*aetas*) is proportional to the whole duration of the universe (*universi saeculi*) of which it is a part…. It is by such an organization of parts according to scale that our world achieves its vast size (*sic habendo omnia magnus est hic mundus*): the world which in the Scriptures is called "heaven and earth"…[13]

In book 11 of his *Confessions,* Augustine's idea of "Judicial Rhythm" in the cosmos, similar to the Ainur's Music, emerges as a creature in its own right through which the Creator's own act of creation is somehow mediated. As Augustine inquires of God:

---

10 Plotinus, *Enneads* 5.9.11, trans. Armstrong.
11 Augustine, *De musica*, trans. Knight.
12 Ibid., 6.7.17–18.
13 Ibid., 6.7.19.

> But how did you speak [in creation]?... The utterance came through the movement of some created thing, serving your eternal will but itself temporal. And these your words, made for temporal succession, were reported by the external ear to the judicious mind whose internal ear is disposed to hear your eternal word. But that mind would compare these words, sounding in time, with your eternal word in silence.[14]

Another well-known passage from Augustine dealing with music as a metaphor for cosmic order comes from a letter in which he compares the way a good song-writer "knows how to distribute the length of time allowed to each word so as to make the song flow and pass on in most beautiful adaptation to the ever-changing notes of the melody," to the way that God in his wisdom ensures

> that not one of the spaces of time allotted to natures that are born and die — spaces which are like the words and syllables of the successive epochs of the course of time — shall have, in what we may call *the sublime psalm of the vicissitudes of this world*, a duration either more brief or more protracted than the foreknown and predetermined harmony requires!... Every man's life on earth continues for a time, which is neither longer nor shorter than God knows to be in harmony with the plan according to which he rules the universe.[15]

Something further to note about these passages is the way they also add a linear or progressive element or dimension to the idea of cosmic music that we also find in the *Ainulindalë*, but which is absent in the comparatively a-temporal and static "music of the spheres" tradition of the Pythagoreans and Platonists.[16] In his commentary on the above letter of Augustine, for example, and whose application to Tolkien I trust will be clear, Spitzer describes Augustine's notion of a transcendent, cosmic pattern both behind and unfolding within creation as a "hymn scanned by God" and a "poem of the world" that, "like any poem, can

---

14 Augustine, *Confessions* 11.6, trans. Chadwick.

15 Augustine, *Letters of St. Augustine* 166.5.13, trans. Cunningham (emphasis added). See also Houghton, "Augustine in the Cottage of Lost Play," 178.

16 Thanks to Stephen Maddux for drawing my attention to this difference. Spitzer, incidentally, points to another important shift from the pagan to the Christian and especially Augustinian understanding of world harmony: "According to the Pythagoreans, it was cosmic order which was identifiable with music; according to the Christian philosophers, it was love. And in the *ordo amoris* of Augustine we have evidently a blend of the Pagan and the Christian themes: henceforth 'order' is love." Spitzer, *Classical and Christian Ideas of World Harmony*, 19–20. See also Hart, *Beauty of the Infinite,* 276.

only be understood in time by a soul which endeavors to understand the action of Providence, which itself unfolds in time…. The God-Artist, creating in time, realizes his *idea*, his providential decisions, like a musician."[17]

Yet, perhaps an even more important Augustinian influence for Tolkien's music imagery is to be found less in Augustine's writings on music *per se* than in his highly original and influential interpretation of the creation event itself. Although Augustine does not make use of any music imagery in his literal commentary on the Genesis creation-account, *De Genesi ad litteram libri duodecim*, the extent of the structural parallels between the latter and Tolkien's *Ainulindalë* are quite remarkable, as John Houghton has shown. Houghton begins by pointing out, from the early version of the *Ainulindalë* from *The Book of Lost Tales*, Tolkien's original intention of representing his creation-narrative as an alternative, "asterisk" or hypothetical cosmogony putatively discovered in England sometime in the early Middle Ages. As this conceit would have it, the *Ainulindalë* would have constituted for the medievals, along with Genesis and Plato's *Timaeus*, a third creation-account.[18] Against the supposition that, because the modern reader may find "the *Ainulindalë* very different from Genesis," medieval thinkers must therefore also "have found it equally strange," Houghton argues, on the contrary, that owing to the commentary tradition stemming from Augustine, "had medieval theologians encountered the *Ainulindalë*, they would have found its picture of a double creation — creation as music in the song of the Ainur and then as fact in the word of Ilúvatar — reassuringly easy to fit into the scheme of Augustine's Christian-Neoplatonist synthesis."[19] In his breakdown of Augustine's *De Genesi,* Houghton discerns five distinct stages in Augustine's analysis of the creation-event:

1. God's eternal intention to create, enunciated in the Word;
2. God's Creation in the minds of the angels of a knowledge of what is to be made;
3. God's creation of things, some of them (like the angels) in full existence, but most of them (like trees, plants, and human beings) in the potentials called "causal reasons";
4. The angels' perception of the created things; and
5. God's eternal support of the Creation through the Holy Spirit.[20]

17 Spitzer, *Classical and Christian Ideas of World Harmony*, 31.
18 Houghton, "Augustine in the Cottage of Lost Play," 171.
19 Ibid., 171–72.
20 Ibid., 176.

Although Tolkien's account emphasizes music imagery and the sub-creative role of the Ainur, whereas Augustine, following Genesis, emphasizes the metaphors of speech and light and God's role as sole Creator, Houghton points out that each of Augustine's five stages finds an important place in the *Ainulindalë*:

> In both cases, God first creates the angels and then reveals to them the further elements of Creation; the angels' own knowledge reflects ideas in the divine mind. In both cases, as well, after the revelation, God gives real existence to what the angels have perceived, upholding that existence in the void; yet that real existence has only the undeveloped potential of what it will become in the unfolding of time, and God reserves to God's self the introduction of elements unanticipated in the basic design.[21]

To Houghton's fine analysis I would only add the further parallel, touched on in chapter one, that, as with Augustine and Genesis, in the *Ainulindalë* it is specifically the Spirit of God, under the guise of the "Secret Fire," that is the agent for bringing the world into being and sustaining it so.

The next influential thinker after Augustine to teach on music was the sixth-century Boethius.[22] Possibly the most influential treatise ever written on the subject of music, it was through Boethius's *De institutione musica* that classical musical theory was primarily transmitted to the Middle Ages and Renaissance.[23] Toward the beginning of his treatise, Boethius distinguishes three kinds of music: cosmic (*musica mundana*, or "music of the spheres"), human (*musica humana,* the music of the human body and soul), and instrumental (*musica instrumentalis*).[24] The three primary examples of the cosmic music distinguished by Boethius include the movement of the heavenly bodies, the combination of the physical elements, and the changing of the seasons. Of the heavenly bodies, for example, Boethius thinks it impossible that "so swift a heavenly machine moves on a mute and silent course" and "that such extremely fast motion of such large bodies should produce absolutely no sound," and in a later chapter Boethius even correlates each of the planetary spheres with the various standard musical strings ("the hypate meson is assigned to Saturn, whereas the parhypate is like the orbit of Jupiter," etc.).[25]

---

21 Ibid., 178.

22 Eden, "The 'Music of the Spheres': Relationships between Tolkien's *The Silmarillion* and Medieval Cosmological and Religious Theory," 183–93.

23 Godwin, *The Harmony of the Spheres: A Sourcebook of the Pythagorean Tradition in Music,* 86.

24 Boethius, *Fundamentals of Music,* 1.2, trans. Bower. See also Godwin, *The Harmony of the Spheres,* 86.

25 Boethius, *Fundamentals of Music,* 1.27.

Although it is with the classical idea of the "music of the spheres" that commentators have most often compared the Music of the Ainur, it is worth noting at this point that the *Ainulindalë* itself does not in fact ever refer to the heavenly bodies, nor are they elsewhere in Tolkien's mythology ever described as producing any kind of sound or music.[26] To this extent, accordingly, Boethius's second and third examples of cosmic music, those of the harmony of the elements and seasons, might justifiably be seen to have an even greater relevance to the *Ainulindalë*. Of the harmony of the elements in particular, Boethius asks: "If a certain harmony did not join the diversities and opposing forces of the four elements, how would it be possible that they could unite in one mass and contrivance?"[27] It is interesting to note that, in the *Ainulindalë*, it is in a state of Boethian harmony that the four elements first appear to the Ainur in the Vision:

> And they observed the winds and the air, and the matters of which Arda was made, of iron and stone and silver and gold and many substances: but of all these water they most greatly praised. And it is said by the Eldar that in water there lives yet the echo of the Music of the Ainur more than in any substance else that is in this Earth; and many of the Children of Ilúvatar hearken still unsated to the voices of the Sea, and yet know not for what they listen. (S 19)

As for his third category of cosmic music, Boethius compares the "consonance" of the four seasons with the attunement of lower and higher strings of an instrument, so that "the whole corpus of pitches is coherent and harmonious with itself": "For what winter confines, spring releases, summer heats, and autumn ripens, and the seasons in turn either bring forth their own fruit or give aid to others in bringing forth their own."[28] And again, in a comparable expression found in the *Ainulindalë* of the accord between seasons and weather patterns, upset only by the disruptions of Melkor, Ilúvatar informs the Valar Ulmo:

> "Behold the snow, and the cunning work of frost! Melkor hath devised heats and fire without restraint, and hath not dried up thy desire nor utterly quelled the music of the sea. Behold rather the height and glory of the clouds, and the everchanging mists; and listen to the fall of rain upon the Earth! And in these clouds thou art drawn nearer to Manwë, thy friend, whom thou lovest."

26 Thanks again to Stephen Maddux for this point.
27 Boethius, *Fundamentals of Music*, 1.2.
28 Ibid., 1.2.

Then Ulmo answered: "Truly, Water is become now fairer than my heart imagined, neither had my secret thought conceived the snowflake, nor in all my music was contained the falling of the rain. I will seek Manwë, that he and I may make melodies for ever to thy delight!" (S 19)

St. Thomas's
Metaphysics of Beauty

AS IMPORTANT AS THE ABOVE BIBLICAL, CLASSICAL, AND EARLY medieval sources may have been in helping shape Tolkien's conception of the Music of the Ainur, my purpose in the remainder of this chapter is to draw attention to some of the ways in which Tolkien's creational music reflects an appreciably and specifically Thomistic aesthetical and metaphysical sensibility. There are three aspects of Thomas's thought in particular that I wish to develop here: the first is Thomas's own occasional remarks on the nature of music; the second consists in select elements of Thomas's theory of beauty or aesthetics more generally; and the third concerns the broader metaphysical "existentialism" and realism involved in Thomas's aesthetics. At each of these three levels, as I hope to show, Thomas has an important contribution to make where the proper interpretation of the significance of Tolkien's music imagery is concerned.

Perhaps the first thing that might be said is that, unlike Tolkien, the music imagery of Augustine, Boethius, and the whole *musica universalis* tradition actually seems to have made very little impression on St. Thomas's metaphysical imagination: fire and light, as we have seen, are certainly to be found in his philosophy of being, but there is admittedly very little music. Drawing attention to this lacuna, Spitzer remarks how Thomas does not seem to have had "the Augustinian ear for world harmony, ascribing to music a holy character only insofar as it was an element of the liturgy; as an Aristotelian he 'reflects' the world as it is, rather than attempting to re-create it by forging it together into a unit."[29] Thomas's personal interest in music, such as it was, would likely

---

29 Spitzer, *Classical and Christian Ideas of World Harmony*, 74. If so, the alleged tone-deafness of St. Thomas in matters of metaphysics might be related to the general absence of an explicit aesthetics in Thomas's thought. John Milbank, for example, observes on the one hand that "just because there was no aesthetics in Aquinas's theological philosophy, the aesthetic is therein everywhere present," while on the other hand suggesting that "the latency of fundamental beauty in Aquinas meant that it was also for him a blind spot: one could even say that Aquinas probably supposed his own theology to have more to do with abstract reason than was really the case. This blindness invited a later rationalistic reduction by nominalism and neo-scholasticism of the Patristic legacy in which

have been informed by his direct experience with sacred music as part of his religious devotion and duties as a priest, a subject he addresses, for example, in ST 2–2.91, "Of taking the divine name for the purpose of invoking it by means of praise."[30] More than this, Thomas's educational and general cultural milieu would have meant some familiarity on his part with both Boethius's *De Institutione* and Augustine's *De Musica*.[31] (His command of some of the more technical and mathematical details of the latter work in particular, for example, may be found in his commentary on Aristotle's *De anima*.[32]) And while Thomas does not seem to have had much use in his cosmology or meta-physics for the Pythagorean notion of a musical world harmony, neither was he completely insensible to the notion's explanatory force, as his treatment of divine power in the *Summa* indicates. While expanding on how the universe cannot be improved, given the order already bestowed upon it by God, Thomas gives an argument echoing that of Augustine cited earlier: "For if any one thing were bettered, the proportion of order would be destroyed, just as if one string were stretched more than it ought to be, the melody of the harp would be destroyed" (ST 1.25.6 ad 3).

As we shall see, however, the relevance of Thomas's views on music for Tolk-ien lies less in his appreciation of music as a principle of cosmic harmony than it does, ironically, in his view of music as exhibiting an exceedingly abstract, almost mathematical, kind of existence. In his commentary on Boethius's

---

he stood, and to resist this one indeed requires a more explicit aesthetics, conjoined to a more explicit poetics." Milbank, "Scholasticism, Modernism, and Modernity," 670.

Related to this is Francesca Aran Murphy's observation that, unlike Franciscans such as St. Bonaventure, none of the Dominican scholastics, including Albert the Great and St. Thomas, ever explicitly listed beauty as a transcendental and therefore convertible property of being. On the other hand, Murphy points out that, "whilst both Albert and Thomas say little of beauty in the main body of their writings, they both succumb to its lure in their respective Commentaries on *The Divine Names* of Pseudo-Dionysus. In these texts, each of these writers speaks of the universal extent of beauty, and names God as its first cause. In *The Divine Names*, Dionysius defines the beautiful as one of the sources of being." Murphy, *Christ the Form of Beauty: A Study in Theology and Litera-ture*, 213. Also, as Milbank is concerned to show, Thomas's aesthetic vision, however blurred by his intellectualism, was to his credit at least sufficiently clear to inspire, through the work of Jacques Maritain, the "more explicit poetics" of twentieth-century Catholic artists and writers such as David Jones, G.K. Chesterton, Flannery O'Connor, and J.R.R. Tolkien.

30 On this passage, see Eco, *The Aesthetics of Thomas Aquinas*, 131–32.

31 Ibid., 131.

32 Bullough, "St. Thomas and Music," 14, 19–21. Thomas F. O'Meara, incidentally, has also made the observation, in his study of Aquinas's "cultural milieu" of thirteenth-century Paris, that it was only the century prior that polyphony had been introduced and developed in Gothic music, whose "rhythmical motion of independent parts," together with the Gothic illustrated window and the Scholastic *Summa*, constitutes a third example of the period's "love of plurality ordered." O'Meara, "Paris as a Cultural Milieu of Thomas Aquinas's Thought," 709.

De Trinitate, Thomas closely associates music with mathematics on account of the way music derives its first principles from arithmetic and applies these principles to natural things.[33] Music thus represents an "intermediate" between mathematics and natural science, yet Thomas says it bears "a closer affinity to mathematics," since music is more "formal" and thus more separated from matter and motion than is the case in natural science: "music considers sounds, not inasmuch as they are sounds, but inasmuch as they are proportionable according to numbers."[34] Behind Thomas's argument here is his teaching that, although concepts of both mathematics and natural objects involve an act of mental abstraction separating their intelligible principles from the physical, sensible substances in which these principles are actually experienced, mathematics and natural science nevertheless differ in their respective *degrees* of abstraction.[35] In the case of a mathematical object such as a circle, there is no reference in the concept of a circle to the kind of matter that real (i.e., non-mental) circles are actually made of, since circles can be made out of virtually anything. The case is otherwise with concepts of natural substances such as man, for which the kind of matter the thing is made out of comprises an integral part of the substance's essence or form. Thus, while the concept of man, like the concept of a circle, is produced by the mind's abstracting it from the determinate or "signate" matter out of which individual men or circles are actually made, the concept of man nevertheless retains a notional reference to the kind of matter out of which real men are made, namely flesh and bones. To return to the question of music, then, for Thomas, while music as we experience it is, of course, an inherently physical, sensible, and sensuous phenomenon, in terms of the formal qualities that constitute its sounds as *musical* sounds, the comparative indifference of music to the particular material environment, circumstances, or conditions under which it is played makes it similar, in Thomas's mind, to the heightened degree of mental abstraction involved in mathematics. For Thomas, in short, music is a highly abstract reality that is ultimately concerned with sound, not *as* sound (i.e., an inherently physical phenomenon), but as a peculiarly mathematical and proportionate kind of sound.

One of the implications of Thomas's comparatively abstract, formalist approach

33 "In another way, one science is contained under another as subalternated to it. This occurs when in a higher science there is given the reason for what a lower science knows only as a fact. This is how music is contained under arithmetic." Thomas Aquinas, *The Division and Methods of the Sciences: Questions V and VI of his Commentary on the "De Trinitate" of Boethius,* trans. Maurer, 5.1 ad 5.

34 Ibid., 5.3.

35 Ibid., 5.1–2.

to music, and a point that will also have an important application to the Ainur's Music, concerns what some scholars have suggested to be a kind of proto-Kantian, metaphysical "disinterest" involved in Thomas's view of music in particular and his aesthetics in general. The concept of disinterest is a central tenet in the idealist aesthetics of the eighteenth-century Enlightenment philosopher Immanuel Kant. According to Kant's "Copernican Revolution" in epistemology, since we can never know things as they exist in themselves and apart from us (the *noumena*), but only as they appear to us (the *phenomena*), if true objectivity in knowledge is to be possible, it is to be found not in the mind's conformity to the objects of its knowledge but in the known object's conformity to the mind's particular ways or "categories" of knowing. Kant was led to a similarly extreme and idealistic theory of beauty, according to which the "pure" aesthetic experience is one that is entirely "disinterested" in the question of the object's mind-independent existence, which can't really be known and which therefore must be irrelevant to the question of beauty. In detaching pure aesthetic pleasure from the question of the object's existence in this way, Kant's goal was to free the object's beauty to be enjoyed for its own sake and without threat of being subsumed within and exploited by what Kant held to be the alien, heteronomous needs or ulterior purposes of the perceiving subject.[36]

An example of this latter "impure" aesthetic experience for Kant was what he called the merely "agreeable," defined as anything that pleases the senses. By referencing the aesthetic experience to the senses, the agreeable causes the subject to take an "interest" in the thing's existence, inasmuch as a thing must actually exist for it to have an effect on the senses. The consequence of such interest, however, is that, in referencing it to one's own self via the senses, the aesthetic experience ceases or fails to be something truly universal, autonomous, free, and rational, and becomes instead something narrowly human, subjective, heteronomous, and constrained. In such cases, the aesthetic object is treated not as an *end* to be contemplated, but as a *means* to be subordinated to dictates of the human subject's sub-rational inclinations, with the result being that the independence of the aesthetic object is negated. For Kant, the pure aesthetic experience, by contrast, is one that is concerned only with the sheer structural or formal qualities of the object's appearances and the state of cognitive free-play or balance these appearances help establish between the mind's faculties

---

36 As Kant writes, interested pleasure "presupposes a *need* or gives rise to one; and, because interest is the basis that determines approval, it makes the judgment about the object *unfree*." Kant, *The Critique of Judgment*, trans. Pluhar, 52 (emphasis added).

of imagination and understanding.[37] Such objects or appearances are said to be truly "beautiful." At the other extreme, and now on the other side of the simply beautiful, Kant distinguished an even more ineffable aesthetic experience that he labeled the "sublime," in which the imagination is entirely, even violently, overwhelmed by the immensity of the aesthetic object, or more accurately, by the immensity of the *mind's* capacity to present an appearance in this concept-defying and awe-inspiring way.[38] In both the sublime and the beautiful, therefore, and consistent with Kant's broader idealist epistemology, yet arguably revealing what we shall see for Tolkien is the metaphysically tragic motive latent within that epistemology, pure aesthetic pleasure is a function of the mind alone rather than of any supposed extraneous and (aesthetically speaking) unnecessary relationship between the mind and an externally existing, mind-independent reality.

As more than one scholar has argued, moreover, there are some notable parallels or similarities between Aquinas's conception of beauty and Kant's. Be that as it may, what cannot be disputed is that there is an intractable, objective or mind-independent character to beauty as Thomas conceives it, such that, the more beauty a thing has, the more existence or being will be implicated in that beauty.[39] One aspect to this principle for St. Thomas is his definition of beauty as "that which pleases when seen" (ST 1.5.4 ad 1). In direct contrast to Kant, therefore, Thomas establishes as one of the defining features of beauty the pleasure or delight the object of beauty is able to bestow on its perceiver through the senses, and in so doing makes beauty to presuppose the existence of a perceiver-independent object capable of acting on the senses in this aesthetically pleasing manner. For Thomas, human sense faculties have as their proper activity and end the perception of sensible objects, especially beautiful sensible objects, and aesthetic pleasure or delight consists in this activity being brought to completion — that is to say, in the sensible properties of the object of beauty first

37 On Kant's aesthetics, see Wood, *Placing Aesthetics: Reflections on the Philosophic Tradition*, 117–51.

38 "When we speak of the sublime in nature we speak improperly; properly speaking, sublimity can be attributed merely to our way of thinking, or, rather, to the foundation this has in human nature. What happens is merely that the apprehension of an otherwise formless and unpurposive object prompts us to become conscious of that foundation, so that what is subjectively purposive is the *use* we make of the object, and it is not the object *itself* that is judged to be purposive on account of its form." Kant, *The Critique of Judgment*, 142.

39 Eco, for example, interprets Aquinas's aesthetics in a proto-Kantian light. See Eco, *The Aesthetics of Thomas Aquinas*, 87–88 and 134. Related to this is a debate that has raged over whether Thomas's aesthetics ultimately stresses the subjective or the objective side of beauty, along with the related debate over whether or not beauty for Thomas technically qualifies as a true transcendental property of being. On this debate, see, for example, Delfino, "The Beauty of Wisdom: A Tribute to Armand Maurer," 42; Santoro-Brienza, "Art and Beauty in Antiquity and the Middle Ages," 69; and Williams, *Grace and Necessity: Reflections on Art and Love*, 12–13.

stimulating and gratifying the senses, and in their turn effecting a corresponding intellectual apprehension of the physical object and satisfaction in its form or internal structure. In this manner a harmonious, pleasing, and nature-fulfilling correspondence is established between the object and the perceiving subject and between the subject's own perceptual and intellective faculties.[40]

As to what it is in the beautiful object that is responsible for eliciting this affective response in the individual, Thomas lists three objective properties of beauty — integrity, proportion, and clarity — which we touched on at the end of the previous chapter. By integrity or perfection, Thomas means something close to what Tolkien has in mind in his requirement that sub-created, secondary worlds exhibit the "inner consistency of reality." Integrity, in other words, refers to a thing's completeness, wholeness, or togetherness, its having and displaying the structure and requisite parts proper to a thing of that particular essence or nature. The second aesthetic property of proportion, sometimes referred to as harmony or consonance, is of Pythagorean origin and designates in Thomas's usage a sense of qualitative proportion that he calls *convenientia*, or what Liberato Santoro-Brienza describes as an "intrinsic attunement" or "correspondence between inner and outer reality, appearance and essence, matter and form."[41] It is the *harmony* of beauty, in other words, that is especially involved in the aforementioned pleasing correspondence obtaining both between the parts and metaphysical principles within the object and between the object and the sensory faculties of the perceiver.[42] Finally, there is the aesthetic criterion of clarity, or brightness or "splendor," i.e., the shining forth of form or radiating of intelligible light from the beautiful object, an idea that Robert Wood suggests is further linked to the Greek word *doxa* or "glory"[43] and that Tolkien gives us an apt image of in the *Ainulindalë* when the Ainur first glimpse the world, newly created by the Flame Imperishable of Ilúvatar, as "a cloud with a living heart of flame" (S 20).

We can see, then, that, while Thomas is certainly keen, in the words of G.B. Phelan, to give "due consideration for the rôle of the perceiving subject in the apprehension of the beautiful," going so far as to define "the beautiful as having a necessary reference to a subject," there is nevertheless an "intransigent objectivism" to his account of beauty.[44] This leads us, finally, to a consideration of

---

40 Santoro-Brienza, "Art and Beauty," 70.
41 Ibid., 72.
42 Wood, *Placing Aesthetics,* 109.
43 Ibid., 105.
44 Phelan, "The Concept of Beauty in St. Thomas Aquinas," 162.

the existential realism underlying Thomas's theory of being. Existentialism in this context refers to the insight — one of the principles, if not the central one, of Thomas's metaphysical thought — that the act of existence, signified by the Latin infinitive *esse*, is the "actuality of all acts and the perfection of all perfections." In any event, as the existential Thomists of the twentieth century argued, in identifying a thing's act of existence as the "act of acts," Thomas inaugurated a veritable revolution in metaphysics and the theory of knowledge, at the heart of which was the realization that, contrary to the "essentialism" of much of the metaphysical tradition both before and after him, it is not a thing's intelligible, contemplatable essence or form, but its actual, real, concrete existence in the world that, in the words of Armand Maurer,

> holds the primary place in the order of being. While not neglecting other aspects of being, such as form and essence, St. Thomas offers a radically new interpretation of being by emphasizing its existential side. This was a decisive moment in the history of Western metaphysics, for St. Thomas was transforming previous Greek and mediaeval conceptions of being, which gave primary place to form.[45]

Related to Thomas's existentialism is his concomitant doctrine of metaphysical *realism*, by which is meant Thomas's stress on the irreducibly real, mind-independent, yet for that reason mind-obtruding and seducing character of things. We saw something of Thomas's and Tolkien's agreement on this point in the last chapter's consideration of their shared doctrine of "theological truth," captured in Tolkien's emphatic claim that things "ARE, they would exist even if we did not" (L 399). What I particularly want to draw attention to here is the positive attitude towards the alterity or "otherness" of things entailed in Thomas's doctrine. On the one hand, it is quite true for Thomas that "natural things…have being absolutely in the divine mind more truly than in themselves, because in that mind they have an uncreated being, but in themselves a created being" (ST 1.18.4 ad 3).[46] In other words, there is a fundamental sense for St. Thomas in which things are more real in the divine mind than they are in their own created being. However, far from this implying the kind of Neoplatonic, tragic metaphysics discussed earlier, on the contrary, as I shall develop further in a moment, it is precisely the inferiority of created being in comparison to their divine origin

---

45 Maurer, "Introduction," in Aquinas, *On Being and Essence,* trans. Maurer, 10.
46 See also *De veritate* 6.4.

that renders the act of creation for Thomas not metaphysically tragic, but comic. Even so, immediately following his above statement that, "absolutely" speaking, things more truly exist in the divine mind than in themselves, Thomas goes on to say that, nevertheless, "to be this particular being, a man, or a horse, for example, *is realized more truly* in its own nature than in the divine mind, because it belongs to the truth of man to be material, which, as existing in the divine mind, he is not." As Thomas further explains in a passage that will have an important application to Tolkien's Music of the Ainur, "even so a house has nobler being in the architect's mind than in matter; yet a material house is called a house more truly than the one which exists in the mind, since the former is a house in act, the latter only in potency" (ST 1.18.4 ad 3). Things, in short, have more truth, more being, more perfection or goodness, and therefore more actuality in God than they do in themselves. The issue, however, is that in the divine mind, "things" enjoy this super-eminent truth, being, perfection, and actuality *not as themselves,* that is, not as *created* beings, but as certain aspects of God's own, uncreated being. To have any kind of reality *as* themselves, of course, things must be given their own being *as* individual things, the kind of being, in other words, that they do not have in the divine mind, a point Thomas finds especially illustrated in the case of material substances.[47] And if this is true of the divine mind, how much more must it be true with respect to finite human minds? Thus Thomas, writing of the purely "logical existence" that mathematical entities have in the mind and yet upon which, as we saw, music is based, says that they clearly "do not subsist as realities" — otherwise "they would be in some sort good if they subsisted" (ST 1.5.3 ad 4) — and that an individual man, because he includes individual matter, therefore "has something in it" which the intelligible essence of man alone does not (ST 1.3.3). Thomas's positive evaluation of matter as a created, intelligible, and objectifying force, combined with the role he reserves for the body in the sensual perception of beauty, means that, as Michael Sweeney has put it in a passage in keeping with our theme, "instead of rendering philosophy tragic, the inescapable corporeality of human life makes philosophy comic because matter is no longer an irrational given contrary to intelligibility but the created principle to which all human thought must return."[48]

47 As we shall see in chapter five's discussion of evil, moreover, for Aquinas, even to wish for a thing to have the kind of being that God has is to wish for that thing to have a different essence than it has, which is in effect to wish the thing to cease to exist. Thus, there is a kind of nihilism implied in any kind of evaluative comparison of the being of creatures to the being that God alone has and that God alone can have.

48 Sweeney, "*Stat rosa pristine margine*: Umberto Eco on the Role of the Margin in Medieval Hermeneutics and Thomas Aquinas as a Comic Philosopher," 266.

Yet even when viewed as a finite, superfluous, and in that sense "inferior" reduplication of the divine being, the entirely voluntary, unnecessary, and gratuitous character of creation — in contrast, as we saw in the last chapter, to the impersonal necessity of Neoplatonic emanation of reality from the One — again has the tendency of rendering creation more comic than tragic. In ST 1.19.2, for example, Thomas reasons from the benevolent nature of voluntary agents in general to the conclusion that it belongs especially to God to will the existence of "things apart from himself" (*alia a se*), which serve no other purpose than to give him something to which he might communicate his own inherent goodness. It is not for his own sake, in other words, that God wills the existence of things other than himself, but for their sake, since God is already perfect and stands to gain nothing from his creative efforts. The result is a profound irony at the heart of Thomas's account of creation, and one that at least one of his more rationalist commentators has sought to avoid, and yet without which creation loses its essential quality of playfulness and gratuitous excess: God creates, in short, to benefit that which would otherwise not even exist unless he first created it.[49] As Thomas charmingly puts it in one passage, God "alone is the most perfectly free giver, because he does not act for his own profit" (ST 1.44.4). Chesterton captures well the basic difference between the kind of tragic rationalism and causalism of Neoplatonic emanationism, reviewed earlier, and the comic freedom of Christian creationism in the contrast he draws in *Orthodoxy* between the madman and the sane man: "The last thing that can be said of a lunatic is that his actions are causeless. If any human acts may loosely be called causeless, they are the minor acts of a healthy man; whistling as he walks; slashing the grass with a stick; kicking his heels or rubbing his hands. It is the happy man who does the useless things; the sick man is not strong enough to be idle."[50] The doctrine of creation, in short, represents a kind of metaphysical strength and health, for it teaches a God who creates and loves that which is "useless" or needless to himself. For Thomas, creation is not a metaphysical decadence: it is a divine extravagance.

If God's own goodness, finally, leads him to desire and to effect the existence of things other than himself, the same must invariably hold true for those rational beings whom he has made especially after his own image. As Thomas puts it in his *Summa Contra Gentiles*,

---

49 Norman Kretzmann, for example, takes issue with the voluntarism of St. Thomas's doctrine of creation in *The Metaphysics of Theism*, 220–25, and *The Metaphysics of Creation*, 101–3, 120–26, and 134.

50 Chesterton, *Orthodoxy*, 23.

a thing approaches to God's likeness the more perfectly as it resembles him in more things. Now, goodness is in God, and the outpouring of goodness into other things. Hence, the creature approaches more perfectly to God's likeness if it is not only good, but can also act for the good of other things, than if it were good only in itself; that which both shines and casts light is more like the sun than that which only shines. But no creature could act for the benefit of another creature unless plurality and inequality existed in created things. For the agent is distinct from the patient and superior to it. In order that there might be in created things a perfect representation of God, the existence of diverse grades among them was therefore necessary.[51]

God creates other things to communicate his own goodness, but part of that goodness which he gives to other things is precisely his own propensity for bestowing goodness on others. Thus, in order for creatures to receive God's goodness, they themselves must have things other than themselves onto which they in their turn, yet in imitation of God, might pass on this goodness. The fulfillment of the nature of created things, therefore, necessitates the existence of things other than themselves towards which they might manifest their (and their Creator's) benevolence. Again, and as Thomas's great Florentine student Dante well recognized, creation constitutes not a metaphysical tragedy, but a veritable "divine comedy":

> the greater the proportion of our love,
> the more eternal goodness we receive;
> the more souls there above who are in love
> the more there are worth loving; love grows more,
> each soul a mirror mutually mirroring.[52]

Metaphysics of the Music

WITH THIS ACCOUNT OF THOMAS'S VIEWS ON MUSIC, BEAUTY, and the realism of created being in hand, we are in a position to consider more precisely the metaphysical significance of the music imagery of Tolkien's creation-myth. Perhaps the first point to be made, for all its obviousness, is the unique fact that Tolkien places at the origins of his fictional cosmos an act of divine music,

---

51 *Summa Contra Gentiles* 2.45, trans. Anderson.
52 Dante, *The Divine Comedy: Purgatorio* 15.71–75, trans. Musa.

which is to say, an act of divine *play*. This point is made even more clearly in the early edition of the *Ainulindalë* found in *The Book of Lost Tales,* in which it is said explicitly that Ilúvatar "sang into being the Ainur" (BLT 52).[53] It is also possible to connect the Creator's music-making at the outset of the *Ainulindalë* with what we saw in chapter one to be the proto-Trinitarianism of Tolkien's mythical theology. As we found Tolkien putting it in one commentary, "the possibility of complexity or of distinctions in the nature of Eru" is already to be glimpsed in the *Ainulindalë,* particularly in the Flame Imperishable, which he identifies as being "in some sense distinct from or within" Eru (MR 335, 345). Linking the orthodox doctrine of the Trinity with the *musica universalis* tradition behind the *Ainulindalë,* Hart has suggested that the "complexity or distinction" of the Christian godhead means that, behind the cosmic music played out in the world *by* the Creator is the prior divine music, which *is* the Creator, constituting the Creator in his own being:

> the image of cosmic music is an especially happy way of describing the analogy of creation to the Trinitarian life. Creation is not, that is, a music that explicates some prior and undifferentiated content within the divine, nor the composite order that is, of necessity, imposed upon some intractable substrate so as to bring it into imperfect conformity with an ideal harmony; it is simply another expression or inflection of the music that eternally belongs to God, to the dance and difference, address and response, of the Trinity.[54]

In keeping with this point is Ilúvatar's explanation to the Ainur that it is because they have been kindled with the Flame Imperishable that they are, as it were, to "kindle" their own music, "show[ing] forth [their] powers in adorning this theme, each with his own thoughts and devices, if he will" (S 15). It is the overflowing harmony within, which makes up the divine nature, in other words, that is the basis and originating source for the sub-created harmonies to be produced by the Ainur. So real is their Music and its participation in the divine music that is Ilúvatar that the latter, notwithstanding his infinite transcendence and perfection, does not remain passively indifferent or oblivious to it and its

---

53 As to why the later editions of the *Ainulindalë* exclude this reference to Ilúvatar's singing the Ainur into being, Michaël Devaux has suggested that it had to do with Tolkien's concern to distinguish Ilúvatar's act of creation from the Ainur's act of sub-creation. Devaux, "The Origins of the *Ainulindalë*: The Present State of Research," 94, 101.

54 Hart, *Beauty of the Infinite,* 276.

existence (as the Neoplatonic One arguably is and must be, for example, with respect to his emanations), but is rather depicted by Tolkien as a connoisseur of their Music, delighting in the new state of affairs their Music has brought about: "But I will sit and hearken, and be glad that through you great beauty has been wakened into song" (S 15).

When Ilúvatar first begins teaching the Ainur their Music, it is neverthe-less the case that they are unable to grasp completely the theme in its unity or wholeness: "but for a long while they sang only each alone, or but few together, while the rest hearkened; for each comprehended only that part of the mind of Ilúvatar from which he came, and in the understanding of their brethren they grew but slowly" (S 15). As we have seen previously, however, the Ainur mature in their comprehension and skill over time, so that, "as they listened they came to deeper understanding, and increased in unison and harmony," and yet despite the Ainur's challenges in learning the initial theme, Ilúvatar follows it with a second, "mighty theme, unfolding to them things *greater* and *more* wonderful than he had yet revealed; and the glory of its beginning and the splendor of its end amazed the Ainur, so that they bowed before Ilúvatar and were silent" (emphasis added). Where Ilúvatar's own music-making is concerned, therefore, it turns out to resemble less a Neoplatonic pattern of iterative decay (as some com-mentators have suggested) than it does the gradual, eschatological progression described, for example, in the Book of Genesis, where creation's initial status as merely "good" gradually gives way to its later consummation as "very good."

More remarkable still is that, despite the surpassing beauty of Ilúvatar's sec-ond theme, this time the Ainur are not told to repeat (however unsuccessfully) its pattern, but as was just noted, are instead exhorted to "adorn" it; instead of imitating Ilúvatar's theme, in other words, they are to interpret, improvise, and improve upon it, much as the biblical Adam and Eve are told to complete the work that the Lord God, for all its initial goodness, had already begun. And while the resulting Music is said to have been so beautiful that not even the Ainur themselves have since "made any music like to this music," in the same breath the narration anticipates a day when "a greater still shall be made before Ilúvatar by the choirs of the Ainur and the Children of Ilúvatar after the end of days." Finally, even the discord introduced into the Music by Melkor ultimately serves not to lessen its overall beauty, but becomes yet another instrument and occasion whereby Ilúvatar is able to enter again into the Music and make it more beautiful still.[55] Here we have yet another parallel to what Hart observes

---

55 On this, see chapter five's study of Tolkien's metaphysics of evil.

in the Bible to be the Holy Spirit's "power to redeem discordant lines" and "the promise of Christian faith that, eschatologically, the music of all creation will be restored."[56]

Metaphysics of the Vision

IN ADDITION TO THIS PROGRESSIVE, ESCHATOLOGICAL ELEMENT of the Ainur's Music, and, again, notwithstanding the exceeding level of beauty achieved within it, Tolkien depicts a similar transformation from glory to greater glory taking place in the transition from the Music to the Ainur's Vision of the world's history following after it. Next to the Music of the Ainur, the second stage of creation, the Vision, has been a comparatively neglected subject in discussions of Tolkien's *Ainulindalë,* yet in some ways it is just as an important a reality, if not even more important, where the underlying metaphysics of Tolkien's mythology is concerned. As was noted in the last chapter, in the ear- liest editions of the *Ainulindalë* Eru had created the world, unbeknownst to the Ainur at the time, simultaneously with their playing and singing of the Music, with the Vision of the world's history being given only after the fact. Yet in the revised edition published in *The Silmarillion,* the dramatic role of the Vision is significantly heightened by the fact that Tolkien places it chronologically between the initial Music and what is now Eru's later act of actually creating the world. As to the Vision's significance, on the one hand there is a sense in which it merely represents the visual counterpart to and interpretation of the Music, as seen in Ilúvatar's statement to the Ainur that in the Vision he has given them "sight where before was only hearing," and a little later, when he further explains that "each of you shall find contained herein, amid the design that I set before you, *all those things* which it may seem that he himself devised or added" (S 17, emphasis added).

As the Ainur quickly realize, however, the Vision is no mere superfluous repe- tition of the Music, but goes radically beyond the Music in its representation of a reality not at all anticipated by the Music. One place where we can see this is in the Ainur's differing responses to these two stages of the creation-process. In contrast with the avarice and presumption of Melkor, who alone during the Music foresees the possibility of his thoughts being given their own existence, the humility of the rest of the Ainur is reflected in their utter astonishment at the Vision:

56 Ibid., 281.

> And so it was that as this vision of the World was played before them, the
> Ainur saw that it contained things which they had not thought. And they saw
> with amazement the coming of the Children of Ilúvatar, and the habitation
> that was prepared for them; and they perceived that they themselves in the
> labour of their music had been busy with the preparation of this dwelling,
> and yet knew not that it had any purpose beyond its own beauty. (S 18)

Not only does the Vision, then, contain "all those things" that the Ainur "devised
or added" in the Music, it also contains "things which they had not thought"
in the Music.

There are a number of distinguishable dimensions to the Vision's superiority
over the Music, one of which is the Vision's increased theological or divinely
revelatory character. Although the Music itself had been a means by which the
Ainur could grow in their knowledge of Ilúvatar, in the foreknowledge of the
Children of Ilúvatar afforded in the Vision, by contrast, the Ainur are said to
be able to see "the mind of Ilúvatar reflected anew, and learned yet a little more
of his wisdom, which otherwise had been hidden even from the Ainur" (S 18).
Through the Vision, in short, the Ainur receive a greater revelation of the Creator
than what the Music alone had provided.[57] Related to this is the greater theodical
power the Vision also wields in comparison to the Music, providing the Ainur
with a greater disclosure of Ilúvatar's ability to bring about good from Melkor's
evil. In the Ainur's Music, to be sure, the Ainur witnessed "the most triumphant
notes" of Melkor's rebellious music being continually taken up by Eru's music
"and woven into its own solemn pattern" (S 17).[58] Yet it is in the Vision that

57 As Tolkien stresses in his letters, it is precisely because the Ainur had so little to do with that
portion of the Music and Vision corresponding to the Children of Ilúvatar that makes the latter so
intriguing and desirable to the Ainur: "The Children of God are thus primevally related and akin,
and primevally different. Since also they are something wholly 'other' to the gods [i.e., the Ainur],
in the making of which the gods played no part, they are the object of the special desire and love
of the gods" (L 147). In another letter Tolkien stresses the "primeval kinship" of the Ainur and the
Children of Ilúvatar in these words: "The uncorrupted Valar, therefore, yearned for the Children
before they came and loved them afterwards, as creatures 'other' than themselves, independent of them
and their artistry, 'children' as being weaker and more ignorant than the Valar, but of equal lineage
(deriving being direct from the One); even though under their authority as rulers of Arda" (L 285).

58 In a discussion that could almost be a direct commentary on this passage, Hart applies the
metaphor of music to the question of theodicy: "For Christian thought…true distance is given in
an event, a motion, that is transcendent…it even makes space for the possibilities of discord, while
also always providing, out of its analogical bounty, ways of return, of unwinding the coils of sin,
of healing the wounds of violence (the Holy Spirit is a supremely inventive composer).… Within
such an infinite, the Spirit's power to redeem discordant lines is one not of higher resolution but of
reorientation, a restoration of each line's scope of harmonic openness to every other line. It is the
promise of Christian faith that, eschatologically, the music of all creation will be restored not as a

the Ainur first experience in a concrete way the Creator's power to subvert and transform Melkor's corrupted themes. As Ilúvatar explains to Melkor in particular after the closing of the Music, in the Vision he will

> see that no theme may be played that hath not its uttermost source in me, nor can any alter the music in my despite. For he that attempteth this shall prove but mine instrument in the devising of things more wonderful, which he himself hath not imagined…. And thou, Melkor, will discover all the secret thoughts of thy mind, and wilt perceive that they are but a part of the whole and tributary to its glory. (S 17)

In addition to the Vision containing things that the Ainur had not thought, it also reveals to them the ultimate truth of those things which they previously had thought. It is not the prior Music, in sum, that embodies the essential truth of the later Vision, but rather the later Vision that embodies the essential truth of the prior Music. The later encompasses and thus gives added meaning to the earlier.

In addition to its greater theological and theodical character relative to the Music is its apparent aesthetic superiority, a point brought home during the Vision when Ilúvatar explains to Ulmo, the Ainur who would later assume dominion over the sea, that the "bitter cold immoderate" caused by Melkor has not in fact destroyed "the beauty of [Ulmo's] fountains, nor of [his] clear pools," but has instead managed only to contribute to "the height and glory of the clouds," "the everchanging mists," and "the fall of rain upon the Earth." To this disclosure Ulmo responds with appropriate awe: "Truly, Water is become now *fairer* than my heart imagined, neither had my secret thought conceived the snowflake, nor in all my music was contained the falling of the rain" (S 19, emphasis added). In the aesthetic categories of St. Thomas, the essential visual character of the Vision, "giving sight where before was *only* hearing," means that to the integrity and proportionality or harmony of the Music the Vision adds the further aesthetic property of *clarity* or splendor, the radiance of created form.[59]

Behind each of these respects in which the Vision surpasses the Music, however, is the now explicitly metaphysical point that the Vision simply implicates a greater

---

totality in which all the discords of evil necessarily participated, but as an accomplished harmony from which all such discords, along with their false profundities, have been exorcised by way of innumerable 'tonal' (or pneumatological) reconciliations. This is the sense in which theology should continue to speak of the world in terms of a *harmonia mundi*, a *musica mundana*, or the song of creation." Hart, *Beauty of the Infinite*, 280–81.

59 For an application of Thomas's three qualities of beauty of integrity, proportion, and clarity to the art of the Elves, see Alison Milbank, *Chesterton and Tolkien as Theologians*, 23–24.

degree of reality or being. In contrast to the Vision, as we shall see, the Ainur are represented as having enjoyed the Music for its own sake, not knowing "that it had any purpose beyond its own beauty." Through the Ainur's Music, accordingly, Tolkien dramatizes the kind of "perfect self-contained significance" and "inner consistency of reality" that he attributes in his essay to the true fairy-story, qualities I have already suggested to embody a literary application of Thomas's aesthetic principle of the integrity or wholeness of the work of art. However, unlike the fairy-stories of his essay, one of whose functions, to be discussed later, is also to direct the individual's attention back towards reality, the Ainur's Music does not suggest to the Ainur before the fact any existential significance or possibilities beyond its own self, much less creatively or productively render those possibilities actual.[60] In one letter Tolkien goes so far as to describe the Ainur's Music as a mere "abstract form" (L 284), a quality that may bring to mind Thomas's analysis of music as an incidentally or accidentally physical embodiment of otherwise ideal mathematical harmonies or proportions. As with Thomas's theory of music, moreover, the Ainur's Music likewise seems to imply on their part a kind of Kantian disinterest, inasmuch as the Ainur are represented as having enjoyed their Music, while it lasted, purely and selflessly on its own terms in their stoic oblivion to the possibility of their Music also being able to serve some ulterior, utilitarian "purpose beyond its own beauty." In Melkor's desire for the Flame Imperishable, whereby he might interestedly bring into existence the objects of his thought, Tolkien may be seen, by contrast, to treat us to a rather profound image of Kant's concern that, failing to enjoy the beauty of a thing at a disinterested distance, we lapse into the interested desire of seeing the objects of our aesthetic enjoyment brought under our own dominion.

If Tolkien, however, portrays the other Ainur as enjoying an almost Kantian moment of aesthetic disinterest in their own Music, it is only so that this same disinterest might subsequently be surmounted by the exceedingly interested aesthetic enjoyment elicited from them by the surpassingly sublime and existential beauty of the Vision. Thus, while in the Music, it is true, the Ainur were able gradually to come into greater contact and communion with each other, it is not until the Vision that they are for the first time confronted with the startling awareness of the possibility of things "other than themselves, strange and free" (S 18). This theme of the love of and delight in otherness for its own sake, touched on previously, is itself a central theme in Tolkien's writings and

---

60 As Houghton observes of the Children of Ilúvatar, in the Music "the Ainur had had no hint of their existence until they saw the vision." Houghton, "Augustine in the Cottage of Lost Play," 178.

one that has its roots in the metaphysical realism of St. Thomas, as Alison Milbank, for example, has pointed out.[61] In the *Ainulindalë*, moreover, the place
where this interested and intentional orientation towards the other first really
becomes manifest is not in the Music, but in the Vision, in which the Ainur
really for the first time are forced outside of their own immediate community
of fellow rational aesthetes and are confronted with the prospect of a reality
whose intractable physicality and externality refuse to be reduced to the formal
properties of the aesthetic presentation alone.[62]

Thus, if the Music in its comparative abstractness should resemble St. Thomas's
account of mathematics, to continue the analogy, the Vision of the Ainur might
be instructively compared to Aquinas's account of natural science, whose intelligible forms abstract from individual matter while retaining an intentional or
notional reference to the kind or species of matter out of which natural substances
are actually made. As Robert Collins has put it in an apt application of the Aristotelian terminology of Boethius and Aquinas, "whereas the music had established
an abstract pattern, the vision had indicated the nature of Ilúvatar's translation of
form to matter."[63] This "translation of form to matter" anticipated in the Vision
but not in the Music, moreover, far from involving a tragic "fall" of ideal form
into matter, implies rather the future realization, perfection, or actualization of

---

61 "There is one further element in this metaphysics [of Chesterton and St. Thomas] that we
need in order to understand Tolkien's philosophy.... [T]he element I would stress is the otherness
or objectivity of things. Only through the reality of the world can the mind, according to Thomas,
reach out to otherness and become the object. As Maritain writes, 'it is in its totality reaching out
towards the object, towards the other *as* other; it needs the dominating contact of the object,
but only that it may be enriched by it...fertilized by being, rightly subjected to the real.' To sum
up, Aquinas, according to Chesterton, teaches 'the reality of things, the mutability of things, the
diversity of things'.... [T]his is a philosophy that can be found at every level of Tolkien's fictional
project.... The world Tolkien invents is, of course, fictional, but it is famously realistic in its density
and completeness of realization.... To invent a world at all, as fantasy writers continue to do, is to
commit to metaphysics.... For the fantasy writer not only mimics the divine act of creation but he
or she, by creating a self-consistent, independent world also witnesses to the existence of an Is: to
Ens." Milbank, *Chesterton and Tolkien as Theologians*, 17–18.

62 Thus the Ainur's Vision would seem to embody what Maritain argues on Thomistic grounds
to be one of the essential elements of all imitative art: "art as ordered to beauty refuses — at least
when its object permits it — to stop at forms or colors, or sounds or words grasped in themselves and
as things (they must first be grasped in this manner — that is the first condition), but it grasps them
also as making known something other than themselves, that is to say, *as signs*.... [T]he more the
object of art is laden with signification..., the greater and richer and higher will be the possibility of
delight and beauty. The beauty of a painting or a statue is thus incomparably richer than the beauty
of a carpet, a Venetia glass, or an amphora. It is in this sense that Painting, Sculpture, Poetry, Music,
and even the Dance, are imitative arts, that is, arts which effect the beauty of the work and procure the
delight of the soul by making use of imitation, or by rendering, through certain sensible signs, something other than these signs spontaneously present to the spirit." Maritain, *Art and Scholasticism*, 55.

63 Collins, "'Ainulindalë': Tolkien's Commitment to an Aesthetic Ontology," 261.

those forms in and through the material substances which they are the forms of.[64] Thus, in the Vision we see the comparative "disinterest" of the Music transcended by a new kind of form that is not indifferent to, but is intentionally oriented towards, the real, mind-independent and material realization through which the actual existence of these realities must ultimately have its being. Much as the Music represents a state of potency with respect to its corresponding actuality in the Vision, so the later physical world is the actuality with respect to which the Vision is merely the corresponding state of potency. In both cases, the *Ainulindalë* undergoes not the tragic motion from a higher existence and actuality to a lower, but dramatizes in a temporal fashion the otherwise logical relationship of the comic and Thomistic trajectory from intelligible potency to existing actuality.

The psychological consequence of the Vision's implying a greater degree of being than the Music is that, more than merely calling the Ainur's attention to an abstract or hypothetical *possibility* of the extra-mental, physical world it portrays, the Vision is also conspicuous in its eliciting in the Ainur the intense *desire* that this world should be made real, that it should be given the gift of its own independent act of existence. When the Vision is concluded, it is interesting that the Ainur's wish is not that the Vision, much less the Music, should be renewed, but rather that what they have seen in the Vision should be made real: "Then there was unrest among the Ainur; but Ilúvatar called to them, and said: 'I know the desire of your minds that what ye have seen should verily be, not only in your thought, but even as ye yourselves are, and yet other'" (S 20). Hart again captures rather precisely the tension between what I'm suggesting is the Kantian disinterest of the Music and the Thomistic desire for the real found in the Vision:

> Beauty evokes desire...precedes and elicits desire, supplicates and commands it (often in vain), and gives shape to the will that receives it. Second, it is genuinely desire, and not some ideally disinterested and dispirited state of contemplation, that beauty both calls for and answers to: though not a coarse, impoverished desire to consume and dispose, but a desire made full at a distance, dwelling alongside what is loved and possessed in the intimacy of dispossession. Whereas for Kant, for instance, "interested" desire figures as the negation of the aesthetic and the ethical alike, as incompatible with contemplative dispassion in the former case and with categorical obligation in the latter, for Christian thought desire — which includes

---

64 Or, as Flieger puts it using similarly scholastic terminology, "the Music is not the physical act of creation, but only its blueprint. It is the pattern for the world *in potentia*." Flieger, *Splintered Light*, 58.

interest — must be integral to both. It is the pleasingness of the other's otherness, the goodness that God sees in creation, that wakes desire to what it must affirm and what it must not violate, and shows love the measure of charitable detachment that must temper its elations; it is only in desire that the beautiful is known and its invitation heard. Here Christian thought learns something, perhaps, of how the Trinitarian love of God — and the love God requires of creatures — is *eros* and *agape* at one: a desire for the other that delights in the distance of otherness.[65]

The Vision, then, depicts a physical reality the realization or perfection of which necessarily requires that it be something *more* than a mere Vision. This means that, in their love for the things portrayed in the Vision, the Ainur necessarily have an *interest* or concern to see that the possibilities exhibited there should be given their full metaphysical due. In this way, the Ainur may be seen to give expression to much the same desire we find at play in St. Thomas's metaphysics of beauty, namely that, as W. Norris Clarke has put it, "what we really desire when we desire a possible being is its actuality, not its possibility."[66]

This issue of desiring things for their otherness — conjured in the Vision but absent, in retrospect, from the Music — is also notable in the way it provides a mythical dramatization of the related, literary distinction he draws in his essay between fairy-stories and what he simply calls the "Dream." As Tolkien explains, the Dream and the fairy-story are alike in that in both "strange powers of the mind may be unlocked," yet Tolkien says he would nevertheless strongly distinguish the two and "condemn" the Dream as

> gravely defective: like a good picture in a disfiguring frame.... [I]f a wak-
> ing writer tells you that his tale is only a thing imagined in his sleep, he
> cheats deliberately the primal desire at the heart of Faërie: the realization,
> independent of the conceiving mind, of imagined wonder.... It is at any
> rate essential to a genuine fairy-story, as distinct from the employment
> of this form for lesser or debased purposes, that it should be presented as
> "true."...But since the fairy-story deals with "marvels," it cannot tolerate
> any frame or machinery suggesting that the whole story in which they
> occur is a figment or illusion. (TR 41–42)[67]

---

65 Hart, *The Beauty of the Infinite*, 19–20.
66 Clarke, "What is Really Real?," 82.
67 Tolkien's critique of the dream-device here might be further compared with Nietzsche's similar critique in *The Birth of Tragedy* of the dramatic prologue introduced by Euripides into

Tolkien's argument concerning the dream-device is interesting on a number of levels, not the least of which is its connection with other literary Thomists of his day for whom the dream represented something of a foil to the nature of true art. In *Art and Scholasticism*, for example, Jacques Maritain had contrasted genuine artistic inspiration — defined along the Thomistic lines of "reason superelevated by an instinct of divine origin when it is a question of human works ruled according to a higher measure" — with the mere "seeking the law of the work...in dream and in the whole organic night below the level of reason."[68] This concern, as we have just seen, Tolkien parallels in his statement about how in dreams "strange powers of the mind may be unlocked."[69] After her own reading of Maritain, however, for American novelist and self-described "hill-billy Thomist" Flannery O'Connor, the dream-image was less a metaphor for a *sub*-rational and therefore illegitimate source of artistic inspiration, than it was, again as for Tolkien, a symbol of the artist's temptation to impose his own, alien purposes, whether rational or otherwise, onto the work of art, instead

---

ancient Greek tragedy. Similar to Tolkien, Nietzsche speaks of this dramatic device as depriving man of the exercise of a human emotion or experience that he believes to be foundational to man's being. For Nietzsche, of course, it is not the experience that Tolkien hungers for, namely the desire or hope that the imaginative and marvelous worlds of Faërie should be made real, a hope that ends in joy in the metaphysical event of the Incarnation and Resurrection of Jesus; rather, Nietzsche speaks of the tragic prologue as "interfering" with the audience's pathos, passion, and "pleasurable absorption" in the tragic, Dionysian scenes being represented on the stage. With the introduction of the Euripidean prologue, however, "so long as the spectator has to figure out the meaning of this or that person, or the presuppositions of this or that conflict of inclinations and purposes, he cannot become completely absorbed in the activities and sufferings of the chief characters or feel breathless pity and fear." Nietzsche, *The Birth of Tragedy*, trans. Kaufmann, 84. For both Tolkien and Nietzsche, the artistic experience is ultimately about man being reminded of and reconciled to the ultimate nature of things, of allowing ultimate reality, however conceived, to break into man's routine existence and to revisit and revivify the ordinary with a sense of the extraordinary. It is this fundamental openness to a transcendent (in Tolkien's case) or immanent/subterranean (in Nietzsche's) reality that the dream-device for Tolkien and the Euripidean prologue for Nietzsche works to impede.

68 Maritain, *Art and Scholasticism,* 183n101.

69 Ironically, the negative connotations that the dream-image has for Maritain and Tolkien contrasts with the much more positive role it serves, for example, in the word's first appearance in the *Summa*, where Thomas uses it positively as a metaphor for the redeemed human soul's superior, post-mortem, disembodied, and hence abstract knowledge of God in his essence. As Thomas writes in ST 1.12.11, "the more our soul is abstracted from corporeal things, the more it is capable of receiving abstract intelligible things. Hence in dreams and estrangements from the bodily senses divine revelations and foresight of future events are perceived the more clearly. It is not possible, therefore, that the soul in this mortal life should be raised up to the uttermost of intelligible objects, that is, to the divine essence." For Augustine, by comparison, and notwithstanding his own tendency to view the physical realm along the "tragic" lines he inherited from Neoplatonism, the dream was a metaphor for the diminished degree of reality things have in the mind in comparison to the reality they have in the real world: "everything that occurs in the spirit is not necessarily better than everything that occurs in the body. The true is better than the false. Thus a real tree is better than a tree in a dream, although a dream is in the mind." Augustine, *De musica* 6.7.

of letting the work's own form come to the fore. As O'Connor explains to one correspondent to whom she had sent a copy of *Art and Scholasticism*: "Strangle that word *dreams*. You don't dream up a form and put the truth in it. The truth creates its own form. Form is necessity in the work of art."[70] And John Milbank, in his essay-review of Rowan Williams's *Grace and Necessity*, itself a study of Maritain's influence on twentieth-century Catholic authors and writers such as O'Connor, also touches on the specifically realist dimension of Tolkien's fairy-story/dream antithesis, when he comments on how "the metaphorical presence of one thing in another alien thing has to be related back to the distinctness of temporal and spatial finite realities if art is to exceed dream."[71]

It is in another reader of Maritain, however, that the most suggestive reference to the dream-image for our consideration of Tolkien appears. In his biography of St. Thomas, Chesterton writes:

> That *strangeness* of things, which is the light in all poetry, and indeed in all art, is really connected with their otherness; or what is called their objectivity. What is subjective must be stale; it is exactly what is objective that is in this imaginative manner strange. In this the great contemplative is the complete contrast of the false contemplative, the mystic who looks only into his own soul, the selfish artist who shrinks from the world and lives only in his own mind. According to St. Thomas, the mind acts freely of itself, but its freedom exactly consists in finding a way out to liberty and the light of day; to reality and the land of the living. In the subjectivist, the pressure of the world forces the imagination inwards. In the Thomist, the energy of the mind forces the imagination outwards, but because the images it seeks are real things. All their romance and glamour, so to speak, lies in the fact that they are real things; things *not* to be found by staring inwards at the mind. The flower is a vision because it is not only a vision. Or, if you will, it is a vision because it is not a dream.[72]

Whether Tolkien ever read Chesterton's biography of St. Thomas is not known for sure, yet the antithesis Chesterton draws between the dream and the vision as metaphors for the opposition between the subjective idealism of much modern

---

70 O'Connor, *The Habit of Being*, 218. In an earlier letter to the same correspondent, O'Connor had written: "The artist dreams no dreams. That is precisely what he does not do, as you very well know. Every dream is an obstruction to his work." Ibid., 216.

71 Milbank, "Scholasticism, Modernism and Modernity," 656–57.

72 Chesterton, *St. Thomas Aquinas: "The Dumb Ox,"* 182–83.

aesthetics and the metaphysical realism of Thomas's aesthetics is certainly striking, and would seem to corroborate further my suggestion that behind the relationship between the Ainur's Music and Vision is the Dream/fairy-story polarity of Tolkien's essay.[73] In contrast to the Music, after all, the Ainur's Vision illustrates Tolkien's belief that fairy-stories tap into a "primal desire" inherent in human beings, namely that, whatever the reality might be, there at least *should* exist things other than ourselves. Where the question of desire is concerned, therefore, the Music would seem to be more akin to the Dream in at least the limited sense that, in it, the Ainur's desire-for-the-other, if not exactly "cheated," is at least largely unrecognized, to say nothing of it being unrealized. The Music was certainly beautiful for its time, "unlocking strange powers" in the minds of the Ainur, yet the logic of the *Ainulindalë* is hard to mistake: had Ilúvatar followed the Vision, not with the creation of the actual, physical world, but instead with a repetition of the Music which had preceded it, the Ainur would have perceived its self-contained, disinterested beauty by comparison as a mere "figment or illusion," as Tolkien put it, i.e., as a *dream*.

Also of interest here is the way Tolkien develops in his essay the implicit realism of fairy-stories — much as Chesterton does with the metaphysical "vision" of St. Thomas — in juxtaposition with the idealism of modern philosophy, in a passage that more than one commentator has related back to Tolkien's own unspoken Thomism. In saying that fairy-stories accomplish a "regaining of a clear view" of things, Tolkien explains that he does not necessarily mean "'seeing things as they are' and involve myself with the philosophers, though I might venture to say 'seeing things as we are (or were) meant to see them' — as things apart from ourselves" (TR 77). Commenting on this, Paul Kocher has suggested that the "philosophers" Tolkien probably has in mind are "those of the idealist school from Berkeley down to our modern phenomenologists who, each in his own way, echo Coleridge's dejection, '...we receive but what we give / And in our life alone does Nature live.'"[74] As we saw Kocher point out in chapter one, however, his assumed posture of reticence notwithstanding, Tolkien of course cannot and ultimately has no intention to "escape metaphysics," and what is more, the metaphysics behind Tolkien's philosophy of fairy-stories is "best understood when viewed in the context of the natural theology of Thomas Aquinas."[75]

---

73 The sequencing of the publication of Chesterton's biography of St. Thomas in 1933, Tolkien's Andrew Lang address "On Fairy-Stories" at the University of St. Andrews in 1939, and his revision of the *Ainulindalë* in the early 1950s to give the Vision (now named for the first time as such) a much more prominent place in the narrative (MR 24–26), is consistent at any rate with the possibility of Tolkien having read and been influenced by Chesterton's biography.

74 Kocher, *Master of Middle-earth: The Fiction of J.R.R. Tolkien*, 76–77.

75 Ibid., 77.

More recently, Alison Milbank has also commented on this same passage from Tolkien's essay, this time explicitly contrasting the realist metaphysics common to St. Thomas, Maritain, Chesterton, and Tolkien, with the idealism of Kant in particular, and in the process introduces a further dimension to the problem represented by idealist metaphysics and its corresponding aesthetics:

> The "things in themselves" to which Tolkien alludes are those elements of phenomena to which Kant, a critical idealist, believes we have no access, and to which he gives the term, "noumena." Despite his apologetic tone, Tolkien is actually saying something quite radical: that fiction in the form of fantastic recreation of the world can give us access to the real by freeing the world of objects from our appropriation of them. Maritain states that Kant's mistake was in believing "that the act of knowing consists in *creating* the other, not in *becoming* the other; he foolishly reversed the order of dependence between the object of knowledge and the human intellect and made the human intellect the measure and law of the object."[76]

To return to Tolkien's discussion of the Dream, however, his characterization of this literary device as a piece of "machinery" is also of some note. In Tolkien's bestiary, the "Machine" is typically a symbol of the tyrannical domination of nature. As we observed in the last chapter, however, and this is a subject to which we will return again in chapter five, the technological or instrumental mastery and manipulation of nature is not the only way in which one can exercise a kind of tyranny over things, for, as Tolkien explains elsewhere in his essay, it is also possible to "appropriate" and "possess" things "mentally" or even artistically and aesthetically (TR 77). It is in this sense, I think, that the Dream as a device "cheats" the primal desire for otherness; by deliberately suspending the question of the story's reality or truthfulness, the Dream becomes a kind of instrument of intellectual domination, suppressing the objectifying otherness of the things and the world its story serves to relate. In this way, and as John Betz for example has argued in the case of Kant, "disinterest" in the aesthetic object's mind-independent existence is really an indirect form of *self*-interest, and the refusal to recognize and enjoy the existence of an "other" becomes the occasion for a form of self-enjoyment.[77] One of the questions implicitly raised by the Ainur's Music, consequently, is whether the temptation or at least possibility towards the

---

76 Milbank, *Chesterton and Tolkien as Theologians*, 19.
77 Betz, "Beyond the Sublime," 379.

"interested" and self-idolatrous quest of Melkor for the power to give being to his thoughts might already be latent within the kind of pure conceptual or mental mastery the Ainur enjoy and exercise in their Music. For, as Betz also points out, in a passage evocative of Melkor's retreat to the Void to seek the Imperishable Flame, or his refusal later in the *legendarium* to leave the endless halls of his subterranean kingdom, Angband, "once beauty no longer inspires a sense of transcendence, a love for an other, it can only conduct one more deeply and despairingly into the chambers of the modern subject and its 'horizons,' i.e., into the bad infinite of its 'mirror halls.'"[78] At the risk of overstatement, there would seem to be a very limited yet important respect in which the Ainur's Vision of the physical world in all its desirable otherness not only fulfills and surpasses the disinterested conceptuality of their Music, but in doing so to an extent even saves the Ainur from it.

Tolkien's Metaphysics of Eucatastrophe

THUS FAR, WE HAVE SEEN HOW THE *AINULINDALË* DRAMATIZES the distinction between what Tolkien identifies in his essay, on the one hand, as the mere contented, dream-like disinterest in the possibility of a mind-independent reality, and, on the other hand, the awakening of the fairy-desire for real, mind-independent existence. Yet, while Tolkien in his essay refrains from stating outright that our "primal desire" for the existence of things other than ourselves is any necessary indication of the way things actually are, as the Aristotelian tradition of Aquinas would suggest, such desires would indeed be in vain if there were no true means for their being fulfilled. Consistent with this, accordingly, is what Tolkien writes of the Elves in his commentary on the *Athrabeth,* namely that they "insisted that 'desires,' especially such fundamental desires as are here dealt with, were to be taken as indications of the true natures of the Incarnates, and of the direction in which their unmarred fulfillment must lie" (MR 343). Thus, in some ways, an even more important moment in the *Ainulindalë* than the progression from the Music to the Vision is the movement it portrays from the world as it exists in mere thought to the real, extra-mental existence the world comes to enjoy as a gift from the Creator himself.

Indeed, if the opening page of the *Ainulindalë*—and hence of Tolkien's entire *legendarium* as a whole—is any indication, the above progression from a merely

78 Ibid.

mental to an extra-mental existence is in a very real sense the underlying theme
and meaning of all creation history. Having barely just recounted the earliest
moment of the world's primeval past, the *Ainulindalë* already anticipates its
end when it prophesies how, "after the end of days[, t]hen the themes of Ilúvatar
shall be played aright, and take Being in the moment of their utterance, for all
shall then understand fully his intent in their part, and each shall know the
comprehension of each, and *Ilúvatar shall give to their thoughts the secret fire,
being well pleased*" (S 15–16, emphasis added). In the *Ainulindalë*'s story, then,
about the beginning of history, in which Ilúvatar gives to the Ainur's Vision the
Flame Imperishable and so brings the world imagined by them into being, is
already encapsulated the end of history, when Ilúvatar promises to do the same
thing for all his Children who have remained faithful to his purpose.

It is this dialectic of mental vs. extra-mental reality that we also find operative
behind the rebellion of Melkor, for his own fall begins with his vain quest(s) into
the Void to find the "Flame Imperishable" of Ilúvatar, whereby he might "bring
into Being" the thoughts of his own mind (S 16). Yet the fullest expression of
not only this distinction between thought and reality, but, what is more, the
implicit desire and orientation that the former contains for and toward the latter
comes when Ilúvatar first informs the Ainur of his intention to create the world
of Eä: "I know the desire of your minds that what ye have seen should verily be,
not only in your thought, but even as ye yourselves are, and yet other" (S 20).[79]
Ilúvatar can even be heard speaking somewhat diminishingly of both the Music
and Vision together when he says how the Music had "been *but* the growth and
flowering of thought in the Timeless Halls, and the Vision *only* a foreshowing,"
whereas the task of the Valar, after the physical world has actually been created,
is to "achieve it" (S 20, emphasis added). In the *Athrabeth,* finally, Finrod clearly
presupposes the physical world's intended metaphysical superiority over the Music
and Vision, when he tells Andreth that the "errand of Men" in history is "to
enlarge the Music and *surpass* the Vision of the World!" (MR 318, emphasis added).

In his many commentaries on the *Ainulindalë* found in his letters and elsewhere, moreover, Tolkien repeatedly emphasizes this dialectic of the merely

---

79 Later on in *The Silmarillion* Ilúvatar repeats this point, reminding the Ainur how he "gave
being to the thoughts of the Ainur at the beginning of the World" (S 44). And a few pages later, the
contrast between the Music and Vision on the one hand and the actual history of the world is drawn
in these terms: "Thus it was that the Valar found at last, as it were by chance, those whom they had so
long awaited. And Oromë looking upon the Elves was filled with wonder, as though they were beings
sudden and marvelous and unforeseen; for so it shall ever be with the Valar. From without the World,
though all things may be forethought in music or foreshown in vision from afar, to those who enter
verily into Eä each in its time shall be met at unawares as something new and unforetold" (S 49).

mental existence of the Music and Vision taken together, and the later, real existence enjoyed by the created physical world. In one letter, to begin, Tolkien analyzes his creation narrative in terms of the "story" of the world as contained in the Music and the Vision on the one hand, and the story as it later becomes "realized" in the creation of the physical world.[80] In another letter, he similarly speaks of the Music and Vision together as a "cosmogonical drama" that is "perceived…as in a fashion we perceive a story composed by some-one else," to which he contrasts the world we see "later as a 'reality'" (L 146). In another letter still, Tolkien passes over the Vision entirely to speak of the Ainur's Music as their

> work of Art, as it was in the first instance, [in which the Valar] became so engrossed with it, that when the Creator made it real (that is, gave it the secondary reality, subordinate to his own, which we call primary reality, and so in that hierarchy on the same plane with themselves) they desired to enter into it, from the beginning of its "realization." (L 259)

Here Tolkien goes so far as to suggest that the independent existence of the physical world actually makes it more like the spiritual being of the Ainur than the purely mental and hence derivative being of the Music: the physical world enjoys the kind of "primary reality" that places it on "on the same plane" as the Ainur. The same point is made in another letter that describes the Music and Vision as a "Design" communicated to and then "interpreted" by the Ainur, "propounded first in musical or abstract form, and then in an 'historical vision,'" after which "the One (the Teller [of the story]) said *Let it Be*, then the Tale became History, on the same plane as the hearers" (L 284). Tolkien goes on to contrast the story of the Music as "it 'exists' *in* the mind of the teller, and derivatively in the minds of hearers, but not on the same plane as the hearers," with the realized world that the hearers "could, if they desired, *enter into*" (emphasis original). And, in his commentary on the *Athrabeth,* Tolkien once again juxtaposes the "Great Music, which was as it were a rehearsal, and remained in the stage of thought or imagination," with the "Achievement" it receives in the final act of the creation drama when it is at last made real (MR 336).

As the above passages overwhelmingly demonstrate, the fundamental logic of Tolkien's understanding of creation, at least as he depicts it in the *Ainulindalë,* consists in this progression from the mere mind-dependent thought-existence

---

80 "According to the fable Elves and Men were the first of these [divine] intrusions, made indeed while the 'story' was still only a story and not 'realized'; they were not therefore in any sense conceived or made by the gods, the Valar, and were called the Eruhíni or 'Children of God'" (L 235–36).

of the Ainur's Music and Vision to the "realized" or "achieved" existence the
world later receives in its own ontological right. In doing so, I submit, Tolkien
provides a cogent, mythical dramatization of much the same principle we found
to lie near the heart of the existential realism and revolution of St. Thomas,
namely the recognition that the intelligible form or essence of a thing is a
mere potentiality in comparison with which its real existence is the actualizing
fulfillment. As Kocher has put it, the Ainur's wish is that Ilúvatar should give
to the world contained within the Vision its own "full metaphysical Being (in
the Thomistic sense)."[81]

   And it is this same Thomistic desire for being, finally, that Tolkien identifies
in his essay "On Fairy-Stories" as being at play in our own world and history.
In chapter one, we touched on Tolkien's concept of eucatastrophe, the "sudden
joyous 'turn'" and "miraculous grace" of the happy ending that he holds to be
essential to all "true fairy-stories." Yet, as Tolkien explains in the epilogue to his
essay — and where he abandons his earlier hesitation to "involve [him]self with
the philosophers" — the ultimate significance of these eucatastrophic moments
is not limited to the highly desirable emotional or psychological effect it has on
the reader, but in the fact that in them we are treated to a "sudden glimpse of
the underlying reality or truth" of the world:

> But in the "eucatastrophe" we see in a brief vision that the answer may
> be greater — it may be a far-off gleam or echo of *evangelium* in the real
> world.... God redeemed the corrupt making-creatures, men, in a way fitting
> to this aspect, as to others, of their strange nature. The Gospels contain a
> fairy-story, or a story of a larger kind which embraces all the essence of
> fairy-stories. They contain many marvels — peculiarly artistic, beautiful and
> moving: "mythical" in their perfect, self-contained significance; and among
> the marvels is the greatest and most complete conceivable eucatastrophe.
> But this story has entered History and the primary world; the desire and
> aspiration of sub-creation has been raised to the fulfillment of Creation.
> The Birth of Christ is the eucatastrophe of Man's history. The Resurrection
> is the eucatastrophe of the story of the Incarnation. This story begins and
> ends in joy. (TR 88–89)

According to Tolkien, in the Christian Gospel of the Incarnation, death, and
Resurrection of Jesus Christ, what has happened is that the Creator has taken

---

81 Kocher, *A Reader's Guide to The Silmarillion*, 18.

up the "essence of fairy-stories" in their otherwise "perfect, self-contained significance," these stories about hope and the unlooked-for "sudden joyous turn," and he has made them *real* by giving them the reality of "History and the primary world," raising them "to the fulfillment of Creation" — by giving them, in Kocher's above expression, "full metaphysical Being (in the Thomistic sense)." The Gospel, in other words, is not merely a real-life story containing a eucatastrophe or happy ending, but precisely in being real it constitutes for Tolkien the eucatastrophe or happy ending of all other fairy-stories, for in it all other fairy-stories have, in a sense, become *true*, have been graced with the special dispensation of real, historical, physical, created being.

Conclusion

IN SUMMARY, THEN, WE SEE THAT THE FUNDAMENTAL MOVEMENT of the *Ainulindalë* from the world as it exists in the Ainur's Music and Vision to the world as it exists in its own created right is no Neoplatonic, emanationist story of a gradual metaphysical decay or demise (as some readers have supposed), but is the same comic, or rather "eucatastrophic," metaphysical pattern that Tolkien, following St. Thomas, saw as constituting the being of our own world. In its representation of the Ainur's own "fairy-story" being gifted with the "fulfillment of Creation," as well as its prophecy of a day when Ilúvatar will give the thoughts of his children the "secret fire," so that they shall "take Being in the moment of their utterance," we see that for Tolkien the *Ainulindalë* is as much a mythical retelling and foreshadowing of the Christian story of salvation, or re-creation, as it is a rehearsal of the original story of creation itself. In Tolkien's hands, the creation event itself has become a kind of *protoevangelion*: if the Music is a beautiful, yet abstract, metaphysically disinterested "Dream," and the Vision a desire-inducing "fairy-story," then the sublime, concept-defying joy of the Ainur in response to the creation of the actual world reveals the latter as nothing less than an image of the Gospel itself. With the angelic doctor and over against the essentialism and idealism of much Greek and modern thought, Tolkien shares the metaphysical insight that a thing in its act of existence enjoys a higher status in the order of being — and, as the Ainur exemplify, a consequent higher status in the order of *desirability* — than what a thing's essence, form, or concept alone provides, precisely because the act of existence is what completes or perfects that essence. The move from Music to Vision to Reality, from intelligible or con-ceived essence to existing, mind-independent being, is metaphysically speaking not a tragedy, but a eucatastrophe, not a Fall, but a Fulfillment. Through his Thomistic creation-myth, Tolkien thus portrays the real existence or being of things as a surpassing and gratuitous gift, anticipated in but never necessitated by their forms or essences alone, hoped for in the promising and received with joy in the giving, a gift freely given by a good, all-powerful, personal God, who himself must transcend all conceptuality because he is Being itself. To see, finally, what Tolkien in his creative interpretation of Thomas's theory of angelic power allows the Ainur actually to accomplish in this newly created world, we must take up a consideration of the fifth and final stage of Tolkien's creation-myth, to which we now turn.

FOUR

The Metaphysics of the Valar

But this condition Ilúvatar made, or it is the necessity of their
love, that their power should thenceforward be contained
and bounded in the World, to be within it for ever, until
it is complete, so that they are its life and it is theirs.

Introduction

WE COME NOW IN OUR STUDY OF THE CREATION-MYTH of J.R.R. Tolkien in light of the creation-metaphysics of St. Thomas Aquinas to the final stages of the *Ainulindalë*. In what Tolkien refers to as "the Achievement" (MR 336), Eru the Creator brings the world — formerly only foreshadowed and foresung in the Ainur's Vision and Music — at last into being and invites those Ainur who so choose, the "Valar," to enter the world and prepare it for the coming of the "children of Ilúvatar" (Men and Elves) by shaping it and filling it with every manner of plant, animal, and celestial being. So great a role do the Valar play in fashioning the world that, similarly to what many commentators have thought concerning the Ainur's Music, many readers have assumed that it is the Valar rather than Eru who are the true or at least proximate "creators" of the world of Middle-earth. Part of my purpose in this chapter, accordingly, will be to show that, while his angelic beings exercise vast world-shaping and creature-fashioning powers — powers far in excess of anything St. Thomas, as we shall see, entertained as possible — Tolkien nevertheless reserved a rather precise and traditional meaning for the term *creation*, and what is more, one that remains entirely true to Thomas's distinctive, historic position that it is the Creator and the Creator alone who creates.

What the Valar are capable of doing in Tolkien's fiction, accordingly, is not an act of *creating*, but an act of *making*, a distinction drawn by early Christian thinkers to distinguish God's act of creating the world *ex nihilo* from the origin

myths of paganism, in which the world was often depicted as being formed out
of some pre-existing matter or substance. Not surprisingly, then, given what we
have seen previously of his intent to associate the Valar with the "gods of higher
mythology," Tolkien in several places refers to the Valar's world-shaping activity
as "demiurgic," an allusion to the divine world-craftsman of Plato's famous
origins myth, the *Timaeus*. The second part of this chapter, accordingly, will
involve us in a study not only of the striking similarities, but also the equally
remarkable dissimilarities, between Tolkien's and Plato's respective creation
stories. At the end of this comparison, I conclude that Tolkien's *Ainulindalë*
represents not only a modern recovery and retelling of Plato's creation-myth,
but at the same time a powerful Christian and Thomistic re-writing of it. In
the third part of the chapter, we will look at how the Valar's demiurgic labors,
in their more allegorical capacity, serve further to illustrate the very same principle of the metaphysical dependency of sub-creation in particular and free will
in general upon the prior divine act of creation that St. Thomas develops in his
own discussion of creation in the *Summa Theologiae*.

Following this analysis, finally, I wish to consider the metaphysical significance
of Tolkien's fictional angels, not as merely allegorical or symbolic representations
of his theory of sub-creation, but as hypothetical or possible beings in their own
right. Here I will argue that, while Tolkien's angels differ in significant respects
from the more conservative angelology of St. Thomas, even in their relative
novelty, not only the Valar, but also Tolkien's Elves, betray a kind of Thomistic
sensibility, insofar as Tolkien conceived them as realizing distinct theoretical
possibilities or gaps otherwise left open and unconsidered in St. Thomas's celestial
and terrestrial hierarchies. Accordingly, using Thomas's angelology and anthropology as a kind of foil, I will attempt to elucidate the metaphysical principles
that seem to have implicitly structured and guided Tolkien's imagination as he
developed, defined, and, in some cases, continually refined his account of the
principal inhabitants of his fictional world.

Thomas and the
Question of Angelic Creation

FROM THE EARLIEST DAYS OF THEIR ENCOUNTER WITH PAGAN
philosophy and religion, the question of angelic "creation" has been a subject
of great concern to Christian theologians. As David Keck explains in his study
on *Angels and Angelology in the Middle Ages*:

The question of the creation of the angels was problematic for Philo and the church Fathers primarily because several schools of pagan philosophy advocated doctrines concerning uncreated spirits that somehow mediated between God and the corporeal creation. Aristotle's spirits were eternal and uncreated (as was the universe itself). The Neoplatonists' scheme of emanations from the divine as the source of eternally uncreated spiritual beings provided these philosophers with angellike spirits who were the real creators of the universe. In addition to the philosophers, the Gnostics of the patristic era also saw the angels and their own peculiar beings, the aeons, as participating in the creation. Their God was quite removed from the created, material universe, which the Gnostics regarded as evil.[1]

In response to the pagan representation of the world as having been created by spirits or "gods," early Christian thinkers defended the inherent goodness of creation and the one true God's identity as the sole "maker of heaven and earth and of all things visible and invisible," as the Nicene Creed of 325 had put it.[2] Thus, whereas, in the first and second centuries, Jewish and Christian commentators were still able to read the *us* in the "Let us make man" of Genesis as referring to the Lord God's angelic assistants, later theologians such as the Cappadocians in the East and Augustine in the West felt compelled to argue that this was instead a reference to the persons of the Trinity.[3] In the *City of God*, moreover, the Bishop of Hippo denied that the angels were creators at all, though he confessed ignorance as to "what kind of service the angels, who were made first, afforded to the Creator in the rest of his creation."[4] However, with the later medieval renewal of interest in Platonic and Neoplatonic origin myths, especially in the school of Chartres in the twelfth century, along with the recovery of Aristotle's cosmological writings, which occurred about the same time, the question of angelic creation and governance once again came to the fore.[5]

An especially important and influential position articulated on the issue was the one formulated by Peter Lombard in his *Book of Sentences*, a work that became the standard theological textbook for the next several centuries, and

---

1 Keck, *Angels and Angelology in the Middle Ages,* 17.

2 Ibid., 17–18.

3 Ibid., 20. See also Pelikan, *What has Athens to Do with Jerusalem? "Timaeus" and "Genesis" in Counterpoint,* 105–6.

4 Augustine, *City of God* 12.26, trans. Bettenson.

5 Keck, *Angels and Angelology in the Middle Ages,* 18–21. On late medieval angelology, see also Colish, "Early Scholastic Angelology." On the medieval reception of Plato, see Gersh, ed., *Platonic Tradition in the Middle Ages: A Doxographic Approach.*

thus the context in which subsequent thinkers such as Aquinas were introduced to the problem of angelic creation.[6] In his treatment of the subject, Lombard cites as definitive Augustine's opinion in his *Literal Commentary on Genesis* that neither good nor evil angels create, but at most help in the "making" of things.[7] Curiously, however, in his later discussion of the power of baptism granted by God to his ministers, Lombard draws an analogy between the way in which God bestows the power to forgive sins upon his ministers and the power of creation that God is supposedly able to communicate to his creatures.[8] As we shall see shortly, it was over against this latter admission of Lombard that St. Thomas would in part stake out his own distinctive position on the question of angelic creation.

According to James Collins in his study, *The Thomistic Philosophy of the Angels,* St. Thomas's response to the Neoplatonic supposition of mediated, angelic creation was largely determined by his Christian belief (touched on in chapter two) that creation is fundamentally an act of divine *will* and therefore not something God was compelled to do by any necessity imposed by the divine nature. If creation is a free act of God, then not only is God free to create or not to create in the first place, but he must also be free to create *more* than simply one single effect, meaning that God can be the direct and unmediated cause of the being of all things, contrary to the fundamental premise of much Neoplatonic philosophy.[9] Even after removing the machinery of Neoplatonic necessity, however, Thomas, in the early part of his career represented by his commentary on Lombard's *Book of Sentences*, continued to allow that it was at least metaphysically possible for God to have used the help of angelic secondary agents in the act of creation, even if this was not how God did in fact choose to create.[10]

Later on, however, Thomas's reflections on the nature of the creative act led

6 On the history of Lombard's *Book of Sentences*, see Rosemann, *The Story of a Great Medieval Book: Peter Lombard's "Sentences."*

7 Lombard, *Sententiae in IV Libris Distinctae* 2.7.8.

8 Ibid. 4.5.3.

9 Collins, *The Thomistic Philosophy of the Angels*, 262. According to Plotinus, by contrast, the One does not and cannot produce all the lower orders of reality at once, but is, in a sense, dependent upon the higher intermediate orders to produce their respective lower orders: "If there is anything after the First, it must necessarily come from the First; it must either come from it directly or have its ascent back to it through the beings between, and there must be an order of seconds and thirds, the second going back to the first and the third to the second." Plotinus, *Enneads* 5.4.1, trans. Armstrong. As for later Islamic Neoplatonists such as Avicenna and Al-Ghazali, Collins observes how they "were forced to assert that God created inferior beings by means of superior, because they believed that from the One only one being can proceed immediately, whereas a multitude must proceed from the One through the mediation of the first and subsequent effects." Collins, *The Thomistic Philosophy of the Angels*, 262.

10 Baldner and Carroll, "An Analysis of Aquinas' Writings on the *Sentences* of Peter Lombard, Book 2, Distinction 1, Question 1," 46–47.

him to the much narrower and exclusive conclusion that God not only *does not* but *cannot* use the help of secondary agents in the creative process;[11] put differently, that it was within neither God's "absolute" nor his "ordained" power to delegate the creative act to the intermediate agency of his creatures. Thus, in his treatment on creation in the *Summa Theologiae*, for example, Thomas already begins laying the foundation for this conclusion in his argument that God, as the most universal cause, must therefore be the source of the most universal effect, namely being, which means that God must be the single and exclusive cause of even prime matter itself (ST 1.44.2). St. Thomas juxtaposes this view of creation with those "ancient philosophers" who took matter to be uncreated and the substantial forms of things to have been produced in matter by "certain universal causes, such as the oblique circle, according to Aristotle, or ideas, according to Plato."[12] By allowing even matter to be created in this way, Thomas has been credited with allowing even base matter to enjoy a dim participation in the intelligibility of God's own being. As Robert Miner has put it, because God produces the creature in its whole being, including its matter, his knowledge "extends not only to forms, but also to matter," meaning that "the knowledge of God must also extend to singular things. It cannot be confined to universals."[13]

It is this understanding of creation as the universal cause of being as such that Thomas brings to bear on the question he poses a little later as to "whether it pertains to God *alone* to create" (ST 1.45.5). Because being is the most universal effect, it must be brought about by the most universal cause, namely God, meaning that "creation is the proper act of God alone." Establishing that creation is the *proper* act of God is not to say, however, that it is an act *exclusive* to him, since he says something can act "instrumentally" by participating in the proper action of another. Of those who applied this thinking to the act of creation, Thomas first cites Avicenna, who taught that God created a "first separate substance," through whose mediation the rest of creation was enacted, and secondly Peter

---

11   Ibid. See also Collins, *The Thomistic Philosophy of the Angels*, 268–69.

12   This passage has generated some debate amongst Thomist scholars as to whether Thomas here intended to deny that Aristotle and Plato ever attained to a true doctrine of creation. See Gilson, *Spirit of Medieval Philosophy*, 438–41n4; Pegis, "A Note on St. Thomas, *Summa Theologica*, I, 44, 1–2"; Elders, *The Metaphysics of Being of St. Thomas Aquinas in a Historical Perspective*, 182; Johnson, "Did St. Thomas Attribute a Doctrine of Creation to Aristotle?" and "Aquinas's Changing Evaluation of Plato on Creation"; Hankey, "Aquinas and the Platonists"; and Velde, *Aquinas on God: the 'Divine Science' of the "Summa Theologiae,"* 124 and 142n4.

13   Miner, *Truth in the Making*, 3. On the intelligibility of matter in St. Thomas and its historical significance, see also Maurer, "Form and Essence in the Philosophy of St. Thomas." For a recent interpretation of and debate over this topic, see Pickstock, "Truth and Correspondence," 14, and Hemming, "*Quod Impossibile Est!* Aquinas and Radical Orthodoxy," 79.

Lombard, who held that, whatever the fact of the matter may be, God at least "*can* communicate to a creature the power of creating, so that the latter *can* create ministerially, not by its own power." In the now mature view of Aquinas, however, the very nature of the creative act precludes this possibility. On Thomas's Neoplatonic definition given in ST 1.45.1, creation is *emanatio totius entis a causa universali quae est Deus*, "the emanation of all being from the universal cause that is God." Now in every "particular" emanation or causation, the thing emanated is not presupposed to the act of emanation. Thomas gives the examples of how the emanation or generation of something white presupposes something that is first non-white, and the emanation of man presupposes what is first not man (namely, as we would now understand it, a sperm and unfertilized egg). Applying this same logic to creation, Thomas concludes that, as the emanation of the being of a thing in its entirety or universality, what creation presupposes is the opposite of what is emanated, namely non-being, which is to say, nothing. Creation by definition, therefore, must be *ex nihilo,* "from nothing."[14]

This is the context, finally, for Thomas's critique of Avicenna's and Lombard's teaching concerning angelic creation in ST 1.45.5, where he contrasts the manner in which creation presupposes nothing with the manner in which secondary instrumental agents (including angels) always presuppose some already existing effect, which the secondary cause then "works to dispose" towards the work of the primary cause. Thomas gives the example of a saw, whose cutting action presupposes the existence of the wood it helps to dispose to receive the form of the bench communicated to it by the carpenter. Without the already existing wood, the saw's activity as a secondary cause would have nothing to act upon, and hence would be without effect. Similarly, unless God first brought something into being in the first place through the act of creation, there would be no existing subject over or upon which any secondary instrumental cause, such as an angel, might extend its power. God's own act of creation, therefore, must take place prior to, and is thus presupposed by, the agency of any secondary instrumental cause. In this way Thomas, beginning with his Neoplatonic definition of creation as the emanation of being from the universal first cause, arrives at a uniquely anti-Neoplatonic conclusion: the first cause, and the first cause *alone*, is the direct, unmediated Creator of all that is and all that can be.[15]

---

14   On the history and influence of the doctrine of creation from nothing, see May, *Creatio Ex Nihilo: The Doctrine of "Creation Out of Nothing" in Early Christian Thought* and Gunton, *The Triune Creator: A Historical and Systematic Study,* 65–96.

15   As David Burrell has observed, Aquinas "insisted on employing the term 'emanation' for creation, even after removing and gutting the scheme of necessary emanation enthusiastically

Tolkien and the Question of Angelic Creation

FOR MANY IF NOT MOST OF TOLKIEN'S COMMENTATORS, HOWEVER, the account of creation reflected in the *Ainulindalë* is the pre-Thomistic, classical, and early medieval doctrine of angelic, mediated creation.[16] Yet as we shall see, the term *creation* actually held for Tolkien much the same specific meaning as an exclusively divine activity given it by St. Thomas, and what is more, far from this point being of mere semantic significance, according to Tolkien at least, a right understanding of this matter struck at the very heart of the meaning of his entire mythology. Tolkien's most in-depth discussion of the issue comes in the same reply to Peter Hastings we have examined previously. One of Hastings's further objections to Tolkien's mythology concerned Treebeard's statement in *The Two Towers* that the "Dark Lord" had, in Hastings's words, "*created* the Trolls and the Orcs" (L 187, emphasis added). According to Humphrey Carpenter, editor of Tolkien's published *Letters*, "Hastings suggested that evil was incapable of creating anything, and argued that even if it could create, its creatures 'could not have a tendency to good, even a very small one'; whereas, he argued, one of the Trolls in *The Hobbit*, William, does have a feeling of pity for Bilbo" (L 187). On Hastings's assumption, evil cannot create, because *creation* means the production of something good, whereas evil can only produce

---

adopted by the Islamic thinkers al-Farabi and Ibn Sina." Burrell, "Aquinas's Appropriation of *Liber de causis* to Articulate the Creator as Cause-of-Being," 76. This complexity in Thomas's relationship to Neoplatonic emanationism has been missed by some of his critics, as Fergus Kerr, for example, has pointed out with respect to Colin Gunton, who faults Aquinas on the one hand for his Neoplatonic definition of creation in emanationist terms, while on the other hand finding a "disturbing symptom" of Thomas's allegedly deficient doctrine of creation in the latter's rejection of Peter Lombard's "view that power to create can be delegated to a creature which works ministerially, in apparent neglect of the pattern displayed in Genesis 1, where God does precisely that — 'Let the earth bring forth.'" Gunton, *Triune Creator,* 100. Thus, the very thesis Aquinas defends in the *interest* of the Christian understanding of God as a personal, free Creator who brings the world into being from nothing, Gunton criticizes as being insufficiently Christian. Interestingly, however, when Gunton encounters what I argue in this chapter to be the same Thomistic doctrine of unmediated creation present in Tolkien's own writings, he is far more appreciative of the view. As Gunton observes in the case of Tolkien, "the artist is not so much creator as *sub-creator.* Such a distinction is essentially theological in content, for it suggests a belief that there is only one to whom we can ascribe the act of creation. The human artist can operate only at a secondary, lower level, by divine gift." Gunton, "A Far-Off Gleam of the Gospel," 129–30.

16 See, for example, Flieger, "Naming the Unnameable," 132, and *Splintered Light,* 55; John Cox, "Tolkien's Platonic Fantasy," 57, 59, and 62; Wood, "Tolkien's Orthodoxy: A Response to Berit Kjos" and *The Gospel According to Tolkien,* 12; Kreeft, *The Philosophy of Tolkien,* 72–73; and Whittingham, "The Mythology of the 'Ainulindalë': Tolkien's Creation of Hope," 216.

something like itself, namely evil. It is even possible that Hastings—himself a manager of the Catholic bookshop in Oxford, it may be recalled—had Thomas's well-known discussion of divine goodness at the beginning of the *Summa Theologiae* somewhere in mind. As Thomas argues there, "everything seeks after its own perfection; and the perfection and form of an effect consist in a certain likeness to the agent, since every agent makes its like; and hence the agent itself is desirable and has the nature of good" (ST 1.6.1). Every effect is like its cause, so that whatever is good in the effect must preexist in its cause. But if a cause is wholly evil, as Hastings seems to have assumed to be the case with Sauron and Melkor, then it stands to reason that any effects they might produce, as Hastings put it, "could not have a tendency to good, even a very small one." On purely Thomistic grounds, of course, Hastings's starting premise is problematic, since, for Thomas, as we shall see in the next chapter, no existing thing, including Sauron or Melkor, can in fact be wholly or entirely evil, inasmuch as existence itself is a good, a point that Tolkien also implies toward the end of his letter to Hastings.[17] In any event, Hastings adds the qualification that, even if an evil being *were* allowed to have the ability to create, whatever it created must, like itself, be evil. Thus, notwithstanding his objections to Tolkien, Hastings actually leaves open the possibility of, first, *good* yet finite creatures being able to create, and secondly, of even *evil* finite beings such as Sauron and Melkor being able to create, provided that their creations exhibit the same constitutional tendency towards evil as themselves.

Far from being caught off guard or perplexed by Hastings's metaphysical concerns, Tolkien complacently responded that he had in fact "already considered all the points" raised by him and pointed out that, "since the whole matter from beginning to end is mainly concerned with the relation of Creation to making and sub-creation…, it must be clear that references to these things are not casual, but fundamental" (L 188). As for the doctrine of creation presupposed in his mythology, Tolkien explains:

> I think I agree about the "creation by evil." But you are more free with the word "creation" than I am. Treebeard does not say that the Dark Lord "created" Trolls and Orcs. He says he "made" them in *counterfeit* of certain creatures pre-existing. There is, to me, a wide gulf between the two statements, so wide that Treebeard's statement could (in my world) have possibly been

---

17 "Because by [God's] accepting or tolerating their making — necessary to their actual existence — even Orcs would become part of the World, which is God's and ultimately good" (L 195).

true. It is *not* true actually of the Orcs — who are fundamentally a race of "rational incarnate" creatures, though horribly corrupted, if no more so than many Men to be met today. (L 190)

With Hastings, in other words, Tolkien agrees that evil is incapable of creating anything, but, unlike Hastings, his conviction stems from the much more basic Thomistic conviction that *no* finite created being, whether evil or otherwise, can exercise the power of creation. As he informs Hastings, it is the latter who is too "free with the word 'creation.'" At this point, Tolkien adds in an explanatory footnote perhaps his most precise definition of creation: "Inside this mythical history (as its metaphysic is, not necessarily as a metaphysic of the real World) Creation, the act of Will of Eru the One that gives Reality to conceptions, is distinguished from Making, which is permissive" (L 190n). Creation, in short, is an act of the Creator alone, a point Tolkien reiterates in another letter similarly distinguishing the divine act of creation from the creaturely act of mere making: "they [the Valar] shared in [the World's] 'making' — but only on the same terms as we 'make' a work of art or story. The realization of it, the gift to it of a created reality of the same grade as their own, was the act of the One God" (L 235n). Again, Eru *creates*, the Valar *make* (or what is the same, *sub-create*), which is the same distinction that the early church Fathers made between God's act of creation and the world-fashioning activity attributed to the gods of the pagan mythologies. What is more, Tolkien indicates in this passage that the demiurgic activity of the Valar is in fact something far closer ontologically to our own storytelling than it is to God's act of creating. As Tolkien explains to Hastings, there is a "wide gulf" between the two actions of making and creating, "so wide that Treebeard's statement could (in my world) have possibly been true" (L 190). In other words, while Tolkien holds it to have been metaphysically *possible* (even if in fact this was not the case) that the Dark Lord had "made" the orcs, under *no* circumstances could it have been true that the Dark Lord had "created" the orcs, since creation involves the gift of being, existence, or "Reality," which the Creator alone can bestow. The power to create, Tolkien holds with Aquinas, is the exclusive prerogative of the Creator alone.

It is this same understanding of creation, finally, that Tolkien cogently and consistently illustrates in the *Ainulindalë*. It is Eru, after all, even while the Ainur expectantly look on, who speaks the word of command, "Eä! Let these things Be!" that at last brings the world, previously only foreshadowed and longed for, but not guaranteed in the Music and Vision, into being, thus giving it the

"primary reality" and "fulfillment of Creation."[18] Coinciding with Eru's command, moreover, is his sending forth the Flame Imperishable to "be at the heart
of the World," causing the world simply to "Be." In chapter one, we considered
Tolkien's identification of the Flame Imperishable with "the Creative activity
of Eru (in some sense distinct from or within Him), by which things could be
given a 'real' and independent (though derivative and created) existence" (MR
345). We also saw that this creative power was something sought for by Melkor,
but not found by him, because it was "with Ilúvatar" (S 16). As much in Tolkien's
secondary world as for Thomas in the primary world, "it is manifest that creation
is the proper act of God alone" (ST 1.45.5).

In the *Ainulindalë's* image or concept of the Void, moreover, the place where
the Flame Imperishable is sent to kindle the existence of the created world, Tolkien
also provides an apt depiction of the orthodox doctrine of *creatio ex nihilo* central
to Thomas's account of creation. The Void is an absence, a nothingness whose
identifying — and for Melkor, most provoking — feature is its "emptiness." In one
commentary Tolkien describes the Void as "a conception of the state of Not-being,
outside Creation or Eä," which "the minds of Men (and even of the Elves) were
inclined to confuse…with the conception of vast *space* within Ëa [*sic*], especially
those conceived to lie all about the enisled 'Kingdom of Arda' (which we should
probably call the Solar System)" (MR 403n).[19] For Tolkien, like St. Thomas, because
creation is the *gift* of being itself, of being or "Reality" as such, creation therefore
presupposes the complete and total absence or negation of what it gives, namely
non-being or nothing, which is to say, a Void. This difference, moreover, between
Ilúvatar's creative "Fire" on the one hand, which is capable of kindling created
existence itself out of literally nothing, and all forms of sub-creative making on
the other, which are "guaranteed" by and hence presuppose an (ontologically)
prior act of creation, is illustrated rather well in *The Lord of the Rings* in Gandalf's
terse reply to Legolas's jest below Mount Caradhras that, if the wizard "would go
before us with a bright flame, he might melt a path" for the fellowship: "'If Elves
could fly over mountains, they might fetch the Sun to save us,' answered Gandalf.

18 Michaël Devaux makes the observation that in the first version of the *Ainulindalë* from
The Book of Lost Tales "there is no *Eä*! This equivalent of the *fiat* is actually subsequent…. Eru's
words 'Let these things Be' date only from 1948." Devaux, "The Origins of the *Ainulindalë*: The
Present State of Research," 93. Though Devaux doesn't make the point here, these changes in the
Ainulindalë would appear to be part of what Devaux, following the studies of Nils Ivar Agøy and
Kaj André Apeland, maintains to have been Tolkien's increasing "theologisation" of his mythology
from 1937 onwards. Ibid., 81.
19 David Harvey would thus appear to misinterpret the Void when he describes it as "the Chaos,
which is formless and in disorder" into which "are brought the Ainur." Harvey, *The Song of Middle-earth: J.R.R. Tolkien's Themes, Symbols, and Myths*, 26.

'But I must have something to work on. I cannot burn snow'" (FOTR 305). As Thomas puts it in his argument for its "pertain[ing] to God alone to create," without some already existing effect brought into being through the divine act of creation, the secondary instrumental cause "effects nothing according to what is proper to itself," and is thus "used to no purpose" (ST 1.45.5).

It is worth further noting in this context that, in an earlier version of the *Ainulindalë* from *The Lost Road*, the Ainur's first glimpse of the created world is described in these words: "Then the Ainur marveled seeing the world globed amid the Void, and it was sustained therein, *but not of it*" (LR 159, emphasis added). In his almost scholastic clarification that the world has its being *in* the Void without being *of* it, Tolkien may be seen to echo St. Thomas's own clarification of the doctrine of creation *ex nihilo*: "when anything is said to be made from nothing, this preposition from (*ex*) does not designate the material cause, but only order; as when we say, 'from morning comes midday'—that is, after morning is midday" (ST 1.45.1 ad 3). For both Tolkien and Thomas, in other words, the Void or "Not-being" out of which creation has its existence is not to be conceived as a kind of matter or material cause out of which the being of creation is then composed or made. As for Thomas's argument in ST 1.44.2 that the prime matter from which the world is made is itself created by God, Tolkien may be seen to credit a related belief to the Elves, for whom he writes that "the physical universe, Eä, had a beginning" and that this included its "basic 'matter,' which they called *erma*," and that it was from this "basic matter" that all things else were "made" (MR 338).

Where the doctrine of creation proper is concerned, in summary, careful scrutiny reveals Tolkien's mythology to be in remarkable agreement with St. Thomas's teaching that God and God alone creates, an activity both men understand in the precise metaphysical sense of a "giving," "sending," "sustaining," or "emanation" of the very being, existence, or reality of a thing. What is more, Tolkien's Thomism on this point, far from being of incidental significance, is in fact essential for rightly understanding the *Ainulindalë*, inasmuch as it is precisely through Melkor's mistaken presumption that a creature such as himself can wield the creative power of Ilúvatar, the Flame Imperishable, that evil was first introduced into the world, a point we shall develop at length in the next chapter's study of Tolkien's metaphysics of evil. Finally, as we have further seen, there is a level at which, for Tolkien, the account of creation presented in the *Ainulindalë* is "not casual, but fundamental" to the meaning of his mythology as a whole, inasmuch as "from beginning to end [it] is mainly concerned with the relation of Creation to making and sub-creation" (L 188).

Tolkien's Valar and Plato's Demiurge

NOTWITHSTANDING TOLKIEN'S AGREEMENT WITH AQUINAS
where the doctrine of creation proper is concerned, on the subject of the creaturely power of mere making, particularly of *angelic* making, it has to be said
that Tolkien departs boldly from the more conservative path trodden by his great
theological forebear. Whereas Tolkien in his fiction accords phenomenally vast
sub-creative powers to the Valar, attributing to them the formation of structures
ranging from the celestial bodies on the one hand to the fashioning of plant
and animal life on the other, Thomas, for example, expressly denies that even
the substantial forms of corporeal bodies are the kind of thing that can be communicated by angels (ST 1.65.4). At least in this respect, then, the inspiration
behind Tolkien's notion of sub-creative angels would indeed seem to have been
more directly pre-Thomistic.

Yet in order to make an accurate judgment in these matters, a more precise
understanding of the nature and scope of the activity of Tolkien's sub-creative
angels is necessary. To begin, we note that, although Ilúvatar the Creator is the
one who first brings the world into being, the world he creates is, for the most
part, entirely unformed, consisting of "wastes unmeasured and unexplored" (S
20). The primary responsibility Ilúvatar gives to the Valar, accordingly, is that
they should labor to make the world inhabitable for the coming of the Children
of Ilúvatar, whom Eru will create himself, and all in fulfillment of what the Valar
had seen in the Vision. Thus, at the conclusion of the *Ainulindalë*, it is said that
the Valar delved valleys, carved mountains, and hollowed seas, indicating that
much of the initial geography of the world is to be attributed to their handi-
work. Even more remarkable is that the Valar are also made responsible for the
introduction of plant and animal life in the world. It is Yavanna, for example,
the spouse of Aulë, who

> planted at last the seeds that she had long devised...and there arose a multi-
> tude of growing things great and small, mosses and grasses and great ferns,
> and trees whose tops were crowned with cloud as they were living mountains,
> but whose feet were wrapped in a green twilight. And beasts came forth
> and dwelt in the grassy plains, or in the rivers and the lakes, or walked in
> the shadows of the woods. As yet no flower had bloomed nor any bird had
> sung, for these things waited still their time in the bosom of Yavanna. (S 35)

The most renowned of Yavanna's works are the Two Trees of Valinor, Telperion and Laurelin, from whose golden fruit and silver leaf the Valar later fashion the sun and the moon themselves.[20] As for the rest of the celestial bodies, many of the stars are also accounted as having been "wrought" by Varda, the "Lady of the Stars" and spouse of Manwë (S 26, 39).

It is in the story of Aulë's foolish and futile attempt at making the dwarves, however, that we get the best illustration of both the tremendous magnitude of the Valar's sub-creative power and the intrinsic limits imposed upon it. In the chapter of *The Silmarillion* titled "Of Aulë and Yavanna," it is told how Aulë, out of an otherwise noble desire for there to be "things other" than himself who might enjoy the beauty of the world, in his impatience for the coming of the Children of Ilúvatar, fashioned the dwarves out of earth and stone. Rebuking Aulë afterwards for his presumption, Ilúvatar inquires of him:

> Why hast thou done this? Why dost thou attempt a thing which thou knowest is beyond thy power and thy authority? For thou hast from me as a gift thy own being only, and no more; and therefore the creatures of thy hand and mind can live only by that being, moving when thou thinkest to move them, and if thy thought be elsewhere, standing idle. Is that thy desire? (S 43)

Although Eru alone can give being, Aulë is nevertheless able to turn the earth and stone that Eru had created into, if not a free, rational being, as Aulë had intended, then at least into a living yet witless organism. It is only as a supernatural gift from Ilúvatar, graciously bestowed in response to Aulë's humble repentance, that the dwarves come to have "a life of their own, and speak with their own voices" (S 44). Thus, while in his letter to Hastings, as we saw, Tolkien wanted to leave open the possibility that the Orcs could have been "made" by the dark powers, he also denies the "making of souls or spirits, things of an equal order if not an equal power to the Valar, as a possible 'delegation'" (L 195).[21] Related to Aulë's

---

20 The sun and the moon are actually fashioned long after Ilúvatar's creation of the Elves, a sequence of events Tolkien later came to regret. As he put it in one commentary, "you can make up stories of that kind when you live among people who have the same general background of imagination, when the Sun 'really' rises in the East and goes down in the West, etc. When however (no matter how little most people know or think about astronomy) it is the general belief that we live upon a 'spherical' island in 'Space' you cannot do this any more" (MR 370).

21 Thus, as Tolkien himself concludes in his letter to Hastings, the question of whether the Orcs were "made" or not is a "different question" from whether or not the Orcs had "souls" or "spirits" (L 195).

production of the dwarvish bodies is the idea, later entertained by Tolkien, that the spirits of deceased Elves, instead of becoming reincarnate through a second, physical rebirth, might have their new bodies prepared for them by the Valar (MR 339, 362, and 364).

In his conception of angelic beings with the power and freedom to fashion a world according to their choosing, Tolkien's purpose was, as we have noted, to capture something of the "beauty, power, and majesty" of the gods of the ancient mythologies. One of these ancient myths that he no doubt partially had in mind is the creation-story of Plato's *Timaeus* dialogue, a work that was tremendously influential in both early Jewish and Christian patristic and later medieval thought. In a number of places, for example, Tolkien describes the sub-creative work of the Valar as "demiurgic" (MR 330, 370, 387, and 401), an evident allusion to the divine demiurge of the *Timaeus*, who fashions the changing, visible world by looking to the order, intelligibility, and beauty of the unchanging, invisible, yet eternal and "living model," and reproducing as much as possible that order within the realm of a pre-existing yet hitherto unorganized matter.

In what is probably the most comprehensive comparison to date between the *Ainulindalë* and Plato's *Timaeus*, John Cox has drawn attention to the fact that, like Plato's demiurge, "everything else [besides the Ainur] that Ilúvatar makes, he makes by the agency of the Ainur," a pattern Cox finds paralleled in the *Timaeus's* account of the divine demiurge, "a benevolent and eternal maker, who first creates what Plato calls 'gods' and then charges them with the task of carrying on the creation."[22] Cox finds in both narratives, moreover, the same "progression from the Creator, to intermediate creating powers, to the visible creation."[23] Both creation-myths, accordingly, present worlds of "stark contrasts" between the invisible, eternal, and unchanging divine realm of being on the one hand and the visible, temporal, and changeable realm of becoming on the other.[24] Cox further points to the resulting themes of emanation and imitation associated with these structures as they manifest themselves in both Plato and Tolkien.[25]

In addition to the above similarities noted by Cox, a number of additional parallels between the cosmogonies of Tolkien and Plato may be observed. Plato's demiurge and Tolkien's Eru, for example, are each identified as "father,"

22 Cox, "Tolkien's Platonic Fantasy," 57.
23 Ibid., 57.
24 Ibid., 58.
25 Ibid., 58–59.

and while they both delegate to their respective sub-deities the responsibility of fashioning other living beings — representing the world as imperfect apart from the presence of a hierarchy of beings and thus instructing the sub-deities to produce things according to their ability[26] — in each case the supreme deity nevertheless retains for himself a direct role in fashioning rational, immortal souls.[27] Thus, in the *Timaeus* the demiurge tells his underling gods that the part of man which is "immortal" he himself will begin by "sowing that seed, and then hand it over to you. The rest of the task is yours. Weave what is mortal to what is immortal, fashion and beget living things. Give them food, cause them to grow, and when they perish, receive them back again."[28] In a similar vein, as we saw, although the Valar Aulë is chastised by Ilúvatar for his presumptuous and futile attempt at sub-creating the dwarves, he does manage to fashion for them mortal bodies, bodies that Eru, acquiescing in response to Aulë's repentance, afterwards animates by uniting them with free, rational souls, something Aulë by himself could not do. Even in Aulë's speech of repentance, we find an eloquent and earnest expression of the principle articulated by Plato's demiurge, namely that, until it is properly populated by *all* manner of mortal beings, the world "will be incomplete, for it will still lack within it all the kinds of living things it must have if it is to be sufficiently complete."[29] As Aulë defends himself,

> I desired things other than I am, to love and to teach them, so that they too might perceive the beauty of Eä, which thou hast caused to be. For it seemed to me that there is great room in Arda for many things that might rejoice in it, yet it is for the most part empty still, and dumb. And in my impatience I have fallen into folly. Yet the making of things is in my heart from my own making by thee; and the child of little understanding that makes a play of the deeds of his father may do so without thought of mockery, but because he is the son of his father. (S 43)

In both creation-myths, moreover, just as the presence of beauty and goodness in the world corresponds to the establishment of a divine order, so evil is presented as a form of disorder.[30] And yet, despite the possibility of evil, both Tolkien's

---

26   *Timaeus* 41c5, trans. Zeyl; *Silmarillion* 15.
27   *Timaeus* 41b7–c4.
28   Ibid., 41c8–d4.
29   Ibid., 41b8–c2.
30   As the demiurge informs his sub-deities, "Now while it is true that anything that is bound is liable to being undone, still, only one who is evil would consent to the undoing of what has been well fitted together and is in fine condition." Ibid., 41b1–3.

Ilúvatar and Plato's demiurge remind their respective vassals that the order they have placed in the world cannot be ultimately undone or reversed except by their providential consent.[31] Neither do the Valar nor does the demiurge, furthermore, create *ex nihilo*, but they produce things from already existing matter, which in each writer's account is further analyzed in terms of the four elements of earth, air, fire, and water.

This latter point leads to an especially interesting parallel between Tolkien and Plato, which is that, although both their creation-accounts attempt to attribute as much causality in the world as possible to the agency of their respective demiurges (what Plato represents under the principle of divine "Mind" or *nous*), both mythologies also recognize the existence and role of a counter-principle, one that both Plato and, as we shall see, Tolkien after him represent under the concept of *ananke* or "necessity." In the *Timaeus*, because matter is not created by, but is co-existent with, the demiurge, it has its own intrinsic and even erratic properties that the demiurge is not responsible for and which present an inherent constraint on or obstacle to his world-making activity. The result is that, in the words of Donald Zeyl, there are moments when divine Mind or Intellect "must make concessions to Necessity [*ananke*]."[32] For Tolkien's demiurges, too, the matter out of which they make the world is not indefinitely malleable, but, as we will see later, it has its own inherent potentialities, which the Valar do not themselves make but instead labor to harness and actualize. As for Plato's notion of *ananke* or Necessity, while it does not appear in the *Ainulindalë*, as we saw in chapter one, Tolkien does make a reference to this concept in a letter to his son Christopher explaining his literary device of eucatastrophe. As Tolkien defines it, eucatastrophe involves

> a sudden glimpse of Truth, your whole nature chained in material cause and effect, the chain of death, feels a sudden relief as if a major limb out of joint had suddenly snapped back.... So that in the Primary Miracle (the Resurrection) and the lesser Christian miracles too though less, you have

---

31 As Plato's demiurge declares, "O gods, works divine whose maker and father I am, whatever has come to be by my hands cannot be undone but by my consent" (*Timaeus* 41a8–10), a speech echoed in Ilúvatar's pronouncement to the Ainur at the conclusion of the Great Music: "Then Ilúvatar spoke, and he said: 'Mighty are the Ainur, and mightiest among them is Melkor; but that he may know, and all the Ainur, that I am Ilúvatar, those things that ye have sung, I will show them forth, that ye may see what ye have done. And thou, Melkor, shalt see that no theme may be played that hath not its uttermost source in me, nor can any alter the music in my despite. For he that attempteth this shall prove but mine instrument in the devising of things more wonderful, which he himself hath not imagined'" (S 17).

32 Zeyl, "Introduction," in Plato, *Timaeus*, xxxiv.

not only that sudden glimpse of the truth behind the apparent Anankê of our world, but a glimpse that is actually a ray of light through the very chinks of the universe about us. (L 100–1)

According to Tolkien, part of what makes the rescued joy of eucatastrophe so poignant is the previous sense of the tragic inevitability of an event, the assumption, that is, that the course of nature is locked in an inalterable chain of "material cause and effect, the chain of death," which the Creator must somehow overcome if his purposes are to be realized in the world. As we will see shortly, Tolkien's account of *anankê* does differ significantly from Plato's, yet the point to be appreciated here is that, for Tolkien, the thrill of eucatastrophe, whether in fairy-stories or in real-life miracles, is expressible and experienceable in terms of the Platonic dialectic of a victory of divine benevolence, wisdom, or "Mind" over an apparently competing, impersonal force of brute, causal necessity.

Many more parallels between Tolkien's and Plato's respective creation-myths might doubtlessly be enumerated, but the foregoing examples I think give sufficient evidence of the profound influence Plato's *Timaeus* seems to have exerted on Tolkien's imagination.[33] At the same time, Tolkien's creation-myth makes a number of significant departures from Plato's, to the point that the *Ainulindalë* might be said to define itself over against Plato as much it borrows from him. Implied in Tolkien's association of his Valar with Plato's demiurge, after all, is the claim that the closest approximation to Plato's world-craftsman in Christian theology is not the God of orthodox belief, but the created, finite angels with whom Tolkien also identifies the Valar. And while both Plato's demiurge and Tolkien's Valar fashion the world out of pre-existing matter, both the nature of this matter and, as a consequence, the motivation behind the world-making of their respective demiurges differ in significant ways. In the *Timaeus*, because matter is entirely uncreated and hence eternal, it has no intrinsic, intelligible relation to either the divine mind or the eternal model from which the order and beauty of the cosmos originate. On the contrary, as has been noted, the original state of the uncreated matter is one of disorder, and it is this external condition of primordial chaos that prompts and even necessitates the demiurge's

33 Another, more literary parallel between the *Timaeus* and the *Ainulindalë* might be mentioned here. Like Plato's *Timaeus*, which was to be followed by the *Critias*'s much fuller account (left unfinished at Plato's death) of ancient Athens's defeat of imperial Atlantis and the subsequent destruction of both nations through earthquake and flood — the *Ainulindalë* forms with the rest of *The Silmarillion* an equally ambitious, all-encompassing mythology (also incomplete at Tolkien's death), beginning with the creation of the world and climaxing in Tolkien's own retelling of the fate of ancient Atlantis in the tragic history of Númenor.

benevolent program of communicating to the material world something of his own goodness and order, while at the same time ensuring that this process of beautification remains forever partial and incomplete. In the *Ainulindalë,* by comparison, as we discussed in the last chapter, because the matter out of which the demiurgic Valar make the world is itself created by the Flame Imperishable of Ilúvatar, it also has a small share, as St. Thomas also recognized, in the radiance of his intelligibility.

The inherent order enjoyed by matter in the *Ainulindalë* by virtue of its createdness also makes for an altogether different motivation behind the Valar's demiurgic activity. In the first place, as we have seen previously, the existence of the matter out of which the world is made, far from representing an externally imposed and metaphysically tragic constraint, is instead graciously brought into being by Ilúvatar in response to the Ainur's desire that the world they had seen in the Vision should be given its own mind-independent existence. In fact, as Tolkien indicates in one letter, it is on account of their "love" for the physical world, not despite but precisely because of its materiality, that some of the Ainur choose, as a condition of their demiurgic power laid upon them by Ilúvatar, to become physically "incarnate" within the world (L 286).[34] As for the character of the matter itself, whereas in the *Timaeus* it is indifferent at best and outright resistant at worst to the ordering activity of the divine mind, Tolkien's tale, by contrast, stresses the beauty and order of matter from its very inception. As in the *Timaeus,* a rudimentary division, at least, of matter into the four basic elements appears to precede the sub-creative work of the Valar, but instead of seeing a chaos of conflicting elements calling for demiurgic intervention and harmonization, the Valar's sub-creative work is inspired by an altogether different material first impression:

> But the other Ainur looked upon this habitation set within the vast spaces
> of the World, which the Elves call Arda, the Earth; and their hearts rejoiced
> in light, and their eyes beholding many colours were filled with gladness;

---

34 Later in the same letter Tolkien refers in particular to Aulë's "great love of the materials of which the world is made" (L 287). In this Tolkien seems to have intended his Valar to embody yet another principle of his theory of fairy-stories. As he writes in his essay, "Fantasy is made out of the Primary World, but a good craftsman *loves his material,* and has a knowledge and feeling for clay, stone and wood which only the art of making can give. By the forging of Gram cold iron was revealed; by the making of Pegasus horses were ennobled; in the Trees of the Sun and Moon root and stock, flower and fruit are manifested in glory…. It was in fairy-stories that I first divined the potency of the words, and the wonder of the things, such as stone, and wood, and iron; tree and grass; house and fire; bread and wine" (TR 78, emphasis added).

but because of the roaring of the sea they felt a great unquiet. And they observed the winds and the air, and the matters of which Arda was made, of iron and stone and silver and gold and many substances: but of all these water they most greatly praised. And it is said by the Eldar that in water there lives yet the echo of the Music of the Ainur more than in any substance else that is in the Earth. (S 19)

When the Ainur first see the world in the Vision, accordingly, many of its basic elements and even geological structures appear already to be in place before their demiurgic labor. The three chief Valar — Ulmo, Manwë, and Aulë — come to be particularly linked with the three elements of water, air, and earth respectively, not because they were responsible for bringing them into being, but because they were the ones who happen to have "turned their thought" towards or "pondered" them "most deeply."[35] So the world is not entirely formless and devoid of beauty when the Valar first enter it, but is from its beginning already marked by its own intrinsic being and corresponding beauty, a beauty that serves not as an obstacle or impediment (*ananké*), but a positive incentive or inducement to the Valar's demiurgic labors. In this subtle manner, Tolkien thus embodies in his myth a much more Christian metaphysical attitude toward material reality as good and therefore desirable because created.

One final related difference between Tolkien and Plato needing to be addressed concerns their respective concepts of *ananké*. Similar to Plato's *Timaeus*, as we have seen, Tolkien characterizes the operation of divine providence in his mythology in terms of a benevolent, "eucatastrophic" disruption of Necessity's otherwise tragic course of "material cause and effect." Unlike the *Timaeus*, however — according to which this material, causal determinism comprises an external limit on divine power, originating in an independently existing reality that is co-eternal with the demiurge — as I argued in chapter one, for Tolkien the "chain of death" which binds creation is not only a chain that the Creator shatters, but, more paradoxically still, is a chain that he himself is responsible for forging in the first place. The seemingly impersonal inevitability of causal and historical necessity, in other words, is an artifice, a kind of divine subterfuge, used

---

35 "Now to water had that Ainu whom the Elves call Ulmo turned his thought, and of all most deeply was he instructed by Ilúvatar in music. But of the airs and winds Manwë most had pondered, who is the noblest of the Ainur. Of the fabric of Earth had Aulë thought, to whom Ilúvatar had given skill and knowledge scarce less than to Melkor; but the delight and pride of Aulë is in the deed of making, and in the thing made, and neither in possession nor in his own mastery; wherefore he gives and hoards not, and is free from care, passing ever on to some new work" (S 19).

by an eminently personal God in order to escalate dramatically the *impression* of divine absence, only so that he might then destroy that impression through an even more radical disclosure of his unwavering, abiding, saving presence.[36] Thus, while it is true that, on the one hand, Tolkien ties his concept of euca-tastrophe dialectically to Plato's metaphysically tragic concept of *ananke*, on the other hand he makes it clear, as he puts it in his letter to Christopher, that this impression of the *ananke* behind the world is not so much real as it is "apparent," that behind this apparent reality there is a greater reality still, namely the divine light that shines "through the very chinks of the universe about us." In this way, Tolkien may be seen as attempting to "save the appearances" of Plato's concept of *ananke*, all the while sublating it within his otherwise Christian metaphysics of creation, much as St. Thomas, for example, does when in his own discussion of divine providence he does not deny the existence of chance, but instead affirms it at its own proper level while subordinating it at a higher level to the divine governance (ST 1.103.5 ad 1).[37] As I shall argue in the next chapter, it is with a similar degree of dialectical subtlety that Tolkien will approach the subject of the metaphysics of evil.[38]

36 As Stratford Caldecott aptly describes the basic conflict in Tolkien's fiction, it is "a triumph of Providence over Fate." Caldecott, "Over the Chasm of Fire," 32.

37 Thomas goes so far as to suggest that chance depends for its very possibility or efficacy on its subjection to divine government: "For unless corruptible things of this kind were governed by a higher being, they would tend to nothing definite, especially those which possess no kind of knowledge. So nothing in them would happen unintentionally, which constitutes the nature of chance." In the closely related article of ST 1.103.7, "Whether anything can happen outside the order of the divine government?," Thomas again writes: "Things are said to be fortuitous as regards some particular cause from the order of which they escape. But as to the order of divine providence, 'nothing in the world happens by chance,' as Augustine declares."

38 A further dimension to Tolkien's and Plato's differing views on the relation between divine providence and Necessity might be noted here. Although a number of *Timaeus* scholars have failed to see any intrinsic connection between Critias's introductory speech about ancient Athens's epic victory over Atlantis at the beginning of the dialogue and the creation-myth Timaeus tells in the remainder of the dialogue (see, for example, Welliver, *Character, Plot, and Thought in Plato's "Timaeus-Critias,"* 2–3; Taylor, *Plato*, 440; and Cornford, *Plato's Cosmology*, 20), the two stories in an important respect are concerned with the same fundamental problem, namely the ineradicable limits the gods face in realizing their benevolent purposes in the physical realm of becoming. Thus, while in the defeat of the despotic power of Atlantis by the ideal city of Athens we have an historic example of divine Nous triumphing over the chaos of Necessity, we see the limits of divine power in the fact that not even the patronage of Athena is able to save Athens from being destroyed by the same natural disasters that engulf Atlantis. In Tolkien's retelling of the story at the end of *The Silmarillion*, however, Atlantis is destroyed for a much different purpose, one in keeping with his metaphysical differences with Plato outlined above. In Tolkien's tale, Atlantis is Númenor (*Atalantë* in the Elvish tongue of Quenya, from which the Greek name *Atlantis* is supposed to have derived), an island-kingdom inhabited by a noble but proud race of men who are eventually seduced by Sauron into outright Melkor-worship. When the Númenoreans in their rebellious quest for personal immortality break the ban laid upon them by the Valar and travel to the forbidden land of Valinor,

Sub-Creation, Con-Creation, and Free Will

EVEN IN THEIR DEMIURGIC CAPACITY, THEREFORE, AND DESPITE their possession of vastly greater sub-creative powers than those admitted in Thomas's angelology, Tolkien's Valar are not only consistent with, but actually reinforce, the same Christian and broadly Thomistic metaphysics we have been tracing in the *Ainulindalë* thus far. In the remainder of this chapter I now want to consider in greater detail Tolkien's Valar as quasi-angelic beings in their own right, along with their similarities and differences with those of Thomas's angelology. For the present, however, there are a couple of points regarding the Valar's more allegorical role as mythical embodiments of Tolkien's theory of sub-creation that merit further examination. In chapter two, it was shown how the Ainur in their music-making capacity illustrate Tolkien's view that the source of sub-creative possibility lies in the "infinite variety" of God's own creative possibility and power.

Ilúvatar intervenes directly and destroys both their fleet and the island of Númenor with a flood. Thus, whereas in the *Timaeus* Atlantis simultaneously symbolizes and is obliterated by an impersonal and indiscriminate Necessity that cannot be completely controlled by the gods because it is not created by them, Tolkien has Atlantis destroyed as an act of divine judgment by a personal, omnipotent God for its worship of Melkor, the one who first sought the power of creation for himself, and for its imitation of his presumption by seeking immortality on Man's own terms.

Also worthy of brief comment here is the contrasting evaluations of the truth-capacity of myth implied in Plato's and Tolkien's divergent metaphysics. Nagy has observed that "Plato, like Tolkien, draws heavily on traditional myths, also including his own 'myths' (nowhere else attested and probably written by him) in his dialogues," and that this parallels Tolkien's "mythopoeic enterprise" in its ultimate aim of "show[ing] 'truth,' in Plato always expressed in mythic scenes and language." Nagy, "Plato," in Drout, ed., *J.R.R. Tolkien Encyclopedia*, 513. Similarly, Weinreich emphasizes Tolkien's debt to Plato for his "metaphysics of myth" when he writes how the "quintessence of Tolkien's ontology" behind his theory of myth is "at the core a Platonic one." Weinreich, "Metaphysics of Myth: The Platonic Ontology of 'Mythopoeia,'" 325. For Plato, however, the philosopher uses myths not out of choice, but of necessity. As Plato puts it in the *Timaeus*, "the accounts we give of things have the same character as the subjects they set forth" (29b), meaning that just as the world (on account of the *ananke* or constraint of its pre-existing matter) only ever achieves a tragically partial and thus never fully-realized participation in the divine, so the "likely story" (*eikos mythos*) that Timaeus has to tell about the origins of the cosmos achieves at best a tragic likeness to the ideal *logos* or rational account that the philosopher would prefer. In Tolkien's creation-myth, by contrast, and following the Christian doctrine of creation, while the world's participation in the divine is limited by virtue of its finitude, because creation is from nothing, the world — including its matter — has its entire existence in participation and likeness of the divine without remainder. For Tolkien, in short, the world in its entirety is a story about the divine, a metaphysical reality that at least in principle allows the stories or myths we tell about the world a much greater participation in the truth that remains to be told about that world. As Tolkien puts it in his essay "On Fairy-Stories," myth is no mere "disease of language" (TR 48), but given the inherent and irreducibly storied structure of reality itself, is a uniquely privileged way of communicating the truth of that reality. Indeed, as we have seen, for Tolkien it is through such myth-telling that reality for the first time comes into its own, accomplishing by God's own ordination the "effoliation and multiple enrichment of creation" (TR 89).

In a similar fashion, and connected with Tolkien's Thomistic doctrine that God alone creates, what I want to draw attention to here is how, in their demiurgic or world-making capacity, the Valar also serve to illustrate Tolkien's related belief that all sub-creative *actuality* likewise depends for its being upon an infusion and sustenance of God's own creative actuality or power. In the last chapter, it was noted how in the *Ainulindalë* creation takes place through a process of Ilúvatar giving "Being" or "Reality" to the sub-creative designs previously thought or imagined by the Ainur. As I showed in chapter one, however, for Tolkien, God's act of creation is not a one-time, once-for-all donation, but consistent with St. Thomas's doctrine of divine concurrence, involves rather the continuous influx of created being. Thus, in perhaps his most precise application of this metaphysical reality to his theory of sub-creation, Tolkien writes in his letter to Peter Hastings:

> having mentioned Free Will, I might say that in my myth I have used "sub-creation" in a special way.... Free Will is derivative, and is ∴ [therefore] only operative within provided circumstances; but *in order that it may exist*, it is necessary that the Author should guarantee it, whatever betides: sc. when it is "against his Will," as we say, at any rate as it appears on a finite view. He does not stop or make "unreal" sinful acts and their consequences. So in this myth, it is "feigned" (legitimately whether that is a feature of the real world or not) that He gave special "sub-creative" powers to certain of His highest created beings: that is a guarantee that what they devised and made should be given the reality of Creation. (L 195, emphasis added)

In keeping, then, with Tolkien's doctrine of creation as an act exclusive to the Creator, in order that a finite, creaturely act of sub-creation "may exist," that is, be effective or realized in the real world, the Creator himself, not simply before or after, but *simultaneously* with that action, must graciously concede to that action and its product the gift of being — in the words of the above passage, must "guarantee that what they devised and made should be given the reality of Creation." By having the Ainur first craft the world in or through Music, then intellectually perceive that world in Vision, and, lastly, after the moment of creation, actually give form or shape to the world in real, physical matter, Tolkien essentially mythologizes and so brings into bold relief the fundamentally atemporal relationship of metaphysical dependence of all sub-creation upon a logically and ontologically prior act of creation. Our sub-creations have being because and only because the Creator himself gives them their being, in the very moment of their being.

Thus, although Tolkien's premise of demiurgic angels is, as we have noted, relatively un-Thomistic in its overall conception, the sub-creative principle he purposes to illustrate by means of it, namely the complete and ongoing metaphysical dependence of creaturely sub-creation on the divine act of creation, is certainly one he shared with St. Thomas, as we shall see. Like Augustine before and Tolkien afterwards, St. Thomas, as has been noted, found it necessary to distinguish between *creating* and mere artistic *making*. In the *Summa's* "Treatise on Creation," accordingly, Thomas concludes his argument concerning the nature of creation as the "emanation of all being from the universal cause" by inquiring, in the eighth and final article of the question, into the relationship between creating and making, asking "whether creation is mingled with works of nature and art" (ST 1.45.8). One of the concerns Thomas entertains in his set of objections is that, if creation is defined as bringing into being something from nothing, then art and nature — inasmuch as they produce new *forms* in things, forms that, taken by themselves, are not made from any previously existing material — would seem to involve a kind of "creation." In his response Thomas draws upon a number of arguments he made earlier in the course of the same question. Forms, not being subsisting things themselves (contra Plato), cannot be the proper object of creation (ST 1.45.4). Instead, the proper objects of creation are individual substances which are composed of both form and matter (excepting angels, of course, which according to Thomas have no matter). Citing Aristotle's argument from book seven of the *Metaphysics* that forms, not being subsistent, do not so much *exist* (in the proper sense of the term) as *co*-exist in the substances they *in*form, Thomas argues in an analogous fashion that neither should it be said that forms are *created*, but are rather "*con* created."[39] The forms produced by art and nature, therefore, are not a *creation*, but a *con-creation*, a designation that points to the radical contingency and dependence of art and nature upon the divine act of creation, inasmuch as their forms cannot exist by themselves, but only in substances whose absolute being has been directly caused by the Creator alone. The conclusion of the matter is that creation is therefore not "mingled with" art and nature, but is rather "presupposed" by them (ST 1.45.8).

---

39 It is not clear, however, that Thomas was entirely consistent or systematic in his use of *creation* and *concreation*. In ST 1.7.2 ad 3, for example, Thomas makes the same claim on behalf of primary matter as he does here with regard to form, namely that because it "does not exist by itself in nature, since it is not being in act, but in potency only," therefore "it is something *concreated* rather than created." Yet in ST 1.44.2 Thomas argues, and without any similar qualification, that "thus it is necessary to say that also primary matter," which never exists apart from some form, "is *created* by the universal cause of being" ("Et sic oportet ponere etiam materiam primam creatam ab universali causa entium"). On Thomas's own admission, however, prime matter (i.e., matter considered in abstraction from its form) cannot be *created*, but only *concreated*.

While it might perhaps be objected that Thomas's position concerning sub-creation's radical ontological dependence upon the divine act of creation seems to degrade rather than — as is Tolkien's ultimate purpose — to promote the metaphysical significance of sub-creation, a number of Aquinas scholars have suggested just the opposite conclusion. It is much the same ontological serious-ness with which Tolkien treats the Valar's demiurgic labors in Middle-earth, for example, that Armand Maurer finds implied in St. Thomas's teaching concerning the con-creative dependence of art on God's own act of creation:

> Having supplied mankind with intelligence, God left nature in his keeping, to guard it, cultivate it, make it fruitful and fill it with his offspring. The art of man was meant to serve nature, to make up what was lacking in it, and to continue its creative activity. Man, by his art, was intended to be a co-creator with God, continuing nature's creative activity in the world.[40]

Peter Candler, moreover, in his article situating Tolkien at the "intersection of Aquinas and Nietzsche," likewise suggests that, in dealing with St. Thomas, "one can speak of the human agent as 'concreating' with God in any human making. Any act of human *poiesis*, then, is a participation [in] the creative agency of God — an act which is nevertheless 'creation' by analogy."[41] And Jacques Mar-itain, without using the language of con-creation directly, nevertheless evokes the image when he describes the artist as "an associate of God in the making of beautiful works...he create[s], so to speak, at a second remove.... Artistic creation does not copy God's creation, it continues it."[42] Finally, Robert Miner, as we have seen previously, has made the case that Thomas's account of human

---

40 Maurer, *About Beauty: A Thomistic Interpretation*, 84. Cf. also Delfino, "The Beauty of Wisdom: A Tribute to Armand Maurer," 41.

41 Candler, "Tolkien or Nietzsche, Philology and Nihilism," 10.

42 Maritain, *Art and Scholasticism*, 60–61. Commenting on this same passage by Maritain, Robert Miner has suggested that the "clearest example" of Thomas's "elevation," discussed in chapter two, of human making over the mere technological-making occurs in his "treatment of the human participation in divine providence. Although there are no intermediaries in creation proper, 'there are certain intermediaries of God's providence, for he governs things inferior by superior...not on account of any defect in his power, but by reason of the abundance of his goodness; so that the dignity of causality is imparted even to creatures' [ST 1.22.3]. Providence ensures that creaturely causality will always be something more than it is for an Aristotelian or modern naturalist. All things are created at an instant, through God's knowledge of his own essence and the diverse modes in which it can be imitated. But things *also* 'come to be in time,' as Thomas says [ST 1.14.16 ad 1; 1.15.3]. Humans do not create in the strict sense, but they are not denied a role in the temporal achievement or realization of the idea. This lends creaturely causality a dignity that it would otherwise lack..." Miner, *Truth in the Making*, 9. For a related discussion, see also Velde, *Aquinas on God*, 141.

making as participating in the divine making is precisely what preserves for art the ontological depth and significance of which it has been stripped in more modern, secularized accounts:

> Because Aquinas does not imagine human making to occur within a desa-
> cralized, sheerly human territory, but understands it rather as a mode of
> participation in the divine, it may be said that human construction acquires
> a significance that is difficult for modern secular perspectives to appreciate.
> It becomes a privileged site where God speaks through the creature, the
> agent of divine providence.[43]

For both Tolkien and St. Thomas, then, our acts of sub-creation, far from their being a matter of metaphysical irrelevance or indifference, exist precisely because they have received the Creator's own immediate validating blessing or "guarantee" of creation. They have, as it were, been paid the highest compliment, namely the dignity of gaining a purchase on or place within God's own creative activity. In our acts of sub-creation, God has chosen to create *through* us, as it were, not in the sense that we are made the intermediate agents or instruments of his creation, but in the sense of our sub-creative activity becoming the locus at which God carries on or continues his own work of creation.

As the above passage from his letter to Hastings further indicates, in addition to the metaphysics of art or sub-creation in particular, the demiurgic program of the Valar is also illustrative of the metaphysical principles Tolkien believes to be operative behind *all* free action generally. The concepts of sub-creation and free will are so closely associated in Tolkien's mind that he uses the two almost interchangeably in his letter to Hastings: "having mentioned *Free Will*, I might say that in my myth I have used *'subcreation'* in a special way.... Free *Will* is derivative, and is ∴ [therefore] only operative within provided circumstances." As the paradigmatic instance of free will, sub-creation is for Tolkien something of a model for free action in general. Human *praxis*, as it were, is a kind of human *poesis*, human *doing* a form of human *making*, inasmuch as every human action seeks to bring about an alternative state of affairs, and therefore to realize a "secondary world" or reality that is alternative to the one currently realized.[44]

---

43 Miner, *Truth in the Making,* 18.

44 As Frodo and Sam realize on the stairs of Cirith Ungol, their own heroic quest to destroy the Ring of Sauron and so save Middle-earth is in fact part of an ancient and on-going "tale" that never ends, "but the people in them come, and go when their part's ended" (TT 321).

The theme of free will, and especially its relationship to divine providence, has received a good deal of attention in the literature on Tolkien. What I wish to contribute here is the uniquely metaphysical approach Tolkien also takes to this important issue, an approach that ultimately leads back to his Thomistic doctrine of creation.[45] For Tolkien, not only does sub-creative free will dimly mirror the freedom the Creator himself enjoys in the act of creation, but, as with its specific application in sub-creation, creaturely free will is likewise wholly dependent for its very existence and exercise upon divine providence. This dependence, however, involves much more than the Creator merely passively "allowing" or "permitting" his creatures to make their own choices about things (though Tolkien will also speak of the Creator as "accepting" or "permitting" creaturely sub-creating or "Making").[46] As Tolkien puts it, free will is not absolute, but "derivative," being "only operative within provided circumstances," namely, those circumstances in which the Creator himself "should guarantee it" by giving it the "reality of creation." It is this sense of causal dependency, moreover, that the *Ainulindalë* hints at on its opening page, when Ilúvatar invites the Ainur to develop their Music, explaining to them that, "*since* I have kindled you with the Flame Imperishable, ye *shall* show forth your powers in adorning this theme, each with his own thoughts and devices, if he will" (S 15, emphasis added). For Tolkien, creaturely freedom is not and cannot be threatened by divine providence, for it is the divine Creator who first brings the creaturely free will into being and by whose providence the individual will, its intentions, and its consequent real-world effects are continuously and actively kept in being.

This causal dependency is no less true, Tolkien specifies, when those intentions and their effects happen to be "against His Will," for the Creator "does not stop or make 'unreal' sinful acts and their consequences" (L 195), a point that shall be developed at greater length in the next chapter on Tolkien's metaphysics of evil. Because it is the divine will that gives being to the finite will and its effects, any potential conflict between the two cannot be ultimate but, like Tolkien's concept of *ananke* or Thomas's concept of chance, is only "as it appears on a finite view," implying a higher level at which even sinful actions are invariably made to contribute to the Creator's greater plan. As Tolkien explains elsewhere in his letter to Hastings, "in every world on every plane all must ultimately be under

---

45 On the relationship between free will and divine providence in Tolkien, see Daniel Timmons's article "Free Will" and attached bibliography in Drout, ed., *J.R.R.T. Encyclopedia*.

46 See, for example, L 190n, 195, and 259.

the Will of God" (L 191).[47] This is another point illustrated in the *Ainulindalë* when Ilúvatar tells Melkor that, despite his rebellious music, in the Vision he will discover "that no theme may be played that hath not its uttermost source in me, nor can any alter the music in my despite. For he that attempteth this shall prove but mine instrument in the devising of things more wonderful, which he himself hath not imagined" (S 17).[48] At the heart of Tolkien's under-standing of free will, accordingly, lies the important metaphysical fact that it is the Creator alone who creates, that is, who gives and preserves the being or existence of the finite intellect and will, so that they might in turn carry out those artistic purposes for which they have been made.

In advancing his theory that every event, including the free and even evil acts of creatures, falls of necessity under the divine will, Tolkien repeats in his own way much the same position defended by St. Thomas.[49] The opinion Tolkien expresses to Hastings that "in every world on every plane all must ultimately be under the Will of God" is defended by Thomas, for example, in his answer to the question in ST 1.19.6 as to "whether the will of God must always be fulfilled":

> Since, then, the will of God is the universal cause of all things, it is impos-sible that the divine will should not produce its effect. Hence that which seems to depart from the divine will in one order, is brought back to it in another order, as does the sinner, who by sin falls away from the divine will as much as lies in him, yet falls back into the order of that will when by its justice he is punished. (ST 1.19.6)

Like Tolkien, who often speaks in terms of there being a hierarchy of "planes" in the causality of an event, Thomas recognizes that there are various levels or

---

47 In another place Tolkien writes of the simultaneous transcendence and immanence of the Creator in this way: "He must as Author always remain 'outside' the Drama, even though that Drama depends on His design and His will for its beginning and continuance, in every detail and moment" (MR 335). In this sense Tolkien is willing to speak of the Creator as in fact "the one wholly free Will and Agent" (L 204).

48 A little later Ilúvatar reiterates the point, telling the Ainur: "This is your minstrelsy; and each of you shall find contained herein, *amid the design that I set before you*, all those things which *it may seem* that he himself devised or added. And thou, Melkor, wilt discover all the secret thoughts of thy mind, and wilt perceive that they are but a part of the whole and tributary to its glory" (S 17, emphasis added).

49 Even Tolkien's interchangeable usage of sub-creation and free will has a parallel in Thomas, who, in the preface to ST 1.45 says that the eighth and last "point of inquiry" to be considered will be whether creation is mingled with "the works of nature and of the *will*," yet the form the question actually takes in the eighth article is "whether creation is mingled with work of nature and *art*."

"orders" at which one must distinguish and evaluate the causality of things. Thus, at one level or order of reality, something can be done which is contrary to the divine will, but that nothing can escape the divine will in an absolute sense follows from the fact that "the will of God is the universal cause of all things." In order for an effect to escape God's will completely, it would also have to escape completely the order of being, which is to say it would have to become nothing, and thus cease to be an effect at all.[50] Thus, what departs "from the divine will in one order, is brought back to it in another order."

For Aquinas, moreover, not only does everything depend upon the divine will "in every detail and moment," as Tolkien has it, but, as we saw with the sub-creative will in particular, he also holds that this absolute control represents not a threat to creaturely freedom, but is a necessary condition for it. At the most general level, this is true because God is the concurrent source of the finite will's existence, and therefore of its freedom. Secondly and more particularly, because God has created the will as free, when he acts on the will, he does so in a way consistent with the nature he has given to it. In a passage from question six of his *Disputed Questions On Evil,* Thomas argues that, as the ultimate cause of all things, divine providence always acts in a way consistent with the manner of existence of each thing, so that God can act on the individual free will in a way that leaves the will free. In his commentary on this passage, Brian Davies observes that human beings "are not free *in spite of* God, but *because of* God…. [H]uman freedom is compatible with providence because only by virtue of providence is there any human freedom."[51] It is precisely this Thomistic relationship, as we have seen, between divine providence and free will that we find in Tolkien, as more than one of his commentators have recognized.[52] As to Tolkien's further point that even the evil intentions and effects of a finite free will require the Creator's indulgent gift of being, we will see in further detail in the next chapter that this too has an important precedent in the thought of St. Thomas.

50 As Thomas puts it in ST 1.103.7 ad 1, if something "wholly escaped from the order of the divine government, it would wholly cease to exist."

51 Davies, "Thomas Aquinas," 254.

52 Writing on Tolkien's views on these matters, for example, Kreeft comments that "divine predestination preserves human free will, because God invented it. As Aquinas says, man is free *because* God is all-powerful. For God not only gets everything done that He designs, but also gets everything done in the right way: subhuman things happen unfreely, and human things happen freely." Kreeft, *The Philosophy of Tolkien,* 64. Brad Birzer, in his article on Aquinas in the *J.R.R.T. Encyclopedia,* similarly writes that "Aquinas argued that…free will could only be understood within God's sovereignty and predestination." Birzer, "Aquinas, Thomas" in Drout, ed., *J.R.R.T. Encyclopedia,* 21.

The Thomistic Philosophy of the Angels

IN THEIR MORE ALLEGORICAL CAPACITY, THEN, TOLKIEN'S somewhat un-Thomistic demiurgic angels nevertheless reflect some basic yet important Thomistic insights into the metaphysics involved in sub-creative making and free will. Even when considered in their own right, however, not as fictional embodiments of Tolkien's theory of sub-creation, but as hypothetical beings demarcating and instantiating real metaphysical possibilities in the hierarchy of being, Tolkien's Valar may be seen to exhibit a certain affinity with Thomas's angels. For St. Thomas, according to Howard Kainz, speculation over the angelic nature had real value both in terms of its theoretical truth and its anthropological implications.[53] In terms of Thomas's overall theory of being, for example, Kainz makes the case that

> a philosophy of the angels is of prime importance for throwing light on the "nature of contingent being." When we try to apply the categories of essence/existence, act/potency, substance/accident, etc., to the complexities of composite creatures, our discussion often becomes impeded because of the introduction of multiple contingent factors. But if it is within our power to discuss the same categories in relationship to a state of "pure" creaturehood beyond space and time, we should be able to get more easily beyond obfuscating tangents to grapple with the problem of the truly *necessary* relationship between essence and existence, substance and accident, etc.[54]

As separate (i.e., immaterial) substances, in other words, what angels represented for Aquinas and other scholastics, at least in part, was an idealized test case for further exploring the implications and intelligibility of the Aristotelian analysis of created being as a whole.

As for the anthropological dimension of Thomas's angelology, Kainz makes the point, especially apropos to our interest in Tolkien, that it is "profitable for us to discuss the significance of the angels, in terms of their mythical content."[55]

---

53 Kainz, *Active and Passive Potency in Thomistic Angelology*, 16–22. In addition to its theoretical truth and anthropological importance, Kainz comments as well on the significance of Thomas's treatment of angels for the Christian belief in angels generally and its historic synthesis of this belief with the Aristotelian notion of separate substances in particular.

54 Ibid., 16.

55 Ibid., 17.

By "mythical content," what Kainz has in view is the "subjective relevance" of
the angelic beings, first, as "projections" of an idealized human existence, secondly, as "external reflections" of a hierarchy of spiritual values, and thirdly, as
"models" for human political ideals such as equality.[56] In addition to the theoretical significance of the question of their actual existence, therefore, reflection
on angels was understood to provide important insights into human beings as
their immediate yet subordinate neighbors in the hierarchy of being. It was this
anthropological dimension to Thomistic angelology, moreover, that one of
Tolkien's own mentors in the ways of fairy-land, G.K. Chesterton, particularly
stressed in his biography of St. Thomas:

> St. Thomas really was rather specially interested in the nature of Angels,
> for the same reason that made him even more interested in the nature of
> Men. It was a part of that strong personal interest in things subordinate
> and semidependent, which runs through his whole system: a hierarchy of
> higher and lower liberties. He was interested in the problem of the Angel,
> as he was interested in the problem of the Man, because it was a problem;
> and especially because it was a problem of an intermediate creature. I do not
> pretend to deal here with this mysterious quality, as he conceives it to exist
> in that inscrutable intellectual being, who is less than God but more than
> Man. But it was this quality of a link in the chain, or a rung in the ladder,
> which mainly concerned the theologian, in developing his own particular
> theory of degrees. Above all, it is this which chiefly moves him, when he
> finds so fascinating the central mystery of Man. And for him the point is
> always that Man is not a balloon going up into the sky, nor a mole burrow-
> ing merely in the earth; but rather a thing like a tree, whose roots are fed
> from the earth, while its highest branches seem to rise almost to the stars.[57]

As we shall see, it is to this same scholastic tradition of doing anthropology by
proxy—that is, of studying man by studying that which is not man and yet

56 Ibid., 19–22.
57 Chesterton, *St. Thomas Aquinas: "The Dumb Ox,"* 164. David Keck gives a similar account
of the anthropological motive involved not only in Thomas's but in medieval speculation over
angels generally when he writes: "Of all God's creatures, human beings are nearest to the angels,
and angelology thus promises to illuminate anthropology. In the modern world, the impulse to
learn about human nature from closely related beings has shifted subjects from seraphim to simians.
Whereas modern scientists study the origins of the apes to uncover clues about humanity, medieval
theologians investigated angels." Keck, *Angels and Angelology in the Middle Ages,* 16. See also Collins,
The Thomistic Philosophy of the Angels, xii–xiii.

nearest to him (man's "other") — that both Tolkien's fictional angels and his Elves may instructively be seen to belong.

While we cannot enter here into a full survey of Thomas's angelology, we may touch on some of those particular points addressed by Thomas that seem most relevant for understanding simultaneously Tolkien's debt and his originality with respect to Thomas's historic work on the subject. The first point that might be made in this regard concerns the whole imaginative, aesthetic, and rational necessity of the angels in Thomas's thought. Angels are important to Aquinas not only for the light they shed on man, but, as I indicated earlier, because they fill an ontological gap that would otherwise intervene between God and man if they did not exist. As intelligent beings that are both incorporeal (being spiritual substances that are not naturally united to a body) and immaterial (being pure form without any adjoining matter), angels represent a real ontological possibility that, while fundamentally related to human beings, is nevertheless not instantiated or fulfilled by them, so that their existence is necessary for the perfection of the created order as God has made it (ST 1.50.1–2).[58]

As to the exact powers Thomas believes angels capable of exercising, this can be somewhat more challenging to reconstruct. One thing Thomas is quite clear on, as we have seen, is that angels cannot create. As has also been mentioned, neither does Thomas believe that angels can communicate substantial form to already created matter. The primary reason Thomas gives for this in the *Summa* is that, because "like is produced from like," we are not to "look for the cause of corporeal forms in any immaterial form," but rather in something that is itself composite, like its would-be effect (ST 1.65.4). As immaterial and incorporeal entities, angels are not a "proportionate" cause of the forms of material and corporeal substances.[59] At the same time, Thomas is adamant that angelic

---

58 As Étienne Gilson argues in a chapter on Thomas's angelology, "St. Thomas's study of the angels is not entirely or specifically a theological inquiry. Angels are creatures whose existence can be demonstrated.... To disregard them destroys the balance of the universe considered as a whole." Gilson, *The Christian Philosophy of St. Thomas Aquinas*, 160. For a similar summary of the spirit and role of Thomas's angelology, see also Collins, *The Thomistic Philosophy of the Angels*, xii.

59 Collins, in a chapter devoted exclusively to the subject of angelic power, elaborates on this particular Thomistic limit: "While that which is potential in matter is present in a more noble way in separated substances [i.e., angels], yet corporeal matter is not a proportionate potentiality with respect to the act whereby spiritual substances are in act. This follows from the fact that it is the composite itself rather than its components that is properly and essentially generated. Because of this necessary disproportion, no created spiritual substance has the power to effect an immediate substantial change in matter. The intermediate agency of some natural cause is required for such a formal transmutation.... As higher forms, separated substances possess supremely universal active powers to which the passive powers of lower substances are not sufficiently adapted to receive an actualization except through the mediation of natural agents." Collins, *The Thomistic Philosophy of the Angels*, 313–14.

intelligences, as the highest of created beings, are *more* rather than less powerful than lower beings, including even the human soul, which can directly move only the body it is united to and other bodies through it, whereas angels can move bodies they are not naturally united to (ST 1.110.3 ad 3). Thomas's purpose thus seems to be at once to claim on the angels' behalf the most far-reaching power and influence among created beings, without at the same time compromising the integrity and natural operation of the sub-angelic, corporeal order. Thus, whereas angels exert a greater, because more universal, power and influence over bodies than even bodies and human souls are able to do, this angelic power and influence is accomplished not by effecting substantial change in things, but rather through what Thomas, following Aristotle, regards as the most perfect form of motion or change, namely local motion. The local motion of bodies induced by angels, furthermore, is accomplished principally through their moving the celestial spheres, the regular alteration of which causes the cycles of generation and corruption in the sub-lunar sphere of Earth.[60] In this way, the local motion of the heavenly bodies serves as a sort of cosmic diffusing lens through which the otherwise expansive power of the angels is mediated, accommodated, and focused or concentrated to the kind of limited, passive potentialities proper to corporeal existence.

Nevertheless, it is evident that Thomas does not wish to limit angelic power over corporeal bodies entirely to their influence over the heavenly bodies, as he allows them to possess a direct influence as well (ST 1.110.1 ad 2 and 1.110.3 ad 1). One instance of this is when he allows that angels can and sometimes do assume corporeal bodies, not because it is in their nature to have such bodies (ST 1.51.1), but in order that they might be of greater service to men with whom they have "intellectual companionship" and whose salvation they help administer (ST 1.51.2). In such cases, however, the angel is not united to the body as its form, as in the case of the human soul and its body, but acts merely as the body's extrinsic mover (ST 1.51.2 ad 3). A couple of significant remarks made by Thomas on this point are, first, his statement that, when angels do appear to men, the bodies they assume are or can be nothing more than "condensed air" (ST 1.51.2 ad 3).[61] Secondly, although angels cannot produce a human body (the angels

60 Thomas, following Augustine, leaves undecided the historic debate as to whether the angels are joined to the heavenly bodies as their animating forms, i.e., the thesis that the heavenly bodies are "ensouled" by angels — the position of Plato, Aristotle, Origen, and Jerome — or whether the angels are united to them merely as external movers — the view of Anaxagoras, Basil, and John Damascene. Thomas's inclination, however, is towards the latter of the two positions. Collins, *The Thomistic Philosophy of the Angels*, 306–10.

61 Dante, incidentally, in his *Divine Comedy* suggests that the diaphanous bodies of the shades

being themselves incorporeal), Thomas avers that they nevertheless "could act as ministers in the formation of the body of the first man, in the same way as they will do at the last resurrection, by collecting the dust" (ST 1.91.2 ad 1). This would appear to be a particular instance of Thomas's more general principle that, although angels cannot perform miracles, being themselves part of the natural order (ST 1.110.4), they can nevertheless predispose nature to the supernatural and miraculous working of God, their own knowledge of the powers of nature being so acute that they can perform wondrous and unusual even if otherwise natural works.[62] According to Thomas, however, the angelic will cannot command corporeal matter *directly*, but moves it "in a more excellent way" by moving "corporeal agents themselves" (ST 1.110.2 ad 2). As Collins summarizes, in this way corporeal forms may indeed derive from angelic intelligences, not through an immediate "creative influx" (or direct "emanation," as Thomas puts it in ST 1.65.4) on the part of the angelic intelligence, but rather through an "eductive process" of "moving the bodies to their forms."[63] However that may be, Thomas reminds us that, at least as a matter of historical fact, in the original creation of corporeal creatures no such "transmutation from potency to act" by angelic means actually took place, inasmuch as Scripture teaches that "the corporeal forms that bodies had when first produced came immediately from God, whose bidding alone matter obeys, as its proper cause" (ST 1.65.4). As for the rational soul of human beings, this of all corporeal forms, being subsistent in itself and not made of any pre-existing matter, can be made by creation (and therefore by the Creator) alone (ST 1.90.2), a fact that the rational soul shares with the angelic intelligence and which as a consequence establishes a degree of equality between the two.[64]

---

are the effect of the deceased soul giving form to the air surrounding it, making the soul visible as well as giving it organs of sense through which even the deceased souls are able to continue communicating with each other. Dante, *Purgatorio* 25.94–105. On the Thomistic origins of Dante's idea of diaphanous bodies, see Philip Wicksteed, *Dante and Aquinas*, 223–25.

62 As Thomas writes in one place, "angels are better acquainted than men with the active and passive powers of the lower bodies, and are therefore able to employ them effectively with greater ease and expedition seeing that bodies move locally at their command. Hence again physicians produce more wonderful results in healing, because they are better acquainted with the powers of natural things." Aquinas, *On the Power of God* 6.3. Thomas goes so far as to refer to the existence of an *ars angeli* or "art of the angels." On the angelic knowledge of and consequent power over nature, see Collins, *The Thomistic Philosophy of the Angels*, 315.

63 Collins, *The Thomistic Philosophy of the Angels*, 289.

64 According to Collins, the rational souls of human beings are for Aquinas "equal to the good angels in view of a common supernatural end. This equality would be impossible if these souls depended upon the angels as their essential or creative causes." Collins, *The Thomistic Philosophy of the Angels*, 290.

Tolkien's Philosophy of the Angels

MUCH MORE MIGHT BE SAID ABOUT THOMAS'S TEACHING ON
the nature and extent of angelic power, yet I think the above account gives sufficient indication of the scope of both the possibilities and the limits Thomas
places on angelic action in the physical world. As is I hope is also apparent by now,
Tolkien's demiurgic Valar far exceed anything St. Thomas ever entertained as
possible within his angelology. Yet even in their comparative excesses, and taking
into account their mythological, imaginative, and literary purpose, as I intend to
show, Tolkien's Valar, together with his fictional Elves, far from being arbitrary
or merely fanciful in their conception, exhibit an identifiable and intelligible
logic that, for all its originality, may be appreciated in part as a highly creative
application of the Thomistic tradition of angelological speculation.[65]

To begin, we may remind ourselves that, whatever other function they may
serve, it was sufficient for Tolkien that his fictional creatures, like any other aspect
of his stories, should merely succeed and delight on a literary and imaginative
level, and therefore any attempt wholly to reduce either his angels or his Elves to
either their utilitarian or theoretical role is ultimately to deny their status as art.
With that having been said, and as was argued in chapter two, Tolkien himself
recognized that a thing's sub-creability through art was indissociable from its
creability by God, of which it was ultimately a function. Thus, on the one hand
Tolkien writes in his letter to Peter Hastings, addressing the question of Elvish
reincarnation, that the "purpose" of his *legendarium* is at once

> still largely literary (and, if you don't boggle at the term, didactic). Elves
> and Men are represented as biologically akin in this "history," because
> Elves are certain aspects of Men and their talents and desires, incarnated in
> my little world. They have certain freedoms and powers we should like to
> have, and the beauty and peril and sorrow of the possession of these things
> is exhibited in them. (L 189)

Like the Valar, therefore, whom we found above to provide a highly idealized and
mythical dramatization of Tolkien's metaphysics of sub-creation, so too Tolkien
envisioned his Elves as "incarnations" of the human sub-creative "talents and

---

65 For introductory discussions of Tolkien's angelology, see Kreeft, *The Philosophy of Tolkien*,
71–81 and Jared Lobdell, "Angels" in Drout, ed., *J.R.R. Tolkien Encyclopedia*, 18–19.

desires." In both cases, however, we have the same kind of "mythical" role that Kainz assigns to Thomas's angels, namely the projection of an idealized aspect of human existence.

Aside from the artistic, mythical, and anthropological dimension of his Valar and Elves, however, Tolkien, like Thomas with his angels, was also concerned with their purely theoretical significance simply as possible, hypothetical beings in their own right. Thus, in another passage from his letter to Hastings, now defending his conceit of Elvish reincarnation along very different lines, Tolkien insists that he does not think "any theologian or philosopher, unless very much better informed about the relation of spirit and body than I believe anyone to be, could deny the *possibility* of re-incarnation as a mode of existence, prescribed for certain kinds of rational incarnate creatures" (L 189, emphasis original). Being the lay metaphysician that he was, for Tolkien, the literary, mythical, and anthropological function of the Elves was ultimately inseparable from the question of their theoretical plausibility or possibility. As we have seen, for St. Thomas the question of angels was the question whether there could be creatures between men and God. As Peter Kreeft has observed, by comparison, the question for Tolkien is: "Could there be creatures between men and angels, such as Elves?"[66] As Kreeft goes on to indicate, the question itself was not even original to Tolkien, but, like the question of angels, was also medieval in origin. Kreeft cites a passage from *The Discarded Image* by Tolkien's friend C.S. Lewis, in which Lewis makes much the same point in regard to the intermediary and cosmological-aesthetic function of Elves (the *Longaevi* or "longlivers") in medieval literature that we saw earlier being made on behalf of St. Thomas's angels. As Lewis writes of the medieval conception of the Elves: "Herein lies their imaginative value. They soften the classic severity of the huge design."[67] As for Tolkien's Valar, as we shall see below, it is also possible to see them in terms of an implicit effort on Tolkien's part to fill out and further refine the medieval hierarchy of possible beings by asking the question, "Could there be creatures even between *Elves* and angels, or even *above* angels?"

Turning our attention, then, to the Valar, we have seen how, for Thomas, angels are not vaporous beings too ethereal to effect any real change in the world, but rather, for him, the problem is more akin to that of the proverbial

---

66 Kreeft, *The Philosophy of Tolkien*, 78.

67 Lewis, *The Discarded Image*, 122. Kreeft, for his part, goes so far as to say that "the same philosophical arguments for the existence of angels" that Lewis makes in his treatise on *Miracles* "could also be used as probable arguments for the possible existence of Elves or other species between the human and the angelic." Kreeft, *The Philosophy of Tolkien*, 80.

bull in the china shop: the actuality enjoyed by the angels is such that it has to be carefully controlled and accommodated to the kind of potencies possessed by physical beings. With this point in mind, we note that Tolkien too emphasizes not simply the vast sub-creative power the Ainur retain in entering the physical world and becoming the "Valar," but also the substantial power they must give up or at least provisionally suspend as a condition for their doing so. In the *Ainulindalë*, for example, we read:

> Thus it came to pass that of the Ainur some abode still with Ilúvatar beyond the confines of the World; but others, and among them many of the greatest and most fair, took the leave of Ilúvatar and descended into it. But this condition Ilúvatar made, or it is the necessity of their love, that their power should thenceforward be contained and bounded in the World, to be within it for ever, until it is complete, so that they are its life and it is theirs. And therefore they are named the Valar, the Powers of the World. (S 20)

In order to enter the physical world that they love and to help fashion it for the future coming of the Children of Ilúvatar, for whom they long, the Valar are required to make a sacrifice of themselves by relinquishing the use of some of their native powers. In order to carry out their sub-creative tasks, in other words, there must first be a certain reduction or focusing of the Valar's power, making them adequate, adapted, or "proportionate," as Thomas might say, to the new material environment they are to inhabit and govern.[68]

An important part of this angelic sacrifice of power, as Tolkien conceives it, is the necessity laid upon the Valar by Eru that they assume physical bodies within the world they are to fashion and rule, making their power "contained and

---

68 The theme of sacrificial angelic power is particularly associated in Tolkien's letters with the Istari or "wizards," of which Gandalf and Saruman are the most notable members. Of the Istari Tolkien writes: "At this point in the fabulous history the purpose was precisely *to limit and hinder their exhibition of 'power' on the physical plane*, and so that they should do what they were primarily sent for: train, advise, instruct, arouse the hearts and minds of those threatened by Sauron to a resistance with their own strengths; and not just to do the job for them" (L 202, emphasis added). Of Gandalf in particular, Tolkien says that even after his "death" and "resurrection" as "Gandalf the White," he was "still under *the obligation of concealing his power* and of teaching rather than forcing or dominating wills, but where the physical powers of the Enemy are too great for the good will of the opposers to be effective he can act in emergency as an 'angel' — no more violently than the release of St Peter from prison. He seldom does so, operating rather through others, but in one or two cases in the War...he does reveal a sudden power" (L 202-3, emphasis added). Like the Valar in their sub-creative and governing capacity, as a counselor Gandalf is charged with limiting the use of the power that is his by nature. On the theme of angelic sacrifice in Tolkien, see Hood, "Nature and Technology: Angelic and Sacrificial Strategies in Tolkien's *The Lord of the Rings*."

bounded in the World." In a number of his letters, Tolkien refers to the Valar and their servants (both the "Maiar" and "Istari," or "wizards") as "incarnate" angels, spirits, or intelligences (L 202, 259-60, 284-85, and 411), raising the possibility that it is as a consequence of their embodied state, whereby they acquire a limited kinship or proportionality with physical reality, that the Valar are able to exercise their profound, physically transformative, sub-creative power in the world.[69] In this manner, Tolkien echoes something of St. Thomas's conviction that angelic sub-creative action is limited or conditioned by angels' natural immateriality and incorporeality. Whereas Thomas, however, at best recognizes the theoretical possibility of artistic and incarnate angels, leaving the hypothesis largely unexamined and unexplained, Tolkien's Valar may perhaps be appreciated as an extended exercise or experiment in probing, stretching, and generally filling in these lacunae left open by St. Thomas. Thus, it is tempting to see in Tolkien's Valar — whose own sub-creative powers arguably reach their climax in Aulë's fashioning Dwarf-bodies out of earth and stone and in the Valar's forming (under Eru's permission) new bodies for reincarnate Elves — a playful exaggeration of Thomas's much more tentative speculation about angels who could have acted "as ministers in the formation of the body of the first man" and who in any event will assist "at the last resurrection" by gathering the dust of the earth.

As with Thomas's angels, however, Tolkien makes clear that the embodiment of the Valar is not something natural to them, as is the case with Men and Elves, but is undertaken voluntarily, so that they are able to go without their bodies should they wish or the need arise. As Tolkien writes of the Valar in one letter: "They were thus in the world, but not of a kind whose essential nature is to be physically incarnate. They were self incarnated, if they wished, but their

---

69 Jacques Maritain makes the following comment as to the aesthetic and imaginative necessity of embodiment for the possibility of art or "sub-creation": "Art being of man, how could it not depend on the pre-existing structures and inclinations of the subject in which it dwells? They remain extrinsic to art, but they influence it.... But art does not reside in an angelic mind; it resides in a soul which animates a living body, and which, by the natural necessity in which it finds itself of learning, and progressing little by little and with the assistance of others, makes the rational animal a naturally social animal. Art is therefore basically dependent upon everything which the human community, spiritual tradition and history transmit to the body and mind of man. By its human subject and its human roots, art belong to a time and a country." Maritain, *Art and Scholasticism,* 74. In this opinion Maritain was joined by Catholic artist and poet David Jones, who applied Maritain's point about art to the sacraments: "No wonder then that Theology regards the body as a unique good. Without body: without sacrament. Angels only: no sacrament. Beasts only: no sacrament. Man: sacrament at every turn and all levels of the 'profane' and 'sacred,' in the trivial and in the profound, no escape from sacrament." Jones, *Epoch and Artist,* 167, also cited in Candler, "Tolkien or Nietzsche, Philology and Nihilism," 11. On David Jones's sacramental view of art, see Williams, *Grace and Necessity,* 43-90.

incarnate forms were more analogous to our clothes than to our bodies, except
that they were more than are clothes the expression of their desires, moods, wills
and functions" (L 259).[70] It is also indicated that, again like Thomas's angels, it
is because the Valar are especially concerned with the Children of Ilúvatar that
the bodies they assume are of human shape.[71] Furthermore, because the angelic
spirit is united to its body not by nature but by will, the formation of its body
is itself a kind of sub-creative act. Describing the angelic body, Tolkien writes:
"It is mythologically supposed that when this shape was 'real,' that is a physical
actuality in the physical world and not a vision transferred from mind to mind,
it took some time to build up. It was then destructible like other physical organ-
isms" (L 260).[72] Tolkien further explains that, when an angelic spirit's body was
destroyed (as happens twice, for example, in Sauron's case), each time it would
take longer for the spirit to re-fashion its body: "because each building-up used
up some of the inherent energy of the spirit, which might be called the 'will' or
the effective link between the indestructible mind and being and the realization
of its imagination" (L 260). As in Thomas's angelology, Tolkien's angelic beings
are not able to make matter obey instantaneously or effortlessly the dictates of
their will, but are only able to form their own and other bodies through a true
sub-creative effort, one involving the passage of time and an apparently un-re-
newable expenditure of great personal energy and vitality.

The more directly the angelic beings are involved in the affairs of Men and
Elves, moreover, the more they seem to be attached to their bodies, so much so
that they are susceptible to real fatigue and even to a sort of "death," as is Gandalf's fate in *The Lord of the Rings* (L 201). As Tolkien explains the implications
of angelic embodiment, "by 'incarnate' I mean they were embodied in physical
bodies capable of pain, and weariness, and of afflicting the spirit with physical
fear, and of being 'killed,' though supported by the angelic spirit they might

---

70   As it is put in the *Ainulindalë*: "Now the Valar took to themselves shape and hue; and because
they were drawn into the World by love of the Children of Ilúvatar, for whom they hoped, they took
shape after that manner which they had beheld in the Vision of Ilúvatar, save only in majesty and
splendour. Moreover their shape comes of their knowledge of the visible World, rather than of the
World itself; and they need it not, save only as we use raiment, and yet we may be naked and suffer no
loss of our being. Therefore the Valar may walk, if they will, unclad, and then even the Eldar cannot
clearly perceive them, though they be present. But when they desire to clothe themselves the Valar
take upon them forms some as of male and some as of female; for that difference of temper they had
even from the beginning, and it is but bodied forth in the choice of each, not made by the choice,
even as with us male and female may be shown by the raiment but is not made thereby" (S 24). The
voluntary incarnation of the Valar is a recurring theme in Tolkien's *Letters*: see L 235, 284–85, and 411.

71   See the preceding footnote and also L 284–85.

72   See also L 202–3.

endure long, and only show slowly the wearing of care and labour" (L 202).[73] The individual Valar who goes the furthest down the path of incarnating himself in the world is Melkor, whose attachment to physical matter is so complete as to make it "permanent," a fact that makes his later removal from the world nothing less than a form of death or "execution" (MR 394–95 and 399–400). Tolkien's conception of the Valar's sub-creative power, therefore, is more complex and dynamic than simple and static: the more they invest themselves into the material shaping and making of the world, the more power or influence they wield over it, and yet the less power they retain in and for themselves, and thus the more like the conventional governing angels theorized about by St. Thomas they become. Thus, describing the state of the Valar in later days, Tolkien writes that they "are as we should say angelic powers, whose function is to exercise delegated authority in their spheres (of rule and government, *not* creation, making, or re-making)" (L 146, emphasis original), and elsewhere Tolkien writes: "The Valar 'fade' and become more impotent, precisely in proportion as the shape and constitution of things becomes more defined and settled" (MR 401).[74] In this, Tolkien's imagination would appear to be governed by yet another Thomistic metaphysical principle, which is that, the more organization, actuality, determination, or form a given matter receives, the less potentiality there remains in it to become actualized in other ways.[75] Like the Elves who over the course of Middle-earth's history must fade and so make way for the age of Men, so Tolkien's demiurgic Valar, who initially are equivalent to the gods of pagan mythology, likewise fade into the conventional angels known in the Christian era.

Despite their attachment to the physical world, the angelic spirits' relationship to their bodies, and thus to the physical world as a whole, still remains a

---

73 In *The Silmarillion* it is told how the Maiar Melian, after falling in love with the Elf-lord Thingol, became so "bound by the chain and trammels of the flesh of Arda" that she bore him a daughter, Lúthien Tinúviel. At the same time, Melian's greater association with the physical world also meant for her a greater "power over the substance of Arda" (S 234).

74 As Tolkien continues in the same place: "The longer the Past, the more nearly defined the Future, and the less room for important change (untrammeled action, on a physical plane, that is not destructive in purpose). The Past, once 'achieved,' has become part of the 'Music in being.' Only Eru may or can alter the 'Music'.… The Valar were like architects working with a plan 'passed' by the Government. They became less and less important (structurally!) as the plan was more and more nearly achieved. Even in the First Age we see them after uncounted ages of work near the end of their time of work — not wisdom or counsel. (The wiser they became the less power they had to *do* anything — save by counsel)" (MR 401–5). Here we see a further dimension of the sacrifice involved in the Valar's choice to enter the world and shape it and govern it for its own good. Perhaps the clearest expression of Tolkien's view of the sub-creational task in sacrificial terms appears in the Valar Yavanna's statement that "even for those who are mightiest under Ilúvatar there is some work that they may accomplish once, and once only" (S 78).

75 On this principle in St. Thomas, see Pasnau and Shields, *The Philosophy of Aquinas*, 157.

fundamentally dualistic one. As we have seen, Tolkien likens the relationship between the Valar and their bodies to that between human beings and their clothes, a metaphor Plato also used in his account of the human soul's relationship to the body.[76] For Tolkien, however, one interesting implication of the dualism of angelic incarnation is the resultant temptation or proclivity they have towards the domination of other beings. As Tolkien writes in one place:

> But since in the view of this tale & mythology, Power — when it dominates or seeks to dominate other wills and minds (except by the assent of their reason) — is evil, these "wizards" were incarnated in the life-forms of Middle-earth, and so suffered the pains both of mind and body. They were also, *for the same reason*, thus involved in the peril of the incarnate: the possibility of "fall," of sin, if you will. The chief form this would take with them would be impatience, leading to the desire to force others to their own good ends, and so inevitably at last to mere desire to make their own wills effective by any means. To this evil Saruman succumbed. Gandalf did not. (L 237, emphasis added)

In another letter, Tolkien writes of the wizards Saruman and Gandalf that, although angelic, spiritual beings in themselves, "being incarnate [they] were *more likely* to stray, or err," and that it was because of his "far greater inner power" in comparison to his companions that Gandalf's self-sacrifice on the Bridge of Kazad-dum was a true "humbling and abnegation" (L 202, emphasis added).[77] Similar to the physical matter that the angelic spirits do not and cannot control directly, other free rational beings are not — or at least ought not to be — subjected to their dominating will. Rather, these spirits' influence over others must involve the same kind of sub-creative patience that moves their subordinates to action, not by coercion, but by persuasion, a responsibility they share with Thomas's angels, who, he says, cannot directly or violently move another creature's will, but can nevertheless "incline the will to the love of the creature or of God, by

---

76 See, for example, *Phaedo* 87b.

77 A little later in the same letter, Tolkien again writes of the "temptation" of Gandalf's incarnate being: "But if it is 'cheating' to treat [Gandalf's] 'death' as making no difference, embodiment must not be ignored. Gandalf may be enhanced in power (that is, under the forms of this fable, in sanctity), but if still embodied he must still suffer care and anxiety, and the needs of flesh. He has no more (if no less) certitudes, or freedoms, than say a living theologian. In any case none of my 'angelic' persons are represented as knowing the future completely, or indeed at all where other *wills* are concerned. Hence their constant temptation to do, or try to do, what is for them *wrong* (and disastrous): to force lesser wills by power: by awe if not by actual fear, or physical constraint" (L 203).

way of persuasion" (ST 1.106.2).[78] Nevertheless, because their embodiment is not natural but voluntary and therefore provisional or conditional, requiring that they lay aside some of their own native powers, it is possible to see Tolkien as recognizing a sense in which the incarnate angels must of necessity have a much more artificial, extrinsic and utilitarian or pragmatic relationship to their bodies than is the case for Men and Elves, as we will see more fully below. In short, the angelic body is, for the angelic spirits, ultimately a kind of "machine," a form of technology and therefore a mere tool to be used rather than part of their fundamental nature and identity.[79] As the demiurgic sub-creators and masters of their own bodies to which they do not belong by nature, the temptation for the Valar and Maiar, Tolkien almost seems to suggest, will be for them to adopt the same attitude of mastery and domination towards others and towards the physical world they are supposed to shepherd.

If so, in this oblique manner Tolkien touches on something his contemporary, Thomist Jacques Maritain, had criticized in terms of the "angelism" of Cartesian mind-body dualism, regarded by many as having helped lay the philosophical foundations for modern scientism, industrialism, and technocracy — the very developments, in other words, that Tolkien so deplored and from whose evils his fiction was meant to provide some measure of "escape."[80] In his effort to advance human mastery over nature, Descartes radically re-conceived the relationship between the human mind and body, arguing that these represented two completely distinct and isolatable substances corresponding to two completely distinct, irreducible, and independent realities. Descartes famously expressed this dualism thus in his *Discourse on Method*: "I knew that I was a substance the whole essence or nature of which was merely to think, and which, in order

78 Of the Istari Tolkien similarly writes that the mission they were "primarily sent for" was to "train, advise, instruct, arouse the hearts and minds of those threatened by Sauron to a resistance with their own strengths; and not just to do the job for them" (L 202).

79 We perhaps see something of the artificial nature of angelic incarnation, incidentally, in the immediate degeneration of the "angel" Saruman's body after he is "killed" at the end of *The Return of the King*. As Tom Shippey writes, "the body that is left once the 'mist' and the 'smoke' have departed seems in fact to have died many years before, becoming only 'rags of skin upon a hideous skull.'" Shippey, *J.R.R. Tolkien: Author of the Century*, 127. With the departure of Saruman's spirit, in other words, his body is revealed for the tool or instrument that it was and had become.

80 As Fergus Kerr summarizes Maritain's critique: "The 'sin' of Descartes is a 'sin of angelism.' By this Maritain means that Descartes conceived human thought on the model of angelic thought: thought was now regarded as intuitive, and thus freed from the burden of discursive reasoning; innate, as to its origins, and thus independent of material things. What this 'angelist psychology' introduces is nothing less than a revolution in the very idea of mind, and thus of intelligibility, scientific understanding and explanation." Kerr, *After Aquinas: Versions of Thomism*, 24.

to exist, needed no place and depended on no material thing."[81] In freeing the
mind from its involvement or rootedness in the world, thereby allowing it to see
its own body as a kind of machine at its disposal, Descartes is plausibly credited
by some with having uniquely situated the modern subject to assert itself in an
unprecedented manner, both theoretically and practically, over the natural
world. As Maritain's charge of "angelism" is meant to suggest, however, from
a Thomistic standpoint, what Descartes did, of course, was effectively substitute
a properly angelic psychology and epistemology, which do not require a body,
for a properly human one, which does.

If Tolkien's hypothesis of non-naturally but voluntarily incarnate angelic
beings captures something of both the "freedom" but also the problematic
character of modern mind-body dualism, his fictional anthropology of Elves
and Men, by contrast, seems intent on hearkening back to the hylomorphic
theory of the relationship between the body and soul advocated by Aristotle
and Aquinas.[82] According to this tradition, the human soul is not extrinsically
related to the body, as per the soul-body dualism of Plato and Descartes, but is
the formal, final, and efficient cause of the human body, the form and actuality
through which, by which, and for which the body has its very being *as a body*
(ST 1.76.1).[83] According to both St. Thomas and Tolkien, for example, the soul
(or what the Elves call "*fëa*"), while incorporeal and incorruptible in itself and
thus capable of existing apart from the body (the "*hröa*"), nevertheless does not
constitute the whole of man and is even dependent upon the body to carry out its
own proper act of knowing through the senses and imagination.[84] Like Thomas,

---

81 Descartes, *Discourse on Method and Meditations on First Philosophy,* trans. Cress, 18.

82 For a somewhat underdeveloped reflection on Tolkien's anthropology in light of St. Thomas's
philosophy of man alternative to the one I am offering here, see Nimmo, "Tolkien and Thomism:
Middle-earth and the States of Nature," discussed on p. 10.

83 For Aristotle's hylomorphic doctrine of the soul, see book two of his *On the Soul.* For an
explanation and defense of Thomas's hylomorphic anthropology in light of some of its contemporary
criticisms, see Klima, "Man = Body + Soul: Aquinas's Arithmetic of Human Nature."

84 Although Tolkien says in one note that *hröa* and *fëa* are "roughly but not exactly equivalent
to 'body' and 'soul'" (MR 330), he does not exactly specify how they are different, and elsewhere he
simply asserts that *fëa* "corresponds, more or less, to 'soul'; and to 'mind'" in its immaterial aspects
(MR 349). On the incorporeality and incorruptibility of the soul in Thomas and Tolkien, see ST 1.75.2
and MR 223, 245, and 330. For Thomas's arguments on the soul not constituting the whole of man
and depending upon the body for the operation of the senses, see ST 1.75.2 and 1.84.7. As for Tolkien,
he writes that, when a man receives an injury it is not merely the soul-principle, the "Indweller,"
that suffers the wound, but "Man, the whole: house, life, and master" (MR 353). According to
Tolkien, the soul is the principle of "identity" (227), being both "conscious" and "self-aware," yet
he also adamantly affirms the body to constitute part of the "self" of the person (349). Although
it is the soul that has "the impulse and power to think: enquire and reflect," its mental processes,
like Thomas's incarnate soul, are nevertheless "conditioned and limited by the co-operation of the

Tolkien in his mythology expressly rejects Platonic dualism in favor of a view of the soul as "indwelling," "cohering with" (MR 218), and generally "desiring to inhabit" its body (MR 243).[85] Perhaps more intriguingly still, however, is the common hylomorphism implied in Tolkien's account of the differences that otherwise obtain between Men and Elves. What gives Elves their immortality or, more properly speaking, their "serial longevity" (the natural Elvish life being limited only by the lifespan of the Earth, MR 331), is the greater power or strength their souls exercise over their bodies. As a more powerful bodily *form*, in other words, the Elvish soul exercises a greater degree of "command," "control," or "mastery," as Tolkien variously puts it, over its matter, the body (MR 211, 218, 233, 331, and 334).[86] The result is that the Elvish soul is capable of keeping its body indefinitely alive (provided it is not catastrophically injured), strong, and in good health (MR 427), not to mention "by nature continent and steadfast" (MR 211–13).[87] So great is the attachment of the Elvish soul to bodily existence that, if it should be killed, its natural lot — at least according to Tolkien's original but later abandoned idea of Elvish reincarnation — is for it eventually to consent to being born again through natural childbirth, though

---

physical organs" of the body (ibid.).

85 In the *Athrabeth*, Andreth emphatically denies that the body is a mere "inn" that the soul dwells in, as this would suggest "contempt of the body." And while she does, like Plato, refer to the body as a "raiment," she suggests that we should not only speak of the "raiment being fitted to the wearer," but also "of the wearer being fitted to the raiment" (MR 317). St. Thomas, by comparison, criticizes Plato for his view that man was merely an *anima utens corpora*, a "soul making use of a body" (ST 1.75.4). On the soul's "desire to inhabit" its body, consider also the "Doom" pronounced on the Noldor Elves in *The Silmarillion*: "For though Eru appointed to you to die not in Eä, and no sickness may assail you, yet slain ye may be, and slain ye shall be: by weapon and by torment and by grief; and your houseless spirits shall come then to Mandos. There long shall ye abide and *yearn for your bodies*, and find little pity though all whom ye have slain should entreat for you" (S 88, emphasis added).

86 As Ralph Wood has observed in the case of Tolkien's fictional race of Men, "Only men can reunite what Melkor divided in death because they alone, among Ilúvatar's creatures, have souls that can virtually divinize their bodies and thus keep them in perpetual undying life. As Aquinas taught, the souls of men give their bodies their true form, their real existence." Wood, *Gospel According to Tolkien*, 160. Related to this, in another passage Tolkien writes of the Elvish body being "modified by the indwelling *fëa*" or soul (MR 337).

87 As Tolkien writes at some length of the Elvish physiognomy in one place: "They were thus capable of far greater and longer physical exertions (in pursuit of some dominant purpose of their minds) without weariness; they were not subject to diseases; they healed rapidly and completely after injuries that would have proved fatal to Men; and they could endure great physical pain for long periods. Their bodies could not, however, survive vital injuries, or violent assaults upon their structure; nor replace missing members (such as a hand hewn off). On the reverse side: the Elves could die, and did die, by their will; as for example because of great grief or bereavement, or because of the frustration of their dominant desires and purposes. This willful death was not regarded as wicked, but it was a fault implying some defect or taint in the *fëa,* and those who came to Mandos by this means might be refused further incarnate life" (MR 341).

the soul's "memory" of its former body and power over its new body would be so great that over time it would impress upon its new body the same physical appearance as the old (MR 233). It is in this formative power of the Elvish soul over the body, moreover, that Tolkien would eventually find the solution to the problem he, again like St. Thomas, came to see in the idea of reincarnation, namely that the reborn body would still seem to be a *different* body — and there- fore the reborn *person* a different person — from the one that existed before.[88] Instead of reincarnation having to take place through a second physical birth, therefore, why could not the powerful Elvish soul simply fashion for itself (albeit with divine and angelic assistance) and thus *in*form directly its new body? In this way Tolkien's idea of Elvish reincarnation gradually morphed into a more Catholically and Thomistically acceptable case of what Tolkien himself refers to in one place as Elvish "resurrection."[89]

---

88 It was Tolkien's conceit of reincarnate Elves, we may recall from chapter two, that had particularly offended Peter Hastings's Catholic sensibilities and prompted him to write Tolkien to ask if the latter had not in fact "over-stepped the mark in metaphysical matters" (L 187). Tolkien at that time had responded, as we have seen, by asserting that Elvish reincarnation, even if it were "bad *theology*," was nevertheless not bad "metaphysics," since he did "not see how even in the Primary World any theologian or philosopher, unless very much better informed about the relation of spirit and body than I believe anyone to be, could deny the *possibility* of re-incarnation as a mode of exis- tence, prescribed for certain kinds of rational incarnate creatures" (L 189, emphasis original). From a Thomistic standpoint this is an extravagant claim, for in chapter 153 of his *Compendium Theologiae*, for example, Thomas argues that, because the soul is united to its body as its form, meaning that the body is proper to the soul as its matter, in order for the soul to be embodied a second time, it must be united to the numerically same body as before, making its reincarnation in a different body impossible. (On Thomas's critique of reincarnation, see George, "Aquinas on Reincarnation.")

Eventually, however, Tolkien's tacit Thomism seems to have got the better of him, for, despite the confidence of his reply to Hastings, Tolkien shortly thereafter began entertaining his own grave doubts as to the feasibility of Elvish reincarnation. As his son Christopher observes, his father came to see the idea of Elvish reincarnation as "a serious flaw in the metaphysic of Elvish existence" (MR 363). His father himself wrote that the idea "contradicts the fundamental notion that *fëa* and *hröa* were each fitted to the other," whereas the reincarnate body, having different parents, presumably would not be the same but a different body, and therefore a grievance to the reborn Elvish soul (ibid.). In a passage cited by Christopher in *The Peoples of Middle-earth*, Tolkien even goes so far as to claim that the now abandoned belief in Elvish reincarnation was "a false notion, e.g. probably of Mannish origin" (390n17). One solution entertained by Tolkien, as mentioned earlier, was the notion that the Elvish soul or spirit, rather than being re-embodied through natural child-birth, was instead given a new body by the Valar under Eru's guidance and permission, yet a body still "of the same form and shape" as it possessed previously (MR 339, 362, and 364). Tolkien seems, however, to have come to regard even this solution as untenable, as he went on to entertain the further possibility that "the 'houseless' *fëa* was itself allowed (being instructed) to rebuild its *hröa* from its memory...," a process Tolkien described as nothing less than "the resurrection of the body" (MR 364). On Tolkien's developing views on Elvish reincarnation, see Devaux, "Elves: Reincarnation," in Drout, ed., *J.R.R.T. Encyclopedia*, 154–55; idem, *Tolkien, l'effigie des elfes*; and Flieger, "The Curious Incident of the Dream at the Barrow: Memory and Reincarnation in Middle-earth."

89 According to St. Thomas, however, in order for the resurrected body to be the same body,

In addition to its role in first preserving and later reconstructing the body, and, like the Valar, whose sub-creative capacity is a function of their peculiar regard for and relationship with the physical world, another consequence of the greater command of the Elvish soul over its body is the greater artistic control and execution Elves enjoy in comparison with Men: "Their 'magic' is Art, delivered from many of its human limitations: more effortless, more quick, more complete (product, and vision in unflawed correspondence)" (L 146).[90] Both Elvish art and biological longevity, in short, are co-effects of a common cause, namely the soul-as-form's dominion over matter. In the figure of his Elves, accordingly, Tolkien treats us, even if unwittingly, to a rather creative depiction of the analogy St. Thomas, for example, observes in Aristotle when he writes that "the soul is compared to the body as art to the thing made by art" (ST 3.80.1). Through his semi-scholastic, Aristotelian anthropology, in summary, Tolkien not only attempts to return his readers to and so help us to "recover" a proper understanding of human nature as a true union and mutual belongingness of body and soul, but he also imaginatively links two of the central themes of his mythology — the question of creaturely sub-creation on the one hand, and the perplexing question of human mortality on the other — revealing them to be in a very real sense one and the same problem.[91]

---

the same prime matter must be used. As Marie George points out, however, St. Thomas seems not to have been entirely consistent in his adherence to this principle, for in some places he "seems to say that any suitable matter to which the soul could be united would constitute the same body. He acknowledges that the matter constituting the body changes during one's lifetime, and this without prejudice to one's individuality [*SCG* IV, c. 81]. Thus it is puzzling that he would hold that one would need (some of) the matter that had actually constituted one's body in order to have the same body, when new matter, so long as it is of the appropriate sort, would seem to do just as well." George, "Aquinas on Reincarnation," 43–44.

90 Tolkien also touches upon the relationship between Elvish immortality and artistry when he writes that "the Elvish *fëa* was above all designed to make things in co-operation with its *hröa*" (MR 332).

91 Other possible points of comparison between Tolkien's Valar and Thomas's angels might be mentioned here. Tolkien, for example, makes a remark in one letter that "the Valar had no language of their own, not needing one" (L 282), whereas Thomas argues that there is indeed a kind of "speech" among the angels (ST 1.107). (On the language or speech of the Ainur, see Flieger, *Splintered Light*, 61–62, and for a treatment of Thomas's teaching concerning angelic speech, see Goris, "The Angelic Doctor and Angelic Speech: The Development of Thomas Aquinas's Thought on How Angels Communicate.") Also consistent with St. Thomas is Tolkien's insistence that, for all their sub-creative power, the Valar cannot perform miracles, this being something the creator alone can do, indicating that even in their sub-creative capacity the Valar are very much a part of the natural order (L 151, 194, 204, 235, and 411; ST 1.110.4). Finally, there is Tolkien's agreement with Thomas that angels cannot know the mind of another being without the assent of its will (ST 1.57.4, "Whether Angels Know Secret Thoughts"; see also ST 1.111.2). As Tolkien stipulates: "No one, not even one of the Valar, can read the mind of other 'equal beings': that is one cannot 'see' them or comprehend them fully and directly by simple inspection. One can *deduce* much of their thought, from general comparisons leading to conclusions concerning the nature and tendencies of minds and thought, and from particular knowledge of individuals, and special circumstances. But this is

Conclusion

TO CONCLUDE, THEN, IN ADDITION TO THEIR EXEMPLIFYING
something of the "beauty, power, and majesty of the 'gods' of higher mythology"
(L 146), as well as their mythical idealization of Tolkien's Thomistic metaphysics
of sub-creative free will, I have suggested that Tolkien's Valar, together with his
Elves, exhibit a kind of medieval and Thomistic occupation with the question
of "hypothetical psychologies,"[92] not only in terms of their absolute theoretical
possibility, but also in terms of their potential for anthropological illumination.
Similar to Thomas's angelology and anthropology, moreover, Tolkien's reflections
on his Valaric and Elvish creatures are at once deeply rational and metaphysical.
This is not to say, as we have seen, that Tolkien's sub-creative angels, any more
than his reincarnating Elves, have any real counterpart or place in St. Thomas's
own celestial and terrestrial hierarchy — quite the contrary. It is, however, to
suggest that we may better understand both the originality and the intelligibility
of Tolkien's fictional creatures if we see them as presupposing at once both the
boundaries and also the inquisitive spirit of St. Thomas's angelological speculation by pushing beyond those boundaries and imaginatively filling in those
theoretical gaps left open and unexplored in Thomas's great chain of being. As
we shall see in the next chapter, this same traditional and Thomistic hierarchy
of created being, which provided Tolkien with a framework for defining his
fictional creatures, also helped him to structure his equally complex and nuanced
metaphysics of evil.

---

no more reading or inspection of another mind than is deduction concerning the contents of a
closed room, or events taken place out of sight. Neither is so-called 'thought-transference' a process
of mind-reading: this is but the reception, and interpretation by the receiving mind, of the impact
of a thought, or thought-pattern, emanating from another mind, which is no more the mind in
full or in itself than is the distant sight of a man running the man himself. Minds can exhibit or
reveal themselves to other minds by the action of their own wills (though it is doubtful if, even when
willing or desiring this, a mind can actually reveal itself wholly to any other mind)" (MR 398–99).
    92 Wicksteed, *Dante and Aquinas,* 153.

FIVE

The Metaphysics of Melkor

*But being alone [Melkor] had begun to conceive
thoughts of his own unlike those of his brethren.*

Introduction

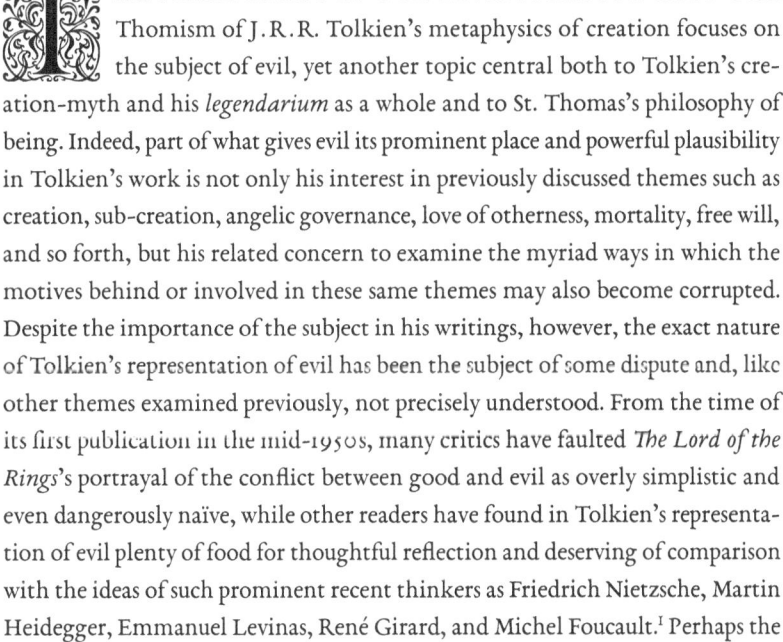

HE FINAL STUDY IN OUR INVESTIGATION INTO THE
Thomism of J. R. R. Tolkien's metaphysics of creation focuses on
the subject of evil, yet another topic central both to Tolkien's creation-myth and his *legendarium* as a whole and to St. Thomas's philosophy of
being. Indeed, part of what gives evil its prominent place and powerful plausibility
in Tolkien's work is not only his interest in previously discussed themes such as
creation, sub-creation, angelic governance, love of otherness, mortality, free will,
and so forth, but his related concern to examine the myriad ways in which the
motives behind or involved in these same themes may also become corrupted.
Despite the importance of the subject in his writings, however, the exact nature
of Tolkien's representation of evil has been the subject of some dispute and, like
other themes examined previously, not precisely understood. From the time of
its first publication in the mid-1950s, many critics have faulted *The Lord of the
Rings*'s portrayal of the conflict between good and evil as overly simplistic and
even dangerously naïve, while other readers have found in Tolkien's representation of evil plenty of food for thoughtful reflection and deserving of comparison
with the ideas of such prominent recent thinkers as Friedrich Nietzsche, Martin
Heidegger, Emmanuel Levinas, René Girard, and Michel Foucault.[1] Perhaps the

---

1 As Tolkien commented in 1954 on the response of some readers to *The Lord of the Rings*,
"Some reviewers have called the whole thing simple-minded, just a plain fight between Good and
Evil, with all the good just good, and the bad just bad. Pardonable, perhaps…" (L 197). On Tolkien
and Foucault, see Chance, *The Lord of the Rings: The Mythology of Power*. On Tolkien and Levinas,
see Eaglestone, "Invisibility," and on Tolkien and Girard, see Head, "Imitative Desire in Tolkien's
Mythology: A Girardian Perspective," both of which are discussed below. On Tolkien and Heidegger, see Malpas, "Home," which considers Tolkien in light of Heidegger's technology-essay and his

most important philosophical debate concerning Tolkien's depiction of evil, however, centers on his relationship not to recent but to very ancient theories of evil. Of particular note is the evident Christian Neoplatonism readers have found Tolkien to share with such eminent thinkers as St. Augustine, Boethius, and St. Thomas, according to whom everything is good to the extent that it exists, so that evil, as the privation of the good, is also the privation of being. On the other hand, Tolkien scholar Tom Shippey has argued that Tolkien's philosophy of evil, as a consequence of his personal effort to come to grips with uniquely modern forms of evil, especially the threats of modern fascism and industrialized warfare, syncretistically combines Neoplatonic monism with its historically contrary position of Manichaean dualism, according to which evil is not a mere absence of being, but is an independently existing force in its own right.

It is chiefly with reference to these two positions that I will compare in this chapter the respective "ponerologies" (the branch of theology dealing with evil, from the Greek word *poneros*, meaning *evil*) of Tolkien and St. Thomas. As we have seen in previous chapters, Tolkien's view of being (of which evil is a privation) is no generic metaphysics, but holds much in common with the specifically Christian and creational metaphysics developed by St. Thomas, according to whom being is not some necessary, impersonal, and highly medi-ated emanative surplus (as per classical and later Islamic Neoplatonism), but a voluntary gift immediately bestowed by an ever-personal God. As I will show in this chapter, it is this unique concept of being that, first, provides the logical structure or coherence to what I argue is for Tolkien a kind of hierarchy of evil, and second (and more paradoxically), that helps at the same time to underwrite rather than contradict the otherwise extreme power and seeming Manichaean independence of evil in Tolkien's mythology, even while allowing Tolkien to reduce this same evil to nothing.

Tolkienian Evil
NEOPLATONIC, MANICHAEAN, OR AUGUSTINIAN?

"IN MY STORY," TOLKIEN UNEQUIVOCALLY WRITES IN ONE letter, "I do not deal in Absolute Evil. I do not think there is such a thing, since that is Zero. I do not think that at any rate any 'rational being' is wholly

---

famous lectures on the poetry of Friedrich Hölderlin. For comparisons of Tolkien and Nietzsche, see Blount, "*Über*hobbits: Tolkien, Nietzsche, and the Will to Power" and Candler, "Tolkien or Nietzsche, Philology and Nihilism."

evil" (L 243).[2] Similarly, in his letter to Peter Hastings, Tolkien contradicts the latter's claim that anything Sauron made "could not have a tendency to good, even a very small one," countering instead that in the Creator's "accepting or tolerating [Sauron's] making—necessary to their actual existence—even Orcs would become part of the World, which is God's and ultimately good" (L 195). In passages such as these, Tolkien may be seen clearly to align himself with the classic Augustinian and Platonic tradition, according to which evil "exists" as a privation of being and consequently as a non-entity in its own right. The Neoplatonist philosopher Plotinus, for example, whose writings had an enormous influence on Augustine's thought, in his *Enneads* makes the characteristic statement that "evil cannot be included in what really exists or in what is beyond existence; for these are good. So it remains that, if evil exists, it must be among non-existent things, as a sort of form of non-existence."[3] While there nevertheless remained certain dualistic tendencies even in Plotinus, as when he sometimes attributes to matter, for example, which for him was the very last emanation from the One and so barely above utter non-being, the primary causation of evil,[4] the overall trajectory in Neoplatonism was nevertheless to reduce as much as possible the ontological status of evil to that of a mere privation of being or existence.

Moving in the near opposite direction to this impetus, on the other hand, was Plotinus's Persian contemporary by the name of Mani, who founded in the middle of the third century the Gnostic religion that came to bear his name. In contrast to both Neoplatonism and Judeo-Christian monotheism (which Mani was raised under), Manichaeism posited a radical dualism according to which good and evil were two equal and equipotent forces in the universe at war with each other. One scholar writes:

> To explain how the intermingling of good and evil took place before the creation of mankind, Mani developed an elaborate and polytheistic cosmogonic myth of a primeval invasion of the Kingdom of Light by the forces of Darkness. The former is ruled over by the Father of Greatness who is the epitome of all that is good, beautiful and honourable and his realm

---

2 Perhaps the closest Tolkien comes in his fiction *per se* to making this kind of claim is Elrond's statement at the Great Council, in regard to Sauron, that "nothing is evil in the beginning" (FOTR 281).

3 Plotinus, *Enneads* 1.8.3, trans. Armstrong.

4 See, for example, ibid. 1.8.3, 6–7, and 5.1.1 and O'Brien, "Plotinus on Matter and Evil," 183–87. On Plotinus's view that the soul is made free from evil by being made free from the material body, see Plotinus, *Enneads* 1.8.3–5 and Elders, *The Metaphysics of Being,* 125. For an effort at reconciling this tension in Plotinus's thought (between viewing evil as non-being and viewing matter as evil), see O'Brien, "Plotinus on Matter and Evil."

is completely insulated from the horrors of war and suffering.... The latter
is the dominion of the Prince of Darkness, who is depicted as a multiform
monster and whose infernal kingdom is characterized by concupiscence
and strife. As the Kingdom of Light is not equipped for war, not even
for its own self-defence, its ruler has to evoke other deities to fulfill this
unaccustomed role.[5]

In the origin myth of Manichaeism, accordingly, the physical cosmos is at once
the product and principal site of this cosmic strife between the Kingdoms of
Good and Evil, Light and Darkness, a conflict in which Light has been partially
imprisoned by Matter in the physical universe but may become freed by those
who, illumined by Mani's *gnosis*, practice virtue and avoid those actions that
contribute to Evil's dominion over the Light.[6]

As for Augustine, before his conversion to Christianity, he, too, had been
attracted to this dualistic account of evil. Eventually, however, through his readings in the "books of the Platonists," he was persuaded of the privation theory
of evil as taught by Plotinus and he rejected the Manichaean account of God as
limited and capable of suffering persecution by the Kingdom of Darkness. As he
would later come to write in his *City of God*, "there is no such entity in nature as
'evil'; 'evil' is merely a name for the privation of good."[7] The Christian doctrine
of creation, moreover, further led him (and here unlike Neoplatonism) to see
even matter as the deliberate creation and thus gift of an all-good and all-wise
God. Thus, Augustine was moved to reduce more completely, than, say, even
Plato did, the question of evil to the psychological question of moral evil or sin
in the individual soul.[8] At the same time, Augustine was also led to introduce
an altogether new mystery that would occupy later thinkers such as Aquinas: if
evil is nothing, it cannot have a cause; yet how can individual evil wills, which
are themselves the cause of all evil, themselves be uncaused?[9]

As for Tolkien's own relationship to this spectrum of historical positions
on the metaphysics of evil, John Houghton and Neal Keesee have documented
how readers realized early on that his portrayal of evil in *The Lord of the Rings*
clearly belongs to a wider and older philosophical tradition. Rose Zimbardo,

5 Lieu, "Christianity and Manichaeism," 282–83.

6 Ibid., 284.

7 Augustine, *City of God* 11.23, trans. Bettenson. Boethius similarly writes: "evil is nothing, since
God, who can do all things, cannot do evil." Boethius, *Consolation of Philosophy*, trans. Watts, 72.

8 Steel, "Does Evil Have a Cause?," 256.

9 Ibid. On Augustine versus Aquinas on the causality of evil, see also John Milbank, "Evil:
Darkness and Silence," 21.

for example, had already remarked in 1969 that, "as in St. Augustine's, so in Tolkien's vision, nothing is created evil. Evil is good that has been perverted,"[10] and in the following year Clyde Kilby observed that, in regard to Tolkien's work, "we can mention the inability of evil to create anything but only to mock.... Philosophers and theologians have often noted the inessentiality of evil."[11] To this testimony, finally, might be added Paul Kocher's remarks, in 1972, in which he connected Tolkien's ponerology with Aquinas in particular:

> Some of Thomas' less specifically Christian propositions about the nature of evil seem highly congruent with those which Tolkien expresses or implies in laymen's terms in *The Lord of the Rings*.... Literally and figuratively, light is exchanged for darkness. Sauron's every change is a deterioration from those good and healthy norms with which he began. Aquinas would call them all losses of Being. Evil is not a thing in itself but a lessening of the Being inherent in the created order.... [T]he losses cry out for ontological interpretation.... Over and over Tolkien's own words connect Sauron and his servants with a nothingness that is the philosophical opposite of Being.[12]

Since these commentators first penned their remarks, moreover, many readers and critics have continued to locate Tolkien's representation of evil in his fiction within the broadly Augustinian tradition according to which evil, as the privation of the good, is also a privation of being and therefore something lacking any real substance or existence in its own right.

More recently, however, eminent Tolkien scholar Tom Shippey has significantly altered the discussion of Tolkien's account of evil by arguing, on the contrary, that it is precisely the Augustinian reduction of evil to a sheer nothingness and therefore (in his view) to an almost illusory status that makes it ultimately an inadequate account of all that Tolkien has to say on the subject. Thus, despite Tolkien's clear disavowal of the existence of an "absolute evil," Shippey has compellingly argued that Tolkien also presents in his fiction an ambiguous, even contradictory, vision of evil, one that holds in deliberate tension, on the

---

10 Houghton and Keesee, "Tolkien, King Alfred, and Boethius: Platonist Views of Evil in *The Lord of the Rings*," 131, citing Zimbardo, "Moral Vision in *The Lord of the Rings*," 73.

11 Houghton and Keesee, "Tolkien, King Alfred, and Boethius," 151n1, citing John Warwick Montgomery, ed., *Myth, Allegory and Gospel: An Interpretation of J.R.R. Tolkien, C.S. Lewis, G.K. Chesterton and Charles Williams* (Minneapolis: Bethany Fellowship, 1974), 138.

12 Kocher, *Master of Middle-earth: The Fiction of J.R.R. Tolkien*, 77–79.

one hand, an Augustinian or "Boethian" monism, wherein evil is reduced to a
form of relative non-being; and on the other hand a "Manichaean" dualism,
according to which evil is more than non-being, but a positive, ontological
force in its own right, coequal and equipotent with the good. Shippey attributes
this complex portrayal of evil, moreover, to Tolkien's desire, like that of many
of his fellow authors of the twentieth century,

> to explain something at once deeply felt and rationally inexplicable, some-
> thing furthermore felt to be entirely novel and not adequately answered
> by the moralities of earlier ages (keen medievalists though several of these
> authors were).... [T]his "something" is connected with the distinctively
> twentieth-century experience of industrial war and impersonal, indus-
> trialized massacre…an unshakable conviction of something wrong,
> something irreducibly evil in the nature of humanity, but without any
> very satisfactory explanation for it....Twentieth-century fantasy can be
> seen as above all a response to this gap, this inadequacy. One has to ask
> in what ways Tolkien's images are original, individual, and in what ways
> typical, recognizable.[13]

According to Shippey, the way in which Tolkien achieves this balance of
novelty and traditionalism is by setting up a "running ambivalence" throughout
his *legendarium* that is "at once orthodox and questioning to the whole problem
of the existence and source of evil."[14] As evidence of Tolkien's more Boethian
instincts, Shippey cites Frodo's remark to Sam in *The Two Towers* that evil cannot
create or even make "new things of its own," and, even more discerningly, the
Orc Gorbag's statement in the same chapter that abandoning one's friends was
a "regular elvish trick," a statement implying the recognition of an absolute,
overarching moral order.[15] On the other hand, Shippey sees a latent dualism
or "Manichaeism" in certain aspects of Tolkien's portrayal of evil. Whereas on
the Boethian view, as Shippey interprets it, evil is primarily "internal, caused by
human sin and weakness and alienation from God," in his more Manichaean
moments Tolkien represents evil as an objective, "external" force. Two examples
Shippey notes are Tolkien's depiction of, first, the Ring as a thing evil in and of
itself, and second, those moments in the story when Frodo's will feels the Ring
beating down upon him as a force coming from without, as in the climactic

13 Shippey, *J.R.R. Tolkien: Author of the Century*, 120–21.
14 Ibid., 130.
15 Ibid., 131–33.

Sammath Naur scene toward the end of *The Return of the King*. In representing evil as having a certain ontological independence, Shippey summarizes, Tolkien's intention is not so much to flirt with heresy as it is to express an empirical fact about the universe and human experience, a fact Shippey believes to be unaccounted for in a one-sidedly Boethian perspective on evil.[16]

Shippey's dualistic reading has met both criticism and approval from other Tolkien readers. Hayden Head, for example, in his Girardian interpretation of Tolkien's ponerology, cites sympathetically Shippey's claim that "evil for Tolkien is both an absence and a presence; theologically speaking, evil is both Boethian and Manichaean."[17] Bringing the matter directly to bear on our present reading of Tolkien, Lee Oser likewise follows Shippey when he pits Tolkien's allegedly dualistic account of evil against the Augustinianism of St. Thomas:

> There are grounds to suggest that Tolkien, like C.S. Lewis, had a strong intuition of positive evil, verging on dualism. Lewis found evidence for dualism in the New Testament. He recognized the danger of Manichaeism and, while stopping short of heresy, conceded ambiguity. The same kind of metaphysical problem exists in *The Lord of the Rings*…. What is peculiarly modern in Tolkien's intuition of evil is how he differs from Aquinas with regard to the orthodox Augustinian teaching that positive evil does not exist. He is closer to Kierkegaard, to Nietzsche, and to Yeats, all of whom recognize a creative element in the conflict of psychological drives or, as Nietzsche called them, "*inspiring* spirits."[18]

Similarly, Verlyn Flieger's interpretation of Tolkien, although not dealing directly with Shippey's Manichaean-Boethian thesis, is worth mentioning here, as it gives a somewhat similar and even complementary account. Agreeing with Tolkien's biographer Humphrey Carpenter that Tolkien was a "man of antitheses," Flieger, like Shippey, attributes Tolkien's complex account of evil to significant aspects and events in Tolkien's own personality and experience, especially the death of his mother when he was still a young boy. Speaking of the tension "between belief and doubt" she finds in Tolkien's writings, Flieger writes:

16 Ibid., 141. Shippey's argument concerning Tolkien's ambivalence towards the traditional, Augustinian privation theory of evil parallels the more general critique a number of recent philosophers such as Slavoj Žižek and Jean Luc Nancy have made of the privation theory in light of the "radical evil" of the twentieth century. For an overview and response to this critique defending privation theory, see John Milbank, "Evil: Darkness and Silence."

17 Head, "Imitative Desire," 145.

18 Oser, "Enter Reason and Nature," 118–19.

They are emblematic of the poles of his emotional life. Even more, they are the boundary markers of his worlds — both the world he perceived around him and the world he created in his fiction. No careful reader of Tolkien's fiction can fail to be aware of the polarities that give it form and tension. His work is built on contrasts — between hope and despair, between good and evil, between enlightenment and ignorance — and these contrasts are embodied in the polarities of light and dark that are the creative outgrowth of his contrary moods, the "antitheses" of his nature. Carpenter describes him as a man of extreme contrasts, one who was "never moderate: love, intellectual enthusiasm, distaste, anger, self-doubt, guilt, laughter, each was in his mind exclusively and in full force when he experienced it."[19]

One place where Flieger particularly finds the "extreme contrast" of Tolkien's temperament on display is in the conflicting pessimism and optimism of his two famous essays, "Beowulf: The Monsters and the Critics" and "On Fairy-Stories," the one representing the tragic spirit of "dyscatastrophe" at one end of Tolkien's emotional spectrum, the other a spirit of hope and joy or "eucatastrophe" at the other end. Together, the two essays are "devoted to exploration of dark and light, and to affirmation of both."[20]

To return to Shippey's thesis in particular, however, while many readers, as has been said, have found it persuasive, others have not. Theologian Colin Gunton, for example, writes that he finds "somewhat more consistent a theology of evil in *The Lord of the Rings* than does Shippey," whom Gunton faults for making "the mistake of drawing too absolute a distinction between 'inner' and 'objective' evil."[21] Scott Davison has similarly repudiated Shippey's thesis in favor of a consistently Augustinian and hence anti-Manichaean reading of Tolkienian evil, according to which, in Davison's words, "the more evil something is, the more nearly it approaches nothingness."[22] John Houghton and Neal Keesee have taken a slightly different approach, arguing that the alleged tensions and ambiguities identified by Shippey in Tolkien's account of evil are

19 Flieger, *Splintered Light*, 129.

20 "Although one speaks movingly of man's defeat by 'the offspring of the dark' and the other celebrates 'the joy of deliverance,' each essay acknowledges that both light and dark are elements held in interdependent tension. The darkness that is the focus of the first passage needs the 'little circle of light' to give it meaning; the 'Joy' of the second passage is consoling only in light of the possibility of sorrow.... In the *Beowulf* essay dark heavily outweighs light; heroes go from the circle of light into the surrounding dark and down to final defeat. In the fairy-story essay, light is victorious and joy triumphs over sorrow." Ibid., 12–13.

21 Gunton, "A Far-Off Gleam of the Gospel," 140n6.

22 Davison, "Tolkien and the Nature of Evil," 102.

in fact already present in Neoplatonism, thus making the introduction of a distinctly Manichaean element unnecessary. Although Houghton and Keesee do not touch on the tendency already inherent in Platonism and Neoplatonism of viewing matter as an eternal and even necessary source of evil, they do note that the Platonic tradition recognizes that evil

> can nonetheless be both internal temptation and real external threat, leaving the evildoer both dead and alive, corrupted to the point of intangibility and yet truly dangerous, something to be *both* pitied for what it has lost *and* fought for what it is.... From Plato on, those who defend the position that Evil is nothing make consciously paradoxical, openly counter-intuitive, statements.... The Neo-Platonic tradition, then, would teach us to see evil synoptically, if paradoxically.[23]

As for the climactic Sammath Naur scene at the end of *The Return of the King* discussed by Shippey, Houghton and Keesee show how Tolkien's own interpretation of the scene in light of the sixth and seventh petitions of the Lord's Prayer ("lead us not into temptation, but deliver us from evil") belongs squarely within the tradition of Christian-Neoplatonic exegesis of this passage represented by St. Augustine and St. Thomas.[24] Houghton and Keesee conclude their study by affirming with Shippey that Tolkien does indeed offer "a complex and nuanced assessment of the nature of evil." Yet they object that "this view is not a departure from Boethius; it is consistently paradoxical rather than ambiguous or contradictory. Rooted firmly in the Neo-Platonic tradition, Tolkien...perceives evil's true nature: nothing, yet paradoxically powerful."[25]

St. Thomas, Evil, and Creation

MY OWN THESIS, TO BE DEFENDED HERE, IS THAT, LIKE HOUGHTON and Keesee and against Shippey, I too see Tolkien as presenting a consistent metaphysics of evil, but that with Shippey I think Tolkien deliberately, provocatively, and paradoxically flirts with Manichaeism far more than the one-sidedly Christian-Neoplatonic interpretations of Tolkien have hitherto allowed. In short, my argument is that Tolkien's theory of evil exhibits both a greater internal

23 Houghton and Keesee, "Tolkien, King Alfred, and Boethius," 134–38.
24 Ibid., 148–51.
25 Ibid., 151.

coherence *and* dialectical subtlety than either of these two camps have perhaps recognized, a coherence and subtlety, moreover, that I think is best accessed and elucidated in light of what we have found to be Tolkien's profoundly Thomistic metaphysics of creation.

In many respects, of course, St. Thomas's own ponerology is quite conventional in its development of an Augustinian, Neoplatonic account of evil. Thomas's discussion of evil in question 48 of the *Summa*, for example, begins familiarly enough with his denial in the first article that evil is a nature, since every nature has its attendant perfection and goodness, whereas "by the name of evil is signified a certain absence of good" (ST 1.48.1). Thomas goes on to explain in the second and third articles how evil exists in those things that have been corrupted from or fail to attain their intended goodness: the "subject" of evil is some good thing of which the evil constitutes a privation or absence of form that the subject is supposed to have (ST 1.48.3). In the fourth article, much as we saw Tolkien denying earlier that any "'rational being' is wholly evil," Thomas argues that, because evil only exists in a subject that is otherwise good, no evil is or can be completely successful in corrupting the whole good (ST 1.48.4).

Where Thomas does finally depart from, or at least improvise upon, the traditional Augustinian reckoning of evil, according to Carlos Steel, his innovations are more Aristotelian (and therefore still Socratic and Greek, in Steel's view) than they are distinctly Christian. To resolve the perplexity left open by Augustine and earlier Neoplatonists as to how evil actions are caused, Thomas in question 49 of the *Summa* applies the Aristotelian distinction between *per se* and accidental causality.[26] In contrast to classical Neoplatonism's characteristic denial that evil has an efficient cause, Thomas begins the corpus of his first article with an emphatic affirmation that "every evil in some way has a cause" (ST 1.49.1). As the "absence of the good which is natural and due to a thing," there must be a cause to explain why anything should "fail" or be "drawn out" from its "natural and due disposition." Thomas nevertheless agrees with the Neoplatonic premise that "only good can be a cause, because nothing can be a cause except in so far as it is a being, and every being, as such, is good." The question, then, is how something good can cause evil. Thomas's answer is that what is good is able to cause evil, not insofar as it is good in itself (*per se* causality), but only "accidentally." An accidental cause of an effect is a cause that produces an effect not intentionally, but by producing some first, intended effect with which the second, unintended effect is somehow accidentally or coincidentally connected. As we will see later,

---

26 Steel, "Does Evil Have a Cause?," 259.

it is this Aristotelian distinction between *per se* and *per accidens* causality that Aquinas applies to the question of how the rational will is ever able to do or choose evil while nevertheless intending something in and of itself good.

Although Aristotle's causal distinction enabled Thomas to answer the question of how evil may be caused by the good, Thomas's solution came with its own set of difficulties, the chief of which, as we shall see, has an important application to the question of Tolkien's portrayal of evil in his fiction. The problem, in short, is one of reconciling Thomas's claim that evil "has no direct cause, but only an accidental cause" (ST 1.49.1 ad 4) with the reality of malicious or "radical" evil — those instances, that is, when evil actions would appear to be deliberately perpetrated by their agent for evil's own sake. The classic example of such deliberate evil is Augustine's famous story of the pear-theft recounted in his *Confessions*. Augustine eventually does attribute, at least in part, his desire to steal and destroy the pears (he had no desire to eat them) to the influence of his friends, friendship and community being themselves good and therefore a possible source of action, even wrong action. In his initial account of his motive, however, Augustine puzzlingly suggests that, in stealing the pears, the evilness of the action itself was the cause: "I became *evil for no reason.* I had no motive for my wickedness except *wickedness itself.* It was foul, and I loved it… the self-destruction…my fall, not the object for which I had fallen but my fall itself…. I was seeking not to gain anything by shameful means, but *shame for its own sake.*"[27] Although Thomas refers to this very passage in his only work devoted exclusively to the subject of evil, *De malo* 3.12, the fact that Augustine's extreme remarks appear, at least to the modern reader, to challenge directly the basic premise of his philosophy of action — namely that evil cannot be desired or pursued for its own sake — does not seem to have occurred to him.[28] Steel, accordingly, concludes that there is thus a deep tension between, on the one hand, Thomas's Socratic optimism, which ultimately seeks to rationalize and reduce all evil to an instance of mere "*hamartia*, to miss the mark, to fail in one's purpose, to go wrong, to make a mistake, to err, a shortcoming, a defect, a privation"; and, on the other hand, something like Søren Kierkegaard's arguably more biblical and (in this respect, at least) more complicatedly Augustinian thesis that evil involves an inexplicable, yet deliberate, knowing intention and "positive choice" to do evil for evil's own sake.[29]

27 Augustine, *Confessions* 2.9, trans. Chadwick (emphasis added).
28 Steel, "Does Evil Have a Cause?," 268.
29 Ibid., 267–73. On this, compare Lee Oser's similar opposition, noted earlier, between Aquinas's "orthodox Augustinian teaching that positive evil does not exist" and Tolkien's allegedly

214 THE FLAME IMPERISHABLE

Be that as it may, it needs to be recognized that there are other respects in which Thomas's theory of evil was uniquely indebted to his Christian metaphysics of creation. According to Brian Davies, who has written at length on Thomas's theory of evil,[30] Thomas's Christianity was of central importance to his ponerology. Thomas, it may be recalled here, was a deeply committed friar whose Dominican order had been founded earlier in the thirteenth century partly in response to the Manichaeism of the Albigensian or Catharist heresy,[31] and Thomas's own preoccupation with the Manichaean heresy was both personal and profound, as most famously and humorously illustrated in his legendary outburst at the banquet hall of King Louis of France. Presumably lost in his thoughts and oblivious to his surroundings, Thomas stunned his host and fellow guests when he brought his fist crashing down on the table and triumphantly shouted, "And *that* will settle the Manichees!"[32] We also see Thomas's concern with the question of evil in the fact that he convened an entire *disputatio* on the subject, the lengthy proceedings of which he published under the succinct title *De malo*, "On Evil." Commenting on the significance of this work, Bonnie Kent observes: "Later medieval thinkers, as a rule, did not write treatises or conduct disputations dedicated to a topic so diffuse as evil. There is, however, one notable exception: Aquinas's disputed questions *De Malo (On Evil)*."[33]

As for his general orientation regarding the question of evil, Davies writes how for St. Thomas

the world is created and governed by a perfectly good God who is also omnipotent and omniscient. And he writes about evil in the light of this belief. In the *De malo* he is not concerned with scientific descriptions and scientific accounts of the causes of particular instances of evil (though he has things to say about them). Rather, he is out to focus on badness or evil in general. And he seeks to understand it as part of a world made by God. Hence, for example, he asks if God can be thought of as causing evil. And his account of human wrongdoing treats it chiefly as sin and as fallings short with respect to God. Hence, too, he touches on specifically Christian

---

Kierkegaardian "strong intuition of positive evil, verging on dualism." Oser, "Enter Reason and Nature," 118.

30 See, for example, Davies, *The Reality of God and the Problem of Evil*, which treats the problem of evil from a Thomistic perspective.

31 Lambert, *The Cathars*, 1.

32 Chesterton, *St. Thomas Aquinas: "The Dumb Ox,"* 100–1.

33 Kent, "Evil in Later Medieval Philosophy," 182.

notions such as the doctrine of original sin. In other words, the *De malo* is very much a work of Christian theology.[34]

Further indication of the fundamentally Christian and creational perspective of Thomas's ponerology may be found in the less occasional, more systematic (if less comprehensive) treatment of evil Thomas provides in the *Summa Theologiae*, where he broaches the topic of evil within the context of his broader address on the subject of creation (ST 1.48–49). When approaching evil in the context of the system of Christian doctrine as a whole, in other words, Thomas views it first and foremost as a distinction *within creation*, reinforcing the point that the being of which evil is a privation is not some bland, theologically neutral concept of being, much less the necessary, mediated, and impersonal emanation of the Neoplatonic One who is "beyond being" that we discussed in chapter one, but the voluntary, personal, and immediate gift shared by the One who is Being himself. Evil for Aquinas, in sum, is first and foremost a privation of *created* being, an insight that, as we shall see presently, is crucial for understanding some of the subtleties of Tolkien's own depiction of evil.

Tolkien's Hierarchy of Evil

AS IT WILL SERVE AS THE ORGANIZING PRINCIPLE FOR THE analysis to follow, the first point of comparison I want to make between Aquinas's and Tolkien's respective doctrines of evil concerns their similar views on the hierarchical nature of reality as a whole, a view St. Thomas, for example, raises toward the beginning of his discussion of evil in the *Summa*. As we have seen in previous chapters, for St. Thomas the hierarchical structure of creation is necessitated by the fact that God's purpose or end in creating the world is to communicate his own goodness, meaning that the created order, if it is to emulate adequately God's goodness towards creation, must itself consist in a hierarchy of diverse and unequal beings. Only in this way can the divine drama of a higher reality ministering to and bringing to perfection a lower order of being be carried out on a finite scale. As I suggested in the last chapter, moreover, it is this same kind of drama that Tolkien illustrates through the Valar Aulë, who, impatient with the relative emptiness and lack of diversity and inequality at that point in the world, attempts to make the Dwarves, and who justifies his action by saying

---

34 Davies, "Introduction," in Aquinas, *On Evil*, trans. Regan, 14–15.

that he merely desired beings upon whom he could exercise something of Ilúvatar's own fatherly care. As I further suggested, one way in particular of viewing
Tolkien's invented races of the Elves and the Valar is to see them as refinements
upon or further iterations within an otherwise Thomistic hierarchy of being.
Because the perfection of the universe requires that there should be, as Thomas
puts it, "inequality in things, so that every grade of goodness may be realized,"
and because one "grade of goodness" consists in things that can nevertheless fail
to achieve the level of goodness intended for it, it follows for St. Thomas that
the perfection of the universe "requires that there should be some which can
fail in goodness, and thence it follows that sometimes they do fail" (ST 1.48.
2). As Thomas goes on to conclude, it is in this failure of a thing to achieve its
goodness that evil consists.

Because evil does not have its own nature, and so does not have its own proper
place in the hierarchy of being, but "exists" only as a privation of the perfection
proper to those natures that do exist within the hierarchy, we might expect the
kinds of evil or privation there are to be differentiated according to the same logic
or structure of the hierarchy of goods which that evil corrupts. And consistent
with this expectation is the way Tolkien does indeed often depict his characters
as tending towards a form of evil unique to the nature of the particular species
to which that character belongs, and therefore to the particular ways in which
that species can fail to realize its true being. As Tolkien writes in one place, "every
finite creature must have some weakness: that is some inadequacy to deal with
some situations. It is not sinful when not willed, and when the creature does
his best (even if it is not what should be done) as he sees it — with the conscious
intent of serving Eru" (MR 392n). Thus it is that the Ainur and Valar have their
Melkor, the Maiar their Sauron, the Wizards their Saruman, the Elves their Orcs,
Men their Wormtongues and Denethors, the Ents their Old Man Willow, and
the Hobbits their Gollum. The almost perfect symmetry with which Tolkien
counterpoises each good being with its corresponding form of evil, far from
suggesting a kind of Manichaean dualism and equipotency between good and
evil, should remind us instead that evil owes even its otherwise extraordinary
variety and subtlety to that authentic variety and subtlety that creation has by
virtue of its participation in the "infinite variety" of the Creator.

My present purpose, however, is not to take stock of all the ways in which
each of the race of rational beings in Tolkien's mythical world can or might fail
to fulfill their nature. Instead, what I want to draw attention to are five distinct
classes or types of evil emphasized by Tolkien as particularly important in his
fiction, which, taken together, comprise what I will here refer to as Tolkien's

"hierarchy of evil," a hierarchy that is nevertheless unified by or organized around a common theme. The first class or manifestation of evil, first both in terms of the order of Tolkien's narrative, and also in terms of its being implicit (or so I shall argue) in every instance of evil, centers on the theme of *creation*. The mode of evil involved here is one in which a creature possesses an illicit and, as Thomas will put it, "unnatural" aspiration for what we saw in the last chapter to be the Creator's own exclusive power to create, that is, to bring things into being. The second motive in Tolkien's hierarchy of evil involves the corruption of the creature's legitimate or *natural* powers of *sub-creation*. Third, an important subdivision of this sub-creative evil in Tolkien's world concerns an obsession with what he calls "*preservation*," or the prevention of one's legitimate sub-creations from changing, decaying, and so eventually falling into oblivion, a motive that is associated with the Valar and especially the Elves. Fourth, we will see that the sub-creation/preservation motive corrupts further still into a form of evil that Tolkien identifies under the heading of *domination*. (At this point in the argument we will also take a moment to consider the metaphysics of Tolkien's polemic against technology or "the Machine" as one of the key instruments by which domination is exercised.) Fifth and finally, even more extreme and desperate in Tolkien's hierarchy of evil, and yet a topic that has hitherto received far less attention in discussions of Tolkien's metaphysics of evil, is the flip-side of creation, namely the impulse of *annihilation*, or the desire, failing the power to *give* being, for at least the power to *obliterate* it. Together, these five opportunities or instances of evil — creation, sub-creation, preservation, domination, and annihilation — constitute what I am here referring to as Tolkien's "hierarchy of evil."

Evil and Creation

AS WE SAW IN THE LAST CHAPTER, AN IMPORTANT DEPARTURE Tolkien makes from the classical and medieval Neoplatonism of Plotinus, Avicenna, and Peter Lombard is in his Thomistic conviction that only the Creator can create, that is, give or "emanate" being directly. In view of this distinction, it is surely not insignificant that the first instance of evil in Tolkien's mythical history occurs when the Ainur Melkor presumptuously aspires to exercise for himself the exclusively divine power of creation. Despite having "been given the greatest gifts of power and knowledge" and having "a share in all the gifts of his brethren," Melkor is reported to have "gone often alone into the void places seeking the Imperishable Flame; for desire grew hot within him to bring into Being things of his own" (S 16). In terms of at least the narrative sequence of Tolkien's mythology, then, the very first thing we learn about evil is that it *begins with the creaturely aspiration for the Creator's own power to create.* As we shall see, there is a significant respect in which, for Tolkien, not only does evil begin here, but this is all that evil ever is.

In making the desire for creative power the primeval sin, Tolkien again strikes a familiar chord with St. Thomas, who argues in the *Summa*'s discussion of the angels that the latter fell by seeking in an "unnatural" way to be like God (ST 1.63.3). Although Thomas is careful, in the absence of any clear teaching from Scripture on the topic, not to assert with certainty the exact circumstances of the angelic fall, the one example he gives of an "unnatural" angelic desire to be like God is the "desire to create heaven and earth, which is proper to God; in which desire there would be sin. It was in this way that the devil desired to be as God." In the conclusion to his argument in the *Summa Contra Gentiles* that the power of creation is proper to God alone, Thomas cites favorably John Damascene's rather caustic remark that "all those who say that the angels are creators of any substance whatever have the devil as their father, for no creatures in existence are creators."[35] For Thomas, it would seem, it is not only the *desire* of a creature to share in God's own power to create that is in some sense "demonic," but even the very *doctrine* that a creature can do so. James Collins has likewise observed that Thomas's example of the unnatural desire to create is not without special significance: "to wish to create heaven and earth…. The strategic import of this example must not be overlooked, since it neatly characterizes as encroachments upon God's unique power all theories which in any way admit that the creative act can be shared by lesser agents."[36] Clearly then, the questions of the power of creation and the primal fall of the angels were closely linked in Thomas's mind.

At the same time, unnatural though it may be for a finite being to desire the infinite Creator's power of creation, taken by itself the power of creation is of course infinitely good. Moreover, the *end* for which Melkor desires this power, namely that there should exist things other than himself, is a desire noble in itself and very much a virtue in Tolkien's Thomistic realism. In these two examples from Tolkien's *Ainulindalë*, we have illustrated a recurring theme in Tolkien's presentation of evil and an important principle in Thomas's metaphysics of evil as well, which is that *evil always involves the (misdirected) desire for some good.*

---

35 *Summa Contra Gentiles* 2.21, trans. Anderson.
36 Collins, *The Thomistic Philosophy of the Angels*, 261.

According to St. Thomas, because what we desire is by definition something desirable, and because what is desirable is, taken by itself, by definition good, it is impossible for the will to desire something evil *because* it is evil. Evil on this view, as we have seen, is nothing and therefore cannot in and of itself be the cause of anything, including desire. Rather, and to use Aquinas's Aristotelian distinction introduced earlier, evil is sought after only "accidentally, so far as it accompanies a good." The examples Thomas gives in the *Summa* are, first, a lion who kills the stag, not because it desires to kill simply, but because it desires food, to which the killing of the stag is accidentally joined, and, second, a man who fornicates not because he desires the sin of fornication *per se*, but because he desires the otherwise God-given sexual pleasure or enjoyment to which the sin of fornication is accidentally related or conjoined (ST 1.19.9; see also 1.5.1). As for those aforementioned, diabolical cases of radical evil where the evil-doer would seem intent on acting wickedly for its own sake and in deliberate opposition to God, Frederick Copleston explains that even here "it is some apparent good, complete independence, for example, which is the object of the will: the evil defiance of God appears as a good and is willed *sub specie boni*. No will, therefore, can desire evil precisely as such."[37] As we shall see, not even Melkor at his most nihilistic extreme completely succeeds in escaping this truth — indeed, one might almost say that it is precisely his inability to escape this truth that fuels as much as it frustrates his nihilistic destructiveness.

Evil and Sub-creation

IF MELKOR'S "FIRST FALL" (AS WE MIGHT VIEW IT) INVOLVES him in the futile and unnatural desire for the Creator's own power of creation, his later, sub-creative fall, in which he makes music in conflict with the original theme propounded by Eru, involves instead the exercise, however misdirected, of powers that are at least natural to him as a free, rational, yet finite being. This leads us to the second level or stage in Tolkien's hierarchy of evil, namely the evil of a corrupted or at the very least *defective* sub-creative will (I say "defective," for not all sub-creative deficiencies necessarily involve or require moral negligence or culpability). Thus, in the *Ainulindalë* it is interesting that it is only *after* Melkor goes into the Void to find the Imperishable Fire that, "being alone, he had begun to conceive thoughts of his own unlike those of his brethren,"

---

37 Copleston, *Medieval Philosophy*, 91.

and from his self-imposed isolation it then "came into the heart of Melkor to interweave [into the Music] matters of his own imagining that were not in accord with the theme of Ilúvatar" (S 16). Melkor's sub-creative deviations, in other words, are not unrelated to, but are the next manifestation of, his original lust for the Flame Imperishable. In a letter generalizing on this relationship between sub-creation and creation, Tolkien writes how the sub-creative desire "has various opportunities of 'Fall'. It may become possessive, clinging to the things made as 'its own,' the sub-creator *wishes to be the Lord and God of his private creation*. He will rebel against the laws of the Creator" (L 145, emphasis added). For Thomas and Tolkien, as has been said, sub-creation presupposes, is guaranteed by, and so is dependent upon a prior divine act of creation. Consistent with this premise, Tolkien recognizes that, should the sub-creative impulse become rebellious or aberrant, implicit in its corruption is the primeval desire for the kind of creational power that makes sub-creation possible in the first place.

The fact that it is and always remains God's deliberate act of creation that underlies sub-creation, even in its corrupted forms, reminds us that, even in the very act of evil itself, it is God who sustains the malefactor and his action in existence. As we observed in Tolkien's letter to Peter Hastings in the last chapter, the sub-creative free will is

> derivative, and is ∴ [therefore] only operative within provided circumstances; but in order that it may exist, it is necessary that the Author should guarantee it, whatever betides: sc. when it is "against His Will," as we say, at any rate as it appears on a finite view. He does not stop or make "unreal" sinful acts and their consequences. So in this myth, it is "feigned" (legitimately whether that is a feature of the real world or not) that He gave special "sub-creative" powers to certain of His highest created beings: that is a guarantee that what they devised and made should be given the reality of Creation. Of course within limits, and of course subject to certain commands or prohibitions. But if they "fell," as the Diabolus Morgoth did, and started making things "for himself, to be their Lord," these would then "be." (L 195)

Here in particular we can see the importance of Tolkien's Thomistic doctrine of creation for his metaphysical understanding not only of sub-creation and free will, but also of those circumstances in which they become corrupted by evil. Although a privation of being in itself, for Tolkien evil is very much *real*, having as the very source of its possibility and power the provisional "guarantee" of created being made by the infinite Creator himself.

This naturally raises the question: how is it that God, if he is responsible for metaphysically bankrolling, as it were, the evil, sub-creative investments of his creatures, is not himself the *cause* of evil? Although Tolkien himself (so far as I am aware) does not anywhere directly answer this question, as we see in his letter to Hastings, he is certainly aware of the problem. As he states matters even more expressly in another letter, "the problem of evil, and its apparent toleration, is a permanent one for all who concern themselves with our world" (L 280). As I hope to show, moreover, the general picture implied in Tolkien's fiction as to the question of God's causality with respect to evil, as we may by now have come to expect, bears a certain affinity with St. Thomas's position on the matter. In the *Summa,* Thomas explains that, in voluntary things, whenever there is an evil effect, it is always the result of some pre-existing evil in the agent, specifically, some pre-existing defect in the *will* of the agent, so that, when the agent acts, "it does not actually subject itself to its proper rule" (ST 1.49.1 ad 3). Thus, Thomas implicitly distinguishes two dimensions to every evil action: first, there is the action itself, caused by the will itself, both of which, taken by themselves, are good; second, there is the *defect* in the action, the result of the defect in the will causing the action. Now God in no way, says Aquinas, is the cause of the defects in the will of voluntary agents, since God is altogether perfect and thus incapable of causing an imperfection in the will (ST 1.49.1). Having parsed out the evil action in this manner, Thomas is able similarly to parse out the responsibility for it: "whatever there is of *being* and *action* in a bad action is reduced to God as the cause, whereas whatever *defect* is in it is not caused by God, but by the deficient secondary cause" (ST 1.49.2 ad 2). In a well-known illustration, Thomas compares God's creative power by which he gives being to an otherwise evil action with the "moving power" of a lame leg: while the moving power is the cause of the leg's motion, it is not the cause of the leg's motion being a *limping* motion. What causes the latter is the curvature of the lame leg, which in Thomas's illustration is analogous to the "curvature" or defect of the agent's will. In a passage that parallels closely Tolkien's statement to Hastings that God "guarantees" even "sinful acts" with the "reality of Creation," Leo Elders explains Thomas's argument:

> It is true that God is the cause of the content of being in any human act, just as all beings exist by participating in the First Being. But a human act is not God's action and a human choice is not God's choice. God gives only the entitative content and occurrence of an action without being the cause which does something through this action. Hence God is [in] no way,

not even *per accidens*, the cause who commits this action and so he is in no way the cause of the moral evil. He permits sin to take place in that he grants his causal support to the will to enable it to perform an act, despite its deviation from the rule of reason. The person who performs the evil action is *per accidens* the cause of the privation of subordination to moral law. To clarify this St. Thomas gives an example: if a cripple walks, the cause of his crippled gait is not his power to move, but his leg which is too stiff or too short. Therefore all of the entity in an evil action goes back to God as to its First Cause whereas the privation which renders it evil comes from the acting person who does not conform himself to moral law.[38]

Jacques Maritain similarly explains the same argument of St. Thomas, but in terms of what he distinguishes as the "unshatterable divine action" of creation and the "shatterable activations" of the individual human will, a metaphor evocative of the images of kindling fire and splintering light at the heart of Tolkien's mythology. According to Maritain, the creative "activations or motions" given by the First Cause to his individual free agents

contain within themselves, in advance, the permission or possibility of being rendered sterile *if* the free existent [agent] which receives them takes the first initiative of evading them, of not-acting and not-considering, or nihilating under their touch…. [B]efore the *unshatterable* divine action, by which the will to good of creative Liberty infallibly produces its effect in the created will, the divine activations received by the free existent must first be *shatterable* activations. It depends solely upon ourselves to shatter them by making, upon our own deficient initiative, that thing called nothing (or by nihilating).[39]

The soul or will, in short, is like a window pane or, to use another image shared by Tolkien and Maritain (see chapter two), a "prism": the light it receives is God's creative, activating, "moving" power; the light it admits or which shines through the window is the actions of the soul. Should the light it admits become shattered (as distinguished, say, from its being beautifully refracted through the sub-creative act), it is the fault, not of the light it receives, but of the cracked or shattered soul or will that receives it.

---

38 Elders, *The Metaphysics of Being*, 135.
39 Maritain, *Existence and the Existent,* trans. Galantiere and Phelan, 100–1.

God, therefore, is not in any way the *cause* of evil, but he does permit and even "preserve" (Thomas's language) or "guarantee" (Tolkien's language) the actions of evil wills, much as the source of light preserves or guarantees the broken light emitted through a cracked prism or piece of glass, yet without becoming on that account responsible for the light's brokenness. But the question still remains as to why God should choose to preserve or guarantee such broken wills and actions. One important answer for both Thomas and Tolkien, as the last chapter discussed, is that the Creator desires that there should be such a thing as free will, even if what those free wills choose should be evil. This, however, is only a partial explanation, for, as we have also seen, even and especially the free choices of creatures fall under the providence of God as things willed by him or, if the choices be evil, permitted by him, so that for Aquinas, at least, God could have willed that there be no evil in the world while still leaving the human will to be free.[40] For both Thomas and Tolkien, a further explanation for God's permission of evil concerns our next proposition in Tolkien's metaphysics of evil, which is that *evil makes possible the realization of even greater good*. Thomas makes this point in response to the objection that evil cannot reside in those things made by God, because, just as "white unmixed with black is the most white," as Aristotle says, so "the good unmixed with evil is the greater good. But God makes always what is best, much more than nature does" (ST 1.48.2 obj. 3). While Thomas agrees that God, like nature, makes "what is best in the whole," that is, in the "universe of creatures," as with nature, this does not necessarily mean that God makes "what is best in every single part" of the whole. According to Thomas, rather, the universe of creatures is in fact "better and more perfect if some things in it *can* fail and *do sometimes* fail, God not preventing this" (ST 1.48.2 ad 3). The greater good of the universe, or at least of *this particular* universe as it has been divinely ordered, requires not only the *possibility* of evil, but even its actuality, suggesting that, for the sake of the greater perfection of the world as a whole, the emergence of evil in the world was in some sense inevitable. As Thomas concludes his response, quoting Augustine's *Enchiridion*:

> "God is so powerful that he can even make good out of evil." Hence many good things would be taken away if God permitted no evil to exist; for fire would not be generated if air was not corrupted, nor would the life of a lion

---

40 This is a point, however, upon which not all Thomist scholars appear to agree. For varying viewpoints on this topic, see, on the one hand, Oesterle, "Preface," in Thomas Aquinas, *On Evil,* trans. Oesterle, xvii, and on the other hand, McCabe, *God Matters,* 38.

be preserved unless the ass were killed. Neither would avenging justice nor the patience of a sufferer be praised if there were no injustice. (ST 1.48.2 ad 3)

Some, however, have found such rational theorizing cold and unfeeling towards the cruel realities of human suffering in the world,[41] yet for Tolkien this truth was the source of deep personal comfort, as may be seen in the following, unflinching encouragement he offered his son Christopher while the latter was in South Africa training as a pilot during the Second World War:

> I sometimes feel appalled at the thought of the sum total of human mis-ery all over the world at the present moment: the millions parted, fret-ting, wasting in unprofitable days — quite apart from torture, pain, death, bereavement, injustice. If anguish were visible, almost the whole of this benighted planet would be enveloped in a dense dark vapour, shrouded from the amazed vision of the heavens! And the products of it all will be mainly evil — historically considered. But the historical version is, of course, not the only one. All things and deeds have a value in themselves, apart from their "causes" and "effects." All we do know, and that to a large extent by direct experience, is that evil labours with vast powers and perpetual success — in vain: preparing always only the soil for unexpected good to sprout in. So it is in general, so it is in our own lives. (L 76)

Like St. Thomas, then, Tolkien too held to a kind of greater-good theodicy, though it was one that he affirmed in the face of seemingly overwhelming evi-dence to the contrary, namely the "vast powers and perpetual success" of evil, which nevertheless, in the final analysis, will be seen as having labored "in vain." So important is this promise that evil will indeed result in greater good that it is given expression in the *Ainulindalë* by none other than Ilúvatar himself, who, after bringing the Ainur's Music to its climactic, triumphant resolution, declares:

> Mighty are the Ainur, and mightiest among them is Melkor; but that he may know, and all the Ainur, that I am Ilúvatar, those things that ye have sung, I will show them forth, that ye may see what ye have done. And thou, Melkor, shalt see that no theme may be played that hath not its uttermost source in me, nor can any alter the music in my despite. For he

---

41 See, for example, Hart's critique in *The Doors of the Sea*, referenced earlier (although as I have mentioned, Hart fails to see how Aquinas likewise falls under his indictment of such Leibni-zian, greater-good theodicies).

that attempteth this shall prove but mine instrument in the devising of things more wonderful, which he himself hath not imagined…. And thou, Melkor, wilt discover all the secret thoughts of thy mind, and wilt perceive that they are but a part of the whole and tributary to its glory. (S 17)[42]

As Ilúvatar explains to Melkor, the ultimate meaning of his rebellion will prove to be entirely different from the one intended by him. Not only is Ilúvatar the only one who can create and therefore give being to the sub-creative designs of his creatures, but for that same reason he is also the one who determines the ultimate meaning and outcome of the sub-creative choices of his creatures, whether they be good or evil.[43] It is this peculiar power of turning evil inexorably to good, in short, that distinguishes Ilúvatar as the one and only true Creator, allowing Melkor and all the Ainur to "know" that he is Ilúvatar. In addition to Melkor's rebellious music succeeding by Ilúvatar's design in making the Music more beautiful, and similar to what we saw in St. Thomas, there is a respect in which the beauty achieved in the Music through Melkor's evil could not have been realized in any other way. As it is described in the *Ainulindalë*, Ilúvatar's musical response to Melkor's discord was "deep and wide and beautiful, but slow and blended with an immeasurable sorrow, from which its beauty chiefly came." It is this idea, moreover, of the necessity of sorrow for the possibility of a certain kind of joy that lies at the heart of Tolkien's concept of eucatastrophe, "the joy of the happy ending" or "sudden joyous 'turn'" that "does not deny the existence of *dyscatastrophe*, of sorrow and failure," inasmuch as "the possibility of these is necessary to the joy of deliverance" (TR 85–86).[44]

---

42 See also MR 383.

43 Ilúvatar's speech is referred to later on in *The Silmarillion* in the Valar Manwë's response to the Elf-lord Fëanor's declaration that the Noldor Elves would leave their refuge in Valinor and return to Middle-earth to wage war against Melkor: "But at that last word of Fëanor: that at the least the Noldor should do deeds to live in song for ever, [Manwë] raised his head, as one that hears a voice far off, and he said: 'So shall it be! Dear-bought those songs shall be accounted, and yet shall be well-bought. For the price could be no other. Thus even as Eru spoke to us shall beauty not before conceived be brought into Eä, and evil yet be good to have been.' But Mandos said: 'And yet remain evil. To me shall Fëanor come soon'" (S 98). Robert Collins has also touched on the necessity of evil for the achievement of certain kinds of goods in Tolkien's writings: "Tolkien has embedded not only an analog of the 'progressive' Hegelian dialectic, but also an aesthetic analog of the Christian paradox of the 'fortunate fall.' Unopposed, the forces of concord may not conceive the beauty of the snowflake. Untempted, unfallen, man may not achieve the glory of sainthood." Collins, "'Ainulindalë': Tolkien's Commitment to an Aesthetic Ontology," 260.

44 To return to the Ainur's Music, inasmuch as it contains within itself a preview of subsequent world history, we also find in Tolkien something of the Thomistic thesis that the eventual existence of evil in the world was not only a possibility, but in some sense an inevitability. "In this Myth," as Tolkien explains in one letter, "the rebellion of created free-will precedes creation of the World (Eä);

Evil and Preservation

ONE PARTICULAR MANIFESTATION OF SUB-CREATIVE "EVIL" IN
Tolkien's stories involves not only the sub-creation of things in overt conflict
with the Creator and what he has made, but also the well-meaning but ill-judged
attempt at "preserving" or "possessing" the things around us and produced by
us in a way that is nevertheless contrary to their ultimate nature and divine
purpose. It is this motive that is operative in the otherwise unfallen Valar, for
example, when, instead of pursuing their primary task after first giving shape
to the world, namely the continued resistance of Melkor and the governance
of the world according to the Music for the benefit of the Children of Ilúvatar,
they fell rather into the practice of trying to preserve just one isolated area of
the world, Valinor, not only against the onslaughts of Melkor, but also against
the otherwise natural processes of time and change themselves. Thus, Tolkien
describes Manwë's "own inherent fault (though not sin)" as a matter of having
become "engrossed...in amendment, healing, re-ordering — even 'keeping the
status quo' — to the loss of all creative power and even to weakness in dealing
with difficult and perilous situations" (MR 392).[45] Addressing the Valar more
generally, Tolkien says of the Two Trees of Valinor that one of their objects

> was the healing of the hurts of Melkor, but this could easily have a *selfish*
> aspect: the staying of history — not going on with the Tale. This effect it had
> on the Valar. They became more and more enamoured of Valinor, and went
> there more often and stayed there longer. Middle-earth was left too little
> tended, and too little protected against Melkor. (MR 377, emphasis original)[46]

---

and Eä has in it, subcreatively introduced, evil, rebellions, discordant elements of its own nature
already when the *Let it Be* was spoken. The Fall or corruption, therefore, of all things in it and all
inhabitants of it, was a possibility if not inevitable" (L 286–87). In holding that, given free will,
the existence of evil was probable if not inevitable, Tolkien was in basic agreement with his good
friend C.S. Lewis, who in his *Problem of Pain*, as Elizabeth Whittingham points out, argues that,
"if God creates people with free will, suffering and evil will probably exist, but their existence does
not contradict God's existence." Whittingham, "The Mythology of the '*Ainulindalë*': Tolkien's
Creation of Hope," 218.

45 Tolkien's distinction between an "inherent fault" that has not yet become a "sin" might
be compared to the important distinction Thomas draws in *De Malo* 1.3, where he argues that evil
begins with a defect in the will that is voluntary but not yet morally culpable. For an explanation
of Thomas's argument and its historic significance in the debate over the question of the causality
of evil, see Steel, "Does Evil Have a Cause?," 260–62.

46 In one letter Tolkien refers to this as the "fainéance" (i.e., inactivity, idleness, or indolence)
of the Valar (L 202).

Preoccupied with mere preservation, the Valar fail to apply and so lose the important sub-creative skill of adaptation, of adjusting to the conditions of growth
and change, and hence of growing into maturity, qualities that are necessary in
a material world that is ultimately not of one's own creating.

The species of being, however, for whom the motive of preservation becomes
especially troublesome are the Elves, who, as exaggerated embodiments of otherwise human artistic and technical excellence, also find therein their peculiar
temptation to go astray. Tolkien writes of the Elves in one place that their

> "magic" is Art, delivered from many of its human limitations: more effortless,
> more quick, more complete (product, and vision in unflawed correspon-
> dence). And its object is Art not Power, sub-creation not domination and
> tyrannous re-forming of Creation. The "Elves" are "immortal," at least
> as far as this world goes: and hence are concerned rather with the griefs
> and burdens of deathlessness in time and change, than with death. (L 146)

As I argued in the last chapter, these two dimensions of the Elves — their artistic
superiority and their immortality — are metaphysically and psychologically
linked through Tolkien's hylomorphic anthropology: the powerful Elvish soul,
or *fëa*, that exerts so formative an influence over the Elvish body, or *hröa*, making it immortal or at least undying, is also what gives their art its heightened
spiritual command over matter — in short, its "magic" (in the positive sense of
"enchantment"). As with Tolkien's incarnate angels, however, whose voluntary
and extrinsic relation between spirit and body can tend towards a domineering
stance in relation to physical reality in general, so also the Elvish relationship
of soul and body is simultaneously its glory and its liability, its peculiar virtue
when well-ordered and peculiar vice when not.

The reason this "unflawed correspondence" between "product and vision"
(or between the will executing the product and the intellect first envisioning
it[47]) becomes a source of temptation for the Elves is that it can of course never
approximate the absolute identity of will and intellect (and thus perfect artistic
execution) enjoyed by the Creator by virtue of the divine will's unrivaled capacity
of giving being to things exactly as conceived in the divine mind. James Collins
makes this point in a discussion of the inherent limitation on angelic causality
that, *mutatis mutandis*, finds equal application to Tolkien's Elves:

---

47 Elsewhere Tolkien refers to the sub-creative will as "the effective link between the indestructible mind and being and the realization of its imagination" (L 260).

The limitation placed upon direct angelic causality is based ultimately on the finiteness of created separated substances. While they act through intellect and will, they can move other things only in a way proportioned to their natures. Unlike God, the angel is not its own will; it has will in a determinate nature, and the effect proceeds from this faculty according to the mode of the finite nature. Hence angelic power is subject to the conditions of categorical action and passion. As higher forms, separated substances possess supremely universal active powers to which the passive powers of lower substances are not sufficiently adapted to receive an actualization except through the mediation of natural agents. As pure act, God is determined neither in His being nor in His operation to any particular genus or species. His action is transcendental and His will can do indifferently anything that can be done by any created will or natural agent. Hence God requires no preliminary proportioning of His power to the receptive capacity of the material subject. Immediate formal transmutation or substantial change of material substances, then, is possible only for that immaterial substance Whose power is identical with His infinite act of being.[48]

The temptation inherent in the greater correspondence between will and intellect enjoyed by the Elves (and even more so by Thomas's angels) is the increased possibility that they will covet the absolute identity of will and intellect that belongs to the Creator alone.[49] Again, the corruption of the sub-creative motive involves the implicit coveting of God's own power to create.

Corresponding to the gap between will and intellect in created, rational beings is another point made in the last chapter, namely, that, whereas the Creator gives being in its entirety, creaturely sub-creating or "making," by contrast, always presupposes some already existing and therefore somewhat recalcitrant (from the finite point of view) external matter, what for Plato fell under the principle of *anankê* or necessity. This lack of total control over one's artistic medium and product becomes an issue, as Leo Elders points out in a passing but apropos comment relating Thomas's doctrine of evil to the problem of art, inasmuch

---

48 Collins, *The Thomistic Philosophy of the Angels*, 314–15.

49 As Hayden Head aptly puts it in his Girardian interpretation of Tolkien, "the mighty, those who apparently possess more substance, more 'being,' than the rest of us, are those most susceptible to the temptation to rise against God," to give way to the "primeval impulse to appropriate the prerogatives of God.... Gazing into the pure ontology of God, the strong man discovers anew his own contingency, and his pride of strength dissolves in the cauldron of envious desire.... The fall is that sudden recognition of the incommensurability between God and man." Head, "Imitative Desire," 140–41.

as "in a world which consists of limited and perishable things it will never be possible to avoid all failure" in art, because "the possibility of decay and passing away is imprinted in the essence of material things."[50] And this is the Elvish dilemma and paradox: by nature undying and unchanging, striving to carry out their sub-creative task while consigned to live forever in—and if they die, to return to—an ever-changing world, the Elves, like the Valar, become obsessed with, as Tolkien puts it, "the prevention or slowing of *decay* (i.e., 'change' viewed as a regrettable thing), the preservation of what is desired or loved, or its semblance—this is more or less an Elvish motive" (L 152, emphasis original).

In *The Lord of the Rings*, the places where we see this idealization of unchanging timelessness and preservation are of course in the otherwise idyllic yet static Elvish enclaves of Rivendell and Lothlórien. For all their beauty and enchantment, Tolkien nevertheless indicates something at the same time questionable about them when he writes of his Elves in a 1956 letter:

> Mere change as such is not represented as "evil": it is the unfolding of the story and to refuse this is of course against the design of God. But the Elvish weakness is in these terms naturally to regret the past, and to become unwilling to face change: as if a man were to hate a very long book still going on, and wished to settle down in a favorite chapter. Hence they fell in a measure to Sauron's deceits: they desired some "power" over things as they are (which is quite distinct from art), to make their particular will to preservation effective: to arrest change, and keep things always fresh and fair. (L 236)[51]

---

50 Elders, *The Metaphysics of Being*, 134–35. McCabe makes a comparable point in his discussion of the necessity of "evil suffered" (Thomas's *malum poenae*, the "evil of pain") in a world composed of corruptible beings: "In general, it seems to me that you cannot make material things that develop in time without allowing for the fact that in perfecting themselves they will damage other material things." McCabe, *God Matters*, 31.

51 Thus, in the *Athrabeth*, Finrod may be found to articulate a more balanced Elvish perspective on the matter: "Other creatures also in Middle-earth we love in their measure and kind: the beasts and birds who are our friends, the trees, and even the fair flowers that pass more swiftly than Men. Their passing we regret; but believe it to be a part of their nature, as much as are their shapes or their hues" (MR 308). Flieger, in an excellent discussion of the necessity of change in Tolkien's philosophy and fiction, indicates something of the complexity and even self-critical nature of Tolkien's emphasis on this point. While Tolkien was himself an Elf of sorts, and his "psychological and emotional yearning was nostalgia for aspects of his world that had vanished or were vanishing in his lifetime, still, his philosophical and religious position was that change is necessary." Flieger, *Splintered Light*, 170. Flieger also makes my above point about "evil" in this regard involving the desire for some good when she writes: "Desire to preserve a present good inevitably becomes desire to keep it from passing, but this leads to stagnation. The process of change is part of the design, and must continue if the design is to be fulfilled." Ibid., 170. Finally, Peter Kreeft has also written perceptively on the problem of Elves and change, describing them as "bad conservatives: they want to embalm the

The point to be made here is that, in the Elvish motive of preservation, it is possible to see the primal sin of desiring God's own power of creation resurfacing again, albeit in a highly muted form, in the context of Elvish art and immortality: instead of resting content in the Creator's own power and "design" by limiting their art to cultivating and culling those properties already inherent in things by virtue of their createdness, the Elves were persuaded to accept Sauron's promise of godlike "'power' over things *as they are* (which is quite distinct from art)." In desiring "to make their particular will to preservation effective" through art, the Elves were essentially coveting, like Melkor, Eru's power of creation, that is, the total and immediate effectiveness of his will over created being. To cite the passage quoted earlier, the sub-creative desire having thus "become possessive, clinging to the things made as 'its own,' the sub-creator wishes to be the Lord and God of his private creation" (L 145). And, as Tolkien puts it in another place still, "individual Elves might be seduced to a kind of minor 'Melkorism': desiring to be their own masters in Arda, and to have things their own way, leading in extreme cases to rebellion" (MR 334). Even in the comparatively innocuous Elvish motives of possessiveness and preservation, therefore, we see the residue of the primeval lust of Melkor for the Creator's power to give being.

In criticizing the Elvish motive of preservation and possessiveness, we should at this point remind ourselves, one of Tolkien's purposes of course is to draw attention to and comment on what for him was in fact a distinctly human temptation in the real world. We have seen how, through the Elvish quality of loving things for their "otherness," Tolkien positively displays the role of "recovery" that all fairy-stories have, the "regaining of a clear view," as Tolkien puts it in his essay "On Fairy-Stories," a "'seeing things as we are (or were) meant to see them'—as things apart from ourselves" (TR 77). What we see here, accordingly, is that the Elves, as "the artistic, aesthetic, and purely scientific aspects of the Humane nature raised to a higher level than is actually seen in Men" (L 236), at the same time represent some of the very human motives that these same fairy-stories are meant to deliver us from. For as Tolkien continues in the same passage from his essay,

> We need, in any case, to clean our windows; so that the things seen clearly
> may be freed from the drab blur of triteness or familiarity—from posses-
> siveness. Of all faces those of our *familiars* are the ones both most difficult
> to play fantastic tricks with, and most difficult really to see with fresh

present. Seeing the downward slant of the present, they try to preserve the past. They are not *evil* like Sauron, who always wants to sing 'I Did It My Way,' but they are *foolish* because they sing 'I Believe in Yesterday.'" Kreeft, *The Philosophy of Tolkien: The Worldview Behind the Lord of the Rings*, 80.

attention, perceiving their likeness and unlikeness: that they are faces, and yet unique faces. This triteness is really the penalty of "appropriation": the things that are trite, or (in a bad sense) familiar, are the things that we have appropriated, legally or mentally. We say we know them. They have become like the things which once attracted us by their glitter, or their colour, or their shape, and we laid hands on them, and then locked them in our hoard, acquired them, and acquiring ceased to look at them. (TR 77)

It is important to note that Tolkien is not yet critiquing here the kind of practical, technological mastery and "appropriation" of things that, as we shall see, he warns us against elsewhere. His target in this passage, rather, is the much more subtle, intellectual, and even aesthetic and artistic form of possessiveness that, left unchecked, can lead and in modern times arguably has led to the outright domination and tyranny of nature. Nevertheless, the two forms of "appropriation," however dissimilar, are closely related in Tolkien's mind, as may be seen when he refers in his essay to the dissimulating dream-device in fairy-stories as a "machine" that "cheats deliberately the primal desire at the heart of Faerie: the realization, independent of the conceiving mind, of imagined wonder" (42). In other words, the dream-device, not unlike the genre of allegory as a whole, is a literary device that effectively domesticates and so controls the narrative by denying or at least suppressing its possible real-world truth or wider applicability. That Tolkien should liken such intellectual and aesthetic appropriations to an act of "locking" things up in our mental "hoard" is itself interesting, moreover, in that it bears some resemblance to Martin Heidegger's critique in *Being and Time* of the modern, Cartesian view of human perception:

> the perceiving of what is known is *not* a process of returning with one's booty to the "cabinet" of consciousness after one has gone out and grasped it; even in perceiving, retaining, and preserving, the Dasein which knows *remains outside*, and it does so *as Dasein*. If I "merely" know about some way in which the Being of entities is interconnected, if I "only" represent them, if I "do no more" than "think" about them, I am no less alongside the entities outside in the world than when I *originally* grasp them.[52]

For Tolkien as for Heidegger, we must avoid reducing the existence of things to only that aspect which lends itself to conceptual or perceptual apprehension

---

52 Heidegger, *Being and Time,* trans. Macquarrie and Robinson, 89–90 (emphasis original).

and representation (this is why, as I argued in chapter three, it is so important that the Ainur eventually move beyond the abstract formalism of the Music to a love for the existing reality of Eä itself). Instead, our task, in the language of Heidegger, is to remain "open" to things "disclosing" themselves to us in new and even unexpected ways. It is precisely such openness, finally, that Tolkien attempts to model for us through the Elvish love of nature and "things other," while at the same time warning how the things we are open to and value today in their unfamiliarity can quickly become the things we possessively render familiar and trite tomorrow.

If Tolkien should begin to sound like an existentialist on this point, however, German Thomist Josef Pieper would tell us that it is perhaps because the existentialist critique of the modern reduction of life and reality to what is "fathomable, fully accessible to rational comprehension, and, above all,…permissible to change, transform, or even destroy" is the one sounding a lot like St. Thomas.[53] For, as Pieper points out, it is the doctrine of creation that, on the one hand, accounts for the inherent intelligibility of things (denied by atheistic existentialists, but affirmed, as we saw in chapter two, by Tolkien), while at the same time guaranteeing the mind's ultimate inability to completely "grasp" or comprehend them on the other:

> This common root, to express it as briefly as possible, is the *createdness* of things, i.e., the truth that the designs, the archetypal patterns of things, dwell within the Divine Logos. Because things come forth from the eye of God, they partake wholly of the nature of the Logos, that is, they are lucid and limpid to their very depths. It is their origin in the Logos which makes them knowable to men. But because of this very origin in the Logos, they mirror an *infinite* light and can therefore not be wholly comprehended. It is not darkness or chaos which makes them unfathomable. If a man, therefore, in his philosophical inquiry, gropes after the essence of things, he finds himself, by the very act of approaching his object, in an unfathomable abyss, but it is an abyss of *light*.[54]

53 Pieper, *The Silence of St. Thomas*, 92. For an introduction to some of the concerns shared by Tolkien and the modern existentialist movement, particularly as represented by Jean-Paul Sartre and Martin Heidegger (though Heidegger himself rejected the label), see Robert Eaglestone's article "Existentialism" in Drout, ed., *J.R.R. Tolkien Encyclopedia*, 179–80. Below I touch on some of Heidegger's and Tolkien's shared concerns with regard to the problem of modern technology.

54 Pieper, *The Silence of St. Thomas*, 96.

Pieper's discussion serves to remind us that, in an important sense, the kind of intellectual "appropriation" or "possessiveness" of reality cautioned against by Tolkien is at heart a denial of reality's createdness, or, to state matters differently, it is to affirm it as one's *own* creation. In a remote, yet real, Melkorian manner, it is to make the power and light of the Flame Imperishable coextensive with the light of one's own intellect.

Evil and Domination

THIS, OF COURSE, IS TO STATE MATTERS RATHER STRONGLY, for, however misguided and defective it may be or become, the Elvish and Valaric "will to preservation" is, for Tolkien, not yet necessarily evil in itself, inasmuch as it still has the good of another in view.[55] We see the preservation motive corrode into full-fledged evil only when it devolves further into *domination*, when the plan or program one has for the good of the other ceases to be a means to an end and becomes an end and good in itself, even at the eventual expense of the object the plan was originally intended to benefit. The principal embodiment and representative of this fourth phase of evil in Tolkien's literature is Sauron, "the Enemy" who

> in successive forms is always "naturally" concerned with sheer Domination, and so the Lord of magic and machines; but the problem: that this frightful evil can and does arise from an apparently good root, the desire to benefit the world and others — speedily and according to the benefactor's own plans — is a recurrent motive. (L 146)[56]

Similar to the Elvish motive of preservation, the Sauronic will to dominate has its origin in the desire for an otherwise good end, and, like preservation, domination involves the desire to control other beings, to make their being more directly conformable to the desires or dictates of one's own will. In this respect, domination emerges as simply a more extreme form of coveting God's own absolute unity of will and intellect that is his by virtue of his status as Creator.

55 Despite their inherent tendency towards this form of "possessiveness," Tolkien says in one place that the Elvish race, taken as a whole and in contrast with Men, is "unfallen" (MR 334).

56 As Tolkien writes in another place of Sauron's originally good intentions, he had "gone the way of all tyrants: beginning well, at least on the level that while desiring to order all things according to his own wisdom he still at first considered the (economic) well-being of other inhabitants of the Earth. But he went further than human tyrants in pride and the lust for domination, being in origin an immortal (angelic) spirit" (L 243).

The difference between preservation and domination, however, is that, whereas the sub-creative, artistic impulse of Elvish preservation seeks to establish, protect, and set things free in their divinely-given "otherness" and independence — even if to the sometimes counterproductive point of wrongfully denying them their natural tendency for change and decay — *the evil of domination lies in its deliberate suppression of otherness*, in its attempted reduction of otherness, as it were, to sameness, to a complete univocity of subjective intention and objective existence. In the *Ainulindalë,* this will to sameness manifests itself, first, in the unvarying and highly repetitive music of Melkor, which "had now achieved a unity of its own; but it was loud, and vain, and endlessly repeated; and it had little harmony, but rather a clamorous unison as of many trumpets braying upon a few notes," in contrast to the music of Ilúvatar, which "was deep and wide and beautiful, but slow and blended with an immeasurable sorrow, from which its beauty chiefly came" (S 16–17).[57] After the world has actually been created, Melkor similarly focuses his efforts on undoing the diversity and distinction of being introduced into the world by the other Valar: "they built lands and Melkor destroyed them; valleys they delved and Melkor raised them up; mountains they carved and Melkor threw them down; seas they hollowed and Melkor spilled them; and naught might have peace or come to lasting growth, for as surely as the Valar began a labour so would Melkor undo it or corrupt it" (S 22). Here again it is instructive to relate Tolkien's portrayal of evil to his Thomistic metaphysics of creation. As we have seen in earlier chapters, creation involves the communication of divine goodness, which necessitates on the part of the finite, created order a plurality of unequal beings. Failing to achieve the creative power whereby he might bring into being things other than himself, Melkor resorts to a kind of anti-creation, to reducing the otherness of those things already created to the sameness of his own increasingly empty self. In creation, in other words, the Creator in his generosity gives real, distinct, albeit participatory, being to things that were not there before, whereas

57 Compare the *Ainulindalë's* contrast between Melkor's and Ilúvatar's music with the contrast Hart develops between the Dionysian aesthetic of Nietzsche and Gilles Deleuze and that provided by Christian theology: "A Dionysian rhythm…embraced within the incessant drumbeat of being's *unica vox* as it repeats itself endlessly, from whose beat difference erupts as a perpetual divergence; and even if Dionysus allows the odd irenic caesura in his dance — the occasional beautiful sequence — it constitutes only a slackening of a tempo, a momentary paralysis of his limbs, a reflective interval that still never arrests the underlying beat of difference. Theology, though, starting from the Christian narrative of creation out of nothingness, effected by the power and love of the God who is Trinity, might well inquire whether rhythm could not be the prior truth of things, and chaos only an illusion, the effect of a certain convulsive or discordant beat, the repetition of a sinful series." Hart, *The Beauty of the Infinite,* 276–77.

the envy of domination works in the reverse direction by reducing the independence of things into a state of dependence upon oneself. At the same time, and in keeping with our earlier point about evil always involving some good, domination reveals itself as a parody of creation, for, in an important sense, the Creator has no true otherness or "outside" where creation can exist, inasmuch as he already embodies within himself the infinite source and plenitude of all actuality and perfection.

Central to Tolkien's representation of the evil of domination, of course, is the Ring of Sauron itself, about which there are three main points I would like to make in regard to its general symbolism of Tolkien's metaphysics of domination. The first point concerns the Ring's mythic power to render its wearer invisible, a property Robert Eaglestone has capably analyzed in light of Emmanuel Levinas's application of the Ring of Gyges from Plato's *Republic* to the problem of the modern self. As Eaglestone points out, Levinas sees "in the gesture of seeing without being seen, both the phenomena of evil and one of the defining and unavoidable features of modernity."[58] For Levinas, Eaglestone explains, "our thought and daily lives are first in a relationship to the others that populate the world. Everything else is built on this fundamental relationship to the other, which 'happens' to us before we choose it."[59] This fundamental, mutual participation in the life of others "involves giving up one's rights and acknowledging both the rights of the other and one's own responsibility to them over and above yourself."[60] In modernity, however, Levinas argues that a decidedly new attitude emerged, especially in Descartes's methodical doubt, which posited a radical theoretical distance between the thinking subject and the world, thus rendering the subject "invisible" to it. As Eaglestone summarizes Levinas's argument, the modern isolation of the subject

> creates the illusion that one's subjectivity is, like Gyges, not derived from one's relation with others but rather existing independently without society or recognition from others. Levinas continues and argues that the "myth of Gyges is the very myth of the I" which stands alone. "Seeing without being seen" is at the same time an illusion of radical separation and uprootedness from others, and the grounds of the possibility of "inner life".... Invisibility

58 Eaglestone, "Invisibility," 75.
59 Ibid., 75.
60 Ibid.

seems to turn the world into a world of spectacle, in which the observer is
disengaged and free from bounds or restraint.[61]

As Eaglestone continues, in this illusion of separation at the heart of modernity,
"others are turned from people into objects."[62] Like the modern conception of the
subject, Sauron's Ring, in making its wearer invisible to others and thus detaching him from his rootedness and participation in the world, in principle denies
the claim that other beings have on him by virtue of their otherness. Invisible
to all others while all others remain visible to him, the Ring-wearer assumes a
quasi-transcendence in which their being effectively becomes an extension of
his own.[63] In this, Sauron's Ring may be said to reverse the pattern of the Ainur's Vision, the joyous eucatastrophe that consists of giving to the *appearance*
of "things other," which do not yet exist, the *reality* that is later granted as a
divine gift. The tragedy or dyscatastrophe of Sauron's Ring, by contrast, is that
it takes the reality of an already existing thing and belies that reality by denying
its appearances. However, because things are what they are on account of their
otherness, to deny a thing its appearance and its consequent relationship with
those beings to whom it appears is also to deny its reality, as we see in the case

61 Ibid., 76.

62 Ibid., 81.

63 As Stratford Caldecott has similarly observed, the Ring's "gift of invisibility symbolizes this
ability to destroy all natural human relationships and identity, to become untouchable by light. The
person who places himself within the golden circle of the Ring seeks not to be seen, and thereby to
have power over others.... Its circular shape is an image of the will closed in upon itself. Its empty
center suggests the void into which we thrust ourselves by using the Ring. Once there, unseen by
others, we are cut off from human contact, removed from the reach of friendship or companionship, anonymous and isolated.... In that world of evil there is no room for two wills: the wearer
is either absorbed and destroyed, or he defeats Sauron and becomes another Dark Lord himself."
Caldecott, *The Power of the Ring: The Spiritual Vision Behind "The Lord of the Rings,"* 57–58. Peter
Kreeft gives a slightly more theological analysis of the problem of invisibility: "Invisibility also
means isolation. God alone can endure this (and only because He is a Trinity of persons, a society
in Himself). He is God alone; there is no other. Yet He is other in Himself and never alone. God *is* a
community. That is why He needs no community, as we do. The Ring cuts us off from community,
and contact. We are alone with the Eye. There is no room for an Other in the One Ring. This is
why the Ring surrounds emptiness. If We-ness, or Relationship, or Love, or Trinity is the name of
ultimate reality, then the Ring makes us unreal by isolating us. It plunges us into its own emptiness,
like a Black Hole. Its circular shape is an image of that emptiness: it encloses nothingness with its
all-encompassing circle of power." Kreeft, *The Philosophy of Tolkien,* 181. Finally, Jane Chance has
approached the visibility-invisibility issue raised by Tolkien in light of Michel Foucault's discussion
of Jeremy Bentham's Panopticon, "a ring-shaped building enclosing a tower that oversees cells that
might contain a convict — or a lunatic, a patient, a worker, or a student. It is the same model used
by Tolkien to locate the nature of Sauron's power.... Visibility — the searching Eye of Sauron — is
necessary to ensure access to all individuals; it is this same visibility that insists on a rigorous and
universal power." Chance, *"The Lord of the Rings": The Mythology of Power,* 21.

of the Ring-wraiths and all those who possess Sauron's Ring for too long. As Gandalf explains to Frodo, if one "often uses the Ring to make himself invisible, he *fades*: he becomes in the end invisible permanently, and walks in the twilight under the eye of the dark power that rules the Rings.... Yes, sooner or later... the dark power will devour him" (FOTR 56).[64] The only person over whom the Ring seems to have no power, even to render him invisible, is Tom Bombadil, one of the earthiest characters in Tolkien's fiction and one whose whole identity is most tied to his love of and devotion to things other.[65]

The connection between modern mind-body dualism and the Platonic and Tolkienian theme of invisibility drawn by Levinas and Eaglestone brings us to the second point I would make about Sauron's Ring, which is that it is precisely one's material or physical appearance which is suppressed in wearing the Ring, a point leading Alison Milbank to suggest a certain Manichaeism behind the domination of Sauron and Melkor. They are Manichaean "not just because they wish to claim equal if not superior power for evil, but because they denigrate the material and physical world and 'save' their subjects from it. The Nazgûl, for example, have lost bodily form as a result of their subjection to the power of Sauron, while he himself is reduced to a single eye."[66] Tolkien himself may possibly allude to the presence of a kind of Manichaean impulse behind the Rings of Power when he describes their power as a capacity to render "invisible the material body, and making things of the invisible world visible" (L 152). As Milbank further observes, although *The Lord of the Rings* is almost entirely devoid of religious practice, in the tragic history of the Númenóreans recorded in *The Silmarillion,* we see the Manichaeism of Sauron and Melkor actually

---

64 And as Bilbo complains to Gandalf in a well-known passage earlier on, showing the effect the Ring has had on him, "'I am old, Gandalf. I don't look it, but I am beginning to feel it in my heart of hearts. *Well-preserved* indeed!' he snorted. 'Why, I feel all thin, sort of *stretched*, if you know what I mean: like butter that has been scraped over too much bread. That can't be right. I need a change, or something'" (FOTR 41).

65 Tolkien writes of Bombadil: "he is an 'allegory,' or an exemplar, a particular embodying of pure (real) natural science: the spirit that desires knowledge of other things, their history and nature, *because they are 'other'* and wholly independent of the enquiring mind, a spirit coeval with the rational mind, and entirely unconcerned with 'doing' anything with the knowledge" (L 192, emphasis original).

66 Milbank, *Chesterton and Tolkien as Theologians,* 80. On the other hand, Milbank notes a tendency in Tolkien to attribute physical imperfections to his evil characters, something she sees, however, as the result not of a Manichaean but of a peculiarly Thomistic influence: "It is because Tolkien has an Augustinian attitude to evil as a privation — and not a positive force in itself — and a Thomist understanding of evil as a deficiency in being, which he shares with Chesterton, that he presents his evil human characters as physically warped and grotesque in the manner of medieval devils, who were represented in ugly and hybrid forms with bestial characteristics. Since human embodiment is a positive thing in itself, evil must be a warping of that nature." Ibid., 71.

established as a formal religion.[67] Brad Birzer has similarly observed that it is a "Gnostic interpretation and reading of what was left of traditional Númenórean theology" that is given by Sauron when he seduces the Númenóreans into worshipping Melkor instead of Eru:

> Ilúvatar was the false god, the "God of Darkness," said the dark prophet and priest Sauron. Melkor was the true god, the "Giver of Freedom" to men. "The wretched soul has strayed into a labyrinth of torment and wanders without a way out," ancient Gnostic writings teach, "it seeks to escape from the bitter chaos, but knows not how to get out." In Tolkien's mythology, Sauron presents himself as the Gnostic savior, urging the Númenóreans away from the labyrinth of Ilúvatar's time and space and toward the "true god" Melkor.[68]

Whether or not Melkor and Sauron succeeded in convincing themselves of this fact, they at least seem to have found the promulgation of this lie expedient as a means for corrupting Elves and Men. Tolkien writes in a commentary that their "cunning motive is probably best expressed thus. To wean one of the God-fearing from their allegiance it is best to propound another *unseen* object of allegiance and another hope of benefits; propound to him a Lord who will sanction what he desires and not forbid it" (MR 398). Long before the rise of Númenor, however, Men had already been lulled by Melkor into such Manichaeism, for, as Andreth informs Finrod in the *Athrabeth*, "still many Men perceive the world only as a war between Light and Dark equipotent. But you will say: nay, that is Manwë and Melkor; Eru is above them" (MR 321). Thus, it would seem that Shippey is in fact more correct than he realizes when he discovers a certain Manichaeism in Tolkien's representation of evil, for it is not an implicit but an explicit Manichaeism that Tolkien embodies in his fiction. Yet surely it weighs heavily against Shippey's claim that Tolkien's own views on evil were Manichaean when the principal representatives of the Manichaean outlook within his fiction are themselves the greatest agents of evil and the ones standing to gain the most from the spread of its doctrine. Instead, and as we shall see more fully below, Tolkien's purpose seems rather to have been to illustrate the point John Milbank makes in his account of the privation theory of St. Thomas and Augustine: "For evil to be at all, it must still deploy and invoke some good, yet it would like to

---

67   Ibid., 80.
68   Birzer, *Tolkien's Sanctifying Myth*, 98.

forget this: evil as positive is evil's own fondest illusion."[69] Thus, while Tolkien does expressly touch on the question of Manichaeism in his writings, he does so in such a manner as to suggest its ultimately demonic nature.[70] As we will see later in the chapter, Tolkien was also deeply interested, as Shippey is again right to observe, in the seeming independence and autonomy of evil recognized by the Manichees; yet, as we will also see, he gives this seeming independence and autonomy of evil a very different and arguably even more powerful source than what ancient Manichaeism was able to account for.

If the aim of domination is the reduction of the being of another to the image or extension of one's own being, the principal means for accomplishing this end is what Tolkien refers to as "Magic," not now in the sense of a generous "Enchantment," but in its negative, occult, and manipulative sense, or, as its modern counterpart has it, "the Machine," which leads to the third aspect of the Ring I wish to consider here. Although Tolkien famously discouraged his readers from allegorizing the Ring (the Ring as nuclear power or the atomic bomb, for example), in one letter he nevertheless says that the "primary symbolism of the Ring" is "the will to mere power, seeking to make itself objective by physical force and mechanism, and so inevitably by lies" (L 160).[71] Note that Tolkien does not say that the Ring symbolizes technology or mechanization, but that it symbolizes the *will* or intent to dominate through the production and use of these means. Thus, if the Ring in Tolkien's fiction should appear as a thing inherently evil, as Shippey points out, I submit that it is less because Tolkien has momentarily lapsed into a Manichaean, evil-objectifying dualism than it is an issue of the Ring in this instance embodying symbolically and mythically an inherently problematic attitude towards reality. Also, as the mythical incarnation of Sauron's corrupt will, the Ring possesses (ironically) a personal dimension or connection that sets it apart from ordinary inanimate objects. The reason the Ring cannot be *used* for any good whatsoever, in other words, is not because it is an objectified form of independently existing evil, but because the Ring represents and embodies a

---

69 John Milbank, "Evil: Darkness and Silence," 22.

70 In this Tolkien may be seen to reverse what Candler has suggested is Nietzsche's own "implicit suggestion" in *Thus Spake Zarathustra* that "Judaism and Christianity are themselves corruptions of an originally pure [pre-Christian and proto-Gnostic] Zoroastrianism which can be redeemed by more forcefully saying 'yes' to that particular past, while negating its false images…" Candler, "Tolkien or Nietzsche, Philology and Nihilism," 27.

71 That Tolkien may have had Nietzsche's notion of the will to power particularly in mind here is further implied in his statement, in the same passage, that one "moral" of *The Lord of the Rings* is, consistent with Nietzsche, "the obvious one that without the high and noble the simple and vulgar is utterly mean," and yet, contrary to Nietzsche, "without the simple and ordinary the noble and heroic is meaningless."

person, and even evil persons such as Sauron are (as Kant recognized) ultimately to be treated as ends and never as means only.

Yet, even considered as a material object, Sauron's Ring might be compared to what Thomas describes in his *Summa,* in an article on "Whether the adornment of women is devoid of mortal sin," as a case of "art directed to the production of good which men cannot use without sin" (ST 2–2.169.2 ad 4), a passage Jacques Maritain refers to in his *Art and Scholasticism* and thus one that Tolkien may have been at least indirectly familiar with.[72] In such cases, Thomas argues, "it follows that the workmen sin in making such things, as directly affording others an occasion of sin; for instance, if a man were to make idols or anything pertaining to idolatrous worship." In addition to it being the mythical embodiment of Sauron's corrupted will, therefore, the Ring in and of itself is evil in the sense that it is was made for one purpose alone, namely the tyrannous domination of others, and therefore has this evil as its only "proper" use (for which it is indeed useful, and therefore in that sense "good").[73]

As to the "physical force and mechanism" whereby the will to domination makes itself "objective," Tolkien explains elsewhere in the same letter quoted above that he means by this

> all use of external plans or devices (apparatus) instead of development of the inherent inner powers or talents — or even the use of these talents with the corrupted motive of dominating: bulldozing the real world, or coercing other wills. The Machine is our more obvious modern form though more closely related to Magic than is usually recognized. (L 145–46)

The difference between true art and the tyranny of domination is that the one seeks to shepherd things as they are, cultivating and adorning those properties already inherent in them by virtue of their createdness, whereas the other imposes upon things one's own godlike order and purposes. This is where the necessity

---

72 Maritain, *Art and Scholasticism,* 71. On the possibility of Tolkien's having read *Art and Scholasticism,* see the Introduction.

73 Another passage from St. Thomas, this time from the *Summa*'s discussion of evil proper, that might possibly inform a reading of Sauron's Ring is found in his explanation, discussed earlier, as to how good can be the cause of evil (ST 1.49.1). When there is a "defect" or "ineptitude" in the instrument or matter of the agent, Thomas argues, then there will be a corresponding defect in the action or effect of the action. And this is the problem with the Ring: designed as a means for dominating others, in addition to it being the literal embodiment of a corrupt or defective will, the Ring has an inherent defect that must corrupt every action, no matter how well intentioned, in which it is used. (For a related discussion on how "Aquinas also has something to contribute to the problem of the Ring of Power," see Alison Milbank, *Chesterton and Tolkien as Theologians,* 24.)

of Magic or the Machine comes in, for, by their instrumentality, the natural limitations of both agent and things may be transcended: "enhanc[ing] the natural powers of a possessor" (L 152) and thus "making the will more quickly effective" in the world (L 145), Magic and Machines, by the reduction "to a minimum (or vanishing point) of the gap between the idea or desire and the result or effect" (L 200), help the creature approximate the kind of absolute power and efficacy of will possessed by the Creator.

And this, incidentally, I submit is the relevant mythological, theological, and metaphysical context for Tolkien's whole polemic against modern industrialization: its lust after "devices" and "apparatuses" for the more efficient control of nature is nothing less than a continuation of what for both Tolkien and St. Thomas was the primeval and diabolical quest for the creational power of God, whereby one might "bring into Being things of his own." As Tolkien puts it in another letter, in contrast to "art which is content to create a new secondary world in the mind," the Machine "attempts to actualize desire, and so to create power in this World; and that cannot really be done with any real satisfaction" (L 88). This theological subtext to Sauron's Ring, which is in its own turn a symbol of all forms of tyrannous technology, also helps make further sense of Tolkien's claim that the central conflict in *The Lord of the Rings*, a book that never mentions the Creator, is nevertheless "about God, and His sole right to divine honour" (L 243). The question posed by the Ring, in essence, is the question of who among creatures has the right to "play God," to which the entire quest of the Fellowship to destroy the Ring is the implicit answer, namely, that only God has the right to play God.[74]

---

74 Though it takes us beyond the immediate concern of this chapter, some comment might be made here comparing Tolkien's metaphysics of the machine with the most influential philosophical essay on the subject, Martin Heidegger's "The Question Concerning Technology." (For a comparison of Tolkien and Heidegger, see also Malpus, "Home," referred to earlier.) In his essay Heidegger calls into question the adequacy of the instrumental definition of technology in terms of a system of means and ends, of causes and effects, the approach, in other words, implicit in Tolkien's characterization of the Machine as an instrument for "making the will more *effective*." The problem with the instrumental, means-and-ends, cause-and-effect analysis of technology, according to Heidegger is that the system of causality is already part of the technological perspective, and thus fails to get at its true essence. The instrumental definition of technology, in other words, defines technology *technologically*. Heidegger includes in his critique of the insufficiency of the instrumental definition of technology any attempt (such as Tolkien's) to understand technology theologically or metaphysically. Heidegger's critique, for example, of Tolkien's view of technology primarily as a means for domination, and domination (as I have been arguing) in turn as a desire for God's own power of creation, would be that this views God in terms of "causality and making, without ever considering the essential origin of this causality," and thus loses "all that is exalted and holy, the mysteriousness of [God's] distance." Heidegger, *The Question Concerning Technology*, 26. The problem with Tolkien's ultimately theological analysis of the problem of technology, in short, is that it already naively partakes of and presupposes the technological.

Evil and the
Objectification of the Self

DOMINATION, THEREFORE, INVOLVES THE ATTEMPTED REDUCTION
or assimilation by means of Magic or Machinery of the being of others to the
being of oneself. As Tolkien's stories also aim to illustrate, and as a number of his

---

Tolkien, of course, would see things quite differently, arguing perhaps that it is precisely in its lust
for the Creator's own power of creation that domination, manifesting itself in technology, denies
the exaltedness, holiness, and mysteriousness of divine distance. Notwithstanding his critique, for
Heidegger, technology, for all its dangers, remains a valid and even inevitable mode in which being
"reveals" itself to human beings, one in which things present themselves in terms of an orderable or
controllable "standing-reserve" for human use, as energy that can be extracted and stored, unlocked
and transformed, regulated and secured, ready-at-hand to be called on when needed (14–17). The
real problem, in Heidegger's view, arises when this inevitable mode of revealing comes to exclude
other modes of revealing. As in Tolkien's discussion of the effects of the domination motive, for
Heidegger the revealing of technology is one in which "the object disappears into the objectlessness
of standing-reserve" (19). Heidegger points out, however, that this becomes even more problematic
when "man in the midst of objectlessness" becomes "nothing but the orderer" of a now objectless,
standing-reserve, and so "comes to the very brink of a precipitous fall; that is, he comes to the point
where he himself will have to be taken as standing-reserve" (27), an insight that, as we shall see
later, has an important place in Tolkien's polemic as well. Despite his reservations, Heidegger may
even be seen to approach the kind of theological critique implicit in Tolkien when he writes that,
"Meanwhile man, precisely as the one so threatened, exalts himself to the posture of lord of the
earth…. This illusion gives rise in turn to one final delusion: It seems as though man everywhere
and always encounters only himself" (27). What, then, is the solution for Heidegger? Part of the
answer is that, because of its inevitability, rather than demonizing it, technology is a reality we
must resign ourselves to and whose essence we must simply seek to understand.

For Tolkien, by contrast, when it comes to technology, if not exactly an evil *per se* (since nothing,
insofar as it has being, is in itself evil), much of the motivation behind it, especially in modernity, is
not just figuratively but literally, in Heidegger's words, the "work of the devil." The second part of
Heidegger's solution, however, is to re-cultivate a "more primally granted revealing that could bring
the saving power into its first shining forth in the midst of the danger," and Heidegger finds this saving
power in what the Greeks called *poiesis* and *techne*, or art, whereby they "brought the presence of the
gods, brought the dialogue of divine and human destinings, to radiance" (34). What we need, then,
is a "decisive confrontation" between technology and "a realm that is, on the one hand, akin to the
essence of technology and, on the other, fundamentally different from it. Such a realm is art" (35). For
Tolkien, too, as we have seen, the opposition is between art and the Machine, between Magic understood
as "enchantment" and Magic understood as power and control, though he certainly draws the line of
kinship between these two differently than Heidegger does: for Heidegger, art and technology are two
species belonging to the same genus of *poiesis*; for Tolkien, the Machine is most often the result of the
corruption of the artistic impulse. As to the particular task Heidegger suggests that art must assume,
namely reinvigorating the world with a sense of divine "presence," Tolkien couldn't agree more, as
this is what his own art sets forth to do. Finally, even if Tolkien is less sanguine than Heidegger is about
the intrinsic validity or worth of technology, he could also agree with Heidegger's conclusion to his
essay, even if giving it an interpretation different from the one meant by Heidegger himself, namely
that "the more questioningly we ponder the essence of technology, the more mysterious the essence
of art becomes" (35). As Tolkien might prefer to put it, it is in contrast to the darkness (and evil) of
technology that the light (and goodness) of true art is made all the more manifest.

commentators have noted, one of the great ironies of modern industrialization, technology, and its related consumerism is the way in which they have rendered human beings so helplessly dependent upon the very things that were supposed to set them free. This is certainly the case with Sauron, the objectification of whose power in the One Ring makes him simultaneously able to conquer Middle-earth and that much more vulnerable to eventual defeat. As Tolkien explains:

> The Ring of Sauron is only one of the various mythical treatments of the placing of one's life, or power, in some external object, which is thus exposed to capture or destruction with disastrous results to oneself. If I were to "philosophize" this myth, or at least the Ring of Sauron, I should say it was a mythical way of representing the truth that *potency* (or perhaps rather *potentiality*) if it is to be exercised, and produce results, has to be externalized and so as it were passes, to a greater or less degree, out of one's direct control. A man who wishes to exert "power" must have subjects, who are not himself. But he then depends on them. (L 279)[75]

Tolkien's reasoning here calls to mind Hegel's famous master-slave dialectic, according to which it is the master who, in his dependence upon the slave, is in fact the slave to the slave. As Kreeft observes, if today we do not have slaves it is only

> because we have substitutes for them: machines. The Industrial Revolution made slavery inefficient and unnecessary. But our addiction is the same whether the slaves are made of flesh, metal, or plastic. We have done exactly what Sauron did in forging the Ring. We have put our power into things in order to increase our power. And the result is, as everyone knows but no one admits, that we are now weak little wimps, Shelob's slaves, unable to survive a blow to the great spider of our technological network. We tremble before a nationwide electrical blackout or a global computer virus.... In our drive for power we have deceived ourselves into thinking that we have become more powerful when all the time we have been becoming less. We

---

75 In a parallel passage from another letter, Tolkien writes: "But to achieve this [i.e. Sauron's dominion] he had been obliged to let a great part of his own inherent power (a frequent and very significant motive in myth and fairy-story) pass into the One Ring. While he wore it, his power on earth was actually enhanced. But even if he did not wear it, that power existed and was in 'rapport' with himself: he was not 'diminished.' Unless some other seized it and became possessed of it. If that happened, the new possessor could (if sufficiently strong and heroic by nature) challenge Sauron, become master of all that he had learned or done since the making of the One Ring, and so overthrow him and usurp his place" (L 153).

are miserable little Nietzsches dreaming we are supermen. For in gaining
the world we have lost our selves.[76]

Approaching Tolkien's Ring from a related direction, Alison Milbank has
compared Tolkien's insight into the estrangement between agent and artifact
with Karl Marx's critique of capitalism (based in its turn on Hegel's master-slave
analysis). According to Marx, capitalist economies alienate the worker from his
labor by treating the commodities he produces as having an independent life
or existence of their own,[77] a relationship which, at any rate, certainly obtains
between Sauron and his Ring, wherein we see the Manichaean aspirations of evil
as the will-to-dominate seeking to make itself "objective" and so independent.

More than us merely becoming dependent upon our technology or artifacts,
however, Tolkien implies that there is a sense in which, in the process, we have
surrendered to them something of our own *being*. Thus, in transferring much of
his power and purposes into the One Ring, the instrument of his domination,
Sauron is also mythically depicted, in a kind of parody of the Incarnation, as
placing part of his own *self* in the Ring, so that, when the Ring is destroyed,
that part of Sauron tied to the Ring is destroyed along with it: "if the One Ring
was actually *unmade,* annihilated, then its power would be dissolved, Sauron's
own being would be diminished to vanishing point, and he would be reduced
to a shadow, a mere memory of malicious will" (L 153, emphasis original). In
Sauron's mythic identity of subjective self and external, objective instrument
or commodity, Tolkien makes the serious, real-world metaphysical point that,
in the process of aggrandizing ourselves through materialistic acquisitiveness
and the scientific mastery of nature, we have in fact emptied ourselves, denied
our own nature, and sacrificed something of our own inherent and authentic
being.[78] Domination comes at a price, for, in reducing the other to oneself, one
is required to reduce his self to his other.

An even more extreme example of this phenomenon is Tolkien's notion of
"Morgoth's Ring," the idea that

---

76 Kreeft, *The Philosophy of Tolkien,* 187–88. For a similar analysis, see Caldecott, *The Power
of the Ring,* 43–45.

77 Alison Milbank, "'My Precious': Tolkien's Fetishized Ring," 36–37.

78 As Kreeft writes, in the "idolatry and fetishism" of modern Sauronism, the self has been
"'unselfed' — not filled but emptied, not enhanced but devastated. The object grew into a god, and
we shrank into slaves. We exchanged places: we became the objects, the its, and it became the subject, the I. We found our identity in what was less than ourselves, in what we could possess. We were
possessed by our possession, or by our possessiveness. We who began as the Adam (Man) became the
golem, the 'Un-man.'" Kreeft, *The Philosophy of Tolkien,* 110.

to gain domination over Arda, Morgoth had let most of his being pass into the *physical* constituents of the Earth — hence all things that were born on Earth and lived on and by it, beasts or plants or incarnate spirits, were liable to be "stained".... Melkor "incarnated" himself (as Morgoth) permanently. He did this so as to control the *hröa*, the "flesh" or physical matter of Arda. He attempted to identify himself with it. A vaster, and more perilous, procedure, though of similar sort to the operations of Sauron with the Rings. Thus, outside the Blessed Realm, all "matter" was likely to have a "Melkor ingredient," and those who had bodies, nourished by the *hröa* of Arda, had as it were a tendency, small or great, towards Melkor: they were none of them wholly free of him in their incarnate form, and their bodies had an effect upon their spirits.... Sauron's relatively smaller power was *concentrated*; Morgoth's vast power was *disseminated*. The whole of "Middle-earth" was Morgoth's Ring. (MR 394–95, 400, emphasis original)

If Sauron's Ring is a parody of the Incarnation, Melkor's "Ring" might be said to be a parody of the creation act itself: in dispersing his own being throughout the material creation, Melkor attempts to make the world participate not in Ilúvatar but in himself for its being, a point that would again seem to reveal the subliminal aspirations to divinity behind the modern impetus for the mastery of nature.[79]

The idea that Melkor had "disseminated" part of his own evil self into the very material being of the Earth is by itself somewhat peculiar and may again seem to lend support to Shippey's identification of a Manichaean dualistic strain in Tolkien's thought. While there are a number of different levels at which Tolkien's notion of Morgoth's Ring might be evaluated, for the present we may simply note Tolkien's emphatic denial, and in overt contradiction with one of the central tenets of Manichaean thought, that matter in his fiction is by any means inherently evil. On the contrary, in good Augustinian fashion

---

79 And as in the case of Sauron's Ring, through his concept of "Morgoth's Ring" Tolkien again reinforces the principle that domination ends up ultimately diminishing rather than augmenting one's own power and being. As Tolkien writes of Arien, the Maiar-spirit to whom the Valar gave the charge of the sun: "And Arien Morgoth feared with a great fear, but dared not come nigh her, having indeed no longer the power; for as he grew in malice, and sent forth from himself the evil that he conceived in lies and creatures of wickedness, his might passed into them and was dispersed, and he himself became ever more bound to the earth, unwilling to issue from his dark strongholds. With shadows he hid himself and his servants from Arien, the glance of whose eyes they could not long endure; and the lands near his dwelling were shrouded in fumes and great clouds" (S 101–2).

Tolkien writes: "'Matter' is not regarded as evil or opposed to 'Spirit.' Matter was wholly good in origin. It remained a 'creature of Eru' and still largely good, and indeed self-healing, when not interfered with: that is, when the latent evil intruded by Melkor was not deliberately roused and used by evil minds" (MR 344). One statement Tolkien would appear to be making through his concept of Morgoth's Ring, accordingly, is that, if material being should at least *seem* to have an inherent tendency towards evil, as per the Manichaean explanation, this tendency is in fact not inherent in matter at all, but is adventitious, the result of a Fall that *all* creation, and not just its free, spiritual or moral beings, has partaken in. If so, then the dualism we find in Tolkien might perhaps best be compared with the "provisional dualism" David Bentley Hart finds present in the New Testament: matter "stained" by a "Melkor ingredient" would be comparable to the *stoicheia* of which the Apostle Paul speaks (Gal. 4:3), the "rudimentary elements" of an otherwise good world subject for a time to futility, groaning for its redemption, and awaiting the "manifestation of the sons of God" (Rom. 8:19–23)—a world, that is (and as Tolkien put it in his letter to his son Christopher), in which "evil labours with vast powers and perpetual success—in vain" (L 76). By means of his Morgoth's Ring concept, accordingly, Tolkien again would seem to concede at most the *appearance* of a kind of Manichaean dualism on the one hand, while at the same time attempting to give an orthodox cause or explanation of the *reality* behind this appearance, much as we found him in the last chapter affirming an "apparent Anankê" of "nature chained in material cause and effect, the chain of death," all the while positing the existence of an absolute divine providence working behind this "apparent Anankê" and governing all things towards their own higher, "eucatastrophic" purpose. To this point we will return shortly.

Evil and Annihilation

THE LAST STAGE IN TOLKIEN'S HIERARCHY OF EVIL, ALREADY anticipated somewhat in his account of domination and thus revealing the latent motive within it, is that of outright *annihilation*, the will not simply to *control* the being of others, but to destroy it all together. In the *Ainulindalë*, although Melkor is initially content, when the Vision of the world is first given, with making himself the lord and master over it, failing this, by the end of the tale, he falls into utter nihilism, as when we read earlier of his efforts to undo all the demiurgic work of the other Valar. In a commentary titled "Notes on motives in *The Silmarillion*,"[80] Tolkien distinguishes the domination of Sauron from the later annihilationism of Melkor in this way:

> When Melkor was confronted by the existence of other inhabitants of Arda, with other wills and intelligences, he was enraged by the mere fact of their existence.... Hence his endeavor always to break wills and subordinate them to or absorb them into his own will and being, before destroying their bodies. This was sheer nihilism, and negation its one ultimate object: Morgoth would no doubt, if he had been victorious, have ultimately destroyed even his own "creatures," such as the Orcs, when they had served his sole purpose in using them: the destruction of Elves and Men.... [L]eft alone, he could only have gone raging on till all was leveled again into a formless chaos....
>
> Sauron had never reached this stage of nihilistic madness. He did not object to the existence of the world, so long as he could do what he liked with it. He still had the relics of positive purposes, that descended from the good of the nature in which he began: it had been his virtue (and therefore also the cause of his fall, and of his relapse) that he loved order and coordination, and disliked all confusion and wasteful friction....
>
> Morgoth had no "plan": unless destruction and reduction to *nil* of a world in which he had only a *share* can be called a "plan." But this is, of course, a simplification of the situation. Sauron had not served Morgoth, even in his last stages, without becoming infected by his lust for destruction, and his hatred of God (which must end in nihilism). (MR 395–97)

The will to dominate, as typified by Sauron, still at least admits the existence and therefore at some level the desirableness of other things, provided they can be made to enlarge oneself. This ambition, however, is never wholly achievable, inasmuch as the otherness of things is ultimately an irreducible, transcendental prerogative and gift of all being, and so the unwavering pursuit of absolute domination must invariably devolve into annihilationism, the will to power, in other words, into the will to obliterate. In his suggestion that, following the success of his own domination, Melkor "could only have gone raging on till all was leveled again into a formless chaos," Tolkien articulates the same logical progression of evil that he would have observed in Maritain's *Art and Scholasticism*, which

---

80 A variant manuscript of the same commentary, according to Tolkien's son Christopher, bears the title "Some notes on the 'philosophy' of *The Silmarillion*" (MR 394).

contains this account of Thomas's discussion in the *Summa* of the potentially
infinite hunger of the concupiscible appetite (ST 1–2.30.4):

> Material progress may contribute [to the production of art], to the extent
> that it allows man leisure of soul. But if such progress is employed only
> to serve the will to power and to gratify a cupidity which opens *infinite*
> jaws — *concupiscentia est infinita* — it leads the world back to chaos at an
> accelerated speed; that is its way of tending toward the principle.[81]

In summary, in Melkor we see the misguided, primeval attempt at making things
other than himself, after passing through the Sauronic desire to assimilate all
other things to his own self, devolve finally into its complete antithesis in the
desire to unmake those things other than himself, the feeling, that is, of one's
own being as threatened by and impinged upon by the mere fact of their existence.
In this, moreover, Tolkien treats us to a stinging indictment of where modern
industrial and mechanized culture is headed. The Sauronic "will to mere power"
(L 160), according to Tolkien (and in contrast to Nietzsche), is not the solution
to, but the presage of, the Melkorish will to nothingness.[82]

Given our earlier point about evil always involving the desire for some
good, it may well be wondered how the Melkorish will to annihilation is even
psychologically possible. How can someone *will* nothing, that is, find the utter
absence of anything desirable, given that the proper object of the will is always
some real or perceived good, and that what is good is always something that
has being? *Nothing*, in short, cannot be a cause, even of desire.[83] To answer this
question, we may recall how the Sauronic desire to suppress the *alterity* of things
is in fact a desire for something of the *aseity* of God, and even the express desire
to rebel against God is a desire for an apparent good, namely independence. In
the same way, the desire to annihilate, like the desire to create, is a desire for
a power that God alone has, and therefore, taken by itself, is something good.
Indeed, the power to create is identical with the power to annihilate, the power
to give existence being one with the power also to take it away. In his discussion of divine government in the *Summa*, in an article on "whether God can

---

81 Maritain, *Art and Scholasticism*, 75.

82 On Tolkien and Nietzsche's concept of "will to power," see Blount, "*Über*hobbits: Tolkien,
Nietzsche, and the Will to Power."

83 As Umberto Eco has remarked in the different but not unrelated case of the modern affirmation of non-being or nothingness over being or existence as the simpler or primary metaphysical
explanation of things, "if we aspire to nothingness, by this act of aspiration we are already in being."
Eco, "On Being," 16.

annihilate anything," Thomas explains that, just as God is free to create and preserve things in their being in the first place, "so after they have been made, he is free not to give them being, and thus they would cease to exist; and this would be to annihilate them" (ST 1.104.3).[84] And although Thomas does not make the point expressly, because things exist as a result of God immediately and "continually pouring out being into them" (ST 1.104.3), it stands to reason that nothing but God could ever bring it about that they altogether cease to exist (ST 1.104.4).[85]

It is to this same realization that Melkor is forcibly brought, for, as Tolkien further explains in his "Notes on motives in *The Silmarillion*," for all his efforts at obliterating the being of things, Melkor "was aware, at any rate originally when still capable of rational thought, that he could not 'annihilate' them: that is, destroy their being…. Melkor could not, of course, 'annihilate' anything of matter, he could only ruin or destroy or corrupt the forms given to matter by other minds in their sub-creative activities" (MR 395 and note). Continuing on, Tolkien writes that Melkor nevertheless "became so far advanced in Lying that he lied even to himself, and pretended that he could destroy them and rid Arda of them altogether. Hence his endeavour always to break wills and subordinate them to or absorb them into his own will and being, before destroying their bodies. This was sheer nihilism, and negation its one ultimate object" (396). Thus, even in Melkor's rage to level all "into a formless chaos," Tolkien finds a glimmer of hope, for "even so he would have been defeated, because it [i.e., the world] would still have 'existed,' independent of his own mind, and a world in potential." As to the reason why the ultimate "destruction and reduction to *nil*" must be impossible, the closest Tolkien comes to explaining this directly is his statement that it was "a world in which [Melkor] had only a *share*" (397), something that may remind us of Ilúvatar's speech to the Ainur in the *Book*

84 Were God in fact to annihilate things in this way, of course, Thomas argues that God wouldn't exactly be "causing" it to cease to exist, inasmuch as "non-being has no cause *per se*," and God as pure being can only *cause* something like himself, namely being. Rather, by virtue of their being created from nothing, creatures already have a constitutional "tendency" toward non-being, so that, if they were annihilated, it would not be by God actively "causing" it to be, but "by withdrawing his [creative] action from them" (ST 1.104.3 ad 1). As Thomas explains further, "if God were to annihilate anything, this would not imply an action on God's part, but a mere cessation of his action" (ST 1.104.3 ad 3).

85 Even so, as Thomas argues in this same article, God in fact does not and will not annihilate anything, for in the order of nature things may become corrupted, but then the matter out of which things are made would still exist. Nor does annihilation occur according to the *supernatural* order of the "manifestation of grace, since rather the power and goodness of God are manifested by the preservation of things in being. Therefore we must conclude by denying absolutely that anything at all will be annihilated."

of Lost Tales version of the *Ainulindalë* (discussed in chapter one) that he has made all things to "*share* in the reality of Ilúvatar myself" (BLT 55).[86] Things have their being by participating in God, by having God, as Thomas puts it, "continually pouring out being into them." Creaturely existence is a font that, having the divine being and power itself as its infinite reservoir, only God can turn off. The same power to "send forth" the Flame Imperishable that Melkor seeks at the beginning of creation is also one with the power to withdraw it, so that Melkor can no more prevent the Creator from communicating being to his creatures through annihilation than Melkor could successfully replace the Creator as the source of their being through their domination. Again we find that evil in Tolkien's fictional world not only begins with, but also returns to and climaxes in, a futile defiance of the kind of theological metaphysics of creation articulated by St. Thomas.

There is nevertheless a sense in Tolkien's world in which one can at least ritually enact, after a fashion, the annihilation of the world through suicide, through the "annihilation" of one's own self. Evil may never be able to "corrupt the whole good," as Thomas says, yet, because evil is the privation of being, it follows that every act of evil succeeds in eroding something of the evil-doer's own being, causing him to be less than what he is. For Aquinas, as Philipp Rosemann observes, "to do evil, or to sin, means to act against one's own conscience, that is to say, against the innermost core of one's own being. This split *within* the human being, this division of the self against itself, is at the same time a split *outside* the human being, that is to say, a division between the sinner and God."[87] One way of striking out at God, accordingly, is to strike at oneself as his image-bearer, and one way of obliterating the world is, so to speak, to obliterate oneself. We see an aspect of this, of course, in Sauron and Melkor, who, in their desire to dominate and destroy, are willing and even required to do violence to their own selves, rending their own spirits in an act that for Tolkien, as has been suggested, mythically dramatizes the spiritual suicide of the modern self, and all in order that they might invest part of themselves in the instruments and objects of their domination.[88] The link between the destruction of the world and the

---

86 That the will to annihilate is ultimately in rivalry with God may be further seen in Tolkien's equivalence, quoted earlier, between Melkor's "lust for destruction" on the one hand and "his hatred of God (which must end in nihilism)" on the other (MR 397).

87 Rosemann, *Understanding Scholastic Thought with Foucault*, 170.

88 This idea has been revisited recently in J.K. Rowling's popular *Harry Potter* series, in which the "Dark Lord" Voldemort, in an effort to make himself immortal and invincible, creates "horcruxes" by violently splitting his own soul into seven different parts and putting each part into some fetish-object held to be of great value or lineage in the wizarding-world.

self-destruction of suicide is made particularly perspicuous in the grim nihilism of Denethor, Steward of Gondor, who, when asked by Gandalf what he would have if his will could have its way, answers:

> "I would have things as they were in all the days of my life," answered Denethor, "and in the days of my longfathers before me: to be the Lord of this City in peace, and leave my chair to a son after me, who would be his own master and no wizard's pupil. But if doom denies this to me, then I will have *naught*: neither life diminished, nor love halved, nor honour abated." (ROTK 130, emphasis original)

When it becomes evident that he cannot have things as they once were, Denethor indeed chooses "naught" and sets himself on fire (like one of the "heathen kings," as he puts it), thus revealing the will to annihilation or nihilism latent not only within the will to domination, but even within the will to mere preservation examined earlier.[89]

It is also tempting to see this link between suicide and world-annihilation behind an early, alternative climax Tolkien envisioned to *The Lord of the Rings*, in which Gollum, rather than falling accidentally into the fires of Mount Doom with the Ring (as the final, published version has it), instead "commits suicide" by leaping into the fires with the Ring of his own accord, but not before pronouncing to Frodo that, in doing so, "I will destroy you all" (SD 5). It is possible that in stating this Gollum is merely referring to the fact that, in destroying the Ring along with himself, he would also succeed in killing Frodo and Sam in the conflagration to follow. However, as it is not evident that Gollum could or would have known that the destruction of the Ring would result in such a cataclysm, another more tantalizing possibility is that Gollum's declaration is intended to have a more symbolic significance. Throughout the passage, it is worth noting, Tolkien emphasizes the state of Gollum's "wretchedness" (it is referred to twice), and it is perhaps significant that, although Frodo and Sam are the only other individuals present, Gollum does not say "I will destroy you *both*," but "I will destroy you *all*." If Gollum, therefore, in this alternative ending saw his own death as a kind of ritual world-annihilation, together he and Frodo, who by contrast saw his own likely death as the means for saving the world, rather neatly dramatize the radical metaphysical difference between the martyr and

---

89 Another important example of the nihilism of suicide in Tolkien's fiction is the character of Ungoliant, discussed below, of whom it is said "that she ended long ago, when in her uttermost famine she devoured herself at last" (S 81).

the suicide, which Tolkien would have been familiar with from Chesterton's *Orthodoxy*. As Chesterton puts it there:

> a suicide is the opposite of a martyr. A martyr is a man who cares so much for something outside him, that he forgets his own personal life. A suicide is a man who cares so little for anything outside him, that he wants to see the last of everything. One wants something to begin: the other wants everything to end. In other words, the martyr is noble, exactly because (however he renounces the world or execrates all humanity) he confesses this ultimate link with life; he sets his heart outside himself: he dies that something may live. The suicide is ignoble because he has not this link with being: he is a mere destroyer; spiritually, he destroys the universe.[90]

Linking Chesterton's view of suicide with his Thomistic doctrine of creation in a manner no less applicable to Tolkien, Mark Knight writes that "the unique threat of suicide lies in the way that it inverts the act of Creation through an individual's choice to undo that act."[91] Self-annihilation is an act of resentment towards and defiance of the God who alone gives and ultimately controls being.

To return our attention to the *Ainulindalë* and the question of creation, the suicidal division between, in the one instance, self and self, and in the other instance, self and God, may already be seen in Melkor's hubristic desire for the Flame Imperishable. In his discussion of how the devil first "sinned by seeking to be as God," Thomas carefully qualifies his meaning to avoid the suggestion that, in doing so, the devil sought to be "equal" with God. According to Thomas, the angels sought to be "as God" not by "equality," but rather by "likeness," the reason being that, first, the angels would have known equality with God to be intrinsically impossible for any creature, and second, that, even if such equality were possible (or at least *thought* to be possible), in desiring it the angels would have been desiring a nature or essence other than their own, and thus would have been effectively desiring the abolition of their own being, a desire contrary to every nature (ST 1.63.3).[92] "Consequently," Thomas summarizes, "no thing of a lower order can ever desire the grade of a higher nature, just as an ass does not desire to be a horse; for were it to be so upraised, it would

---

90 Chesterton, *Orthodoxy*, 78–79.
91 Knight, *Chesterton and Evil*, 51.
92 As Thomas puts it in his article in the *Summa* on why evil is not or has no nature, "good is everything desirable; and thus, since every nature desires its own being and its own perfection, it must be said also that the being and the perfection of any nature has the character of goodness" (ST 1.48.1).

cease to be itself." For Thomas, in short, the desire that the devil may have had for God's own power to create nevertheless could not have involved a desire to be equal with God, inasmuch as he would have known such an eventuality to have entailed his own non-existence. Yet Thomas himself is arguably not entirely consistent when he claims that no being can desire the realization of circumstances that would entail its own destruction. In any event, Thomas goes on in the same passage to recognize that there are moments (not applicable to the angels, given their incorporeality) when the "imagination plays us false," leading a man to believe that by acquiring a "higher grade as to accidentals, which can increase without the destruction of the subject, he can also seek a higher grade of nature, to which he could not attain without ceasing to be." Toward the beginning of the *Summa*, however, in his discussion of "whether good is prior in idea to being," Thomas entertains the objection that good must be prior to being because it is more universal, as in the case of Judas, of whom Scripture says that it would have been better for him not to have been born, to which Thomas replies that it is not the non-being of a thing itself that is ever desired, but rather its non-being is desired for the sake of the removal of some other evil in something else, which is to say, for the sake of the *being* of something else, and so "even non-being can be spoken of as relatively good" (ST 1.5.2 ad 3). Thus, it would seem consistent with Thomas's own principles to say that the devil, in desiring to create, desired to be equal with God, and thus in a sense desired his own non-being, not for its own sake, but as a perceived condition for his gaining something good in itself.

This, at any rate, is how Satan's fall has been interpreted by René Girard, whose theory of mimetic desire Hayden Head has applied to Tolkien's depiction of evil. According to Girard, the suicidal desire for the essence of an "other" is implicitly involved in all such imitative desire: when we desire objects, things, people, status, or the like, we do not desire them so much for themselves as we do for the much more sordid, envious reason that they are possessed by an "Other." This means that desire for the object is in essence a desire for or towards the rival possessor of the object, meaning further that it is in fact the possessor who is the true object of desire. Entailed in this desire is an awareness that the rival, as the desired object, also stands in a position of superiority over the desirer. This acute awareness of one's own inferiority Girard refers to as the "ontological sickness": in coveting what the other desires, a person is in fact coveting the other's own "essence," and so sacrifices something of his own being. In his application of Girard's analysis of mimetic desire to Tolkien's fiction, Head writes of Melkor in particular that he is driven by a desire to imitate Ilúvatar and wishes to claim the ultimate prerogative of Eru, which is the capacity to create. And though he possesses as much "being" as a contingent creature can possess, though he is more powerful than his fellow Ainur, nevertheless, Melkor is not content with any "being" less than Eru's ultimate being. Like Satan's doomed attempt to rival God, however, Melkor's attempt to emulate Eru only serves to bring about his fall…. Having failed to acquire the light of Ilúvatar, Melkor… is left with the bitter consolation of "fire and wrath," dim parodies of Ilúvatar's creative fire.[93]

Implicit in Melkor's desire for the Flame Imperishable, in short, is the desire to supplant and to become his "rival" Eru. His desire is the "ontologically sick" and self-annihilating one of wanting an essence and being other than his own. As Thomas points out, however, such a desire is in effect a desire for the annihilation of one's own being, or as Tolkien himself puts it, it is the envy and "hatred of God…[that] must end in nihilism."

Perhaps an even more poignant example of evil's nihilistic bent than Melkor, and arguably the closest Tolkien at least *appears* to come to a Manichaean affirmation of evil as an ontologically independent force, is the spider-demon Ungoliant, the former servant of Melkor and the presumable ancestor to Shelob of *The Lord of the Rings*.[94] To lead up to Ungoliant's introduction in *The Silmarillion*, however, we might begin first with the *Ainulindalë*'s account of how, after the Ainur's Vision had been taken away, "in that moment they perceived a new thing, Darkness, which they had not known before, except in thought" (S 19–20). Here Tolkien unambiguously states darkness's status as a mere privation of light and hence its dependence upon the prior existence of light for its very potency. In this Tolkien aptly illustrates the very point St. Thomas makes in the *Summa* in regards to the dependence of evil upon good, not only for its existence, but also for the possibility of evil being known and experienced: as "darkness is known through light," so evil "must be known from the notion of good" (ST 1.48.1). Later in *The Silmarillion*, however, in the chapter "On the Darkening of Valinor," Tolkien would appear to come perilously close to contradicting this relationship of dependence. When first introduced, Ungoliant's existence is described as one of "taking all things to herself to feed her emptiness" and of hiding in a cleft in the mountain, where she "sucked up all light that she could

93 Head, "Imitative Desire," 141–42.
94 For an excellent analysis of Shelob, see Alison Milbank, *Chesterton and Tolkien as Theologians*, 71–80.

find, and spun it forth again in dark nets of strangling gloom, until no light more could come to her abode; and she was famished" (S 73). When solicited by Melkor to aid him in his assault on Valinor, home of the Valar, she veils the two of them in "a cloak of darkness" which was nothing less than "an Unlight, in which things seemed to be no more, and which eyes could not pierce, for it was void" (74). More curious still is Tolkien's account of the aftermath of Melkor and Ungoliant's attack on the Two Trees of Valinor, at that time the two principal sources of light in the world: "The Light failed; but the Darkness that followed was more than loss of light. In that hour was made a Darkness that seemed not lack but a thing with being of its own: for it was indeed made by malice out of Light, and it had power to pierce the eye, and to enter heart and mind, and strangle the very will" (76).

In portraying the darkness and evil of Ungoliant as "more" than a mere "loss" or negation of light, but as a "thing with being of its own," Tolkien would seem to challenge deliberately the Augustinian doctrine of evil as mere non-being in favor of the more dualistic and Manichaean account of evil. Indeed, the whole scene, especially with its emphasis on the imagery of light and darkness, poignantly captures the basic metaphysical drama according to the Manichees, who believed that evil "came from an invasion of the good — the 'Kingdom of Light' — by a hostile force of evil, equal in power, eternal, totally separate — the 'Kingdom of Darkness.'"[95] Or as Tolkien himself bracingly and perplexingly puts it in his "Mythopoeia" poem, "of Evil this / alone is deadly certain: Evil is" (TL 99).

Before concluding, however, as Shippey does, that Tolkien's presentation of evil is ambiguous, incoherent, or contradictory — the result of an effort to make sense of distinctly modern forms of evil by means of quaint or antiquated premodern theories of evil — we should consider whether Tolkien might not have had a deeper purpose in view here. In the last chapter, after all, we considered the not unrelated situation of how Tolkien's metaphysics of eucatastrophe presupposed — not for dramatic effect only, but as an allegedly real, empirical feature of the world — a dualism similar to that posited by Plato's *Timaeus* between the demiurgic powers struggling to do good in the world on the one hand and the countervailing force of an impersonal "Ananke" or causal necessity on the other. Yet we also saw how this tension for Tolkien was not ultimate but only "apparent," finding its perfect resolution in an even more transcendent deity who does not exist side-by-side with the realm of natural and material necessity but who is the very Creator of it. It is in a comparable spirit, I want

---

95 Brown, *Augustine of Hippo*, 47.

to suggest here, that we are to interpret Tolkien's depiction — preeminently in Ungoliant but also to a lesser degree in Melkor and Sauron — of evil's powerful impression of ontological independence.

First, it is important to note in the above episode from *The Silmarillion* that Tolkien does not in fact say that the darkness introduced by Ungoliant was a thing with being in itself, but rather that it "*seemed* not lack but a thing with being of its own" (much as Tolkien identifies it not as a real but an "*apparent* Ananke of our world"). Consistent with this is the passage cited earlier recording the Ainur's first experience of darkness, in which Tolkien writes again not that they had *actually* perceived something altogether new, but rather that "it *seemed* to them that in that moment they perceived a new thing" (S 19, emphasis added). As for the darkness introduced by and surrounding Ungoliant, the explanation given in the narrative for its "seeming" ontological independence is entirely in keeping with Tolkien's creation metaphysics, "for it was made by malice *out of Light*," and thus it had "power to pierce the eye, and to enter heart and mind, and strangle the very will." Ungoliant's evil and darkness, in other words, are powerful precisely because they have as the source of their strength the goodness and light which they negate, and it is this borrowed or exploited strength that in turn provides evil and darkness with even its *appearance* of radical independence. In this, once again, Tolkien may be seen to capture the very kind of phenomenon John Milbank sees as being fully accounted for in the privation theory of evil as taught by St. Thomas, namely "an incremental piling up of small deficient preferences which gradually and 'accidentally' (as Aquinas argued) produce the monstrous."[96]

The point of this analysis, however, is not merely to say that Tolkien's presentation of evil might be coherent after all, but to suggest that Tolkien is in fact doing something much more profound and interesting. Far from vacillating between the Augustinian and Manichaean theories of evil, Tolkien's purpose rather seems to be one of confronting Manichaeism head-on, not by contradicting it outright, but, more intriguingly, by conceding what even the pre-converted Augustine recognized as the superficial cogency, at least, behind Manichaean dualism: evil at times *seems* to have its own independent power and being. As Tolkien's friend C.S. Lewis put it in the context of his own rejection of Manichaeism in favor of the Augustinian privation theory, the Manichaean position does enjoy a certain "obvious *prima facie* plausibility."[97] I think the best way of

---

96 John Milbank, "Evil: Darkness and Silence," 21.
97 Lewis, "Evil and God," 22.

understanding Tolkien, therefore, is to see him as conceding the appearance of Manichaean evil while re-inscribing and accounting for this appearance in the only way in which, for him, it could be accounted for, namely in terms of an otherwise Augustinian and Thomistic metaphysics of creation. This "truth" of Manichaeism, moreover, is one that Thomas himself, after a fashion, defends in the *Summa* when he says that evil is no mere illusion, but has a real existence *in things* (ST 1.48.2), meaning that, in an important respect, evil is as real and present as the things in which it resides. This I also take to be the meaning behind Tolkien's emphatic claim in his "Mythopoeia" poem that "Evil is," for, as the poem also assures us of the eye that will see Paradise,

> Evil it will not see, for evil lies
>
> not in God's picture but in crooked eyes,
>
> not in the source but in malicious choice,
>
> and not in sound but in the tuneless voice. (TL 101)

As we have seen, for both Thomas and Tolkien, evil by itself is a "zero," but therein lies the issue: *evil is never by itself.* As Thomas puts it, "evil is the privation of good, and not pure negation" (ST 1.48.5 ad 1). Evil, in other words, is not isolatable to that small segment of the thing which it negates, for its effects reverberate throughout and might even be said to be amplified by the being that remains.[98] As Mary Edwin DeCoursey aptly put it in a 1948 dissertation on Thomas's metaphysics of evil, the privation of evil "is more than simple non-being. It has definite, malevolent ties with reality; it is the absence that is conspicuous."[99] In this way, as John Milbank has again put it, "it is possible for negativity to take a sublime

---

[98] An apt illustration of this principle occurs in the total devastation that results from Melkor's monstrous wolf, Carcharoth, swallowing the Silmaril jewel of fire and light when he bit off the hand of Beren, which was holding the jewel. Although the jewel, as a symbol of creative and sub-creative light and existence, is a thing beautiful and good in itself, inside the belly of Carcharoth, its powerful effect is only to magnify the madness, terror, and destruction of Carcharoth's rampage: "Of all the terrors that came ever into Beleriand ere Angband's fall the madness of Carcharoth was the most dreadful; for the power of the Silmaril was hidden within him" (S 182).

[99] DeCoursey, *The Theory of Evil in the Metaphysics of St. Thomas and Its Contemporary Significance: A Dissertation*, 34, also cited in Knight, *Chesterton and Evil*, 51. Herbert McCabe also puts the same point well: "Now does this mean that badness is unreal? Certainly not. Things really are bad sometimes and this is because the absence of what is to be expected is just as real as a presence. If I have a hole in my sock, the hole is not anything at all, it is just an absence of wool or cotton or whatever, but it is a perfectly real hole in my sock. It would be absurd to say that holes in socks are unreal and illusory just because the hole isn't made of anything and is purely an absence. *Nothing* in the wrong place can be just as real and just as important as *something* in the wrong place. If you inadvertently drive your car over a cliff you will have nothing to worry about; it is precisely the nothing that you will have to worry about." McCabe, *God Matters*, 29.

quasi-heroic form."[100] Thus, it is not *in spite* of evil's status as a privation that it seems to be so powerful, but precisely on account of it. To state it differently still, evil doesn't need to be ontologically independent in order for it to be a potent force to reckon with, since it has the very potency of the goodness of being at its disposal. Evil's status as a privation of being is not what mitigates its efficacy, therefore, but what establishes it: it is as a privation of being that evil is able to derive its power and potency from the being it labors, so to speak, to negate.[101] As Thomas again explains, evil is never capable of "corrupting the whole good" (ST 1.48.4), yet this only means that evil always has some remaining good behind it, giving it its very ontological efficacy and metaphysical momentum. One practical consequence of this doctrine is that, the more powerful the being in which evil is found, the greater that being's effects will be.[102]

This does not yet, however, get to the real heart and problem of the matter, for, as we have already touched on, the real scandal and mystery is that the being in which evil resides has the infinite Creator himself as its source, as the one "guaranteeing" and "preserving" evil with its seemingly inexhaustible resource of being (the subliminal realization of which also drives Melkor mad in his nihilistic despair). The ultimate answer to the question of why evil seems so powerful, then, is that evil has, for the time being at least, been given a pur- chase or lease on (or at least *within*) God's own creative power, for, at the heart of created being, including *corrupted* created being, is nothing less than the Flame Imperishable kindling all things into existence. While it may seem that this puts God at evil's disposal, however, ultimately the truth of the matter is quite the reverse: it means that even evil has to be at "God's disposal," as Ilúvatar reminds Melkor in the *Ainulindalë* at the close of the Music: "And thou, Melkor, shalt see that no theme may be played that hath not its uttermost source in me, nor can any alter the music in my despite. For he that attempteth this shall prove but mine instrument in the devising of things more wonderful, which he himself hath not imagined" (S 17). To be sure, evil is an enemy and a destroyer and its presence (by virtue of its negating absence) and causality (by abusing the

---

100 John Milbank, "Evil: Darkness and Silence," 21.

101 As we found John Milbank putting it earlier, "for evil to be at all, it must still deploy and invoke some good." Ibid., 22.

102 Tolkien expresses a related sentiment when he says that Gandalf, being good, had he taken and become corrupted by the Ring, "would have been far worse than Sauron. He would have remained 'righteous,' but self-righteous. He would have continued to rule and order things for 'good,' and the benefit of his subjects according to his wisdom (which was and would have remained great).... Thus, while Sauron multiplied...evil, he left 'good' clearly distinguishable from it. Gandalf would have made good detestable and seem evil" (L 332–33).

causality of the good that is there) are mysteries, mysteries that, in a sense, are inexplicable even for God, "for 'explanation' can pertain only to existence, and here evil is not seen as something in existence."[103] This means that, not having a being, nature, and logic of its own, evil must "borrow itself," so to speak, from the good. To use St. Thomas's distinction, evil may not be "willed" by God, but it is certainly "permitted" by him, so that, if evil should seem so radically powerful, it nevertheless must ultimately labor at its own expense — "in vain," as Ilúvatar puts it — providing as it does the infinite and omnipotent God yet another "instrument" for bringing about his good purposes. Like St. Thomas, Tolkien too, in the words of Brian Davies cited earlier, "seeks to understand [evil] as part of a world made by God."

Seen from this perspective, then, the real objection to Manichaeism is not that it makes evil real, but rather that it denies the existence of the omnipotent, transcendent Creator capable of making evil as real as it is, of giving evil, that is, the only reality to be had — the reality of the *good*. As Aquinas quotes Pseudo-Dionysius in one passage, "evil does not fight against good, *except through the power of the good*; in itself, indeed, it is powerless and weak" (SCG 3.9.4, emphasis added). In summary, then, it is precisely his Thomistic metaphysics of creation that enables Tolkien, through characters such as Ungoliant, Melkor, and Sauron, to take for granted the awesome and terrifying power of evil in the world — and thus allow the Manichaean insight into the radical power and being of evil, really for the first time, to come into its own — while at the same time reducing this same evil to nothing, and thereby holding out the hope of the ultimate futility and "vanity" of evil and hence its inevitable defeat. One can almost hear Tolkien saying, "And let *that* settle the Manichees."

Conclusion

IN THIS CHAPTER I HAVE ARGUED THAT, WHILE SHIPPEY IS quite correct that Tolkien's fictional depiction of evil is far more complex and nuanced than perhaps a one-sidedly Augustinian privation theory of evil has traditionally or typically emphasized, the solution Tolkien arrives at is itself arguably more sophisticated and coherent than the contradictory "running ambivalence" Shippey has characterized it as. Instead, I have argued that Tolkien's ponerology involves a highly original application of St. Thomas's metaphysics

---

103 Milbank, "Evil: Darkness and Silence," 18.

of creation and evil to uniquely modern forms of evil, forms of evil that the thirteenth-century Aquinas, for example, was largely unaware of. Yet it is an application that reveals as much about Tolkien's own dialectical and scholastic subtlety and inventiveness as it does about the profound explanatory power and adaptability of St. Thomas's philosophy of being. At the same time, I have sought to explicate Tolkien's remarkably cogent hierarchy and corresponding logic of evil, one that begins in a primordial, unnatural lust for the Flame Imperishable which gives being, before descending into the inordinate yet natural sub-creative impulse first to produce and then to preserve the things of one's own imagining, and at last devolving into the desire to dominate and then simply to annihilate the being of others. As I have further sought to show, while each of these forms of evil has its own peculiar identity and motives, at another level they are all variations of the same original sin of desiring what for both Tolkien and Aquinas is the Creator's exclusive power to give created being.

FINAL THEME

Of Metaphysics
and Myth

HE THESIS OF THIS BOOK HAS BEEN THAT BEHIND J.R.R. Tolkien's vast and vastly popular mythology of Middle-earth—giving his world a philosophical cogency and sophistication not often recognized by scholars, and certainly not typically associated with the fantasy or science-fiction genre—lies the influential metaphysical thought of Tolkien's great Catholic forebear, St. Thomas Aquinas. Structuring my discussion around Tolkien's creation-myth, the *Ainulindalë*, I have attempted not simply to analyze Tolkien's fiction in light of it, but also to show how the latter purposefully incarnates such important Thomistic themes as the relationship between faith and reason; the being, attributes, and persons of the divine Creator; the simultaneous realism or mind-independence and yet inherent intelligibility of all created being; the realization or fulfillment of intelligible form or essence in and through a thing's real act of existence; the dependence of artistic sub- or "con" creation on the Creator's prior, exclusive act of creation; the anthropological significance of angels; and the metaphysics of evil.

At the same time, my purpose has also been to suggest that, far from Tolkien's metaphysics being narrowly reducible to St. Thomas's, the nature of his Thomism often lies as much in his creative departures from or innovations upon the thought of the angelic doctor as it does in his overt debt to it. Although Tolkien never mentions St. Thomas by name, as we saw in the Introduction, the influence of St. Thomas on the Catholic culture, thought, and art of Tolkien's generation was nigh inescapable, especially for someone attempting to sub-create an alternative world of the philosophical complexity and magnitude of Tolkien's. The way in which I have conceived Thomas's influence on Tolkien, accordingly, has been in terms of his providing the latter with an inherited, trustworthy, yet always tacitly assumed, intellectual benchmark or framework by which Tolkien might both the more effectively determine what was metaphysically *necessary*, and within those parameters the more keenly discern what was metaphysically and therefore sub-creatively *possible*. Thus, in chapter one, for example, we saw how Tolkien's otherwise Thomistic metaphysical theism was (paradoxically) what also allowed his mythology to be fundamentally "about God" even when it scarcely bothered to mention him. We saw further how Tolkien's concept of eucatastrophe, while presupposing the traditional, orthodox view of divine presence and providence defended by St. Thomas, also requires for its full aesthetic and emotional effect a degree of provisional "forgetting" of the Creator and almost despairing of hope, conditions which set the stage for that special "miraculous" act of divine intervention whereby both the reader and the characters are powerfully reminded that, though God may be "never named," he is also the one who is "never absent." In chapter two, we saw how Tolkien similarly presupposes a Thomistic conception of divine and creational possibility in his developing a theory of sub-creative freedom or autonomy and creaturely contingency that is more likely to be associated with the theological voluntarism and counter-factual speculation of a William of Ockham than with the comparatively more reserved theology of Aquinas. In chapter three, we saw how Tolkien stresses the Thomistic insight as to the metaphysical primacy of the act of existence, not by putting the world in its created existence at the beginning of his creation-myth, but precisely by postponing the divine gift of being until the eschatological climax at the end. In the fourth chapter, we witnessed Tolkien at perhaps his metaphysical boldest in his postulation of reincarnating Elves and incarnate, "demiurgic" angels, again, entities that would seem to defy the comparative sobriety of St. Thomas's hierarchy of being on the one hand and yet whose sophisticated natures and powers, on the other hand, seem to presuppose the very logic of Thomas's hierarchy. Finally, in the last chapter I argued that, more than simply favoring the traditional Augustinian and Thomistic view of evil as a relative form of non-being, Tolkien in fact utilizes his Thomistic metaphysics of creation not so much to contradict as to sublate the Manichaean insight into the (apparent) independence and radical power of evil. What we see in each of these cases, accordingly, is I think less an uncritical adoption of Thomistic ideas than it is what one would in fact expect of someone of Tolkien's genius and originality, namely a creative appropriation and adaptation of Thomas's thought for his own literary purposes.

I want to suggest, however, that even here there would seem to be something remotely Thomistic in Tolkien's creative departures from St. Thomas, for the latter's own thought was nothing if not a profoundly creative appropriation and application of the metaphysics of his own intellectual forebears. It was arguably the infallible insight afforded by Christian revelation, after all, that allowed St. Thomas to discern and exploit hitherto unrealized potentialities in the thought of his predecessors, as when he used Aristotle's act-potency distinction, for example, to transcend Aristotle by means of his own essence-existence distinction; or when he utilized Aristotelian arguments to prove the arguably un-Aristotelian conclusion that the soul is both a form and a subsistent being capable of existing independently of the body of which it is the form; or when, in a clever application of the Neoplatonic logic of emanation, he argued the distinctly anti-Neoplatonic conclusion that the Creator alone can create. These are just a few examples of Thomas's own metaphysical innovation and the kind of thing Chesterton may have had in mind when he said, in the first epigraph with which I opened this book, that St. Thomas had "the imagination without the imagery."[1]

In Tolkien, by contrast, I submit that we meet with a metaphysician who had *both* the imagination *and* the imagery, which brings us to the point with which I wish to conclude this study. The primary objective of this book, as has been said, has been to enlist the metaphysical thought of St. Thomas in an effort to better understand an important yet hitherto largely unexamined dimension of Tolkien's literary project. In short, it has been occupied with the question, "What does St. Thomas Aquinas have to offer our understanding of J.R.R. Tolkien?" But Tolkien's own project was the self-conscious one of "recovery," that is, the "regaining of a clear view" of the world, the same world that St. Thomas labored so hard to analyze and understand, and yet whose explanation has become largely lost and to a large extent even unintelligible to the modern world. If so, to the extent to which Tolkien's own project of "recovery" has been successful, and to the extent that his project has been informed and guided by the metaphysical sensibility of St. Thomas, an appropriate question to ask would seem to be this: "What, if anything, does J.R.R. Tolkien have to offer St. Thomas Aquinas?" Might Tolkien, in other words, help us also recover the kind of metaphysical insight possessed by St. Thomas?

John Houghton, in his article on Augustine and Tolkien, has made the point that there are in fact "two moments in the task of theology." On the one hand, the theologian must "de-mythologize" and so render intelligible to his audience the meaning of divine revelation or sacred scripture by explaining it in terms of what they already know.[2] It is this first task of theology with which

---

1 Chesterton, *St. Thomas Aquinas: "The Dumb Ox,"* 152–53.
2 Houghton, "Augustine in the Cottage of Lost Play: The *Ainulindalë* as Asterisk Cosmology," 181.

St. Thomas was primarily involved, translating, as I suggested in the Introduction, the *mythos* of biblical revelation into the *logos* of Aristotle and the
"vernacular" of late medieval scholasticism. "On the other hand," Houghton
continues, "the theologian faces the task of recovery, of restoring the power of
images and stories that have grown weak from cultural change or from mere
familiarity. In this sense the theologian's task is not demythologizing but
mythopoesis as…'re-mythologizing'…"[3] As we have seen, it is this second task
of the theologian to which Tolkien devoted himself and his work. Yet what I
am suggesting here is that the world Tolkien "re-mythologizes" is not simply
the world of bare, ordinary experience, now become mundane or trite through
our constant exposure to and consequent familiarity with it, but includes, in
whole or in part, the specifically religious, theological, and philosophical world
he had inherited from his own Catholic intellectual tradition, and yet which
had also become truly quaint — when not in fact despised — in the eyes of his
modern audience. In short, where St. Thomas translated the biblical *mythos* into
the *logos* of Aristotle, what Tolkien represents in part is an effort to retransplant
the Thomistic *logos* back into the original, mythic soil from which it first took
root. As Tolkien himself writes, in the other epigraph with which I opened this
book, "naturally the stories come first." St. Thomas himself, in the opening
question of his *Summa*, points out the important role that the poetic structure
of metaphor (the stuff of myth), for example, plays in the science of sacred theology: since it belongs to the nature of human knowledge to begin in the senses,
it is "befitting" that spiritual truths should be communicated through sensible
images such as metaphor, and this not for the benefit of the simple-minded
only, inasmuch as the "very hiding of truth in figures is useful for the exercise of
thoughtful minds" as well (ST 1.1.9 corpus and ad 2).[4] Rational science, in other
words, takes as its starting point, and thus is in a dependent relationship upon,
the senses and therefore upon metaphor, much as Thomas's own metaphysics
had its roots in biblical mythology. As Louis Dupré has aptly generalized upon
the relationship between religion, mythology, and poetry on the one hand and
philosophy and metaphysics on the other,

---

3 Ibid.
4 As Owen Barfield, whose views on the interrelationship between language and reality were
influential on Tolkien, comments on Aquinas, he "and others after him, emphasized the importance
of using the humblest and most banal images, as symbols for purely spiritual truths or beings. For
only in this way could a representation be safely polarized into symbol and symbolized, into literal
and metaphorical." Barfield, *Saving the Appearances*: A *Study in Idolatry*, 74.

> Religious believers deepen their faith through metaphysics, while at the
> same time keeping the metaphysical flame alive.... Metaphysics has risen
> from mythology and religion. Without a religious sense of wonder the
> philosopher is rarely inclined to raise the question of Being in its totality,
> against the horizon of emptiness.... Today it is among poets, rather than
> philosophers, that we most commonly find the sense of wonder from which
> metaphysics springs.[5]

Dupré's image of the religious and mythic sensibility as keeping the "flame" of
metaphysical rationality alive is a felicitous one, for it is of course the same image
of a kindling fire that Tolkien uses in the *Ainulindalë* to describe that unique
and all-important event of the Creator, who is Being itself, giving the gift of
being to his creatures, and from which image, accordingly, this book has taken
its title. It is precisely the opacity — or rather, the super-luminosity — of such
images that, in retaining the mythic and numinous character of reality, helps
enliven the mind in the first place to that rational enterprise we call *metaphysics*,
to inspire the mind, that is, to know the world insofar as it can be known. It
takes a fascinating world, and an equally fascinating mind, to foment the kind
of system of thought created by St. Thomas.

But it must also be said that it takes a comparably imaginative and ingenious
mind to render that system of thought of enduring interest, accessibility, and
relevance, especially to the modern mind, which has grown impatient with such
lofty and seemingly impractical matters. This is why, for example, introductions
to St. Thomas such as Chesterton's biography have proven so important and why,
finally, I would like to suggest Tolkien too could prove to be important for St.
Thomas. Thomistic philosophy gives us a rational account of the biblical creation
narrative, translating, as I have said, the biblical *mythos* into the language of
philosophical *logos*. Tolkien offers an implicit validation of Thomas's project by
translating the creation metaphysics of Christian philosophy back into the
mythic mode. By comparing Thomas and Tolkien, I hope to have shown indirectly that, through his concrete and mythic imagery, what Tolkien gives us is
not one more dialectical treatise *arguing* that faith and philosophy have met
and *mythos* and *logos* have kissed, but a radically fresh vision of the world, in
which we might *see* and experience how these things are so. In this manner, my
hope in the end is not only to be able to commend the philosophical insights of
St. Thomas, whether discovered or simply preserved by him, as a profoundly

---

5 Louis Dupré, "Belief and Metaphysics," 10.

helpful guide in plumbing the depths of Tolkien's metaphysical thought, but
conversely to be able to commend Tolkien's literary achievement, given its
extraordinary popularity and influence, as an important and altogether
unique landmark in the history of Thomism, offering us a creative
and powerful contemporary interpretation and application
of Thomistic metaphysics for the twentieth and twenty-
first centuries. In the myths and metaphors of
Tolkien, in brief, we have the hidden
truths of St. Thomas, "useful for
the exercise of thought-
ful minds."

FINIS

Bibliography

AQUINAS: PRIMARY SOURCES

Aquinas on Creation: Writings on the "Sentences" of Peter Lombard: Book 2, Distinction 1, Question 1. Translated by Steven E. Baldner and William E. Carroll. Toronto: Pontifical Institute of Mediaeval Studies, 1998.

Commentary on Aristotle's Metaphysics. Translated by John P. Rowan. Chicago: H. Regnery, 1961.

Commentary on the Book of Causes. Translated by Vincent A. Guagliardo, Charles R. Hess, and C. Taylor. Washington, D.C.: Catholic University of America Press, 1996.

The Division and Methods of the Sciences: Questions V and VI of his Commentary on the "De Trinitate" of Boethius. 4th ed. Translated by Armand Maurer. Toronto: Pontifical Institute of Mediaeval Studies, 1986.

Faith, Reason, and Theology: Questions I-IV of his Commentary on the "De Trinitate" of Boethius. Translated by Armand Maurer. Toronto: Pontifical Institute of Mediaeval Studies, 1987.

Light of Faith: The Compendium of Theology. Translated by Cyril Vollert. Manchester, NH: Sophia Institute Press, 1998.

On Being and Essence. Translated by Armand Maurer. Toronto: Pontifical Institute of Mediaeval Studies, 1968.

On Evil. Translated by Jean T. Oesterle. Notre Dame, IN: University of Notre Dame, 1995.

On Evil. Translated by Richard Regan. Edited by Brian Davies. New York: Oxford University Press, 2003.

On the Power of God. Translated by the Fathers of the English Dominican Province. Eugene, OR: Wipf and Stock, 2004.

St. Thomas Aquinas on Politics and Ethics. Edited by Paul E. Sigmund. New York: W. W. Norton, 1988.

Suma Contra Los Gentiles: Edición bilingüe en dos volúmenes. 2 vols. Madrid: Biblioteca de Autores Cristianos, 1967.

Summa Contra Gentiles: Book One: God. Translated by Anton Charles Pegis. Notre Dame, IN: University of Notre Dame Press, 1997.

Summa Contra Gentiles: Book Two: Creation. Translated by James F. Anderson. Notre Dame, IN: University of Notre Dame Press, 2001.

Summa Theologica. 5 vols. Madrid: Biblioteca de Autores Cristianos, 1961.

Summa Theologica. Translated by the Fathers of the English Dominican Province. Vols. 19–20 of *The Great Books of the Western World*, edited by Robert Maynard Hutchins. Chicago: Encyclopedia Britannica, 1987.

Treatise on Separate Substances. Translated by Francis J. Lescoe. West Hartford, CT: St. Joseph College, 1963.

Truth. Translated by Robert W. Mulligan, James V. McGlinn, and Robert W. Schmidt. Indianapolis, IN: Hackett Publishing Company, 1994.

TOLKIEN: PRIMARY SOURCES

"*Beowulf:* The Monsters and the Critics." In *Beowulf: A Verse Translation*, translated by Seamus Heaney, 130. Edited by Daniel Donoghue. New York: Norton, 2002.

The Book of Lost Tales. Vol. 1, part 1 of *The History of Middle-earth*, edited by Christopher Tolkien. Boston: Houghton Mifflin, 1984.

The Fellowship of the Ring. Boston: Houghton Mifflin, 1994.

The Letters of J. R. R. Tolkien. Edited by Humphrey Carpenter. Boston: Houghton Mifflin, 2000.

The Lost Road. Vol. 5 of *The History of Middle-earth*, edited by Christopher Tolkien. Boston: Houghton Mifflin, 1987.

Morgoth's Ring. Vol. 10 of *The History of Middle-earth*, edited by Christopher Tolkien. Boston: Houghton Mifflin, 1993.

"Mythopoeia." In *Tree and Leaf*, 97–101. London: Unwin Hyman, 1988.

"On Fairy-Stories." In *The Tolkien Reader*, 33–99. New York: Ballantine, 1966.

The Peoples of Middle-earth. Vol. 12 of *The History of Middle-earth,* edited by Christopher Tolkien. Boston: Houghton Mifflin, 1996.

The Return of the King. Boston: Houghton Mifflin, 1994.

Sauron Defeated. Vol. 9 of *The History of Middle-earth*, edited by Christopher Tolkien. Boston: Houghton Mifflin, 1992.

The Silmarillion. Edited by Christopher Tolkien. Boston: Houghton Mifflin, 1977.

The Two Towers. Boston: Houghton Mifflin, 1994.

OTHER SOURCES CITED OR CONSULTED

Adams, Marilyn McCord. "Recovering the Metaphysics: Christ as God-Man, Metaphysically Construed." Chap. 5 in *Christ and Horrors: The Coherence of Christology*, 108–43. Cambridge: Cambridge University Press, 2006.

—. *William Ockham.* 2 vols. Notre Dame, IN: University of Notre Dame, 1987.

Aertsen, Jan. *Medieval Philosophy and the Transcendentals: The Case of Thomas Aquinas.* Leiden, Netherlands: Brill Academic Publishers, 1996.

Agøy, Nils Ivar. "*Quid Hinieldus cum Christo?* —New Perspectives on Tolkien's Theological Dilemma and his Sub-Creation Theory." *Mythlore* 21, no. 2 (1996): 31–38.

Aristotle. *Metaphysics.* Translated by Richard Hope. Ann Arbor, MI: Ann Arbor Paperbacks, 1960.

—. *On the Heavens.* Translated by J. L. Stocks. In *The Complete Works of Aristotle*, edited by Jonathan Barnes, 447–511. Vol. 1. Princeton: Princeton University Press, 1984.

—. *On the Soul* and *On Memory and Recollection.* Translated by Joe Sachs. Santa Fe, NM: Green Lion Press, 2004.

Augustine. *City of God*. Translated by Henry Bettenson. New York: Penguin, 1984.

—. *Confessions*. Translated by Henry Chadwick. New York: Oxford University Press, 1992.

—. *De musica*. Translated by W. F. Jackson Knight. Westport, CT: Hyperion Press, 1979.

—. *Eighty-Three Different Questions*. Translated by David L. Mosher. Vol. 70 of *The Fathers of the Church: A New Translation*. Washington, D.C.: Catholic University of America Press, 1982.

—. *Letters of St. Augustine*. Translated by J. G. Cunningham. In *Nicene and Post-Nicene Fathers*, edited by Philip Schaff, 209–619. Vol. 1. Peabody, MA: Hendrickson Publishers, 1995.

—. *The Literal Meaning of Genesis*. Translated by John Hammond Taylor. Vol. 2. New York: Newman Press, 1982.

Baldner, Steven E., and William E. Carroll. "An Analysis of Aquinas' Writings on the *Sentences* of Peter Lombard, Book 2, Distinction 1, Question 1." In Aquinas, *Aquinas on Creation*, 35–62.

Balthasar, Hans Urs von. *Theology: The Old Covenant*. Translated by B. McNeil. Vol. 6 of *The Glory of the Lord*. San Francisco: Ignatius Press, 1989.

Barfield, Owen. *Poetic Diction: A Study in Meaning*. Hanover, NH: Wesleyan University Press, 1984.

—. *Saving the Appearances*: A *Study in Idolatry*. Hanover, NH: Wesleyan University Press, 1988.

Barr, James. *The Semantics of Biblical Language*. Eugene, OR: Wipf and Stock, 2004.

Bassham, Gregory, and Eric Bronson, eds. *"The Lord of the Rings" and Philosophy*. Chicago: Open Court, 2003.

Betz, John. "Beyond the Sublime: Part I." *Modern Theology* 21, no. 3 (2005): 367–411.

Birzer, Brad. *Tolkien's Sanctifying Myth: Understanding Middle-earth*. Wilmington, DE: ISI Books, 2003.

Blount, Douglas. "*Überhobbits*: Tolkien, Nietzsche, and the Will to Power." Chap. 7 in Bassham and Bronson, *"The Lord of the Rings" and Philosophy*, 87–98.

Boethius. *The Consolation of Philosophy*. Translated by Victor Watts. New York: Penguin, 1999.

—. *Fundamentals of Music*. Translated by Calvin M. Bower. Edited by Claude V. Palisca. New Haven: Yale University Press, 1989.

Boland, Vivian. *Ideas in God According to Saint Thomas Aquinas: Sources and Synthesis*. Leiden, Netherlands: E. J. Brill, 1996.

Boman, Thorleif. *Hebrew Thought Compared with Greek*. New York: W. W. Norton, 1960.

Bratman, David. "The Year's Work in Tolkien Studies 2005." *Tolkien Studies* 5 (2008): 271–97.

Brisbois, Michael J. "Tolkien's Imaginary Nature: An Analysis of the Structure of Middle-earth." *Tolkien Studies* 2 (2005): 197–216.

Brooke-Rose, Christine. "The Evil Ring: Realism and the Marvelous." In *Narratology II: The Fictional Text and the Reader*. Special issue, *Poetics Today* 1, no. 4 (Summer 1980): 67–90.

Brown, Peter. *Augustine of Hippo*. Berkeley, CA: University of California Press, 1969.

Bullough, Sebastian. "St. Thomas and Music." *Dominican Studies* 4 (1951): 14–34.

Burrell, David. "Aquinas's Appropriation of *Liber de causis* to Articulate the Creator as Cause-of-Being." Chap. 4 in Kerr, *Contemplating Aquinas: On the Varieties of Interpretation*, 74–83.

—. "Creation and 'Actualism': The Dialectical Dimension of Philosophical Theology." *Medieval Philosophy and Theology* 4 (1994): 25–41.

Bussanich, John. "Plotinus's Metaphysics of the One." Chap. 2 in Gerson, *The Cambridge Companion to Plotinus*, 38–65.

Caldecott, Stratford. "Over the Chasm of Fire: Christian Heroism in *The Silmarillion* and *The Lord of the Rings*." Chap. 2 in Pearce, *Tolkien: A Celebration*, 17–33.

—. *The Power of the Ring: The Spiritual Vision Behind "The Lord of the Rings."* New York: Crossroad, 2005.

—. "Was Chesterton a Theologian?" *The Chesterton Review* 24, no. 4 (1998): 465–81.

Caldecott, Stratford, and Thomas Honegger, eds. *Tolkien's "The Lord of the Rings": Sources of Inspiration*. Zollikofen, Switzerland: Walking Tree, 2008.

Candler, Peter. "Tolkien or Nietzsche, Philology and Nihilism." University of Nottingham Centre of Theology and Philosophy. http://theologyphilosophycentre.co.uk/papers/~Candler_TolkeinNietzsche.doc (accessed 6/17/2017).

Candler, Peter M., and Connor Cunningham, eds. *Belief and Metaphysics*. London: SCM Press, 2007.

Carpenter, Humphrey. *Inklings*. Boston: Houghton Mifflin, 1979.

—. *Tolkien: A Biography*. Boston: Houghton Mifflin, 1977.

Chance, Jane. *"The Lord of the Rings": The Mythology of Power*. Lexington, KY: University Press of Kentucky, 2001.

—, ed. *Tolkien and the Invention of Myth*. Lexington, KY: University Press of Kentucky, 2004.

—, ed. *Tolkien the Medievalist*. New York: Routledge, 2003.

—, ed. *Tolkien's Modern Middle Ages*. New York: Palgrave Macmillan, 2005.

Chenu, M.-D. "The Platonisms of the Twelfth Century." Chap. 2 in *Man, Nature, Society in the Twelfth Century*, 49–98. Toronto: University of Toronto Press, 1997.

Chesterton, G. K. *Orthodoxy*. San Francisco: Ignatius Press, 1995.

—. *St. Thomas Aquinas: "The Dumb Ox."* New York: Doubleday, 1956.

Clarke, W. Norris. "What is Really Real?" In *Progress in Philosophy: Philosophical Studies in Honor of Rev. Doctor Charles A. Hart,* edited by James A. McWilliams, 61–90. Milwaukee: Bruce Publishing Company, 1955.

Colish, Marcia. "Early Scholastic Angelology." *Recherches de Théologie ancienne et medieval* 72 (1995): 80–109.

Collins, James. *The Thomistic Philosophy of the Angels*. Washington, D.C.: Catholic University of America Press, 1947.

Collins, Robert. "'Ainulindalë': Tolkien's Commitment to an Aesthetic Ontology." *Journal of the Fantastic in the Arts* 11, no. 3 (2000): 257–65.

Coolman, Boyd Taylor and Dale M. Coulter, eds. *Trinity and Creation: Exegesis, Theology and Spirituality from the Abbey of St. Victor*. New York: New City Press, 2011.

Copleston, Frederick. *Medieval Philosophy*. Vol. 2, part 2 of *A History of Philosophy*. Garden City, NY: Doubleday, 1962.

Cornford, Francis. *Plato's Cosmology*. New York: Liberal Arts Press, 1957.

Courtenay, William. *Capacity and Volition: A History of the Distinction of Absolute and Ordained Power*. Bergamo, Italy: Pierluigi Lubrina Editore, 1990.

—. "The King and the Leaden Coin: The Economic Background of 'Sine Qua Non'

Causality." *Traditio* 28 (1972): 185–209.

Cox, John. "Tolkien's Platonic Fantasy." *Seven* 5 (1984): 53–69.

Crowe, Edith L. "Making and Unmaking in Middle-earth and Elsewhere." *Mythlore* 23, no. 3 (2001): 56–69.

Cunningham, Conor. "The Difference *of* Theology and Some Philosophies of Nothing." *Modern Theology* 17, no. 3 (July 2001): 289–312.

—. *Genealogy of Nihilism: Philosophies of Nothing and the Difference of Theology.* New York: Routledge, 2002.

Dante Alighieri. *The Divine Comedy.* In *The Portable Dante,* translated by Mark Musa. New York: Penguin Books, 1995.

Davies, Brian. "Aquinas on What God is Not." Chap. 8 in Davies, *Thomas Aquinas: Contemporary Philosophical Perspectives,* 227–42.

—. *The Reality of God and the Problem of Evil.* New York: Continuum, 2006.

—. "Thomas Aquinas." Chap. 11 in *Medieval Philosophy,* edited by John Marenbon, 241–68. New York: Routledge, 1998.

—, ed. *Thomas Aquinas: Contemporary Philosophical Perspectives.* Oxford: Oxford University Press, 2002.

Davis, Howard. "Ainulindalë: The Music of Creation." *Mythlore* 9, no. 2 (1982): 6–10.

Davison, Scott A. "Tolkien and the Nature of Evil." Chap. 8 in Bassham and Bronson, *"The Lord of the Rings" and Philosophy,* 99–109.

De Armas, Frederick. A. "Gyges' Ring: Invisibility in Plato, Tolkien, and Lope de Vega." *Journal of the Fantastic in the Arts* 3, no. 4 (1994): 120–38.

Deavel, Catherine Jack. "Relational Evil, Relational Good: Thomas Aquinas and Process Thought." *International Philosophical Quarterly* 47, no. 3 (September 2007): 297–313.

DeCoursey, Mary Edwin. *The Theory of Evil in the Metaphysics of St. Thomas and Its Contemporary Significance: A Dissertation.* Washington, D.C.: Catholic University of America Press, 1948.

Deferrari, Roy J., and Inviolata Barry. *A Complete Index of "The Summa Theologica" of St. Thomas Aquinas.* Washington, D.C.: Catholic University of America Press, 1956.

Delfino, Robert A. "The Beauty of Wisdom: A Tribute to Armand A. Maurer." Chap. 4 in *A Thomistic Tapestry: Essays in Memory of Etienne Gilson,* edited by Peter A. Redpath, 37–45. Amsterdam: Rodopi, 2003.

Dennehy, Raymond. "Introduction" to *St. Thomas Aquinas* in *G. K. Chesterton: Collected Works,* 414–17. Vol. 2. San Francisco: Ignatius, 1986.

Descartes, René. *Discourse on Method and Meditations on First Philosophy.* Translated by Donald A. Cress. Indianapolis, IN: Hackett, 1985.

Devaux, Michaël. "The Origins of the *Ainulindalë*: The Present State of Research." Translated by Allan Turner. In *The Silmarillion: Thirty Years On,* edited by Turner, 81–110. Zollikofen, Switzerland: Walking Tree, 2007.

—, ed. *Tolkien, l'effigie des elfes.* Geneva: Ad Solem, 2005.

Dewan, Lawrence. "St. Thomas, James Ross, and Exemplarism: A Reply." *American Catholic Philosophical Quarterly* 65, no. 2 (1991): 221–34.

—. "Thomas Aquinas, Creation, and Two Historians." *Laval Théologique et Philosophique* 50 (1994) 363–87.

Dickerson, Matthew. *Following Gandalf: Epic Battles and Moral Victory in "The Lord of the Rings."* Grand Rapids, MI: Brazos Press, 2003.

Dickerson, Matthew, and Jonathan Evans. *Ents, Elves, and Eriador: The Environmental Vision of J. R. R. Tolkien.* Lexington, KY: University Press of Kentucky, 2006.

Dillard, Raymond B., and Tremper Longman. *An Introduction to the Old Testament.* Grand Rapids, MI: Zondervan, 1994.

Doolan, Gregory T. "Is Thomas's Doctrine of Divine Ideas Thomistic?" In *Wisdom's Apprentice: Thomistic Essays in Honor of Lawrence Dewan, O.P.,* edited by Peter A. Kwasniewski, 153–69. Washington, D.C.: Catholic University of America Press, 2007.

—. *Aquinas on the Divine Ideas as Exemplar Causes.* Washington, D.C.: Catholic University of America Press, 2008.

Drout, Michael, ed. *J.R.R.T. Encyclopedia.* New York: Routledge, 2006.

—. "Towards a Better Tolkien Criticism." Chap. 1 in Eaglestone, *Reading "The Lord of the Rings,"* 15–28.

Dubs, Kathleen E. "Providence, Fate, and Chance: Boethian Philosophy in *The Lord of the Rings,*" *Twentieth Century Literature* 27, no. 1 (Spring 1981): 34–42, reprinted in Chance, *Tolkien and the Invention of Myth,* 133–42.

Dupré, Louis. "Belief and Metaphysics." Chap. 1 in Candler and Cunningham, *Belief and Metaphysics,* 1–10.

Dutton, Paul Edward. "Medieval Approaches to Calcidius." Chap. 9 in *Plato's "Timaeus" as Cultural Icon,* edited by Gretchen J. Reydams-Schils, 183–205. Notre Dame, IN: University of Notre Dame Press, 2003.

—. "The Uncovering of the *Glosae Super Platonem* of Bernard of Chartres." *Medieval Studies* 46 (1984): 192–221.

Eaglestone, Robert. "Invisibility." Chap. 5 in Eaglestone, *Reading "The Lord of the Rings,"* 73–84.

—, ed. *Reading "The Lord of the Rings": New Writing on Tolkien's Trilogy.* New York: Continuum, 2005.

Eco, Umberto. *The Aesthetics of Thomas Aquinas.* Translated by Hugh Bredin. Cambridge, MA: Harvard University Press, 1997.

—. *Art and Beauty in the Middle Ages.* Translated by Hugh Bredin. 2nd ed. New Haven, CT: Yale University Press, 2002.

—. *The Name of the Rose.* Translated by William Weaver. San Diego: Harcourt Brace, 1984.

—. "On Being." Chap. 1 in *Kant and the Platypus: Essays on Language and Cognition,* translated by Alistair McEwan, 9–56. New York: Harcourt Brace, 2000.

Eden, Bradford Lee. "The "Music of the Spheres": Relationships between Tolkien's *The Silmarillion* and Medieval Cosmological and Religious Theory." Chap. 12 in Chance, *Tolkien the Medievalist,* 183–93.

Egan, Thomas M. "*The Silmarillion* and the Rise of Evil: The Birth Pains of Middle-earth." *Seven* 7 (1985): 79–84.

Elders, Leo J. *The Metaphysics of Being of St. Thomas Aquinas in a Historical Perspective.* Leiden, Netherlands: E. J. Brill, 1993.

Ellison, John. "Images of Evil in Tolkien's World." *Mallorn: the Journal of the Tolkien Society* 38 (January 2001): 21–29.

Emery, Gilles. *Trinity in Aquinas*. Ypsilanti, MI: Sapientia Press, 2003.

Evans, Jonathan. "The Anthropology of Arda: Creation, Theology, and the Race of Men." Chap. 13 in Chance, *Tolkien the Medievalist*, 194–224.

Fisher, Matthew A. "Working at the Crossroads: Tolkien, St. Augustine, and the *Beowulf*-poet." In *The Lord of the Rings, 1954–2004: Scholarship in Honor of Richard E. Blackwelder*, edited by Wayne G. Hammond and Christina Scull, 217–30. Milwaukee, WI: Marquette University Press, 2006.

Fitzgerald, Allan D. *Augustine Through the Ages: An Encyclopedia*. Grand Rapids, MI: William B. Eerdmans, 1999.

Flieger, Verlyn. "The Curious Incident of the Dream at the Barrow: Memory and Reincarnation in Middle-earth." *Tolkien Studies* 4 (2007): 99–112.

—."Naming the Unnameable: The Neoplatonic 'One' in Tolkien's *Silmarillion*." In *Diakonia: Studies in Honor of Robert T. Meyer*, edited by Thomas Halton and Joseph P. Williman, 127–32. Washington, D.C.: Catholic University of America Press, 1986.

—. *Splintered Light: Logos and Language in Tolkien's World*. 2nd ed. Kent, OH: Kent State University Press, 2002.

Fornet-Ponse, Thomas. "Freedom and Providence as Anti-Modern Elements." In *Tolkien and Modernity, Vol. 1*, edited by Frank Weinreich and Thomas Honegger, 177–206. Zollikofen, Switzerland: Walking Tree, 2006.

Frame, John. *The Doctrine of God*. Phillipsburg, NJ: Presbyterian and Reformed, 2002.

Funkenstein, Amos. *Theology and the Scientific Imagination from the Middle Ages to the Seventeenth Century*. Princeton: Princeton University Press, 1986.

Garcia, Jorge J. E. "Philosophy in the Middle Ages: An Introduction." In *A Companion to Philosophy in the Middle Ages*, edited by Jorge J. E. Garcia and Timothy B. Noone, 1–11. Malden, MA: Blackwell, 2006.

George, Marie I. "Aquinas on Intelligent Extra-Terrestrial Life." *The Thomist* 65, no. 2 (2001): 239–58.

—. "Aquinas on Reincarnation." *The Thomist* 60, no. 1 (1996): 33–52.

—. "Reincarnation Western-Style: The Resurgence of Age-old Superstition in a Scientific Era." *Faith and Reason* 22, no. 3 (Fall 1996): 155–84.

Gersh, Stephen, ed. *Platonic Tradition in the Middle Ages: A Doxographic Approach*. Berlin: Walter de Gruyter, 2002.

Gerson, Lloyd, ed. *The Cambridge Companion to Plotinus*. Cambridge: Cambridge University Press, 1996.

Gibson, Margaret. "The Study of the *Timaeus* in the Eleventh and Twelfth Centuries." *Pensamiento: revista trimestral de investigacióne e informacio'n filosófica* 25 (1969): 183–94.

Gillespie, Michael Allen. *Nihilism Before Nietzsche*. Chicago: University of Chicago Press, 1995.

—. "Temporality and History in the Thought of Martin Heidegger." *Revue Internationale de Philosophie* 43 (1989): 33–51.

—. *The Theological Origins of Modernity*. Chicago: University of Chicago Press, 2008.

Gilson, Étienne. *Being and Some Philosophers*. 2nd ed. Toronto: Pontifical Institute of Mediaeval Studies, 1952.

—. *The Christian Philosophy of St. Thomas Aquinas*. Translated by L. K. Shook. New York: Random House, 1956).

—.*The Spirit of Medieval Philosophy*. Translated by A. H. C. Downes. Notre Dame, IN: University of Notre Dame, 1991.

—.*Thomist Realism and the Critique of Knowledge*. Translated by Mark A. Wauck. San Francisco: Ignatius Press, 1986.

Godwin, Joscelyn, ed. *The Harmony of the Spheres: A Sourcebook of the Pythagorean Tradition in Music*. Rochester, VT: Inner Traditions International, 1993.

Goris, Harm. "The Angelic Doctor and Angelic Speech: The Development of Thomas Aquinas's Thought on How Angels Communicate." *Medieval Philosophy and Theology* 11 (2003): 87–105.

Gough, John. "Tolkien's Creation Myth in *The Silmarillion* —Northern or Not?" *Children's Literature in Education* 30, no. 1 (1999): 1–8.

Gregory the Great. *Forty Homilies on the Gospels*. Translated by Stephen Chase. In *Angelic Spirituality: Medieval Perspectives on the Ways of Angels*, edited by Steven Chase. Mahwah, NJ: Paulist Press, 2002.

Gregory, Tullio. "The Platonic Inheritance." Translated by Jonathan Hunt. Chap. 2 in *A History of Twelfth-Century Western Philosophy*, edited by Peter Dronke, 54–80. Cambridge: Cambridge University Press, 1988.

Grubbs, David. "The Maker's Image: Tolkien, Fantasy & Magic." http://www.cornerstonemag.com/imaginarium/features/tolkien_magic.html (accessed 9/19/2009).

Gunton, Colin. "A Far-Off Gleam of the Gospel: Salvation in Tolkien's *The Lord of the Rings*." Chap. 10 in Pearce, *Tolkien: A Celebration*, 124–40.

—. *The Triune Creator: A Historical and Systematic Study*. Grand Rapids, MI: William B. Eerdmans, 1998.

Gurney, Shelley. "Falling From Grace." Masters thesis, Otago University, NZ, 2006.

Hankey, Wayne J. "Aquinas's First Principle: Being or Unity?" *Dionysius* 4 (December 1980): 133–72.

—. "Aquinas and the Platonists." In Gersh, *Platonic Tradition in the Middle Ages: A Doxographic Approach*, 279–324.

—. "*Theoria versus Poesis*: Neoplatonism and Trinitarian Difference in Aquinas, John Milbank, Jean-Luc Marion, and John Zizioulas." *Modern Theology* 15, no. 4 (October 1999): 387–415.

Hart, David Bentley. *The Beauty of the Infinite: The Aesthetics of Christian Truth*. Grand Rapids, MI: William B. Eerdmans, 2003.

—. *The Doors of the Sea: Where Was God in the Tsunami?* Grand Rapids, MI: William B. Eerdmans, 2005.

Harvey, David. *The Song of Middle-earth: J. R. R. Tolkien's Themes, Symbols, and Myths*. Boston: George Allen and Unwin, 1985.

Head, Hayden. "Imitative Desire in Tolkien's Mythology: A Girardian Perspective." *Mythlore* 26, no. 1–2 (2007): 137–48.

Heidegger, Martin. *Being and Time*. Translated by John Macquarrie and Edward Robinson. New York: Harper and Row, 1962.

—. *The Question Concerning Technology and Other Essays*. Translated by William Lovitt.

New York: Harper and Row, 1977.

Helms, Randel. *Tolkien's World*. Boston: Houghton Mifflin, 1974.

Hemming, Laurence Paul. "*Quod Impossibile Est!* Aquinas and Radical Orthodoxy." Chap. 6 in *Radical Orthodoxy? —A Catholic Enquiry*, edited by Hemming, 76–93. Burlington, VT: Ashgate, 2000.

Herbert, Gary B. "Tolkien's Tom Bombadil and the Platonic Ring of Gyges." *Extrapolation* 26, no. 2 (1985): 152–59.

Hibbs, Thomas. "Providence and the Dramatic Unity of *The Lord of the Rings*." Chap. 13 in Bassham and Bronson, *"The Lord of the Rings" and Philosophy*, 167–78.

Hood, Gyneth. "Nature and Technology: Angelic and Sacrificial Strategies in Tolkien's *The Lord of the Rings*." *Mythlore* 19, no. 4 (1993): 6–12.

Hood, John Y. B. "Art and Beauty." Chap. 7 in *The Essential Aquinas: Writings on Philosophy, Religion, and Society*, 182–90. Westport, CT: Praeger, 2002.

Houghton, John. "Augustine in the Cottage of Lost Play: The *Ainulindalë* as Asterisk Cosmogony." Chap. 11 in Chance, *Tolkien the Medievalist*, 171–82.

Houghton, John, and Neal K. Keesee. "Tolkien, King Alfred, and Boethius: Platonist Views of Evil in *The Lord of the Rings*." *Tolkien Studies* 2 (2005): 131–59.

Howe, Leroy T. "The Necessity of Creation." *International Journal for Philosophy and Religion* 2 (1971): 96–112.

Hume, David. *An Enquiry Concerning Human Understanding*. Edited by Eric Steinburg. Indianapolis, IN: Hackett Publishing, 1993.

Hyles, Vernon. "On the Nature of Evil: The Cosmic Myths of Lewis, Tolkien, and Williams." *Mythlore* 13, no. 4 (1987): 9–13.

Johnson, Mark. "Did St. Thomas Attribute a Doctrine of Creation to Aristotle?" *New Scholasticism* 63 (1989): 129–55.

—. "Aquinas's Changing Evaluation of Plato on Creation." *American Catholic Philosophical Quarterly* 66, no. 1 (1992): 81–88.

Jones, David. *Epoch and Artist*. London: Faber, 1959.

Jordan, Mark D. "The Intelligibility of the World and the Divine Ideas in Aquinas." *Review of Metaphysics* 38, no. 1 (1984): 17–32.

Kant, Immanuel. *Critique of Judgment*. Translated by Werner S. Pluhar. Indianapolis, IN: Hackett Publishing Company, 1987.

Katz, Eric. "The Rings of Tolkien and Plato: Lessons in Power, Choice, and Morality." Chap. 1 in Bassham and Bronson, *"The Lord of the Rings" and Philosophy*, 5–20.

Keck, David. *Angels and Angelology in the Middle Ages*. Oxford: Oxford University Press, 1998.

Kenny, Anthony, and Sarah Broadie. "The Creation of the World." *Aristotelian Society Supplementary Volume* 78 (2004): 91–92.

Kent, Bonnie. "Evil in Later Medieval Philosophy." *Journal of the History of Philosophy* 45, no. 2 (April 2007): 177–205.

Kerr, Fergus. *After Aquinas: Versions of Thomism*. Malden, MA: Blackwell, 2002.

—, ed. *Contemplating Aquinas: On the Varieties of Interpretation*. Notre Dame, IN: University of Notre Dame Press, 2003.

Kilby, Clyde S. *Tolkien and "The Silmarillion."* Wheaton, IL: Harold Shaw, 1976.

Klima, Gyula. "Man = Body + Soul: Aquinas's Arithmetic of Human Nature." Chap. 10 in Davies, *Thomas Aquinas: Contemporary Philosophical Perspectives*, 257–73.

Klocker, Harry. *William of Ockham and the Divine Freedom*. Milwaukee, WI: Marquette University Press, 1992.

Knight, Mark. *Chesterton and Evil*. New York: Fordham University Press, 2004.

Kocher, Paul H. "Ilúvatar and the Secret Fire." *Mythlore* 12, no. 1 (1985): 36–37.

—. *Master of Middle-earth: The Fiction of J. R. R. Tolkien*. Boston: Houghton Mifflin Company, 1972.

—. *A Reader's Guide to The Silmarillion*. Boston: Houghton Mifflin Company, 1980.

Kreeft, Peter. *The Philosophy of Tolkien: The Worldview Behind "The Lord of the Rings."* San Francisco: Ignatius Press, 2005.

Kretzmann, Norman. *The Metaphysics of Creation: Aquinas's Natural Theology in Summa Contra Gentiles II*. Oxford: Clarendon Press, 2005.

—. *The Metaphysics of Theism: Aquinas's Natural Theology in Summa Contra Gentiles I*. Oxford University Press, 2002.

Kretzmann, Norman, and Eleanore Stump, eds. *The Cambridge Companion to Aquinas*. New York: Cambridge University Press, 1999.

Lacoste, Jean-Yves. "Anges et Hobbits: Le Sens des Mondes Possibles." *Freiburger Zeitschrift für Philosophie und Theologie* 36 (1989): 341–73.

Lambert, Malcolm D. *The Cathars*. Malden, MA: Blackwell, 1998.

Leclercq, Jean. *The Love of Learning and the Desire for God: A Study of Monastic Culture*. Bronx, NY: Fordham University Press, 1982.

Lee, Stuart and Elizabeth Solopova. *The Keys of Middle-earth: Discovering Medieval Literature through the Fiction of J.R.R. Tolkien*. New York: Palgrave MacMillan, 2006.

Leithart, Peter. *Deep Comedy: Trinity, Tragedy, and Hope in Western Literature*. Moscow, ID: Canon Press, 2006.

Leo XIII, *Aeterni Patris*. http://w2.vatican.va/content/leo-xiii/en/encyclicals/documents/hf_l-xiii_enc_04081879_aeterni-patris.html (accessed 06/17/2017).

Levering, Matthew. "Scripture and the Psychological Analogy for the Trinity." Chap. 5 in *Scripture and Metaphysics: Aquinas and the Renewal of Trinitarian Theology*, 144–64. Malden, MA: Blackwell, 2004.

Lewis, C. S. *The Discarded Image: An Introduction to Medieval and Renaissance Literature*. Cambridge: Cambridge University Press, 1995.

—. "Evil and God." Chap. 1 in *God in the Dock*, edited by Walter Hooper, 21–24. Grand Rapids, MI: William B. Eerdmans, 1999.

—. *The Problem of Pain*. New York: Simon and Schuster, 1996.

Lieu, Samuel N. C. "Christianity and Manichaeism." In *Constantine to c. 600*, edited by Augustine Casiday and Frederick W. Norris. Vol. 2 of *The Cambridge History of Christianity*. Cambridge: Cambridge University Press, 2007.

Lombard, Peter. *Sententiae in IV Libris Distinctae*. Edited by Ignatius Brady. Vol. 2. Grottaferrata, Rome: Collegii S. Bonaventurae ad Claras Aquas, 1981.

MacCarthy, Fiona. *Eric Gill: A Lover's Quest for Art and God*. London: Faber, 2003.

MacDonald, Scott. "The Divine Nature." Chap. 6 in Stump and Kretzmann, eds., *The Cambridge Companion to Augustine*, 71–90.

Madsen, Catherine. "Light from an Invisible Lamp: Natural Religion in *The Lord of the Rings*." In Chance, *Tolkien and the Invention of Myth*, 35–47.

Malpas, Simon. "Home." Chap. 6 in Eaglestone, *Reading "The Lord of the Rings": New Writing on Tolkien's Classic*, 85–98.

Maritain, Jacques. *Art and Scholasticism and The Frontiers of Poetry*. Translated by Joseph W. Evans. New York: Charles Scribner's Sons, 1962.

—. *Creative Intuition in Art and Poetry*. New York: Pantheon Books, 1960.

—. *Existence and the Existent*. Translated by Lewis Galantiere and Gerald B. Phelan. Garden City, NY: Doubleday, 1957.

Martin, Aaron. "Reckoning with Ross: Possibles, Divine Ideas, and Virtual Practical Knowledge." *Proceedings of the American Catholic Philosophical Association* 78 (2005): 193–208.

Matthews, Gareth B. "Knowledge and Illumination." Chap. 13 in Stump and Kretzmann, 171–85.

Maurer, Armand. *About Beauty: A Thomistic Interpretation*. Houston: Center for Thomistic Studies, 1983.

—. "Form and Essence in the Philosophy of St. Thomas." *Mediaeval Studies* 13 (1951): 165–75.

—. "James Ross on the Divine Ideas: A Reply." *American Catholic Philosophical Quarterly* 65, no. 2 (1991): 213–20.

—. *The Philosophy of William of Ockham in Light of its Principles*. Toronto: Pontifical Institute of Mediaeval Studies, 1999.

May, Gerhard. *Creatio Ex Nihilo: The Doctrine of "Creation Out of Nothing" in Early Christian Thought*. Translated by A. S. Worral. Edinburgh: T&T Clark, 1994.

McCabe, Herbert. "Aquinas on the Incarnation." Chap. 10 in *God Still Matters*, 107–14. London: Continuum, 2005.

—. *God Matters*. London: Continuum, 2005.

McMahon, Jennifer L., and B. Steve Csaki. "Talking Trees and Walking Mountains: Buddhist and Taoist Themes in *The Lord of the Rings*." Ch. 14 in Bassham and Bronson, *"The Lord of the Rings" and Philosophy*, 179–91.

Milbank, Alison. *Chesterton and Tolkien as Theologians: The Fantasy of the Real*. Edinburgh: T&T Clark, 2007.

—. "Interview with Dr. Alison Milbank author of *Chesterton and Tolkien as Theologians*." Tolkien Library, 10/22/07. http://www.tolkienlibrary.com/press/Chesterton-and-Tolkien-as-Theologians.php (accessed 6/17/2017).

—. "'My Precious': Tolkien's Fetishized Ring." Chap. 3 in Bassham and Bronson, *"The Lord of the Rings" and Philosophy*, 33–45.

—. "Tolkien, Chesterton, and Thomism." Ch. 8 in Caldecott and Honegger, *Tolkien's "The Lord of the Rings": Sources of Inspiration*, 187–98.

Milbank, John. "Evil: Darkness and Silence." Chap. 1 in *Being Reconciled: Ontology and Pardon*, 1–25. London: Routledge, 2003.

—. "Truth and Vision." Ch. 2 in Milbank and Pickstock, *Truth in Aquinas*, 19–59.

—. "Scholasticism, Modernism, and Modernity." *Modern Theology* 22, no. 4 (2006): 651–71.

—. *The Suspended Middle: Henri de Lubac and the Debate Concerning the Supernatural*. Grand Rapids, MI: William B. Eerdmans, 2005.

Milbank, John, and Catherine Pickstock. *Truth in Aquinas.* New York: Routledge, 2001.

Milburn, Michael. "Coleridge's Definition of Imagination and Tolkien's Definition(s) of Faery." *Tolkien Studies* 7 (2010): 55–66.

Miner, Robert. *Truth in the Making: Creative Knowledge in Theology and Philosophy.* New York: Routledge, 2003.

Moevs, Christian. *The Metaphysics of Dante's Comedy.* Cambridge: Cambridge University Press, 2005.

Moonan, Lawrence. *Divine Power: The Medieval Power Distinction up to its Adoption by Albert, Bonaventure, and Aquinas.* Oxford: Clarendon Press, 1994.

Murphy, Francesca Aran. *Christ the Form of Beauty: A Study in Theology and Literature.* Edinburgh: T&T Clark, 1995.

Nagy, Gergely. "Saving the Myths: the Re-creation of Mythology in Plato and Tolkien." Chap. 5 in Chance, *Tolkien and the Invention of Myth*, 81–100.

Nietzsche, Friedrich. *The Birth of Tragedy.* In *Basic Writings of Nietzsche.* Translated by Walter Kaufmann. New York: The Modern Library, 1992.

Nimmo, Andrew. "Tolkien and Thomism: Middle-earth and the States of Nature." *Universitas* 10 (2001). http://www.cts.org.au/2001/universitas10/tolkienandthomism. htm (accessed 6/17/2017).

O'Brien, Denis. "Plotinus on Matter and Evil." Chap. 7 in Gerson, *The Cambridge Companion to Plotinus*, 171–95.

O'Connor, Flannery. *The Habit of Being.* Edited by Sally Fitzgerald. New York: Farrar, Straus, Giroux, 1979.

O'Meara, John F. "Paris as a Cultural Milieu of Thomas Aquinas's Thought." *Thomist: A Speculative Quarterly Review* 38 (October, 1974): 689–722.

Oakley, Francis. *Omnipotence and Promise: The Legacy of the Scholastic Distinction of Powers.* Toronto: Pontifical Institute of Mediaeval Studies, 2002.

Oberman, Heiko. *The Harvest of Medieval Theology: Gabriel Biel and Late Medieval Nominalism.* Cambridge, MA: Harvard University Press, 1963.

Ockham, William. *Philosophical Writings.* Translated by Philotheus Boehner. New York: Bobbs-Merrill Company, 1964.

—. *Quodlibetal Questions.* Translated by Alfred J. Freddoso. 2 vols. New Haven: Yale University Press, 1991.

—. *Scriptum in Librum Primum Sententiarum Ordinatio, Distinctiones* XIX-XLVIII. Edited by Girardus I. Etzkorn and Franciscus E. Kelley. Vol. 4 in *Opera Philosophica et Theologica: Opera Theologica.* St. Bonaventure, NY: St. Bonaventure University Press, 1979.

Olszański, Tadeusz Andrzej. "Evil and the Evil One in Tolkien's Theology." Translated by Agnieszka Sylwanowicz. *Mythlore* 21, no. 2 (1996): 298–300.

Oser, Lee. "Enter Reason and Nature." Chap. 7 in *The Return of Christian Humanism: Chesterton, Eliot, Tolkien, and the Romance of History*, 105–20. Columbia, MO: University of Missouri Press, 2007.

Oziewicz, Marek. "From Vico to Tolkien: The Affirmation of Myth Against the Tyranny of Reason." Chap. 5 in Caldecott and Honneger, *Tolkien's "The Lord of the Rings": Sources of Inspiration*, 113–36.

Ozment, Steven. *The Age of Reform (1250–1550): An Intellectual and Religious History of Late Medieval and Reformation Europe.* New Haven, CT: Yale University Press, 1980.

Panofsky, Erwin. *Gothic Architecture and Scholasticism.* Latrobe, PA: Archabbey Publications, 2005.

Pasnau, Robert, and Christopher Shields. *The Philosophy of Aquinas.* Boulder, CO: Westview, 2004.

Patrick, James. *Magdalen Metaphysicals: Idealism and Orthodoxy at Oxford, 1901–1945.* Macon, GA: Mercer University Press, 1985.

Pearce, Joseph. "Tolkien and the Catholic Literary Revival." Chap. 9 in Pearce, *Tolkien: A Celebration*, 102–23.

—, ed. *Tolkien: A Celebration: Collected Writings on a Literary Legacy.* San Francisco: Ignatius Press, 2001.

—. *Tolkien: Man and Myth.* San Francisco: Ignatius Press, 1998.

—. *Wisdom and Innocence: A Life of G. K. Chesterton.* San Francisco: Ignatius, 1996.

Pegis, Anton. "Concerning William of Ockham." *Traditio* 2 (1944): 465–79.

—. "A Note on St. Thomas, *Summa Theologica*, I, 44, 1–2." *Mediaeval Studies* 8 (1946): 159–68.

Pelikan, Jaroslav. *What has Athens to Do with Jerusalem? "Timaeus" and "Genesis" in Counterpoint.* Ann Arbor: University of Michigan, 1997.

Phelan, G. B. "The Concept of Beauty in St. Thomas Aquinas." In Phelan, *G. B. Phelan: Selected Papers*, 155–80.

—. *G. B. Phelan: Selected Papers.* Edited by Arthur G. Kirn. Toronto: Pontifical Institute of Mediaeval Studies, 1967.

—. *"Verum Sequitur Esse Rerum."* In Phelan, *G. B. Phelan: Selected Papers*, 133–54.

Pickstock, Catherine. "Truth and Correspondence." Chap. 1 in Milbank and Pickstock, *Truth and Aquinas*, 1–18.

Pieper, Josef. *The Silence of St. Thomas.* Translated by John Murray and Daniel O'Conor. South Bend, IN: St. Augustine's Press, 1999.

—. *The Truth of All Things.* In *Living the Truth: The Truth of All Things and Reality and the Good,* translated by Lothar Krauth. San Francisco: Ignatius Press, 1989.

Plato. *Gorgias.* In *Plato: The Collected Dialogues*, edited by Edith Hamilton and Huntington Cairns. Princeton: Princeton University Press, 1989.

—. *Phaedo.* Translated by G. M. A. Grube. 2nd ed. Indianapolis, IN: Hackett, 1980.

—. *The Republic of Plato.* Translated by Allan Bloom. 2nd ed. New York: Basic Books, 1991.

—. *Timaeus.* Translated by Donald Zeyl. Indianapolis, IN: Hackett Publishing Company, 2000.

Plotinus. *Enneads.* Translated by A. H. Armstrong. Loeb Classical Library. 7 vols. Cambridge, MA: Harvard University Press, 1966.

Pseudo-Dionysius. *The Divine Names.* In *Pseudo-Dionysius: The Complete Works*, translated by Colm Luibheid. Edited by Paul Rorem. New York: Paulist Press, 1987.

Purtill, Richard L. "Tolkien's Creation Myth." Chap. 7 in *J. R. R. Tolkien: Myth, Morality, and Religion*, 88–101. San Francisco: Harper and Row, 1984.

Quinn, Patrick. "The Experience of Beauty in Plotinus and Aquinas: Some Similarities and Differences." In *Neoplatonism and Western Aesthetics,* edited by Aphrodite Alexandrakis. Albany, NY: State University of New York Press, 2002.

Ramos, Alice. "Ockham and Aquinas on Exemplary Causality." *Proceedings of the PMR Conference* 19-20 (1994-6): 199-213.

Reilly, R. J. "Tolkien and the Fairy Story." In *Tolkien and the Critics,* edited by Neil D. Isaacs and Rose A. Zimbardo. Notre Dame, IN: University of Notre Dame Press, 1968.

Richard, Jay and Jonathan Witt. *The Hobbit Party: The Vision of Freedom That Tolkien Got and the West Forgot.* San Francisco: Ignatius Press, 2014.

Rocca, Gregory P. *Speaking the Incomprehensible God: Thomas Aquinas on the Interplay of Positive and Negative Theology.* Washington, D.C.: The Catholic University of America Press, 2004.

Rose, Mary Carman. "The Christian Platonism of C. S. Lewis, J. R. R. Tolkien, and Charles Williams." Chap. 17 in *Neoplatonism and Christian Thought,* edited by Dominic J. O'Meara, 203-12. Albany, NY: State University of New York Press, 1982.

Rosemann, Philipp. The Story of a Great Medieval Book: Peter Lombard's "Sentences." Buffalo, NY: Broadview Press, 2007.

—. *Understanding Scholastic Thought with Foucault.* New York: St. Martin's Press, 1999.

Ross, James. "Aquinas's Exemplarism; Aquinas's Voluntarism." *American Catholic Philosophical Quarterly* 64, no. 2 (1990): 171-98.

—. "Response to Maurer and Dewan." *American Catholic Philosophical Quarterly* 65, no. 2 (1991): 235-43.

Santoro-Brienza, Liberato. "Art and Beauty in Antiquity and the Middle Ages." Chap. 4 in *Art and Essence,* edited by Stephen Davies and Ananta C. Sukla, 55-73. Westport, CT: Praeger, 2003.

Seland, John. "Dante and Tolkien: Their Ideas about Evil." *Inklings Forever* 5 (2006): 147-55.

Shippey, Tom. *J. R. R. Tolkien: Author of the Century.* Boston: Houghton Mifflin, 2002.

Spitzer, Leo. *Classical and Christian Ideas of World Harmony: Prolegomena to an Interpretation of the Word "Stimmung."* Baltimore: Johns Hopkins Press, 1963.

Steel, Carlos. "Does Evil Have a Cause? Augustine's Perplexity and Thomas' Answer." *The Review of Metaphysics* 48, no. 2 (November 1994): 251-73.

Stump, Eleonore. "Biblical Commentary and Philosophy." Chap. 10 in Kretzmann and Stump, *Cambridge Companion to Aquinas,* 252-68.

—. "The Metaphysics of the Incarnation." Chap. 14 in *Aquinas,* 407-26. New York: Routledge, 2005.

Stump, Eleonore, and Norman Kretzmann, eds. *The Cambridge Companion to Augustine.* Cambridge: Cambridge University Press, 2001.

Sweeney, Leo. *Christian Philosophy: Greek, Medieval, Contemporary Reflections.* New York: Peter Lang, 1997.

Sweeney, Michael. "*Stat rosa pristina margine*: Umberto Eco on the Role of the Margin in Medieval Hermeneutics and Thomas Aquinas as a Comic Philosopher." *Proceedings of the American Catholic Philosophical Association* 72 (1998): 255-69.

Tatarkiewicz, Wladyslaw. *Medieval Aesthetics.* Vol. 2 of *History of Aesthetics.* Translated by Adam and Ann Czerniawski. Edited by C. Barrett. London: Continuum, 2005.

Taylor, A. E. *Plato: the Man and His Work.* New York: Meridian Books, 1957.

Tornay, Stephen Chak. *Ockham: Studies and Selections.* La Salle, IL: Open Court, 1938.

Torre, Michael. "The Portrait of Evil in *The Lord of the Rings*: Reflections Personal, Literary, and Theological." *Logos* 5, no. 4 (2002): 65–74.

Torrell, Jean-Pierre. *Saint Thomas Aquinas, Volume 1: The Person and His Work.* Translated by Robert Royal. Washington, D.C.: Catholic University of America Press, 1996.

Turner, Denys. "On Denying the Right God: Aquinas on Atheism and Idolatry." In *Aquinas in Dialogue: Thomas for the Twenty-First Century*, edited by Jim Fodor and Frederick Christian Bauerschmidt. Malden, MA: Blackwell, 2004.

Velde, Rudi te. *Aquinas on God: The "Divine Science" of the "Summa Theologiae."* Burlington, VT: Ashgate, 2004.

—. *Participation and Substantiality in Thomas Aquinas.* Leiden, Netherlands: E. J. Brill, 1995.

—. "Understanding the *Scientia* of Faith: Reason and Faith in Aquinas's *Summa Theologiae*." Chap. 3 in Kerr, *Contemplating Aquinas: On the Varieties of Interpretation*, 55–74.

Vine, W. E. *Vine's Complete Expository Dictionary of Old and New Testament Words.* Edited by Merrill F. Unger and William White, Jr. Nashville: Thomas Nelson Publishers, 1996.

Ward, Elizabeth. *David Jones: Mythmaker.* Manchester, UK: Manchester University Press, 1983.

Watson, Francis. "Language, God and Creation." Chap. 8 in *Text, Church, and World: Biblical Interpretation in Theological Perspective*, 137-153. Grand Rapids, MI: William B. Eerdmans Publishing Company, 1994.

Weinreich, Frank. "Metaphysics of Myth: The Platonic Ontology of 'Mythopoeia.'" In *Tolkien's Shorter Works*, edited by Margaret Hiley and Frank Weinreich, 325–47. Zollikofen, Switzerland: Walking Tree, 2008.

Welliver, Warman. *Character, Plot, and Thought in Plato's "Timaeus-Critias."* Leiden, Netherlands: E. J. Brill, 1977.

White, Victor. "Prelude to the Five Ways." Chap. 2 in *Aquinas's Summa Theologiae: Critical Essays*, edited by Brian Davies, 25–44. Lanham, MD: Rowman and Littlefield, 2006.

Whittingham, Elizabeth A. "The Mythology of 'Ainulindalë': Tolkien's Creation of Hope." *Journal of the Fantastic in the Arts* 9, no. 3 (1998): 212–28.

Wicksteed, Philip H. *Dante and Aquinas.* London: J. M. Dent and Sons, 1913.

Wilhelmsen, Frederick D. "The Concept of Existence and the Structure of Judgment: A Thomistic Paradox." Chap. 3 in *Being and Knowing*, 47-71. Albany, NY: Preserving Christian Publications, 1995.

Williams, Rowan. *Grace and Necessity: Reflections on Art and Love.* New York: Continuum, 2006.

Wippel, John. "Thomas Aquinas, Henry of Ghent, and Godfrey of Fontaines on the Reality of Non-existing Possibles." In *Metaphysical Themes in Thomas Aquinas*, 163–89. Washington, D.C.: Catholic University of America Press, 1984.

Wolter, Allen B. "Ockham and the Textbooks: On the Origin of Possibility." In *Inquiries into Medieval Philosophy*, edited by J. F. Ross, 243–73. Westport, CT: Greenwood Publishing Co, 1971.

Wood, Ralph. "Conflict and Convergence on Fundamental Matters in C. S. Lewis and J. R. R. Tolkien." *Renascence* 55, no. 4 (2003): 315–38.

—. *The Gospel According to Tolkien: Visions of the Kingdom in Middle-earth.* Louisville, KY: Westminster John Knox Press, 2003.

—. "Tolkien's Orthodoxy: A Response to Berit Kjos." Leadership University. http://www.leaderu.com/humanities/wood-response.html (accessed 6/17/2017).

Wood, Robert. *A Path Into Metaphysics: Phenomenological, Hermeneutical, and Dialogical Studies.* Albany: State University of New York, 1990.

—. *Placing Aesthetics: Reflections on the Philosophic Tradition.* Athens, OH: Ohio University Press, 1999.

Young, R. V. "Chesterton's Paradoxes and Thomist Ontology." *Renascence* 49, no. 1 (1996): 67–77.

Zimbardo, Rose. "Moral Visions in *The Lord of the Rings.*" In *Understanding "The Lord of the Rings": The Best of Tolkien Criticism,* edited by Rose A. Zimbardo and Neil D. Isaacs, 68–75. Boston: Houghton Mifflin, 2004.

Zimmer, Mary E. "Creating and Re-creating Worlds with Words: The Religion and Magic of Language in *The Lord of the Rings.*" Chap. 3 in Chance, *Tolkien and the Invention of Myth,* 49–60.

Index of Proper Names

www.ingramcontent.com/pod-product-compliance
Lightning Source LLC
Chambersburg PA
CBHW020843020726
47497CB00005B/1236